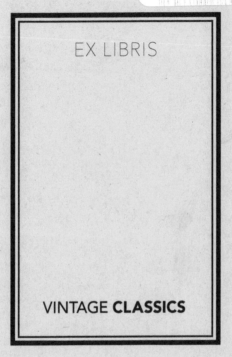

EX LIBRIS

VINTAGE **CLASSICS**

THE NICE AND THE GOOD

Iris Murdoch was born in Dublin in 1919 of Anglo-Irish parents. She went to Badminton School, Bristol, and read classics at Somerville College, Oxford. During the war she was an Assistant Principal at the Treasury, and then worked with UNRRA in London, Belgium and Austria. She held a studentship in Philosophy at Newnham College, Cambridge, and then in 1948 she returned to Oxford, where she became a Fellow of St Anne's College. Until her death in February 1999, she lived with her husband, the teacher and critic John Bayley, in Oxford. Awarded the CBE in 1976, Iris Murdoch was made a DBE in the 1987 New Year's Honours List. In the 1997 PEN Awards she received the Gold Pen for Distinguished Service to Literature.

Iris Murdoch made her writing debut in 1954 with *Under the Net*, and went on to write twenty-six novels, including the Booker prize-winning *The Sea, The Sea* (1978). Other literary awards include the James Tait Black Memorial Prize for *The Black Prince* (1973) and the Whitbread Prize (now the Costa Book Award) for *The Sacred and Profane Love Machine* (1974). Her works of philosophy include *Sartre: Romantic Rationalist*, *Metaphysics as a Guide to Morals* (1992) and *Existentialists and Mystics* (1997) She wrote several plays including *The Italian Girl* (with James Saunders) and *The Black Prince*, adapted from her novels of the same name. She died in February 1999.

ALSO BY IRIS MURDOCH

Fiction

Under the Net
The Flight from the Enchanter
The Sandcastle
The Bell
A Severed Head
An Unofficial Rose
The Unicorn
The Italian Girl
The Red and the Green
The Time of the Angels
Bruno's Dream
A Fairly Honourable Defeat
An Accidental Man
The Black Prince
The Sacred and Profane Love Machine
A Word Child
Henry and Cato
The Sea, The Sea
Nuns and Soldiers
The Philosopher's Pupil
The Good Apprentice
The Book and the Brotherhood
The Message to the Planet
The Green Knight
Jackson's Dilemma

Non-fiction

Sartre: Romantic Rationalist
Acastos: Two Platonic Dialogues
Metaphysics as a Guide to Moral
Existentialists and Mystics

IRIS MURDOCH

The Nice and the Good

WITH AN INTRODUCTION BY
Catherine Bates

VINTAGE BOOKS
London

Published by Vintage 2000

25

First published in Great Britain in 1968 by Chatto & Windus

Vintage
Random House, 20 Vauxhall Bridge Road,
London SW1V 2SA

www.vintage-classics.info

Addresses for companies within The Random House Group Limited
can be found at: www.randomhouse.co.uk/offices.htm

The Random House Group Limited Reg. No. 954009

A CIP catalogue record for this book
is available from the British Library

ISBN 9780099285267

The Random House Group Limited supports the Forest Stewardship
Council® (FSC®), the leading international forest-certification
organisation. Our books carrying the FSC label are printed on
FSC®-certified paper. FSC is the only forest-certification scheme
supported by the leading environmental organisations, including
Greenpeace. Our paper procurement policy can be found at:
www.randomhouse.co.uk/environment

Printed and bound in Great Britain by
Clays Ltd, Elcograf S.p.A.

TO
RACHEL
AND
DAVID CECIL

INTRODUCTION

In a little scene towards the beginning of *The Nice and the Good* a young adolescent boy makes a doomed gesture of love to a young adolescent girl:

> Pierce had covered the table with a complicated pattern composed of hundreds of shells arranged in spirals, tiny ones in the centre, larger ones on the outside. Adjusting the outer edge of the pattern he stopped to select a shell from a heap at his feet.

It is a typically Murdochian moment. Brought up from the nearby beach, the shells invade the household, bringing the sea and the seashore with them and breaking down the normally discrete categories of earth and water, land and sea. Under the influence of love the otherwise warring elements yearn one for the other and the animals, vegetable, and mineral worlds fuse with the human in a sympathetic and almost animistic universe of pre-Baconian correspondences. 'My imagination lives near the sea and under the sea', wrote Iris Murdoch once[1], and in this as in other novels the sea sweeps in on an emotional tide that dissolves all rigid boundaries and in their place creates something rich and strange, an imaginative realm not unlike the 'rich strand' of literary romance. Whether in *Tristan and Iseult*, *The Faerie Queene*, or Shakespeare's late romances, this tideland is a mysterious border-ground that owes allegiance both to land and sea – an ambiguous and ambiguating place where anything and everything might happen. Here things don't go according to plan and the divisions or compartments which normally rationalise life give way to something quite different. It's no accident, in fact, that much of the action of this novel takes place on the beach and in the sea-caves of the idyllic Dorset coast where the story is, for the most part, set.

Though small, light, and infinitely disposable, Pierce's shells are more than just shells. The something-more – the excess that is to be carried over – is the great weight they bear, the whole burden of first (and in this case unrequited, love. For, and again this is one of Murdoch's hallmarks, the physical world is never just the physical world. It is infused with metaphysical meaning, aglow with the extra dimension that is bestowed upon it by the artist's loving gaze. No other writer except perhaps John Donne is so concerned to materialise feelings into things or to ram ordinary objects – shells, stones, pieces of glass – with metaphysical significance. Murdoch often wrote of this 'thingy' quality of the world. To see the world in all its concrete objectivity, its manifest over-there-ness, is a sign of proper attentiveness, of a patient and benevolent regard which, in its direction away from the self and out towards external phenomena, is akin to love. Even the contents of a rubbish bin can be lovingly described as if seen for the first time, the detritus of daily life attended to with a new, even startled eye. The kind of hyper-clarity that results makes us realise how rarely we apprehend reality in this way if, indeed, we ever apprehend it at all.

What makes this scene most characteristic of all, however, is the question it raises about art. For the shell design is, with its careful placements and overall eye to effect, nothing less than a work of art. Pierce's spiral patterns imitate the Fibonacci spirals of the shells themselves, art and nature coinciding for once and testifying to God and man's blessed rage for order in a universe that's otherwise random and utterly prey to contingency. But the beauty does not last. For all its pained solemnity, Pierce's gift is destined to go unheeded, unreceived. Intended as a welcome-home present for Barbara, home from finishing school for the summer holidays, the whole thing is, on her arrival, thoughtlessly, crushingly swept aside. Does its impermanence, its destructibility – the simple fact that it is refused – negate the gift, the labour of love? What is art's place in a violent, uncaring world? Does it have a curative function? Is it there to make good an imperfect nature, to patch up, polish and finesse the raw material of experience, patiently restoring the rents in the fabric of life? Or does art make no difference whatsoever? Is it just another component of a world that is no more nor less contingent for its being there? Do terrible things happen regardless of whether art is there or not? The existence of Shakespeare's plays or Schubert's music did not prevent the Holocaust, after all. Is art – or good art, in any case – an isolated monument, then, one that rises serenely above the chaotic field of human happening, its symbols capturing the cultural memory and with it a whole archaeology of meaning? There are times when, in her reverential attitude to the great classics of literature and of Renaissance painting, Murdoch seems to imply the latter. But there are also moments when art's ability to hold, bind, and even redeem experience are savagely mocked – when elegant patterns and formal contrivances collapse into hideous scenes of complication and sexual muddle which this novelist has made her own special trademark. Is art pointless, then? And, if it is, does that negate art or only affirm it still further? Besides, where in all this does the novelist's own art lie?

The intimate relation between ethics and art is the one issue with which all Iris Murdoch's writing – her philosophy as well as her fiction – is ultimately concerned. *The Nice and the Good* is no exception and its question-begging title draws particular attention to the Socratic quest for the good man. 'What is a good man like? How can we make ourselves morally better? *Can* we make ourselves morally better?' These questions, formulated here in '"On God" and "Good"', an essay published in 1969, a year after *The Nice and the Good*, centre in that novel around the character of John Ducane, a middle-aged civil servant who is perceived by those around him to be a model of the upright man. Ducane does not necessarily share his friends' good faith in him but he sees goodness as a serious aim and 'had from childhood quite explicitly set before himself the aim of becoming a good man'. This ambition takes the form of regular if not always happy self-examination. If morality is intimately linked with art, then Ducane's ethics are best described as theatrical. He early relinquishes a career at the Bar out of a dislike for the histrionics of that trade, but Ducane's practical ethics are, for all that, entirely modelled on the drama. In the puritan mentality of his strict Scottish upbringing he characteristically sees himself as performing if not before the eye of God then before a personalised conscience, and either coming up to scratch or (increasingly) not. He is acutely conscious of the way others perceive him – the figure he cuts in their eyes – and, given that everything revolves around seeing, he is almost more upset at seeming to be a liar or a traitor that at actually being one. All this involves a no doubt laudable exercise of the imagination: the ability to imagine others' views of oneself is co-extensive with the ability to imagine goodness, evil, or other people's feelings, and is a prerequisite, of course, of the creative artist. There is a profound aestheticism in Ducane's nature and when he attempts to perform good actions it is not surprising that the role to which he naturally reverts is that of the dramaturge. In his self-appointed role as *deus ex machina* he takes it upon himself to arrange two marriages (things happen in pairs in this novel), contriving, Prospero-like, to combine imagination with will in the control of otherwise recalcitrant human material. He is only half successful.

The figure with whom Ducane most obviously contrasts is that of Radeechy, the colleague whose mysterious suicide in the office one summer afternoon he is asked to investigate. If Ducane does his best to be a good man, Radeechy, it appears, did the opposite. Already known to have had interests in necromancy and magic, he also dabbled, it turns out, in the occult. A trip to the vaults beneath the government department where he worked – one of two such visits to the underworld in the novel – reveals all the paraphernalia of satanic ritual: bell, book, candle and all. Here Ducane finds the inverted crosses, demonic cryptograms, priestly vestments and dead pigeons of previously celebrated black masses, and these lead him, in turn, to a murky underworld of vice and crime. Radeechy is clearly an evil counterpart in whose studied inversion of the good, Ducane distressingly confronts his own opposite. Yet for all this the moralities of the two men are strangely alike, the one a parodic mirror-image of the other. Radeechy's amateur dramatics have something in common with Ducane's theatre of conscience for both rest to the same degree on the power of the human imagination. Radeechy's posturings recall those of Dr. Faustus who rejects God in return for the supernatural powers that are granted him by magic: "But his dominion that exceeds in this/Stretcheth as far as doth the mind of man" (*Dr. Faustus*, I.i.60-61). Faustus's rhetorical flourish is meant to imply infinitude – the infinite reaches of the human mind. The trouble is that the human mind doesn't in fact stretch all that far and Marlowe's play is dedicated to showing up its pathetic limitations. This is one reason why Faustus's demonic antics are, like those of Radeechy, so unimaginative, so derivative, in the end so downright silly. There is nothing supernatural here, only a pathetic reaching for the extreme. Paltry, dreary, and depressing are exactly how Ducane, when he gets to the bottom of the affair, finally judges Radeechy's goings-on. But there is also a judgement of himself in this assessment. It is not that Ducane's morality is bad. It's rather that his goodness – fussy, humane, managerial as it is, a thing to be worked at and practised, a busyness that's prone to ineptitude and self-consciousness – shares an essential quality with Radeechy's evil. In both cases, good and evil are an inspiration, something to 'become', to be enacted and *willed*. This good and evil can be spoken and spoken about. It can be decided on and planned – arranged as deliberately and carefully as the artist disposes his characters or orders his creative material. Good and evil here have a familiar, homely, man-made quality. They are all too human – not other, not divine. They represent small evil and small good – opposite to one another, for sure, but, for all that, equal in scale.

The figure with whom Ducane contrasts more subtly is that of Uncle Theo – an enigmatic man whose uncertain past is divulged only at the very end and who is virtually the only character not to be paired off in the multiple couplings that make up the novel's positively Shakespearean ending. Inscrutable from the beginning, Theo succeeds in deflecting others' interest and curiosity in himself: 'this lack of interest seemed to be caused in some positive way by Theo himself, as if he sent out rays which paralysed other people's concern about him. It was like a faculty of becoming invisible'. Pointless, undetectable and distinctly uncharismatic, Theo is either a very boring man or, as one of the other characters shrewdly suspects, someone who has, in the course of his undisclosed life, been through the inferno and arrived on the far side of despair. With his odd canine features and marked bond of mutual empathy with the family pet, Mingo, Theo appears to the others as a kind of dog-man. But this is not some demonic, Radeechy-style reversal of God. Rather, Theo embodies the paradoxical non-god of a resolutely godless world. 'All metaphysics is devilish, *devilish*', he says to the refugee scholar, Willy Kost:

'There is no good metaphysics?'
'No. Nothing about that can be *said*'.

'Sad for the human race, since we are such natural prattlers'
'Yes. We are natural prattlers. And that deepens, prolongs, spreads and intensifies our evil'.

Theo, it is gradually revealed, has indeed progressed past good and evil into the Nietzschean beyond. And into the Freudian yonder, too – beyond the pleasure principle of a great copulating Nature which, in the animal as well as the human kingdom, he sardonically observes rutting all around him, out into the blankness and galactic silence of the death drive. Here, in the nothingness of Zen, Theo has confronted 'the other face of love, its blank face'. All is vanity, and the pointlessness of existence is grasped – if emptiness can be said to be grasped – for what it is. At this point, the busy, self-justifying chatter of human ethics drops quite naturally away. From this beyond has nothing whatever to do with goodness, at least not with a goodness that can be spoken about, prayed for, or even made into art. It defies language, thought, and self. 'The Good has nothing to do with purpose'. wrote Iris Murdoch in '"On God" and "Good"', indeed it excludes the idea of purpose, "All is vanity" is the beginning and the end of ethics. The only genuine way to be good is to be good "for nothing" in the midst of a scene where every "natural" thing, including one's own mind, is subject to chance, that is, to necessity. That "for nothing" is indeed the experienced correlate of the invisibility or non-representable blankness of the idea of Good itself'. This is quite different from the homely, practical, well-meaning – in a word, 'nice' – ethics of a John Ducane. How small and insignificant they seem by comparison!

We may think we all know what goodness is and that we'd have no trouble in recognising it if we saw it. But the concept of the Good is, it turns out, difficult to understand, the more so for being haunted by a host of false doubles – power, freedom, purpose, reward, judgement – all of which, with Murdoch's love of chiastic pairings, doubles and opposites, offer themselves as not-so-shadowy surrogates for a more obscurely grasped virtue. *The Nice and the Good* is, like all her novels, full of characters earnestly trying, hoping, and not infrequently praying to be good, all (sometimes comically, sometimes tragically) to no avail. For goodness is not a matter of will – or , as soon as it becomes so, it ceases to be goodness and becomes self. 'Mystics of all kinds have usually known this', she writes in another essay, 'and have attempted by extremities of language to portray the nakedness and aloneness of Good, its absolute for-nothingness' ('The Sovereignty of Good Over Other Concepts', 1967). By comparison with their noisier, self-justifying, and generally more meddlesome cousins, Murdochian saints are usually recognised by their quietness and inconspicuousness. Unlikely (and often unlikeable) characters, they tend to exist unparticipatingly at the very edges of the plot, and they frequently turn out to have some kind of discreet mystical leanings. Uncle Theo, though not quite a saint, is the nearest thing to it in *The Nice and the Good*, and only at the very end do we learn of his youthful adventures in a Buddhist monastery in India.

The unspeakability of the Good – an article of faith in the mystical traditions of both the east and the west – also makes its appearance in western philosophy, or, more properly, in that branch of philosophy most concerned with questions of goodness, namely ethics. Wittgenstein enunciated it most austerely, perhaps, when he said that 'ethics cannot be put into words. Ethics is transcendental'.[2] The only things which language can meaningfully express are the propositions of natural science – verifiable statements of fact, in effect. Anything else – any statement of value, any 'ought' or 'Thou shalt' or 'that is good' or 'that is bad' – has no verifiable status and is therefore strictly nonsensical or, as Wittgenstein would prefer, unsayable. This unsayability is indeed the very condition of ethics. 'This running up against the limits of language is *ethics* . . . In ethics we are always making the attempt to say something that cannot be said, something that does not and never will touch the essence of the matter'.[3] The philosopher's most eloquent statements are, consequently, what he does not say. 'My work consists of two parts: the one presented here [in the *Tractatus*] plus all that I have *not* written', Wittgenstein wrote to Ludwig Ficker in 1919:

'And it is precisely this second part that is the important one. My book draws limits to the sphere of the ethical from the inside as it were, and I am convinced that this is the ONLY *rigorous* way of drawing those limits. In short, I believe that where *many* others today are just *gassing* I have managed in my book to put everything firmly into place by being silent about it'.[4]

The indefinability, ineffability and mysteriousness of the Good – the fact that it lies "beyond", is uninteresting, invisible, will-less and not there to be "experienced" – is a topic to which, in her philosophical writings, Iris Murdoch reverts again and again. It creates something of a problem for the writer, however. If you cannot speak of the Good, how are you supposed to write moral books? The problem is rather different depending on whether you look at it as a moral philosopher or a moral novelist. Basically, the philosopher won't and the novelist can't. Enjoined to speak truth, the moral philosopher is bound not to utter falsehood or nonsense and so can only, when it comes to the unsayable, lapse into silence. The moral novelist, however, is not so enjoined. On the contrary, she is busy saying the unsayable. She has made her business that special realm of discourse in which propositions are neither true nor false because they are fiction. This is a most dangerous realm, as Plato warned, for, liberated from strict truth-content, words can do anything you like. The writer is free – as free to create the bad as the good, the false as the true. As Murdoch wrote in her long essay on Plato's aesthetics, 'we are able meaningfully and plausibly to say what is not the case: to fantasise, speculate, tell lies, and write stories...for truth to exist falsehood must be able to exist too' (*The Fire and The Sun: Why Plato Banished the Artists*, 1976). As far as philosophy is concerned, all art is morally compromised and fiction in particular suffers an irredeemable taint.

As a philosopher Murdoch is enough of a puritan and a Platonist to share this view. But as a novelist she doesn't hold back. She is down there in the world with her characters – the unsaintly ones, that is – right in the thick of it, saying the unsayable, getting her hands dirty, and getting fascinatedly caught up in the web of words, irresistibly intrigued, charmed – *tempted* is perhaps the word – by all that is most false. Moreover, she shares her medium with her characters who are busy doing exactly what she is doing – dreaming up plots, setting things in motion, manipulating others, acting parts, making things happen, ordering people around. In the embroiled and complicated histories of those characters who use language and the structures of art for their own worthy or unworthy ends, the novelist looks critically, quizzically at her own procedures. Her vision of the corrupting power of words reflects necessarily upon her own practice. There's a sense in which she is no better than her characters, no closer than they are to speaking or realising the Good. She is on a level with them – the level of ego, art, and lies which makes for so busy, justified, sentimental, just plain *interesting* a world. Down there in the human muddle of compromise and untruths she is able equally to create good and bad, to exercise the same magical powers, black or white, as a Joseph Radeechy or a John Ducane.

The novelist cannot speak of the Good any more than the philosopher can. Given that she has opted for speech rather than silence, moreover, she condemns herself to the vain human prattling that is at bottom only falsehood or nonsense: 'just gassing'. She shares the same fallen human world as her characters, joining in their jostling, moody, generally unsatisfying existence. She can only write of the nice and the bad, in effect. But there is one important difference – and it is a crucial one. The novelist is no closer to speaking of goodness than anyone else, but this does not cancel or negate her art. She has one unique advantage over the philosopher. She is able to *show* the Good by means of her carefully implied comparisons – the nice and the bad versus the good, the conspicuous versus the inconspicuous, the interesting versus the uninteresting. To this extent the novelist is able to rise above her characters. As they tie themselves in knots or go wrong or get absolutely nowhere she is able to show – without of course saying it in so many words – that language creates misunderstandings and that human efforts to organise, improve upon, and simply make sense of life offer only the false consolations of fantasy – of hopefully-cast narratives, of pre-existing role-models (caricatures for the most part) into which we'd like to see ourselves fit. It's all hopeless. Being good doesn't lie that way. But the novelist is able to reveal this in a uniquely truthful and even didactic way by virtue of her comparisons. Indeed, unnoticed, absent, 'for-nothing' as it is, the Good can be indicated in no other way.

This is where the novelist has the edge over the philosopher. The philosopher will not speak what cannot be spoken, but the novelist speaks it in the only way that's left open to human beings – through the force of negative example. For Iris Murdoch this is infinitely preferable to not saying anything at all. Indeed, it's a kind of having it both ways. Art knowingly speaks falsehood. It acknowledges – even celebrates – the familiar human mish-mash and recognises that we are sinners all. When art points towards the transcendental or the sublime, therefore, it does so without spiritual pride. This is why, for Murdoch, the compromises of art ultimately win out over the purity of philosophy: 'For both the collective and the individual salvation of the human race art is doubtless more important than philosophy and literature most important of all' ('"of God" and "Good"'). Literary fiction is perhaps the most morally compromised of all the art forms. But, in the tumble of novels that speak so eloquently of her decision to opt for fiction over everything else, Iris Murdoch has bequeathed one of the most seriously examined oeuvres in the English language, and for that if for nothing else she has given her readers something most profound to be grateful for.

CATHERINE BATES 2000

1 Iris Murdoch, '*Crest of a Wave*', *Daily Mail*, 23 November 1978.
2 *Tractatus Logico-Philisophicus* (1921), trans. D. F. Pears and B. F. McGuinness (1961), 6.421.
3 *Wittgenstein and the Vienna Circle: conversations recorded by Friedrich Waismann*, ed. Brian McGuinness (1979), pp.68-69.
4 Paul Englemann, ed., *Letters from Ludwig Wittgenstein with a Memoir* (1967), p. 143.

THE NICE
AND THE GOOD

One

A HEAD of department, working quietly in his room in Whitehall on a summer afternoon, is not accustomed to being disturbed by the nearby and indubitable sound of a revolver shot.

At one moment a lazy fat man, a perfect sphere his loving wife called him, his name Octavian Gray, was slowly writing a witty sentence in a neat tiny hand upon creamy official paper while he inhaled from his breath the pleasant sleepy smell of an excellent lunch-time burgundy. Then came the shot.

Octavian sat up, stood up. The shot had been somewhere not far away from him in the building. There was no mistaking that sound. Octavian knew the sound well though it was many years since, as a soldier, he had last heard it. His body knew it as he stood there rigid with memory and with the sense, now so unfamiliar to him, of confronting the demands of the awful, of the utterly new.

Octavian went to the door. The hot stuffy corridor, amid the rushing murmur of London, was quite still. He wished to call out "What is it? What has happened?" but found he could not. He turned back into the room with an instinctive movement in the direction of his telephone, his natural lifeline and connection with the world. Just then he heard running steps.

"Sir, Sir, something terrible has occurred!"

The office messenger, McGrath, a pale-blue-eyed ginger-haired man with a white face and a pink mouth, stood shuddering in the doorway.

"Get out." Richard Biranne, one of Octavian's Under Secretaries, pushed past McGrath, propelled McGrath out of the door, closed the door.

"What on earth is it?" said Octavian.

Biranne leaned back against the door. He breathed deeply for a moment and then said in his usual high-pitched and rather precise voice, "Look, Octavian, I know this is *scarcely* credible, but Radeechy has just shot himself."

7

"Radeechy? Good God. Is he dead?"

"Yes."

Octavian sat down, He straightened out the piece of cream-coloured paper on the red blotter. He read the unfinished sentence. Then he got up again. "I'd better come and—see." He moved to the door which Biranne held open for him. "I suppose we'd better call Scotland Yard."

"I've already taken the liberty of doing so," said Biranne.

Radeechy's room was on the floor below. A little crowd of people stood at its closed door, arms pendant, mouths open. They were being addressed by McGrath.

"Go away," said Octavian. They stared at him. "Go to your rooms," he said. They moved slowly off. "You too," he said to McGrath. Biranne was unlocking the door.

Through the opening door Octavian saw Radeechy lying with his head turned sideways upon the desk. The two men went in and Biranne locked the door on the inside and after a moment's thought unlocked it again.

The reddish brown flesh of Radeechy's neck was bulging out over his stiff white collar. Octavian wondered at once if his eyes were open, but the shadowed face could only have been seen by peering. Radeechy's left arm hung down toward the floor. His right arm was upon the desk with the gun, an old service revolver, near to the hand. Octavian was finding it necessary to take a deliberate grip on himself, to respire slowly and assemble his senses and tell himself who he was. He had seen many dead men. But he had never seen a dead man suddenly on a summer afternoon in Whitehall with his flesh bulging out above a stiff collar.

Octavian quickly informed himself that he was the head of the department and must behave calmly and take charge.

He said to Biranne, "Who found him?"

"I did. I was nearly outside his door when I heard the shot."

"I suppose there's no doubt he's dead?" The question sounded weird, almost embarrassed.

Biranne said, "He's dead all right. Look at the wound." He pointed.

Octavian moved nearer. He moved round the desk on the side away from Radeechy's face and leaning over the chair saw a round hole in the back of the head, a little to the right

8

of the slight depression at the base of the skull. The hole was quite large, a dark orifice with blackened edges. A little blood, not much, had run down inside the collar.

"He must have pointed the gun into his mouth," said Biranne. "The bullet went right through."

Octavian noticed the neatness of the recently clipped grey hair upon the warm vulnerable neck. He had an impulse to touch it, to touch the material of Radeechy's jacket, to pulp it timidly, curiously. Here were the assembled parts of a human being, its clothes and carnal paraphernalia. The mystery appalled him of the withdrawal of life, the sudden disintegration of the living man into parts, pieces, stuff. Radeechy, who muffed most things, had not muffed this.

Octavian had never particularly liked Radeechy. He had never particularly known him. Radeechy was one of those eccentrics, found in every Government department, who though highly intelligent, even brilliant, lack some essential quality of judgment and never rise above the rank of Principal. Radeechy was considered to have, in a mild way, "a screw loose". He had seemed content, however. He had interests elsewhere. He was always asking for special leave. On the last occasion, Octavian recalled, it was to investigate a poltergeist.

"Has he left a note?"

"Not that I can see," said Biranne.

"That's not like him!" said Octavian. Radeechy was an indefatigable writer of circumstantial minutes. "I suppose now we shall have the police here for the rest of the day, and just when I wanted to get away for the weekend." He knew from the deepening of his voice that the dreadful moment had passed. Now he could be cool, business-like, soberly jocular.

"I'll deal with them if you like," said Biranne. "I suppose they'll want to take photographs and all that." He added, "I must remember to tell them that I touched the gun. I moved it just a little to see his face. They might find my finger-prints on it!"

"Thanks, but I'd better stay myself. Poor devil, I wonder why he did it."

"I don't know."

"He was a pretty odd man. All that conjuring with spirits."

"I don't know," said Biranne.

"Or perhaps—Of course, there was that awful business with his wife. Someone told me he hadn't been the same since she died. I thought myself he was getting very depressed. You remember, that terrible accident last year—"

"Yes," said Biranne. He laughed his high-pitched little laugh, like an animal's yelp. "Isn't it just like Radeechy's damn bad taste to go and shoot himself in the office!"

"Kate, darling." Octavian was on the telephone to his wife in Dorset.

"Darling, hello. Are you all right?"

"I'm fine," said Octavian, "but something's happened in the office and I won't be able to get down till tomorrow morning."

"Oh dear! Then you won't be here for Barbie's first evening home!" Barbara was their daughter and only child, aged fourteen.

"I know, it's maddening and I'm very sorry, but I've just got to stay. We've got the police here and there's a terrible to-do."

"The police? What's happened? Nothing awful?"

"Well, yes and no," said Octavian. "Someone's committed suicide."

"God! Anyone we know?"

"No, no, it's all right. No one we know."

"Well, thank heavens for that. I'm so sorry, you poor dear. I do wish you could be here for Barbie, she'll be so disappointed."

"I know. But I'll be along tomorrow. Is everything OK at your end? How is my harem?"

"Your harem is dying to see you!"

"That's good! Bless you, sweetheart, and I'll ring again tonight."

"Octavian, you are bringing Ducane with you, aren't you?"

"Yes. He couldn't come till tomorrow anyway, so now I can drive him down."

"Splendid. Willy was wanting him."

Octavian smiled. "I think *you* were wanting him, weren't you, my sweetheart?"

"Well, of course I was wanting him! He's a very necessary man."

"You shall have him, my dear, you shall have him. You shall have whatever you want."

"Good—ee!"

Two

"YOU must put all those stones out in the garden," said Mary Clothier.

"Why?" said Edward.

"Because they're garden stones."

"Why?" said Henrietta.

The twins, Edward and Henrietta Biranne, were nine years old. They were lanky blonde children with identical mops of fine wiry hair and formidably similar faces.

"They aren't fossils. There's nothing special about them."

"There's something special about *every* stone,"said Edward.

"That is perfectly true in a metaphysical sense," said Theodore Gray, who had just entered the kitchen in his old red and brown check dressing gown.

"I am not keeping the house tidy in a metaphysical sense," said Mary.

"Where's Pierce?" said Theodore to the twins. Pierce was Mary Clothier's son who was fifteen.

"He's up in Barbie's room. He's decorating it with shells. He must have brought in a ton."

"Oh God!" said Mary. The sea shore invaded the house. The children's rooms were gritty with sand and stones and crushed sea shells and dried up marine entities of animal and vegetable origin.

"If Pierce can bring in shells we can bring in stones," reasoned Henrietta.

"No one said Pierce could bring in shells," said Mary.

"But you aren't going to stop him, are you?" said Edward.

"If I'd answered back like that at your age I'd have been well slapped," said Casie the housekeeper. She was Mary Casie, but since she had the same first name as Mary Clothier she was called "Casie", a dark pregnant title like the name of an animal.

"True, but irrelevant, Edward might reply," said Theodore. "If it's not too much to ask, may I have my tea? I'm not feeling at all well."

"Poor old Casie, that was hard luck!" said Edward.

"I'm not going to stop him," said Mary, "firstly because it's too late, and secondly because it's a special occasion with Barbara coming home." It paid to argue rationally with the twins.

Barbara Gray had been away since Christmas at a finishing school in Switzerland. She had spent the Easter holidays skiing with her parents who were enthusiastic travellers.

"It's well for some people," said Casie, a social comment of vague but weighty import which she often uttered.

"Casie, may we have these chicken's legs?" said Henrietta.

"How I'm to keep the kitchen clean with those children messing in the rubbish bins like starving cats—"

"Don't pull it *all* out, Henrietta, please," said Mary. A mess of screwed up paper, coffee beans, old lettuce leaves and human hair emerged with the chicken's legs.

"Nobody minds me," said Casie. "I'm wasting my life here."

"Every life is wasted," said Theodore.

"You people don't regard me as your equal—"

"You aren't our equal," said Theodore. "May I have my tea please?"

"Oh do shut up, Theo," said Mary. "Don't set Casie off. Your tea's there on the tray."

"Lemon sponge. Mmm. Good."

"I thought you weren't feeling well," said Casie.

"A mere bilious craving. Where's Mingo?"

Mingo, a large grey unclipped somewhat poodle-like dog, was always in attendance upon Theodore's breakfast and tea, which were taken in bed. Kate and Octavian were ribald in speculation concerning the relations between Theodore and Mingo.

"We'll bring him, Uncle Theo!" cried Edward.

A brief scuffle produced Mingo from behind the florid cast-iron stove which, although it was expensive to run and useless for cooking, still filled the huge recess of the kitchen fireplace. Theodore had begun to mount the stairs bearing his tray, followed by the twins who, according to one of their many self-imposed rituals, carried the animal between them, his foolish smiling face emerging from under Edward's arm, his woolly legs trailing, and his sausage of a wagging tail

13

rhythmically lifting the hem of Henrietta's gingham dress.

Theodore, Octavian's valetudinarian elder brother, formerly an engineer in Delhi and now long unemployed, was well known to have left India under a cloud, although no one had ever been able to discover what sort of cloud it was that Theodore had left India under. Nor was it known whether Theodore in reality liked or disliked his brother, his contemptuous references to whom were ignored by common consent. He was a tall thin grey-haired partly bald man with a bulging brow finely engraved with hieroglyphic lines, and screwed-up clever thoughtful eyes.

"Paula, *must* you read at the table?" said Mary.

Paula Biranne, the twins' mother, was still absorbed in her book. She left the disciplining of her children, with whom she seemed at such moments to be coeval, entirely to Mary. Paula had been divorced from Richard Biranne for over two years. Mary herself was a widow of many years' standing.

"Sorry," said Paula. She closed her copy of Lucretius. Paula taught Greek and Latin at a local school.

Meal times were important to Mary. They were times of communication, ritualistic forgatherings almost spiritual in their significance. Human speech and casual co-presence then knit up wounds and fissures which were perhaps plain only to Mary's own irritated and restless sensibility, constantly recreating an approximation to harmony of which perhaps again only she was fully aware. At these points of contact Mary held an authority which nobody challenged. If the household possessed a communal unconscious mind, Mary constituted its communal consciousness. The regularity of breakfast lunch tea and dinner was moreover one of the few elements of formal pattern in a situation which, as Mary felt it, hovered always upon the brink of a not unpleasant but quite irrevocable anarchy.

The hot sun shone through the big windows with their quaint Victorian Gothic peaks and their white cast-iron tracery, greenly shaded on one side by honeysuckle and on the other side by wistaria, and revealed the stains upon the red and white check table-cloth, the cake crumbs upon the stains, and the coffee beans and human hair upon the paved floor.

The position was that the twins had had their tea, Theo had removed his, Pierce had not come down for his, Kate was late for hers as usual, Mary and Paula and Casie were having theirs.

"She's got a new car again," said Casie.

"I wish you'd say who you mean and not call everybody 'she'," said Mary.

"My sister." Casie, having spent most of her life tending her late ailing mother whom she referred to as "the old bitch", could not forgive her younger sister for having escaped this fate and married an affluent husband. Casie, with a red chunky face and a coil of iron grey hair, was much given to crying fits, often set off by sad things she saw on television, which claimed Mary's preoccupied and exasperated sympathy.

"What kind?" said Paula absently. She was still thinking about Lucretius and wondering if a certain passage would be too hard to set in the examination.

"A Triumph something or other. It's well for some people. The Costa Brava and all."

"We saw that flying saucer again today," announced Henrietta, who had come back carrying Barbara's cat, Montrose. The twins often made this claim.

"Really?" said Mary. "Henrietta, please don't put Montrose on the table."

Montrose was a large cocoa-coloured tabby animal with golden eyes, a square body, rectangular legs and an obstinate self-absorbed disposition, concerning whose intelligence fierce arguments raged among the children. Tests of Montrose's sagacity were constantly being devised, but there was some uncertainty about the interpretation of the resultant data since the twins were always ready to return to first principles and discuss whether cooperation with the human race was a sign of intelligence at all. Montrose had one undoubted talent, which was that he could at will make his sleek hair stand up on end, and transform himself from a smooth stripey cube into a fluffy sphere. This was called "Montrose's bird look".

"Don't ask me where they get the money from," said Casie. "It's enough to make a Socialist of you."

"But you are a Socialist, Casie," said Mary. So were they

all, of course, but this seemed notable only in the instance of Casie.

"I didn't say I wasn't, did I? I just said it was enough to make you one."

"Do you know which is the largest of all birds?" said Edward, pushing his way in between Mary and his sister.

"No. Which is?"

"The cassowary. He eats Papuans. He kills them by hitting them with his feet."

"I think the condor is bigger," said Henrietta.

"It depends whether you mean wing-span or weight," said Edward.

"What about the albatross?" said Paula. She was always ready to enter into an argument with her children, whom she treated invariably as rational adults.

"He has the biggest wing-span," said Edward, "but he has a much smaller body. Do you know how big a breast bone we should need to have if we were going to fly? Mary, do you know how big a breast bone we should need to have if we were going to fly?"

"I don't know," said Mary. "How big?"

"Fourteen feet wide."

"Really? Fancy that."

"In the case of the condor—" said Paula.

"Do be careful, Henrietta," said Mary to Henrietta, who was engaged in hitting her brother's face with one of Montrose's paws.

"It's all right, his claws are in," said Henrietta.

"Mine wouldn't be if I were him," said Casie. "When I was your age I was taught not to maul my pets about."

"I do wish you'd do something about those stones," said Mary. "We shall all be falling over them. Couldn't you put them in order of merit, and then we could find a home outside for the less important ones?"

The idea of putting the stones in order of merit appealed at once to the twins. They dropped the cat and settled down on the floor with the pile of stones between them and were soon deep in argument.

"Has Theo been up to see Willy?" asked Paula.

"No. I suggested it, but he just laughed and said he wasn't Willy's keeper."

Willy Kost, a refugee scholar, lived in a bungalow on Octavian's estate which was known as Trescombe Cottage, a little further up the hill from Trescombe House. Willy suffered from a melancholia which was a cause of anxiety to the household.

"I suppose they've quarrelled again. They're like a couple of children. Have you been up?"

"No," said Mary. "I haven't had a moment. I sent Pierce up and Willy seemed OK. Have you been?"

"No," said Paula. "I've had a pretty full day too."

Mary was rather relieved. She felt that Willy Kost was her own special responsibility, practically her property, and it mattered that she was always the one who knew how Willy was. She would go up and see him tomorrow.

"It's just as well Ducane is coming," said Paula. "He always does Willy good."

"Is Ducane coming?" said Mary. "I wish somebody would tell me something sometimes!"

"I suppose you realise the room isn't ready," said Casie.

"I think Kate assumes it's a regular thing now and that's why she didn't tell you."

John Ducane, a friend and colleague of Octavian's, was a frequent weekend visitor.

"Casie, would you mind doing the room after tea?"

"Of course I mind," said Casie, "in my one bit of free time; what you mean is will I, yes I will."

At that moment Kate Gray came into the kitchen, followed by Mingo, and at once as if struck by some piercing stellar ray the scene dissolved into its atoms and reassembled itself round Kate as centre. Mary saw, pinioned in some line of force, Paula's keen smiling dog face, felt her own face lift and smile, her hair tossed, blown back. Mingo was barking, Montrose had jumped on to the table, Casie was pouring more hot water into the pot, the twins, disarranging their careful line of stones, were both chattering at once, fastening brown sandy hands on to the belt of Kate's striped dress.

Kate's bright round face beamed at them all out of the golden fuzz of her hair. Her warm untidy being emphasised the sleekness, the thinness, the compactness of the other two, Mary with her straight dark hair tucked behind her ears and her air of a Victorian governess, Paula with her narrow head and pointed face and the well adjusted surfaces of her cropped brown hair. Kate, herself undefined, was a definer of others, the noise, the heat, the light which flattered them into the clearer contours of themselves. Kate spoke with a slight stammer and a slight Irish accent.

"Octavian isn't coming tonight after all."

"Oh dear," said Mary, "he won't be here for Barb."

"I know, it's too bad. Something's happened at the office."

"What's happened?"

"Some chap killed himself."

"Good heavens," said Paula. "You mean killed himself, there in the office?"

"Yes. Isn't it awful?"

"Who was he?" said Paula.

"I don't know."

"What was his name?"

"I didn't think to ask. He's not anyone we know."

"Poor fellow," said Paula. "I'd like to have known his name."

"Why?" said Edward, who was experimenting with the tendons of one of the chicken's legs.

"Because it's somehow easier to think about somebody if you know their name."

"Why?" said Henrietta, who was dissecting the other leg with a kitchen knife.

"You may well ask," said Paula. "Plato says how odd it is that we can *think* of anything, and however far away it is our thought can hit it. I suppose I can think of him even if I don't know his name—"

"You are right to think of him," said Kate. "You are so right. You reproach me. I feel reproached. I just thought of Octavian and Barbara."

"Why did he kill himself?" said Edward.

"I'll do Ducane's room now," said Mary to Casie.

"No, you won't," said Casie.

They got up together and left the kitchen.

The lazy sun, slanting along the front of the house, cast elongated rectangles of watery gold on to the faded floral wallpaper of the big paved hall, which served as the dining-room at weekends. The front door was wide open, framing

18

distant cuckoo calls, while beyond the weedy gravel drive, beyond the clipped descending lawn and the erect hedge of raspberry-and-creamy spiraea, rose up the sea, a silvery blue, too thin and transparent to be called metallic, a texture as of skin-deep silver paper, rising up and merging at some indeterminate point with the pallid glittering blue of the midsummer sky. There was something of evening already in the powdery goldenness of the sun and the ethereal thinness of the sea.

The two women swept round the white curve of the stairs, Casie clumping, Mary darting, and disputed briefly at the top. Mary let Casie go on to the spare room and turned herself in the direction of Barbara's room.

Mary Clothier and her son Pierce had lived for nearly four years now at Trescombe House. Mary's father, a sickly defeated man, had been a junior clerk in an insurance office, and he and Mary's vague gentle mother had perished together of double pneumonia, leaving their only child, then aged nine, to the care of an elderly and rather needy aunt. Mary had managed, however, by means of scholarships, to win herself a good education, in the course of which she encountered Kate. Kate admired Mary and also quite instinctively protected her. They became firm friends. Much later, at some point in Mary's wanderings of an impecunious and socially uncertain widow Kate had suggested that she should come and live with them, and Mary had come, with many misgivings, for a trial period. She had stayed. Kate and Octavian were well off and enjoyed the deep superiority of the socially secure. Mary, a deprived person who had sometimes come near, rather romantically, to thinking of herself as an outcast, appreciated both these advantages in her friends, and was prepared to be herself propped up by them. But of course she could not have accepted this act of rescue had it not been for an indubitable virtue of generosity in both her hosts, a virtue somehow expressed in their roundness, in Octavian's big spherical bald head with its silky golden tonsure, in Kate's plump face and fuzzy ball of touchable yellow hair. There was a careless magnanimity about them both, something too of the bounty of those who might have been magnificent sinners magnificently deciding for righteousness. They were happily married and spontaneous in their efforts to cause happiness in others. Mary was untroubled by the thought that she was in fact extremely useful to them. Mary ran the house, she controlled the children, she was the one who was always there. But she knew that the benefits to herself were infinitely greater.

The presence, more recently, of foxy-faced Paula was something about which Mary had been, at first, not too certain. Paula was a college friend of Mary's, and not known to Kate until the time, after her divorce, when Paula came to stay. "Everyone invites a divorced woman," Paula had said. Mary had invited her and Kate had adored her. Kate had suggested that Paula should stay with them indefinitely, Octavian had started to make the joke about his harem, and the matter had been fixed up. Paula had been Mary's older and revered college friend. Mary thought it possible that Paula at close quarters might prove exacting; also she was afraid of becoming jealous. Paula was an uncompromising person and at times Mary had experienced her as a sort of unconscious prig. The strength and clarity of her being, her meticulous accuracy and truthfulness, operated as a reproach to the mediocrity and muddle which Mary felt to be her own natural medium. Paula had a hard cool dignity which had been quite unimpaired by her divorce, the details of which Mary never learnt, though it was generally known that Richard Biranne was an irresponsible chaser of women. That both Kate and Paula 'adored' Mary was of course taken, a little too much, for granted. Mary was prepared to watch, in her nervous hyperconscious way, their interest in each other, and in the first few months of Paula's sojourn Mary suffered acute pains of anticipation. However, in the end it was Paula's coolness, her detachment, her peculiar virtue which soothed Mary's nerves, and even provided Mary with the energy which she needed to see the situation exactly as it was. She soon concluded that there was nothing to fear. The mutual affection of Kate and Paula held no threat to her. There was nothing hidden and no possibility of a plot. With this acceptance came a special pleasure in their existence as a free trio which she knew that the others shared.

The quartet of children had also got on reasonably well. They all went away to school now, Pierce to Bryanston, the twins to Bedales and Barbara to La Résidence in Switzerland. Their presence, their absence, together with the alternation of week and weekend made of Mary's existence a chequer-board of contrasting atmospheres. When the children were away Kate often spent part of the week at the Grays' house in London, if she was not absent on a trip with Octavian, who treated airline timetables as most people treat train timetables. The arrival of the weekend changed the house with the introduction into it of the mystery of a married pair. Kate and Octavian, charmingly, ebulliently wedded, took, as it were, the thrones which awaited them. Paula and Mary then wore their status of women without men. They laughed at Octavian's harem jokes and heard late at night behind walls the ceaseless rivery murmur of the conversing couple. When the children were at home the weekend was a less intensive matter just because the house was fuller and more anarchic and less private. But the children too were altered by it, Barbara becoming suddenly "the child of the house", a somewhat purdah-like condition, half privilege, half penalty, the nature of which was never questioned by the other three. The presence of men, Octavian and of late John Ducane (it occurred to no one to count Uncle Theo as a man), also made the conduct of the children not exactly more disciplined, but more coherent and self-conscious.

On the whole Mary Clothier was satisfied, at least she enjoyed a harassed nervous rather dark content which she told herself was the best she was capable of. Alistair Clothier had died when Pierce was a very small child, leaving his wife with no money. Mary, who had abandoned the university to marry, found it hard to earn. She became a typist. Pierce gained a scholarship at his father's old school. They managed; but Mary had never forgiven the fates for so cheating her over Alistair. A spirit took possession of her which was sardonic, sarcastic, narrow. She had come to expect little and to rail on what she had. Kate, who was not even conscious of Mary as a disappointed person, half cured her. Kate, eternally and unreflectively happy herself, made Mary want happiness and startled her, by a sort of electrical contact, into the hope of it. Kate's more demonstrative affections gave Mary the courage of her own. The golden life-giving egoism and rich self-satisfaction of Kate and her husband inspired in Mary a certain hedonism which, puny as it was by comparison, was for her a saving grace. For the rest, she understood very well indeed the things that hurt her, and on the whole she now accepted them.

Mary passed along the top corridor, observing the twins who had emerged on to the lawn in front of the house. They were resuming one of their special games. The twins had a number of private games which they had invented for themselves, the rules of which, though she had many times observed them, Mary was unable to deduce. She sometimes suspected that these games were mathematical in nature, based upon some sort of built-in computer system in those rather remarkable children which they had not yet discovered that other people did not possess. Most of the games had brief and uninformative names such as "Sticks" or "Feathers". The one which was at present being played upon the sloping lawn, in an area of rectangles and triangles marked out with string, was called, no one had ever discovered why, "Noble Mice".

The door of Barbara's room was open and Mary saw through the doorway the intent preoccupied profile of her son as he bent down and peered through horn-rimmed spectacles at the surface of the large table in the window. Pierce, brown-complexioned, brown-haired, brown-eyed, possessed a large nose which descended in a straight line from his brow, giving to his plump waxen face a somewhat animal quality. An impulse to stroke him down over brow and nose like a pony had already troubled, in half conscious form, a number of people, including some of his masters at school. He had a serious staring gaze which, together with a slow pedantic habit of speech, gave him the air of an intellectual. In fact, though clever, he was idle at school and far from bookish. Mary, still unseen, moved closer and saw that Pierce had covered the table with a complicated pattern composed of hundreds of shells arranged in spirals, tiny ones in the centre, larger ones on the outside. Adjusting the outer edge of the pattern he stooped to select a shell from a heap at his feet.

Pierce became aware of his mother and turned slowly to face her. He rarely moved fast. He looked at her without smiling, almost grimly. He looked at her like an animal, cornered but not frightened, a dangerous confident animal. And Mary apprehended herself as a thin dark woman, a mother, a representative somehow of the past, of Pierce's past, confronting him as if she were already a ghost. This came to her in an instant with an agony of possessive love for her son and a blinding pity of which she did not know whether it was for him or for herself. Next moment, as she searched for something to say, she took in the scene, Barbara's pretty room, so tidy and empty now, but already expectant. And with an immediate instinct of her son's vulnerability she saw the huge shell design as utterly untimely. It was something that belonged to the quietness of Pierce's thought about Barbara and not to the hurly-burly of Barbara's actual arrival, which Mary now anticipated with a kind of dread. The careful work with the shells seemed to her suddenly so typical of Pierce, so slow and inward and entirely without judgment.

There was a shout from the lawn outside and then the sound of a car upon the gravel and the ecstatic barking of Mingo. Pierce did not move instantly. He held his mother's anguished look for a moment longer and then as she moved back he went unhurriedly past her and along the landing.

"Mama, it was so marvellous, I had a fab lunch in the aeroplane and they offered me champagne, oh Mary, you mustn't carry my case, must she, mama, just look at Mingo's tail, it's going round and round like like a propeller, down, Mingo, you'll hurt Montrose with your big paws, Montrose knew me, didn't he, mama, where's Uncle Theo gone to, I hardly saw him, Edward don't pull my skirt so, it's new, Henrietta I've got such a sweet dress for you, I got it in Geneva, is Willy all right, I've got him a marvellous pair of binoculars, I *smuggled* them, wasn't I brave, I've got presents for everybody, *laisse moi donc, Pierce, que tu m'embêtes*, mama, I went riding every day and my French is so good now and I practised my flute such a lot, I played in a concert, and aren't I brown, just look how brown I am, I've got some lace for you, mama, and a brooch for Mary, and a clock for papa, Henrietta could you take Montrose, do be careful with that suitcase it's got Italian glass in it, just put it on the bed, could you, Mary, oh it's so heavenly to be home, I do wish papa was here, everything looks so wonderful, I shall walk up and see Willy, what on earth are all those shells doing on my table, just push them up in a pile will you, oh damn they're falling all over the floor, Casie I do wish you'd keep the twins out of my room, now you can put the other suitcase on the table, that's right, thank you so much, and mama it was marvellous I went to such a fab dance, we all had to dress in black and white, and I went up in a helicopter, I was so frightened, it's not a bit like an aeroplane. . . ."

Three

JOHN DUCANE looked into the eyes of Jessica Bird. Jessica's eyes slowly filled with tears. Ducane looked away, sideways, downward. He had not left her then, when he ought to have done, when the parting would have been an agony to him. He was leaving her now when it was less than agony, when it was almost relief. He ought to have left her then. The fact remained that he ought to leave her now. He needed this thought to strengthen him against her tears.

He looked up again, past her blurred suffering head. His imagination, already alienated from her room, perceived its weirdness, Jessica's room was naval in its austerity. No homely litter of books or papers proclaimed its inhabitant and the pattern of clean hard colours and shapes was not merged into any human mess or fuzz. If furniture is handy man-adjusted objects for sitting, lying, writing, putting, the room contained no furniture, only surfaces. Even the chair on which Ducane was sitting, the only chair, was just a sloping surface bearing no friendly curved relation to the human form. Even the bed wherein he had once been used to wrangle with Jessica looked like a board, its rumpled shame ironed smooth. Formica shelves, impersonal as coffee bar table tops, supported the entities, neither ornaments nor works of art, which Jessica made or found. She wandered the rubbish tips at night, bringing back bricks, tiles, pieces of wood, tangles of wire. Sometimes she made these things into other things. Sometimes they were allowed to remain themselves. Most of the entities however were made of newspaper by a method perfected in Jessica's bathroom at a cost of regularly blocked drains. A half-digested mush wherein newsprint was still partly visible was solidified to form neat feather-weight mathematical objects with pierced coloured interiors. These objects, standing inscrutably in rows, often seemed to Ducane to belong to a series the principle of which he had not grasped. They were not intended for contemplation and were soon destroyed.

Jessica taught painting and English at a primary school.

She was twenty-eight and looked eighteen. Ducane, round-blue-eyed, hook nosed, patchily grey, was forty-three and looked forty-three. They had met at a party. Falling in love surprised them both. Jessica, pale, thin, mini-skirted, with long brownish gold hair tangling over her shoulders or pony-tailed with in-twisted ribbons, presented to Ducane an almost unintelligible thing and certainly not his kind of thing. She seemed to him vastly talented and almost totally non-intellectual, an amalgam he had never encountered before. She belonged to a *race* of the young whose foreignness he felt and had never dreamt of penetrating. They had made each other puzzled and happy for a while. Ducane made her presents of books she did not read, jewellery she could not wear, and small expensive *objets d'art* which, placed among her tribal trinkets, took on a truly surrealist air of estrangement. He tried vainly to persuade her to work in permanent materials. She saw him as corrupted, fascinating, infinitely old.

Though Ducane did not fully realise it, his nervous uncertain sensuality needed some sophisticated intellectual encouragement, a certain kind of play, which Jessica was unable to provide. His profound puritanism could not in any case brook a long affair. He had not the temperament to be anybody's lover. He knew this. His adventures had been infrequent and fairly short. He felt a rational guilt too at keeping this young attractive girl for himself when he did not intend to marry her. Ducane, who liked his life to be simple, did not care for concealments and feelings of guilt. In time, the excitements of discovery diminished, he began to find her curious aesthetic more exasperating than charming, and was able to see her less as a rare and exotic animal and more as an eccentric English girl, not after all so young, and well on the way to becoming nothing more mysterious than an eccentric English middle-aged woman. He had then, ashamed of himself for not having had it earlier, the strength to end an affair which he knew should never have been started. It was then, over eighteen months ago, that he ought to have left her. He allowed her tears to move him then and agreed that though no longer lovers they should remain friends, meeting almost as often as before. He was the readier to agree since he was still half in love with her.

There was perhaps in his passion more cunning than he

knew, since when he had released himself from his primary
guilt he found her freshly charming, contemplated and
touched her with an unmarred delight, and half persuaded
himself that he had acquired a child, a friend. He became
gradually and sadly aware that she did not share his new-
found liberty. He had not set her free. She was still in love
with him and indeed still behaved as if she were his mistress.
Her time consisted of seeing him, waiting, and seeing him
again, of presence, absence, presence. She watched him
anxiously, muting her love, instinctively afraid of making
him feel trapped or guilty. She touched him very carefully
with superficial lingering touches as if to extract some essence,
some strong salve, to keep her through those empty absence
times. The world still came to her only through him. He
became aware of a wrought-up intensity of suffering which
she could not forbear occasionally to let him glimpse. He
began to dread his visits to her for fear of these death's head
glimpses. They both became frightened, irritable, quarrel-
some. Ducane at last decided that there was only one
remedy, the brutal one of a complete parting. He had
thought this into clarity. But since he had been talking to
her, trying to explain, they were back again in the familiar
muddled atmosphere of pity and passion.

"What have I done?"

"You haven't done anything."

"Then why can't things go on, why do you suddenly say
this now?"

"I've been thinking. It's a totally wrong situation."

"There's nothing wrong. I just love you."

"That's the trouble."

"There's little enough love in the world. Why do you
want to kill mine?"

"It's not so simple, Jessica. I can't just accept your love."

"I don't see why not."

"It isn't fair to you. I can't keep you cornered?"

"Suppose I want to be cornered."

"What you want isn't the point. Be tough enough to see
that."

"You think you're acting in my best interests?"

"I know I am."

"You've got tired of me, why not say so?"

"Jessica, you know that I love you. I just can't go on making you suffer like this."

"I'll suffer less in time. Why should one live without suffering anyway?"

"It's bad for us both. I must take some responsibility—"

"Damn your responsibility. There's someone else. You've taken a new mistress."

"I haven't taken a new mistress."

"You promised faithfully that you'd tell me if you ever did."

"I keep my promises. I haven't."

"Then why can't things go on as before? I don't ask much of you."

"That's just it!"

"Anyway, John, I'm just not going to let you go away. I honestly . . . don't . . . think . . . I could stand it."

"Oh God," said Ducane.

"You're killing me," she said, "for something that's just—abstract."

"Oh God," he said, and got up, turning his back on her. He was afraid that the girl, who was kneeling on the floor in front of him, would throw herself forward and clasp his knees. The violence of his words, of her surprise, had kept them till now facing each other rigidly.

Ducane said to himself, human frailty, wickedness in me, has made this situation where I automatically have to behave like a brute. She is right to say why kill love, there is never enough. Yet I have to kill this love. Oh God, why is it so like a murder. If I could only take all the suffering on to myself. But that is one of the punishments of wickedness, perhaps the last and worst one, that even if one wills it one cannot do it.

She said behind him, her voice breaking, "Well, I think there must be *some* special reason. Something's happened to you—"

The trouble was that this was true, and Ducane was weakened by a sense of the impurity of his motives. He knew the act was right, and perhaps he could have done it as a naked simple act, but the shadows of his own interests confused him. He wanted to set Jessica free, but he wanted even more to be free himself. For what had happened to John Ducane was Kate Gray.

Ducane had known Kate for a long time; only lately with that easy shifting of consciousness in relation to the utterly familiar which is one of the privileges of growing older, he had found himself somewhat in love with her and had apprehended her as somewhat in love with him. The discovery brought him no dismay. Kate was very married. He was certain that there was no thought in her lovely head which she did not impart, in their long nightly conversations, to her husband. He had no doubt that the married pair had discussed him. He would not have been mocked, but he might have been laughed at. He could hear Kate saying, "John's a bit sweet on me, you know!" Whatever had so beautifully happened was something to which Octavian was privy. There was, in the situation, no danger. There was no question of a love affair. Ducane could tell Jessica truthfully that he had no mistress and no prospect of one. In fact, following some cautious instinct, Ducane had never mentioned Kate to Jessica, nor Jessica to Kate. He knew that Kate, in her new awareness of him, took him to be fancy free, and that this was an important belief. The irony of it was that he *was* fancy free. Only now that his feelings for Kate had become more urgent he felt the imperative need to rid himself of this last vestige of an entanglement.

What John envisaged with Kate, and envisaged fairly clearly, was something which was new in his life, and in his vision of it there was a kind of resignation, an acceptance of himself as no longer young and no longer likely to marry. He needed a resting point, he needed a home, he needed, even, a family. He knew, without her having said it, that Kate understood this perfectly. She had told him, he had told her, in half passionate, often wholly passionate, kisses which they now exchanged quite easily and spontaneously, smiling into each other's eyes, whenever they happened to be alone together. He knew that for Kate there was nothing but joy in the prospect of so caging him. For himself, the relationship would at times be painful, and had already been so. But he could embrace these exact, these detailed pains; and even the pain could be an element in something that was wholly good. Kate's generosity, her happiness, even her love for her husband, perhaps especially her love for her husband, could make a house for John. He liked and respected Octavian, he was fond of all the children and especially of Barbara. He needed to be committed and attached at last and to be able to love in innocence, and he felt certain now that he could commit himself to Kate, and through her to her family and to her whole household. But to do this with a free and truthful heart he would have to end, and end completely, this muddled compromise with Jessica which should never have come into being at all. Kate had never questioned him. When she did he would have to be able to tell the truth. This was the personal urgency which made him feel, as he heard Jessica sobbing behind him, so like a murderer.

Ducane got into his car. He sat in the front of the car next to his chauffeur. He felt exhausted and frantic and unclean. He had given way, he had taken her in his arms, he had promised to see her next week. All was to do again.

To gain some immediate relief of his feelings he said to the chauffeur, "It's awful—I mean an awful day—everything has gone wrong."

Ducane's chauffeur, a Scotsman called Gavin Fivey, slewed his brown eyes round for a moment in the direction of his employer. He said nothing. But something to do with the way in which he now gripped the wheel conveyed sympathy, like a firm pressure of the hand.

Ducane's father had been a Glasgow solicitor, but his grandfather had been a successful distiller, and Ducane had money. His one extravagance, apart from his Bentley, was his manservant. He was aware of the jokes and rumours at his expense which this peculiarity occasioned. But Ducane, who suffered from a physical maladroitness which he connected with his being left handed, had never learnt to drive, and saw no reason why he should not treat himself to a chauffeur. He had in fact been indifferently served by a number of men who had not lived in his house. Fivey, fairly new on the job, was his first experiment with a servant who lived in.

Ducane had been influenced in Fivey's favour by two things, the man's appearance and the fact, discreetly revealed with no further details by the employment agency, that he was a jailbird. Their common Scottishness was a bond too. Fivey had even been to the same primary school in Glasgow that had nurtured Ducane. This revelation, together with the dissimilarity of their subsequent careers, rather charmed Ducane. He had hoped to hear something of Fivey's adventures as a criminal, but so far he had learnt little about his servant's past except for the fact that Fivey's mother, as he announced unexpectedly one day, "was a mermaid". "A mermaid in a circus, you understand," Fivey had added in his slow Scottish voice. Ducane did not ask whether she was a real mermaid or a fake one. He preferred not to know.

Fivey was very unusual to look at. He had an extremely large shaggy head which made him look like a figure in a carnival, or as Ducane sometimes thought, like Bottom under the enchantment. It was never clear to Ducane whether this feature made Fivey look monstrous or beautiful. His copious hair and long drooping moustaches were reddish brown. His complexion was of a brownish apricot hue and covered with abnormally large freckles so that his broad spotted face suggested that of an animal, a spaniel perhaps. His wide-apart eyes, of a rich clear brown, were slightly slanted and if Ducane had not known him to be Scottish he would have taken him for some kind of Slav. Fivey was still new enough to be, for Ducane who would not have dreamt of discussing his servant with anyone else, an object of private speculation and something of a hobby. Fivey was meticulously neat in the house and could cook two or three dishes. He was taciturn and apparently friendless and seemed to spend his time off in his room reading women's magazines. He irritated Ducane by eating peppermint creams in the car and by singing Jacobite songs, rather drearily, as he went about his household tasks. Ducane thought it possible that Fivey did not realise that he was singing aloud. So far he had not had the heart to reprimand him. He hoped, at least, that the fellow was reasonably contented.

Ducane's parents were dead and his only close relation was a married sister who lived in Oban and whom he scarcely saw. Ducane had read history and subsequently law at Balliol, had proceeded to All Souls and had been called to the bar. He had practised briefly as a barrister but he was not enough of an actor to enjoy life in the Courts. He disliked legal wit in serious situations and shunned an exercise of power which he conceived to be bad for his character. In the war he was early posted to Intelligence and, to his regret, spent the war years in Whitehall. He became a civil servant and was at present the legal adviser to the Government department of which Octavian was head. He had maintained his academic interests and was a noted expert on Roman law, a subject on which he lectured intermittently at a London college. He was a busy successful man and aware of himself as a respected figure. People tended to admire him and find him mysterious. Ducane saw his career with a cool eye. He had retained, and now deliberately fostered, the consciousness, as well as the conscience, of a Scottish puritan. He had no religious beliefs. He simply wanted to lead a clean simple life and to be a good man, and this remained to him as a real, and also feasible, ambition.

As the Bentley now turned into Whitehall Ducane, thinking miserably about Jessica, felt, not for the first time, a distinct impulse to lay his hand upon Fivey's shoulder. He noticed that he had already stretched his arm along the seat behind his chauffeur's back. The contact, suddenly so vivid to his imagination, would have brought with it some profound and healing comfort. Ducane smiled to himself sadly. Here was yet another of the paradoxes of life. He withdrew his arm from its dangerous position.

Four

"HELLO, OCTAVIAN. You left a note that you wanted to see me."

Ducane put his head round Octavian's door. It was Saturday morning, the day after Radeechy's suicide.

"Come in, John, come in. You find us in the soup."

Already seated in Octavian's room were Richard Biranne and George Droysen, formerly a journalist and now a young Principal in the department.

Ducane came in and sat down and looked enquiringly at Octavian.

"Look," said Octavian, "you aren't going to be pleased. Well—shall I start to tell him, Droysen, or will you?"

"You tell him," said Droysen.

"It's this matter of bloody Radeechy," said Octavian.

Ducane had heard yesterday about Radeechy's death. He had met Radeechy occasionally in the office, but had little acquaintance with him.

"Yes?"

"Well, it's the press as usual. First the press and then the PM. It would happen on a Saturday. Anyway, to tell the tale as briefly as possible, Droysen was around last night in his old haunts in Fleet Street, and it seems that the press have got hold of some sort of story about Radeechy."

"What sort of story?"

"This is what we haven't found out yet, but it sounds like the usual sort of story, at least it's got the two familiar elements, women and money."

"You mean blackmail?"

"Well, it sounds like it. It features a girl who's known as Helen of Troy. I think we can guess her profession. And there's something about 'a large sum of money changed hands'. That's the phrase, isn't it, Droysen? 'A large sum of money changed hands'."

"Whose hands?" said Ducane.

"Don't know."

"But they haven't published this stuff?"

"No, no, it's far too hot. As far as Droysen could gather one of the larger nastier dailies has bought it. A pretty large sum of money probably changed hands there! And now they're sitting on it to see what happens next, and meanwhile every sort of rumour is going about."

"You don't know who provided the story?"

"No, but it's said to have been someone inside the office. Not nice!"

"Radeechy didn't have access to any secret material, did he?"

"Well, not officially. But that isn't going to impress anybody."

"Have Security been on to you?"

"Not yet. I telephoned to tell them of course, since they're so mad keen to know every little thing, and they just grunted, but the PM's been on to me."

"He'd heard about the story and the rumours?"

"Well, he'd heard *something*, and I told him the rest and he was not pleased."

"It's a bit early to get upset," said Ducane. "We don't even know what this story is."

"No, but you know as well as I do that politicians aren't concerned with justice being done, they're concerned with justice seeming to be done as a result of their keen-eyed vigilance. Apparently he's already being pressed to have an official enquiry."

"Which kind?"

"That hasn't emerged yet, but the point is, this is where you come in."

"Me?"

"Yes. You'd be surprised how well thought of you are amongst our leaders. The PM wants you to conduct an enquiry."

"What status would I have?" said Ducane.

"Well, thank God you're taking it so coolly, I thought you'd explode! Strictly speaking you wouldn't have any status, that is the enquiry would be a purely departmental one. I would instruct you to enquire and you would enquire. The rest would have to be played by ear."

"I see. I suppose quick action is the point."

"Precisely. The PM doesn't want this thing to snowball.

If we can clear it all up quickly, establish what went on if anything, and demonstrate that there's no Security interest, we can avoid an official enquiry which the PM doesn't want any more than we do."

"It's one of those things which it's not easy to demonstrate," said Ducane. "If Radeechy had a fishy private life, and if the press keep dropping hints, people will believe anything. It's become a sort of cliché. However, I'll certainly have a go. It doesn't look as if I've got much choice anyway! I suppose there isn't the faintest chance that poor Radeechy *was* being blackmailed into handing over secret stuff?"

"Not the faintest," said Octavian. "You'd agree, wouldn't you, you two?"

"One never knows about anyone," said Biranne, "but I shouldn't have thought it of Radeechy."

"I agree," said George Droysen. "And I knew him reasonably well as far as meeting in the office goes."

"That doesn't go very far," said Ducane. "However it appears he *was* being blackmailed?"

"So the tale runs."

"And he did shoot himself. Why did he shoot himself?"

"And in the office too," said Octavian. "That does strike me as somehow odd and significant. Why couldn't he shoot himself decently at home?"

"He was terribly depressed about his wife's death," said George Droysen. "You remember she got killed last year, fell out of a window or something. He was quite shattered."

"Well, that's a possible motive," said Ducane. "He didn't leave a note, did he?"

"No," said Octavian. "That's a bit odd too. He was such a one for writing minutes about every damn thing. You'd think he'd have left us a minute about his own death!"

"If we could discover exactly why he did it, that should settle the Security point. It looks as if we shall have to find out a lot about Radeechy. Did you know him well, Biranne?"

"Scarcely knew him at all," said Biranne. "We just met in the office, and not much even there. No, I didn't know him."

"I never saw much of him myself," said Ducane, "but I confess I'm surprised about this Helen of Troy story. I shouldn't have thought Radeechy was that sort of chap."

"Any man is that sort of chap," said Biranne, and giggled.

Ducane ignored him. "He seemed to me much more the cranky scientist type. The last conversation I had with him was about poltergeists. He had some theory about their being connected with the water table."

"He communed with spirits," said George Droysen.

"After all," said Octavian, "spiritualism and magic and all that are connected with sex, always have been. Sex comes to most of us with a twist. Maybe that was just his twist."

Ducane was not sure whether sex came to most of us with a twist. He could not help wondering whether it came to Octavian with one. "Has he any close family?" he asked.

"Apparently there's no one except a sister who's been living in Canada for years."

"I'd better see the police," said Ducane, "and look over whatever they've got, though I imagine that won't amount to much. Would you see that I'm OK'd with Scotland Yard, Octavian? And perhaps you'd get back to Fleet Street, Droysen, and track down that story for us, and also find out who gave it to the press."

"Back to the old pubs!" said Droysen. "It's a pleasure."

"You'd better write me an official letter, Octavian."

"I've already drafted one."

"Well, put into it, would you, that I can use my own discretion about not revealing anything which I think is not germane to the purpose of the enquiry."

"I suppose that's all right?" said Octavian dubiously.

"Of course it is. After all, we aren't investigating poor Radeechy's morals. What was his first name, by the way?"

"Joseph," said Biranne.

"Are you going to Dorset, Octavian?"

"Certainly! What's more, you are too. There's no point in starting in until young Droysen has done his detective work."

"All right. Ring me as soon as you get anything." He gave Droysen the Trescombe telephone number. "Well, that's all, friends."

Ducane stood up. Droysen stood up too. Biranne remained seated, looking at Octavian with a deferential air.

Ducane cursed his own bad manners. He had become so used to being, in his friendship with Octavian, the acknowledged superior that he had for a moment forgotten that this was Octavian's room, Octavian's meeting, and not his. But his chief feeling at that instant was hostility to Biranne. Once, many years ago, across a partition in a restaurant, Ducane had overheard Biranne talking about him, Biranne was speculating about whether Ducane was homosexual. Cursing himself too for the persistence of this memory, Ducane recalled the particular quality of Biranne's mocking laughter.

Five

"HOW did they cook eggs in ancient Greece?" Edward Biranne asked his mother.

"Do you know, I'm not sure," said Paula.

"What's Greek for a poached egg?" said Henrietta.

"I don't know. There are references to eating eggs but I can't recall any references to cooking them."

"Perhaps they ate them raw," said Henrietta.

"Not very likely," said Paula. "Can you remember anything in Homer?"

The twins, taught Greek and Latin from an early age by their mother, were already fairly proficient classicists. However, they could not remember anything in Homer.

"We could try Liddell and Scott," said Henrietta.

"Willy will know," said Edward.

"May we have that seaweed in our bath tonight?" said Henrietta.

"You'd better ask Mary," said Paula.

"There's a letter for you downstairs," said Edward. "May I have the stamp?"

"You pig!" cried his sister. The twins, cooperative in most matters, were competitive about stamps.

Paula laughed. She was just preparing to leave the house. "What kind of stamp is it?"

"Australian."

A cold dark shadow fell across Paula. She went on mechanically smiling and answering her children's chatter as she left her room and moved down the stairs. Of course it might always be from someone else. But she didn't know anyone else in Australia.

The letters were always laid out on the big round rosewood table which stood in the centre of the hall, and which was also usually covered with newspapers and whatever books members of the household were reading and with the paraphernalia of the twins' games. Edward ran ahead and retrieved his copy of *More Hunting Wasps* which he had laid down on top of the letter so that Henrietta should not observe the stamp. Paula saw from a distance Eric's unmistakable writing upon the envelope.

"May I have it, Mummy, please?"

"May I have the next one," cried Henrietta, "*and* the next one, *and* the next one?"

Paula's hand trembled. She tore the envelope open quickly, clawed the letter out and put it in her pocket, and gave the envelope to her son. She went out into the sunshine.

The big sphere, cracked and incomplete at the near end, composed of the sky and the sea, enclosed Paula like a cold vault and she shivered in the sunlight as if it were the ray of a malignant star. She bowed her head, making a movement as if she were casting a veil about it, and bolted across the lawn and into the meadow and along the path beside the hawthorn hedge which led down towards the sea. Now she saw in the same sunny darkness her sandalled feet slithering upon the purplish stones of the beach as she fled forward, as if she were falling, to get to the edge of the water. Here the beach shelved steeply and she sat down, with a rattling flurry of pebbles, upon a crest of stones with the sea just below her. It was so calm today that it seemed motionless, touching the shore with an inaudible lapping kiss and the occasional curl of a Lilliputian wavelet. The sun shone into the green water revealing the stone-scattered sand which was briefly uncovered at low tide, and farther out a mottled line of mauve seaweed. The water surface shadowed and dappled the sand with faint bubbly forms like imperfections in glass.

That she had once been in love with Eric Sears Paula knew from the evidence of letters which she had found. She did not know it from memory. At least, she could remember events and pieces of her own conduct which were only explicable on the assumption that she had been in love with Eric. But the love itself she could not really remember. It seemed to have been not only killed but removed even from the lighted caravan of her accepted and remembered life by the shock of that awful scene.

Eric Sears had been the occasion of Paula's divorce. With the precipitate cruelty of a very jealous man, Richard, whose many infidelities she had tolerated, divorced her for a single lapse. The occasion of it all, her insane passion for Eric, had been erased from her mind, but otherwise she had got over nothing. That terrible time, its misery and its shame, lived within her unassimilated and unresolved. She had acted crazily, she had acted badly, and she had got away with nothing. Paula's pride, her dignity, her lofty conception of herself, had suffered a savage wound and that wound still ached and burned, in the daytime and in the nighttime. She thought that no one knew of this, though she reflected sometimes that of course Richard must know.

Her love affair with Eric—it had been very brief—now seemed to her something so unutterably mean and unworthy that she could not, even when she tried hard to discipline herself to do so, recognise herself as a protagonist. While she was fairly indulgent to others, had been so to Richard, Paula thought that faithfulness in marriage was very important. Infidelity was undignified and usually involved lying or at least half-truths and concealments. Paula cared very much about what might be called "moral style". Someone had once said of her, not quite justly, "She wouldn't mind what awful thing you did so long as you didn't *talk* about it in a certain kind of way." In fact Paula had, by the time their marriage ended, almost succeeded in convincing her husband that she hated his lies about his adventures more than she hated the adventures themselves. And what offended her in memory about her own conduct, was not so much that she had actually gone to bed with Eric but that she had half-lied to Richard about it and that she had played a mean scurrying part and become involved in a situation which she did not understand and could not control. She regretted it all with an undying regret which only continual efforts of her reason prevented from utterly poisoning her life.

What would have happened if there had not been that dreadful scene with Richard she did not know. Richard would probably have divorced her in any case, he was savage with resentment. She could not conceive that she could have gone on loving Eric. He had made her lose too much. But what had really, and it seemed instantaneously, destroyed her love was his crushing physical defeat at the hands of Richard. This was unjust, but with the deep dark logical injustice of forces which govern us at our most extreme moments and which, though they have nothing to do with morality, must sometimes be recognised in our lives like gods. That scene still haunted Paula in sleeping and in waking nightmares, Richard's distorted face, Eric's screams, the blood that seemed to have got everywhere. Of course they had all pretended that it was an accident.

Poor Eric. He knew the dark decision of the god as well as Paula did and he submitted to it. He was utterly subdued by shame. When Paula visited him in hospital she soon knew that he no longer wanted her to come. They scrambled through their adieus. Eric wrote that he was going to Australia. He wrote from Australia in a letter of farewell that he had met a girl on the boat and was going to marry her. That had been nearly two years ago. Paula did not want to hear from Eric again. She did not want to know that Eric still existed.

The sun dazzled angrily upon the water. Frowning against it she slowly unfolded the letter.

My dearest,

You will be surprised at hearing from me again—or perhaps you will not. I somehow know that you have been thinking about me. When I last wrote to you I thought I was going to be married. Well, all that has fallen through. I must admit that I am in a state of utter wretchedness and have been for a long time. I didn't know that such extreme unhappiness could continue for so long. I write to say that I know now that coming here was a mistake, leaving you was a mistake. And I have decided to come home. In fact when you get this letter I shall already be on the ship.

Of course I do not know what may or may not have happened to you since we parted, but my intuition tells me that you will not have rushed into another marriage. Paula, we are bound together. This is the conclusion to which, in these awful months of misery, I have at last come. There are eternal bonds which are made in registry offices and in churches, there are eternal bonds which are made in other and stranger and more terrible ways. You understand what I mean, Paula. I suffered for you, I was wounded for you, and there is a lack which only you can fill and a pain which only you can cure. I thought I would "get over" what happened. I have not. *And I know that you have not either.* (I have had the most *extraordinary* series of dreams about you, by the way.) I think we belong to each other. We must live with what has happened, we must live it into ourselves, and we must do this *together*. (How very strange the human mind is. I have had many new causes for wretchedness since I came to Australia. People have disappointed me and deceived me and let me down. But everything that has made me really miserable has been somehow connected with *that*, has somehow *been that*.) You owe this to me, Paula, and I know that you pay your debts. You cannot be happy yourself or feel pleased with the way you behaved to me when I have been (I use the words ·advisedly) nearly destroyed because I was guilty of loving you. One must acknowledge the past, assimilate it, be reconciled to it. We can heal each other, we can save each other, Paula, and only we can do this for each other. I feel an echo from you deep in my heart and I know that what I say is true. Wait for me, pray for me, receive me, oh my dear. I will write again from the ship. To all eternity *Yours*   Eric

Paula crumpled up the letter. Then she tore it up into very small pieces and strewed it upon the still taut surface skin of the water. How that letter conjured Eric up, in all the detail which she had mercifully forgotten, like a demon figure in front of her shadowing the bright sea: his forced ecstasies, his mystical certainties, his blend, which she had once found so touching, of weakness and menace, the ruthless cunning of his egoism. Of course she had acted badly, not least in abandoning him so rapidly at the very end. But she had forever been emptied of love for him and of the ability to help him. That was her certainty. Was it true though, Paula asked herself, trying to steady her mind, could she still help Eric, ought she to try? Perhaps he was right to say that there was still something which they had to do for each other. Her heart shuddered at it. At the idea of seeing him again she felt nausea, a kind of sick fright. There was something demoniac about Eric. Paula had never been frightened of Richard, although he was a man who was capable of violence. She knew now that she had been very very frightened of Eric. This was the quality of the love which she had so completely forgotten.

Six

"It was an Abyssinian cat
And on its dulcimer it sat,"

chanted Edward, hauling Montrose out of the basket into
which Mingo, repulsed by the cat's cold stare, had been
making tentative and unsuccessful efforts to climb. Mingo
climbed in. Affronted, Montrose escaped from Edward
on to the stove and fluffed himself out into his bird look.

"May we have that seaweed in our bath tonight?"
Henrietta asked Mary Clothier.

"Whatever do you want seaweed in your bath for?" asked
Mary.

"It's our special cure for rheumatism," said Edward.

"You aren't suffering from rheumatism, are you,
Edward?"

"No, it's for Uncle Theo really, but we thought we'd
better test it ourselves in case there were any toxic effects."

"Last time you two had seaweed in your bath it all went
down the plug and it was stopped up for days," said Casie,
who had just come in with a basket of lettuces and tomatoes.

"We *promise* we won't let it go down the plug this time!"

"All right then," said Mary. "Look, I do wish you'd take
those stones out into the garden."

Kate and Ducane who were passing by the kitchen door
smiled at each other and went on into the hall. Ducane
called back to the kitchen, "Oh Mary. Kate and I are just
going up to see Willy."

"Well, don't be late for tea, it's special Sunday tea."

"And how is my little nymph?" said Ducane to Barbara,
whom they met in the doorway.

"*J'aimerais mieux t'avoir dans mon lit que le tonnerre*," replied
Barbara primly.

Ducane laughed, reaching out to pluck her hair as she
skipped for a few paces beside them.

Barbara was round-faced, like her mother, and had the
same shortish slightly fuzzy fair hair, only whereas Kate's
unkempt mop shifted about her like a slightly crazed halo,

43

Barbara's hair, much more carefully cut, cupped her head like an elaborate filigree head-piece. Her complexion was that of a child, rosy and shiny, with that delicious apple-like shininess which usually disappears in adolescence. Short-skirted, long-legged, barefooted, her prancing feet were the same smooth glowing golden-brown colour as her legs.

"Why don't you go and look for Pierce?" said Kate. "I saw him down by the churchyard and he looked rather lonely to me."

Barbara shook her head with a virtuous air. "I must go and practise my flute. I'm going to give Willy a Mozart recital."

"Aren't you going to give me a Mozart recital?" Ducane asked.

"No. Only Willy." She skipped away into the house.

"How that child has grown!" said Ducane. "She's as tall as you. And nearly as pretty."

"Darling! I'm afraid Pierce and Barbara aren't exactly hitting it off since she came back."

"Well, you know what's the matter. They're growing up."

"I know. They do develop early these days. I thought somehow, having been together so much like brother and sister, they'd be sort of inoculated."

"Nothing inoculates them against *that*," said Ducane. And he realised as he spoke that he did not at all like the idea of Barbara being involved in *that*. He would have liked her never to grow up.

"But this poor chap," said Kate, reverting to what they had been discussing earlier. "Why did he do it?"

Ducane had not spoken to Kate about the enquiry. Although he had received the news of his task coolly enough from Octavian he was feeling far from happy about it. It was the sort of thing which could turn into an awful mess. It might be very difficult to find out the truth quickly, and impossible to demonstrate that there was no security interest and no case for a more elaborate investigation. However, it was not just the prospect of failing and being discredited which daunted Ducane. He did not like the idea of investigating another man's private life in this way. Moreover the personality of Radeechy, about whom he had

44

reflected considerably since his arrival in Dorset, now seemed to him both puzzling and sinister. He was sure that the spiritualism, or whatever it was, was connected with the suicide; and he felt instinctively that here, once he had started to pry, he would unearth something very unpleasant indeed.

"I don't know why he did it," said Ducane. "He lost his wife lately. That might have been it."

By this time they had crossed the level lawn behind the house with its two tall feathery acacia trees, climbed over a low palisade of string and sticks which had something to do with the twins, and were climbing a path, made with great labour the previous year by Pierce and Barbara out of pebbles from the beach, between twin hedges of plump veronica bushes. Ducane's hand passed caressingly over the compact curves of the bushes. At this moment his mind was divided into several compartments or levels. At one level, perhaps the highest, he was thinking about Willy Kost, whom he was so shortly to meet and whom he had not seen now for some time, since on Ducane's last two weekends Willy had declared by telephone that he wanted no visitors. At another level Ducane was thinking in an upset nervous way about Radeechy and wondering what George Droysen would find out in Fleet Street. At yet another level, or in another compartment, he was miserably recalling his weakness at the end of the scene with Jessica and miserably wondering what on earth he was going to do about her next week.

However, he did not, today, feel too bad about Jessica. Ducane did not usually believe in waiting for the gods to help him out of his follies with miracles, but just today his worry about Jessica had become a little cloudy, softened by a steamy cloud of vague optimism. Somehow or other it could still turn out all right, he felt. This was possibly because, in an adjoining compartment, he was experiencing a pure and intense joy at the presence beside him of Kate, at the proximity of their two bodies, which touched occasionally with a pleasant, clumsy, friendly jostling as they walked along, and at the knowledge, with him as a physical aura rather than a thought, that he would kiss Kate when they reached the beech wood.

There was also elsewhere, at what was by no means the lowest level, though it was certainly the least articulate, a consciousness of his surroundings, a participation, an extension of himself into nature, into the compact curvy veronica bushes, into the spherical huge-leaved catalpa tree at the end of the garden, into the rosy sun-warmed bricks of the wall, through an archway in which they were now passing. These bricks were so old and worn and pitted, so edgeless and cornerless, that they looked like a natural conglomeration of red stones or playthings of the sea. Everything in Dorset is round, thought Ducane. The little hills are round, these bricks are round, the yew trees that grow in the hedgerows are round, the veronica bushes, the catalpa tree, the crowns of the acacia, the pebbles on the beach, the clump of small bamboos beside the arch. He thought, everything in Dorset is *just the right size*. This thought gave him immense satisfaction and sent out through the other layers and compartments of his mind a stream of warm and soothing particles. Thus he walked on with Kate at his side, conveying along with him his jumbled cloud of thoughts whose self-protective and self-adjusting chemistry is known as mental health.

They were walking now in a narrow lane with high sloping banks up which white flowering nettles and willow herb crawled out of a matrix of tall yellow moss, so dry and dusty-looking in the hot sun that it scarcely seemed like vegetation. There was an old thick powdery smell, perhaps the smell of the moss. A cuckoo called nearby in the wood above, clear, cool, precise, hollow, mad. Kate took hold of Ducane's hand.

"I think I won't come in with you to Willy's," said Kate. "He's been rather down lately and I'm sure it's better if you see him alone. I don't think Willy will ever kill himself, do you, John?"

Willy Kost was given to announcing from time to time that his life was an unbearable burden and he proposed shortly to terminate it.

"I don't know," said Ducane.

He felt that he had not done enough for Willy. Most people who knew Willy felt this. But he was not an easy person to help. Ducane had first met Willy, who was a classical scholar living on a pension from the German government and working on an edition of Propertius, at a meeting in London at which Ducane was reading a rather obscure little paper on the concept of *specificatio* in Roman law. He had been responsible for removing Willy from a bed-sitter in Fulham and installing him at Trescombe Cottage. He had often wondered since whether this was not a mistake. He had conceived of providing his friend with the protection of a household. But in fact Willy was able to be as solitary as he pleased.

"I don't think that if he was really seriously contemplating suicide he would let the children come to him the way he does," said Kate. While adult visitors were often barred, the children came and went freely at the cottage.

"Yes, I think that's true. I wonder, when he won't let any of us see him, if he's really working?"

"Or just brooding and remembering. It's awful to think of."

"I've never felt any inclination to commit suicide, have you, Kate?"

"Good heavens no! But then for me life's always been such fun."

"It's hard for people like us with ordinary healthy minds," said Ducane, "to imagine what it would be like for one's whole mode of consciousness to be painful, to be hell."

"I know. All those things he must remember and dream about."

Willy Kost had spent the war in Dachau.

"I wish Theo would try to see more of him," said Ducane.

"Theo! He's a broken reed if ever there was one. He's just a bundle of nerves himself. *You* should see more of Willy. You can talk directly to people and tell them what to do. Most of us are afraid to."

"Sounds awful!" said Ducane and laughed.

"Seriously. I'm sure it would do Willy good if he were just forced to tell somebody what it was like in that camp. I think he's never uttered a word about it to anyone."

"I doubt if you are right. I can even imagine how difficult that might be," said Ducane. But the same idea had come to him before.

"One must be reconciled to the past," said Kate.

"When one's suffered injustice and affliction on the scale

47

on which Willy's suffered it," said Ducane, "it may just not be possible."

"Not possible to forgive?"

"Certainly not possible to forgive. Perhaps not possible to find any way of—thinking about it at all."

Ducane's imagination had often wrestled in vain with the question of what it must be like to be Willy Kost.

"I used to think he'd somehow break down with Mary," said Kate. "She really knows him best, apart from you I mean. But she says he hasn't talked to her at all about—that."

Ducane was thinking, we've nearly reached the wood, we've nearly reached the wood. The first shadows fell across them, the cuckoo uttered from farther off his crazed lascivious cry.

"Let's sit down here for a minute," said Kate.

There was a clean grey shaft of fallen tree from which a skirt of dry curled golden-brown beech leaves descended on either side. They sat down upon it, their feet rustling the dry leaves, and turned to face each other.

Kate took Ducane by the shoulders, studying him intently. Ducane looked into the intense streaky smudgy dark blue of her eyes. They both sighed. Then Kate kissed him with a slow and lingering motion. Ducane closed his eyes, turning his head now from the intensity of the kiss, and clutched her very closely against him, feeling the wiry imprint of her springy hair upon his cheek. They remained motionless for some time.

"Oh God, you do make me happy," said Kate.

"You make me happy too." He set her away from him again, smiling at her, feeling relaxed and free now, desiring her but not with anguish, seeing behind her the brown carpeted emptiness of the wood, while the sun glittered above them in shoals of semi-transparent leaves.

"You look more like the Duke of Wellington than ever. I love that little crest of grey hair that's coming right in the front. It is all right, isn't it, John?"

"Yes," he said gravely. "Yes. I have thought about it a lot and I do think it is all right."

"Octavian—well, you know what Octavian feels. You understand everything."

"Octavian's a very happy man."

"Yes, Octavian *is* a happy man. And that *is* relevant, you know."

"I know. Dear Kate, I'm a lonely person. And you're a generous woman. And we're both very rational. All's well here."

"I knew it was, John, only I just wanted you to say it, like that. I'm so glad. You're sure it won't be somehow painful for you, sad, you know—?"

"There will be some pain," he said, "but pain that I can deal with. And so much happiness too."

"Yes. One doesn't want to be just painless and content, does one? You and I can *be* so much to each other. Loving people matters, doesn't it? Really nothing else matters except that."

"Come in," said Willy Kost.

Ducane entered the cottage.

Willy was sitting stretched out in a low chair beside the hearth, his heels dug into a spilling of grey wood ash. The gramophone behind him was playing the slow movement of something or other. It seemed to Ducane that Willy's gramophone was always playing slow movements. The noise immediately irritated Ducane, who was unmusical to the point of positively disliking the concourse of sweet sounds. His mood as he approached the cottage had been elevated and intense. The harmony generated by his scene with Kate, the perfect understanding so quickly reached between them, had enabled him to switch his thought with a peculiar singleness of attention to the problem of Willy. The music was now like an alien presence.

Willy, who knew how Ducane felt about music, got up and lifted the playing arm off the record and turned the machine off.

"Sorry, Willy."

"S'all right," said Willy. "Sit down. Have something. Have some tea or something."

Willy limped into his little kitchen where Ducane heard the hiss and then the purr of the oil stove. The single main room of the cottage was filled with Willy's books, some on shelves, some still in boxes. Kate, who could not conceive of life without a large personal territory of significantly deployed objects, constantly complained that Willy had never unpacked. She had forgiven him his shudder when she once suggested that she should unpack for him.

The big table was covered with texts and notebooks. Here at least was an area of significance. Ducane touched the open pages, pretending to look at them. He felt a slight embarrassment as he often did with Willy.

"How goes it, Willy?"

"How goes what?"

"Well, life, work."

Willy came back into the room and leaned on the back of a chair, observing his guest with amused detachment. Willy was a small man, delicate in feature, with a long thin curvy mouth which seemed always a little moist and trembling. He had a great deal of longish white hair and a uniformly brown rather oily and glistening face and sardonic narrow brown eyes. A velvety brown mole on one cheek gave him a curious air of prettiness.

" 'Day unto day uttereth speech and night unto night showeth knowledge'."

Ducane smiled encouragingly. "Good!"

"Is it good? Excuse me while I make the tea."

He returned with the tea tray. Ducane accepted his cup and began to perambulate the room. Willy with a large glass of milk resumed his chair.

"I envy you *this*," said Ducane. He indicated the table. "No, you don't."

It was true that he did not. There was always a period of time, more or less brief, when they met after an interval, when Ducane fumbled, flattered. He was patronising Willy now, and they both knew it. The barrier created between them by this spontaneous, this as it seemed automatic, flattery and patronage could be broken easily by Willy's directness if Willy had the sheer energy to break it. Sometimes he had. Sometimes he had not, and would sit by listlessly while Ducane struggled with their meeting. Ducane in fact could overcome this automatic falseness in himself unaided, but it took a little time and a very conscious measure of seriousness and attention. Willy was always difficult.

"I envy something," said Ducane. "Perhaps I just wish I had been a poet."

"I doubt if you even wish that," said Willy. He lay back and closed his eyes. It looked as if it was one of his listless days.

"To live with poetry is next best," said Ducane. "My daily bread is quite other." He read out at random a couplet from the open page.

> "*Quare, dum licet, inter nos laetemur amantes:*
> *non satis est ullo tempore longus amor.*"

A physical vision of Kate came to him out of the words of Propertius, especially out of that final *amor*, so much stronger than the lilting Italian *amore*. He saw the furry softness of her shoulders as he had often seen them in the evening. He had never caressed her bare shoulders. *Amor.*

"Stuff, stuff, stuff," said Willy. "These were clichés for Propertius. In couplets like that he was talking in his sleep. Well, most human beings are talking in their sleep, even poets, even great poets." He added, "The only *amor* I know anything about is *amor fati.*"

"Surely a manifestation of pure wickedness," said Ducane.

"Do you really believe that?"

"That it's wicked to love destiny? Yes. What happens is usually what oughtn't to happen. Why love it?"

"Of course destiny shouldn't be thought of as purposive," said Willy, "it should be thought of as mechanical."

"But it isn't mechanical!" said Ducane. "We aren't mechanical!"

"We are the most mechanical thing of all. That is why we can be forgiven."

"Who says we can be forgiven? Anyway that needn't imply love of fate."

"It's not easy of course. Perhaps it's impossible. Can a thing be required of us and yet be impossible? I don't see why not."

"Submit to fate but don't love it. To love it one must be drunk."

"And one should not be drunk?"

"Of course not."

"Supposing being drunk is the only way to carry on?"

"Oh stop this, Willy!" said Ducane.

These conversations with Willy frightened him sometimes. He was never sure if Willy meant what he said or meant the opposite of what he said. He felt as if he were being used, as if Willy were using him as a hard neutral surface against which to crush, like insects, the thoughts which haunted him. Like a baffled witness, he was afraid of being deliberately led to make some damaging, some perhaps fatal, admission. He felt both powerless and responsible. He said, "There must be other ways of carrying on."

"Even without a God!"

"Yes."

"I don't see why," said Willy.

Ducane felt, as so often before, yawning between them the terrible gulf which divides the mentally healthy from the mentally crippled.

"But you *are* working?" said Ducane. He knew that he was falling back into the tone of patronising. Yet he feared Willy's obscure intensities and feared that he might be at such moments employed by Willy to confirm unwittingly some final edict of despair.

"No."

"Oh come!" Ducane knew that Willy had looked forward to this visit. He knew too that the visit was rendering Willy unspeakably miserable. This had happened before. In fact it often happened in spite of the fiction kept up briskly by everyone, including the two protagonists, that Ducane was eminently "good for" Willy.

Ducane thought, if I were not the tied-up puritan that I am I would touch him now, take his hand or something.

"What ees eet?" Willy was observing his friend. He spoke the question caressingly, exaggerating his foreign accent. It was a ritual question.

Ducane laughed. Some current flowed again, but flowing away from Willy, leaving him more isolated and unreadable than ever. "Oh, I'm just worrying about you."

"Do not do so, John. Tell me of your own things. Tell me about life at that famous place 'the office'. Do you know I have never been in that place where so many people spend their lives. Tell me about the office."

The wraith of Radeechy rose before Ducane like a physical presence in the room, and with it came the puzzlement and the curious fear which he had felt before. He knew that he must not tell Willy about Radeechy. Suicide is infectious, which is one reason why it is wrong. But he felt too that there was some germ of craziness here, perhaps even of evil, to which he should not expose the organism of Willy's soul, frail in ways which he could not determine or even imagine.

He said "It's very dull in the office. You are well out of it." He said to himself, I must remember to tell the others not to mention Radeechy to Willy. He thought, if Willy were ever to commit suicide I should never forgive myself, I should know it was my fault. Yet his affection was impotent. What could he do? If he could only persuade Willy to talk to him about the past.

He said abruptly, "You sleeping all right these days?"

"Yes, fine, until the cuckoo wakes me up about four thirty!"

"No bad dreams?"

They stared at each other, Ducane still standing with his tea cup and Willy stretched out in the chair. Willy smiled a slow rather cunning smile and began to whistle softly.

There was a sharp rap on the door which then flew open to admit the twins, marching abreast and talking at once.

"We've brought you something!" cried Edward.

"You'll never guess what it is!" cried Henrietta.

They marched up to Willy and laid a light soft spherical object on his knees. Willy straightened up to lean over it exclaiming with interest.

"Whatever can it be? What do you think it is, John?"

Ducane moved over to look at the elongated ball of dull green, a few inches long, which Willy was touching with a curious finger. "Some sort of bird's nest, I suppose," he said. He felt himself *de trop*, a spoilsport, an intruder upon a scene of intimates whose rhythm he could not catch.

"It's a long-tailed tit's nest," cried Edward.

"They've brought up their babies," cried Henrietta. "We watched them building the nest, we watched them all through, and now they've gone away. Isn't it a beautiful nest? You see, outside it's made of moss and lichen, see how

53

they've woven it together, and inside it's all lined with feathers."

"One man counted more than two thousand feathers in a long-tailed tit's nest!" cried Edward.

"It's very beautiful," said Willy. "Thank you, twins!" He looked up at Ducane over the nest which he was holding lightly in his hands. "Goodbye, John, thank you for coming."

"A bad crow tried to drive them away," Henrietta was explaining, "but they were so brave—"

Willy and Ducane smiled at each other. Ducane's smile was ironical and rueful. Willy's smile was apologetic and very sad in some way which Ducane could not fathom. With a salute, Ducane turned to the door.

Willy shouted after him, "I'm all right, you know. Tell them I'm all right."

Ducane walked down the meadow path of clipped grass and into the spotted shade of the beech wood. When he came to the smooth grey tree trunk on which he had embraced Kate he did not sit down upon it. He stood for a moment or two quite still. Then he knelt down in the crisp dry beech leaves, leaning his arms on the warm shaft of the tree. He was not thinking about Willy, he was not being sorry for Willy. He was being infinitely sorry for himself because the power was denied to him that comes from an understanding of suffering and pain. He would have liked to pray then for himself, to call suffering to him out of the chaos of the world. But he did not believe in God, and the kind of suffering which brings wisdom cannot be named and cannot without blasphemy be prayed for.

Seven

"WE haven't sung our bathing song *once* since you came back," Henrietta complained to Barbara.

"Well, you go and sing it."

"No, we must all four sing it or it isn't proper."

"I've forgotten it," said Barbara.

"I don't believe you," said Pierce.

Barbara was lying full length upon the ivy. Pierce was standing a little way off leaning against a tombstone off which he was intently scratching yellow lichen with a finger nail.

"You three go and bathe for heaven's sake," said Barbara. "I don't want to come. I feel far too lazy."

"Mingo's getting too hot," said Edward. "Why don't dogs have the sense to lie in the shade?"

Mingo lay panting on the ivy near Barbara who rocked his warm sheep-like body now and then with a bare foot. Hearing his name uttered he swivelled his eyes, lifted his sausage tail an inch or two and let it languidly fall.

"It makes me hot to look at him," said Henrietta. "I do wish it would rain."

"Take him away then," said Pierce. "Drop him in the sea."

"Go and hunt for flying saucers," said Barbara.

"We *did* see one, *really* we did!"

"Are you coming, Pierce?" said Edward.

"No. You go and bathe, twins, and stop making such a damn fuss."

"*No one* wants to bathe these days!" said Henrietta, quite suddenly close to tears.

"Pierce, you're cross!" cried Edward accusingly. To be cross was traditionally a serious fault.

"No, I'm not. I'm sorry."

"Maybe we won't bathe," said Henrietta to Edward. "We'll play Badgerstown instead."

"Well, I want to bathe," said Edward.

"You two go down," said Pierce. "Maybe I'll follow you. Go on, don't be asses."

"Mingo, come, boy," said Edward.

Mingo got up rather reluctantly. His grey woolly face smiled dutifully, but he was too hot and weary to wag his tail, which swung inertly behind him as he followed the twins, placing his big floppy paws carefully upon the yielding ivy.

The abandoned graveyard was about a quarter of a mile from the house. Together with its hexagonal green-domed church, the empty and padlocked fane of a geometer god, it bore witness to a vivid eighteenth-century life of the region which was now but pyramidally extant. The crowded square sloped down toward the sea and behind it, hazed by trees in small valleys or caught distantly by sunlight through folds in rounded hills, could be seen the pale rectangular façades of houses which had once contained this silent population. There, if they lingered still, they were the discreetest and most mannerly of ghosts. Here they had kept their past time untouched, become a little shadowy perhaps, but subsistent as the real dreams of real sleepers. The draped urns and obelisks, the sublimely truncated columns, the obliquely leaning slabs inscribed with angelic *putti* and confidently lettered with a divinely dictated clarity and proportion, all glittering a faintly blueish white now in the bright sun, quivered between presence and absence with that quality of being perhaps altogether an hallucination which belongs to certain Greek archaeological sites.

Yet for all its compactness the place was not exactly a township. It had the kind of unity which a god might have imposed, a little carelessly, upon some place to which he intended to return and which he later utterly forgot, an attentive inscrutable sort of pattern not like human art. There was a sense of speech, as if something were said which yet, as words in an out-door theatre, was at once devoured by the air. In fact nature had taken the churchyard to herself with a relentlessness that was almost sinister, as if she had set herself to paralyse, to blur and render indistinct, the activity of those too attentive dreamers. A very thick small-leaved ivy had grown over the whole area, covering the smaller stones entirely and clambering up the slender shafts of the taller ones, woven in between into a thick springy matrix which seemed to swing a little off the ground.

From where Pierce and Barbara were, at the top of the graveyard, the thin grey spire of Trescombe parish church, marking the village, could be seen rising from trees a mile to the east, while to the west the roof of Trescombe House was just visible beyond a slope of old yews which had been bent sideways and smoothed along the top by the mingled beating and caress of the strong sea wind. Ahead was a curve of sheep-nibbled green grass which flattened to the stone-strewn meadow which fringed the beach. The twins had just reached the far end of the meadow and slowed their march on to the stones, with frequent pauses now to shake the pebbles out of their sandals. Mingo, his lethargy apparently departed, had run ahead and his sharp excited barks, Mingo's "seabarks" as Edward called them, could be clearly heard from below. Mingo, although a confident and enthusiastic swimmer, never seemed to get over his sheer surprise at the great restless watery phenomenon. A little further on the figure of Uncle Theo could be seen, walking along very slowly with his head bowed. When Uncle Theo went for a walk he seemed to look exclusively at his own feet, as if fascinated by their regular motion. Beyond Uncle Theo were some alien holiday-makers, referred to as "natives" by the children, of whom this part of the shore happily attracted few, because of its rebarbatively stony nature, and because the steeply shelving beach and the strong currents were thought to make bathing dangerous.

Cradled upon a swathe of ivy Barbara now lay full length in the sun. She had kicked off her sandals, and her white cotton dress, spotted with little pale green daisies, carelessly ruffled up as she had tossed herself down on to the dark swinging greenery, displayed a length of bronzed thigh above the knee. Her eyes, barely open, appeared liquid and fugitive between the lashes.

Pierce, with his back to her, was savagely ripping the ivy strands off the face of one of the smaller squarer stones to reveal a relief carving of a sailing ship.

"So you think I tell lies, do you?" said Barbara after a while.

"I don't believe you've forgotten the bathing song. You can't have."

"Why not? When one's in Switzerland this place seems pretty remote."

"This place is more important than Switzerland."

"Who says it isn't?"

"You cried when you went away."

"I'm grown up now. I only cry when I'm bored. You're boring me. Why don't you go and bathe or something."

"I don't want to. Not unless you come too."

"Why do you follow me around all the time? Can't you do anything by yourself now? Why are you here at all, if it comes to that? Aren't you supposed to be staying with those Pember-Smith people and sailing in their yacht?"

"Oh fuck the Pember-Smiths."

"Why are you so bad-tempered?"

"I'm not bad-tempered!"

"Well, don't shout!"

"I'm not shouting!"

Pierce sat down on the ivy with his back against the tombstone. He wanted to lay his head against Barbara's biscuity brown legs, a little above the knee, and moan loudly. He also wanted to destroy something, everything, perhaps himself. He tore at the ivy below him, thrusting his hands down deep and wrenching the strong sinewy resistant lower branches.

Making an effort with himself, he said, "Something's gone wrong with us, Barbie. I expect it's just sex."

"Sex may have gone wrong with you. It hasn't gone wrong with me."

"You're old enough to flirt with John Ducane, anyway!"

"I didn't say I wasn't *old* enough for anything. And I don't flirt with John Ducane. He just happens to be my friend."

"And look at the way you've put your skirt."

"I haven't *put* it. It's just that I don't care, whether you're here or not."

"You're little Miss Important Person now, aren't you!"

"I've always been little Miss Important Person."

"Would you like to see a nuthatch's nest, Barbie?"

"No. You've already told me three times about that nuthatch's nest."

"Well, you've told me five times about your visit to the Château de Chillon."

"I wasn't telling you. I was telling other people and you were just listening. *Que tu es bête*, Pierce!"

"Don't bother to show off your French to me, I'm not impressed."

"It's *natural*, I'm *not* showing off, I've been *talking* this language for months!"

"Don't scream at me. All right, I'm going. It's low tide. I'm going to swim to Gunnar's Cave. I'm going to swim *into* Gunnar's Cave."

Gunnar's Cave held a prime place in the mythology of the children. It opened at the base of the cliff directly into the sea, and although reputedly a smugglers' cave its sole entrance was only above water for a short time at low tide. Mary Clothier, whose vivid subterranean imagination had rapidly extended itself in awful scenes of trappings and drownings, had long ago strictly forbidden the children to swim into the cave at all. Barbara and the twins, who were rather frightened of the cave, always obeyed. Pierce, who was very frightened of the cave, sometimes disobeyed. He had several times swum into the entrance at low tide, and although he had not touched any dry land within, had gained the impression that the cave went upward into the cliff. If this was so it might be that there was an upper cavern which was above water level even at high tide when the mouth of the cave was below the sea, a wonderful hiding place for smugglers. Pierce did not see any method of finding out whether this was so other than by the experiment of climbing up through the cave and waiting to see what happened. Of course if one was wrong, and the high tide completely filled the cave, then one would be drowned, but even this vision, though it filled Pierce with horror, was also curiously exciting, and especially since Barbara's return he had thought constantly about the cave, picturing its blackness as a kind of consummation in which treasure troves and death by drowning blended together into a buzzing vortex of divine unconsciousness. But this belonged to the world of fantasy. In fact his explorations had been brief and timid so far, and he had swum hastily back on each occasion and out of the mouth of the cave well before the tide had come near to covering the entrance, which was only open for a period of about forty minutes.

"Well, go if you want to," said Barbara. "Only I think it's silly to do things that frighten you, it's neurotic."

"I'm not frightened, I'm curious. It's a smugglers' cave. I'd like to find out if there's anything left inside."

"You don't *know* it's a smugglers' cave. You don't *know* Gunnar was a smuggler. You don't *know* Gunnar ever existed at all. It's not like the Romans. Gunnar's just a story."

"The Romans, ha ha! You remember that Roman coin you found in a pool?"

"Yes."

"Well, you didn't really find it. I put it there for you to find. I bought it off a chap at school."

Barbara sat up and dragged her dress down. She glared at Pierce. "I think it's *hateful* of you to tell me that now, *hateful*!"

Pierce stood up. He mumbled, "Well, I did it to please you."

"And now you're telling me to hurt me."

What has happened to us, thought Pierce. We were so happy once.

With a soft fluffy sound Montrose materialised on top of the tombstone with the carving of the sailing ship, and tucking in his paws made himself into a furry ball, looking down at Barbara with insolent narrow eyes.

Pierce scooped the cat into his arms, inhaled from the warm fur a whiff of Barbara's special eau de Cologne, and threw Montrose on to Barbara's lap.

He said, "Oh Barbara, I'm so sorry, don't be cross with me."

Barbara twisted round and knelt in the ivy, hugging Montrose up against her face. Pierce knelt down opposite to her, and reaching out he touched her bare knee with one finger. They looked at each other with puzzlement, almost with fear.

"I'm sorry too," she said. "Do you think we've just become bad?"

"How do you mean, bad?"

"Well, you know. When I was younger, when I read in the papers and in books and things about really nasty people, bad people, I felt so completely good and innocent inside myself, I felt that these people were just utterly different from me, that I could never become bad or behave really badly like them. Did you feel this?"

"I don't know," said Pierce. "I think boys always know about badness." But he was not sure.

"Well," said Barbara. "I'm afraid it's all turning out to be much more difficult than I expected."

"Octavian darling, are you *never* coming to bed?"

"Just coming, darling. Listen to the owl."

"Yes, isn't he lovely. By the way, Mary has fixed for Barbie to borrow that pony."

"Oh good. Kate darling, we're out of toothpaste."

"There's a new tube on the dressing table. Don't fall over all those maps and guide books."

"Darling, I don't think we can afford to go to Angkor."

"I know. I've given up Angkor. I've decided I want to go to Samarkand."

"You know it's in the Soviet Union, darling?"

"Is it? Well, they wouldn't eat us."

"It'd be terribly hot."

"Is Samarkand on the sea?"

"No, I'm afraid not. Wouldn't you rather go somewhere on the sea?"

"Well, we *did* think Rhodes, of course—"

"We might ask Paula about Rhodes, you remember she went on that cruise.. By the way, what's the matter with Paula? I thought she was looking awfully depressed and worried."

"Oh, it's just end of term. She's so conscientious about those exams."

"Ducane did go to see Willy, didn't he?"

"Yes, Ducane saw him and then Mary saw him."

"Is Willy all right?"

"He's fine. He told Mary that Ducane had cheered him up no end."

"Ducane's so nice—"

"He's so *good*—"

"He's certainly good for Willy."

"He's good for all of us. Octavian—"

"Yes, darling?"

"I kissed Ducane in the beech wood."

"Good for you! Was he pleased?"

"He was *sweet*."

"Don't make him fall for you too much, darling, I mean so that it hurts."

"No, no, he won't get hurt. I'll manage him."

"He has plenty of sense actually, I mean as well as being thoroughly decent."

"Yes. It's funny that he's never got married."

"No need to make a mystery of it."

"I don't know. Do you think he's queer, sort of unconsciously perhaps? I've never heard of his being connected with any woman."

"That's because he's so devilish discreet and clam-like."

"He *is* clam-like. You know he never told me about his being appointed to do that enquiry."

"He's jolly worried about that enquiry."

"Then I'm all the more annoyed he didn't tell me! By the way, he thinks we shouldn't tell Willy about that poor chap, what's his name, Radeechy."

"He's perfectly right. It wouldn't have occurred to me."

"He thinks of everything. I suppose there's no chance that Radeechy really was a spy or something?"

"None at all. I think John's just rather unnerved at the idea of probing into somebody's private life."

"I'm afraid I should find it fascinating!"

"I believe it frightens him. He thinks he may discover something—odd."

"You mean—sexually odd?"

"Yes. He *is* an old puritan, you know."

"I know, and I adore it. What do you think he thinks *we* do, darling?"

"He doesn't think about it."

"Octavian, do hurry up. I think Ducane would tell me now, I mean about the women, about his past. He *will* tell me now."

"You mean you'll ask him?"

"Yes. I'm not afraid of Ducane."

"Implying I am? Well, maybe I am in a way. He's a man I'd hate to think ill of me."

"Yes, I know, me too. You don't think it's a bit fishy, his having that manservant?"

"No, I don't. Ducane's not homosexual."

"Octavian, have you ever met that manservant?"

"No."

"I shall ask Ducane about that manservant too. He's incapable of telling a lie."

"He's capable of being embarrassed."

"Yes, well, maybe I'll just *investigate* the manservant. I'll call some time when Ducane's out and inspect him."

"Kate dear, you don't really think—"

"No, no, of course not, Ducane's a man who doesn't make muddles. That's one of the marvellous things about him."

"No muddles? That's a lot to say of any man."

"No muddles. Which is also why he can't be hurt."

"And you can't. And I can't."

"Darling Octavian, I do love it that we tell each other everything."

"I love it too."

"God's in His heaven, all's right with the world. Do come to bed, darling."

"I'm just coming now."

"Darling, you're so round—"

"Are you ready, darling?"

"Yes, I'm ready. Oh darling, just *guess* what Barbie brought you home for a present—she's saving it for your birthday."

"What?"

"A cuckoo clock!"

Eight

DUCANE faced Peter McGrath, the office messenger, across the desk.

Ducane said silkily, "I have information which leads me to suppose that you, Mr McGrath, were connected with the recent sale to the press of a scurrilous story concerning Mr Radeechy."

Ducane waited. It was hot in the room. Outside, London roared quietly. A little silent fly kept circling quickly and alighting on Ducane's hand.

McGrath's very light blue eyes were fixed upon Ducane's face. Then McGrath averted his eyes, or rather rolled them in his head as if he were doing an exercise. Then he blinked several times. He peered at Ducane again and smiled a little confiding smile.

"We—ell, Sir, I suppose it was bound to come out, wasn't it," said McGrath.

Ducane was irritated by McGrath's light Scottish voice, whose exact provenance he could not diagnose, and by the man's colour scheme. A man had no right to have such red hair and such a white skin and such pallid watery blue eyes and such a sugary pink mouth in the middle of it all. McGrath was in very bad taste.

"Now I require some information from you, Mr McGrath," said Ducane, shuffling his papers about in a business-like manner and shaking off the fascinated fly. "I want first of all to know exactly what this story consisted of, which you sold, and then I shall ask you a number of questions about the background to the story."

"Am I going to get the push?" said McGrath.

Ducane hesitated. In fact McGrath's dismissal was a certainty. However, at this moment Ducane needed McGrath's cooperation. He replied, "That is not my province, Mr McGrath. You will doubtless hear from Establishments if your employment here is to terminate."

McGrath put two pale hands, lightly furred with long reddish hairs, on the desk and leaned forward. He said confidentially, "I bet I get the push. Don't you bet?" McGrath's voice, Ducane now noticed, had Cockney overtones.

"We shall require to have, Mr McGrath, a copy of this story. How soon can you provide this?"

McGrath sat back. With a slight quizzical effort he raised one eyebrow. His eyebrows were a light gingery colour and almost invisible. "I haven't got a copy," he said.

"Come, come," said Ducane.

"I swear I haven't got a copy, Sir. You see I didn't *write* the story. I'm not much of a hand at the writing. And you know what those journalist laddies are. I just talked and they wrote things down and then they read out to me what they'd written up about it and I signed it. I never wrote nothing myself."

This is almost certainly true, thought Ducane. "How much did they pay you?"

McGrath's pale face became as smooth as a cat's. "A man's financial arrangements are his own affair, Sir, if I may—"

"I advise you to change your tune a little, McGrath," said Ducane. "You have acted very irresponsibly and you may find yourself in serious trouble. *Why* did you sell that story?"

"Well, Sir, a gentleman like you, Sir, just doesn't know what it's like to need the necessary. I sold it for the money, Sir, and I'll make no bones about it. It was a matter of looking after number one, Sir, as I daresay even you do, Sir, in your own way."

An impertinent fellow, thought Ducane, and I should think a complete rogue. Though Ducane had never fully realised it, one reason why his career as a barrister had been less than totally successful was that he lacked the capacity to conceive of any kind of villainy of which he would not have been capable himself. His imagination reached out into the world of evil simply by prolonging the patterns of his own faults. So that his judgment upon McGrath that he was "a complete rogue" remained unhelpful and abstract. Ducane could not conceive what it could be like to be McGrath. The sheer opacity to him of this sort of roguery in fact had the effect of making McGrath more interesting to him and in a curious way more sympathetic.

"All right. You sold it for the money. Now, Mr McGrath,

I want you to tell me in as much detail as you can what it was you said to the press about Mr Radeechy."

McGrath once more rolled his eyes, taking his time about it. He said, "I can't really remember much—"

"You can't expect me to believe that," said Ducane. "Come on. We shall have the story itself in our hands very shortly. And if you help me now I may be able to help you later."

"Well," said McGrath, who seemed for the first time a little perturbed, "well—" Then he said, "I *liked* Mr Radeechy, Sir, I *liked* him, I did—"

Ducane felt a quickening of interest. He felt closer to McGrath, as a bull-fighter might feel to the bull after he had touched it. "You knew him well—?" said Ducane softly. He had often had occasion to question people, and the sensation which he now had was familiar to him, the sense of spinning in the quietness of the room a web of sympathetic atmosphere for the unwary. Ducane felt a bit guilty at being good at this. This "making people talk" was not just a matter of what was said or even how it was said—it was a talent which depended upon all sorts of intuitive, perhaps telepathic, emanations of an almost physical kind.

"Yes—" said McGrath. He had put his hands on the desk again and was looking at them. His hands were singularly clean. The little fly was visiting him now, but he did not shake it off. McGrath and the fly eyed each other. "He was a nice gentleman to me. I did things for him, like. Things outside the office."

"What sort of things?" said Ducane softly.

"Well, for his magic, see, he needed things. I used to go to his house, you know, out at Ealing."

"You mean you brought him things he needed for his—magic rituals?"

"Yes. He was a rum chap, was Mr Radeechy. Harmless sort of looney, I suppose you'd call him. But he was a clever chap, mind you. He knew all about that magic business, its history and all. You've never seen so many big books as he had about it. He was a real operator, he knew the lot."

"What were the things you brought him?"

"Oh, all kinds. You never knew what he'd be wanting next. Feathers, he wanted once, white feathers. And all kinds of herbs and sorts of oil. I used to get them at the Health Food Stores. And birds he wanted sometimes, and little animals, mice like."

"Live ones?"

"Yes, Sir. I used to get them at the Pet Shop. I think they got suspicious in the end."

Ducane shuddered. "Go on."

"Then there were things he got for himself like weeds, nightshade and that, and he wanted to teach me to recognise them so I could go to the country and pick them for him, but I didn't care for it."

"Why not?"

"I don't like the country," said McGrath. He added, "I was a bit afraid of those plants, actually growing, it's different in a shop, you understand—"

"I understand. Did Mr Radeechy really *believe* in his rituals?"

"Oh Lord, yes," said McGrath in an aggrieved tone. "He wasn't doing it just for fun. He could do it, too, I mean it worked—"

"It worked—?"

"Well, I don't know, I was never *there*, mind you, but Mr Radeechy was a very strange man, Sir, a man you might say who had supernatural powers. There was a very funny atmosphere round about that man."

"Have you any definite evidence of Mr Radeechy's supernatural powers, or was this just something that you felt?"

"Well, as to evidence, no, but you felt it, like—"

"Yes, I can imagine that. Where did you first meet Mr Radeechy?"

"Here in the office, Sir."

"I see. And you did these odd jobs of shopping for him, for which I imagine he paid you?"

"Well, yes, Sir, he did pay me a little for my time—"

"Quite. Did you see anything of Mrs Radeechy?"

"I didn't see much of the lady, Sir, she rather kept out of the way, but I did meet her just to say good evening."

"Did she seem to object in any way to your visiting the house?"

"Oh not a bit, Sir. She knew all about it. A very cheerful lady and very friendly and polite."

"Do you think she and Mr Radeechy got on well together?"

"Devoted, Sir, I should say. I've never seen a gentleman so plain miserable as he was after she died. He didn't do any magic for months."

"Mrs Radeechy wasn't upset by Mr Radeechy's magic?"

"Well, I never saw her upset by anything, but it must have got her down a bit because of the girls."

"The girls—?"

"Yes, you see the magic needed girls."

Now we're coming to it, thought Ducane. He shivered slightly and the room vibrated quietly with electrical animal emanations. "Yes, I understand that many magic rituals involve girls, often virgins. Perhaps you could tell me a little about these ones."

"I don't know about *virgins*!" said McGrath, and laughed a slightly crazy laugh.

Radeechy had him fascinated, it occurred to Ducane. There was a kind of mad admiration in McGrath's laugh. "You mean the girls whom Mr Radeechy—used—were— well, what were they like? Did you meet them?"

"I saw them a bit, yes," said McGrath. He was now becoming cautious. He rocked his hand to disturb the persistent fly. He looked up at Ducane, signalling with his colourless eyebrows. "Tarts, I'd say they were. I never properly saw him at it, mind you."

"What do you think he did with the girls?" said Ducane. He found himself smiling at McGrath, encouragingly, perhaps conspiratorially. The subject matter imposed, almost without their wills, a cosy masculine atmosphere.

"Do with them?" said McGrath, smiling too. "Well, you know I never saw really, though I did creep back once or twice, and I looked through a window. I was curious, you see. You'd have been curious too, Sir."

"I expect I would," said Ducane.

"I mean, I don't think he did any of the usual things, it wasn't that, he was a pretty odd chappie. He had a girl once lying down on a table, and there was a sort of silver cup balanced on her tummy. She had nothing on, mind you."

Ducane thought, a black mass. "Did he have the girls there one at a time or several at once?"

"One at a time, Sir, only they couldn't always come, so there were three or four regulars. Once a week it was, punctual on Sundays, and sometimes a special one extra."

"Anything else that you saw?"

"Not so to speak *saw*. But he had some rather queer things lying around."

"What, for instance?"

"Well, whips and daggers and things. But I never saw him use them, on the girls, I mean."

"I see," said Ducane. "Well, now tell me something about Helen of Troy."

"Helen of Troy?" McGrath's white face turned to a uniform light pink. He withdrew his hands from the desk. "I don't know anybody of that name."

"Come, come, Mr McGrath," said Ducane. "We know you mentioned someone of that name in your story to the press. Who is it?"

"Oh, Helen of *Troy*," said McGrath vaguely, as if some other Helen had been in question. "Yes, I believe there was a young lady of that name. She was just one of the young ladies."

"Why did you say just now you hadn't heard of her?"

"I didn't hear rightly what you said."

"Hmmm. Well, now tell me about her."

"There's nothing to tell," said McGrath. "I didn't know anything about the girls. I didn't really meet them. I just heard that one's name and it sort of stuck in my head."

He's lying, Ducane thought. There's something about this particular girl. He said, "Do you know the names of these girls and where they could be found? The police may want to question them."

"*The police?*" McGrath's face crinkled up as if he were going to cry.

"Yes," said Ducane smoothly. "It's a pure formality of course. They may be needed at the inquest."

This was untrue. It had already been arranged with the police that the inquest, which was to take place tomorrow, would involve no exploration of the more 'rum' aspects of the deceased's mode of existence.

"Well, I don't know their names or where any of them

lived," McGrath mumbled. "I wasn't connected with *them* at all."

He won't tell me any more about that, thought Ducane. He said, "Now, Mr McGrath, I believe that the story which you sold also makes mention of blackmail. Would you kindly tell me what this was all about?"

McGrath's face became pink once more, giving him a somewhat babyish appearance. "Blackmail?" he said. "I didn't say anything about blackmail. I didn't mention that word at all."

"Never mind about the word," said Ducane. "Let's talk about the thing. 'Some money changed hands', did it not?"

"I don't know anything about that," said McGrath. He huddled his head down into his shoulders. "The laddies at the paper were very keen on that, it was their idea really."

"But they can't have simply invented it. You must have told them something."

"They started it," said McGrath, "they *started* it. And I told them I didn't know anything for sure."

"But you knew something or guessed or surmised something? What?"

"Mr Radeechy said something about it once, but I might not have understood him properly. I told the laddies—"

"What did he say?"

"Let me see," said McGrath. He gazed full at Ducane now. "He said, let me see, he said that someone was getting money out of him. But he didn't say who or tell me any more about it. And I might not have understood him, and I realise now I shouldn't have said anything, but those lads were so keen, as if this was really the best bit of the story."

He's lying, thought Ducane. At least he's lying about Radeechy. Then with sudden clarity the surmise came to him: the blackmailer was McGrath himself. That the newspaper had pressed him to endorse the hint of blackmail was probably true. Greed had dimmed McGrath's Scottish cunning. He had doubtless imagined that he could get away with the whole thing. An inefficient rogue, Ducane thought.

"I suppose you imagined that you could get away with the whole thing, Mr McGrath?" Ducane asked, smiling pleasantly. "I mean, that we would never find out who sold the story?"

McGrath looked at him with a kind of relief and actually sighed audibly. "The boys at the paper said no one would ever know."

"Boys at papers will say anything," said Ducane, "if they think they can get a story."

"Well, I'll know next time," said McGrath. "I mean—" They both laughed.

"Am I to understand, Mr McGrath, that what you've just told me is the entire substance of what you told the newspaper men?"

"Yes, Sir, that's the lot, they dressed it up a bit of course in the way they wrote it down, but that's all that I told them."

"You aren't keeping anything back, Mr McGrath? I should advise you not to, especially as we shall shortly have that story in our hands. Are you sure there isn't anything else you would like to tell me?"

"No, nothing else, Sir" McGrath paused. Then he said, "You must be thinking badly of me, Sir. It seems bad, doesn't it, to sell a story about a gentleman when he's just gone and killed himself. But I did need the money, you see, Sir. It wasn't that I didn't like Mr Radeechy, there was nothing personal. He was very good to me, Mr Radeechy was, and I was really fond of him. I'd like you to understand that, Sir. I was real fond of Mr Radeechy."

"I understand that," said Ducane. "I think that's all then, Mr McGrath, for the moment. I won't keep you any longer."

"For the moment?" said McGrath, a bit dismayed. He rose to his feet. "Will you be wanting to see me again, Sir?"

"Possibly," said Ducane. "Possibly not."

"Will I have to come to the inquest, Sir?"

"You probably won't be needed at the inquest."

"Will I be getting the sack from here, do you think, Sir? I've been in the job over ten years. And there's my pension. What happens to that if—?"

"That is a matter for Establishments," said Ducane. "Good day to you, McGrath."

McGrath did not now want to go. The interview had generated a curious warmth, almost an intimacy, and McGrath wanted Ducane to comfort him. He also wanted to find out from Ducane just how gravely his misdemeanour was likely to be regarded, but he could not sufficiently collect his wits to ask the right questions. He stood staring down, opening and closing his pink mouth a little, like a kitten.

"Good day," said Ducane.

"Thank you, Sir, thank you very much, Sir," said McGrath. He turned and rather slowly left the room. The little fly accompanied him.

Well, well, well, thought Ducane, leaning back in his chair. It was probably true that what McGrath had told him about Radeechy and the girls was the substance of what he had told the newspaper men. There was certainly enough there to make an excellent story. About one of the girls, Helen of Troy, there was apparently something which McGrath was concealing, but it might be that this something had been concealed from the newspaper too. McGrath might simply have mentioned her to the journalists because, as he said to Ducane, her *nom de guerre* had 'struck' him, and it added a picturesque detail. And of course the concealed something might be perfectly innocuous, such as McGrath's having become a bit infatuated with this particular girl. Or it might be something important. The devil of it is, thought Ducane, although I told him we shall shortly have the story in our hands, this may just not be so. The newspaper could not, as things stood at the moment, be compelled to hand it over.

About the blackmail, Ducane could not make up his mind. While he had been questioning McGrath he had been led to conjecture that McGrath himself was the blackmailer, or at least *a* blackmailer. The idea now seemed to him less obvious. McGrath had perhaps the personality to be a blackmailer, but, Ducane judged, only to be a small one. Ducane could imagine McGrath leering at Radeechy and suggesting respectfully that the pittance he was paid for the 'shopping' might be somewhat increased. And he could imagine Radeechy, half amused, increasing it. And he could see that McGrath, upon the death of the goose that laid the golden eggs, might well be carried away by the impulse to make a last packet out of his poor employer. What he could not imagine was McGrath extracting enormous sums of money from Radeechy. McGrath would not have the nerve, and also he was not quite unpleasant enough. It was probably true that he had been quite fond of Radeechy and in a way fascinated by him. But if McGrath's blackmail was petty it could scarcely count as a motive for Radeechy's suicide. Was there someone else, the real blackmailer, behind McGrath?

Ducane reminded himself that the purpose of the enquiry was to discover whether there was any 'security interest' in the case. Since Radeechy had no official access to secret material, the mere fact that he had put himself into a position to be blackmailed and possibly was being blackmailed, need not itself suggest such an interest, were it not that his suicide remained unexplained. If Radeechy had, *ex hypothesi*, been persuaded to procure and hand over secret material, and if he feared exposure, and even if he did not, here was a quite sufficient motive for suicide. On the other hand, there was not a shred of evidence that Radeechy had done so, he appeared to have no close relations with anyone who might have passed such material to him, those who knew him best did not see such conduct as being in his character, and Ducane was inclined to agree with them. Of course one did not know what price Radeechy might not have been prepared to pay to conceal some particular thing, perhaps some thing of which McGrath had not spoken, and which McGrath did not know, on the assumption that there was another and more important blackmailer in the picture. But Ducane did not seriously imagine that Radeechy had been spying. There was something else behind it all. He thought, my main task is to find out why he killed himself. And he thought, it may all be terribly simple, he may have done it just because of his wife. And if it is terribly simple it is going to be terribly hard to prove!

There had been no suggestion that Mr and Mrs Radeechy were other than 'devoted' and there was evidence to suggest that they had been happily married. The motive might indeed lie here. How Mrs Radeechy coped with the goings on with the 'girls' Ducane simply could not imagine; but he now understood enough about the mystery of married couples to know that there is practically nothing with which those extraordinary organisms cannot deal. Mrs Radeechy might well have been entirely tolerant about the girls. McGrath had described her as a 'very cheerful lady' and this agreed with other testimony. McGrath himself would, of course, have to be interrogated again and very much more ruthlessly and scientifically. This had been just a preliminary shaking of hands. It should not be too difficult, Ducane thought, to break McGrath down entirely, to threaten him and frighten him. But Ducane did not want to do this until he had made certain whether or not the newspaper could be persuaded to hand over the story. George Droysen had been despatched to conduct this delicate negotiation.

At this point Ducane began to think about Jessica. The connection of thought was as follows. It is impossible to be a barrister without imagining oneself a judge, and Ducane's imagination had often taken this flight. However, and this was another reason for Ducane's ultimate disgust with life in the courts, the whole situation of 'judging' was abhorrent to him. He had watched his judges closely, and had come to the conclusion that no human being is worthy to be a judge. In theory, the judge represents simply the majesty and impartiality of the law whose instrument he is. In practice, because of the imprecision of law and the imperfection of man, the judge enjoys a considerable area of quite personal power which he may or may not exercise wisely. Ducane's rational mind knew that there had to be law courts and that English law was on the whole good law and English judges good judges. But he detested that confrontation between the prisoner in the dock and the judge, dressed so like a king or a pope, seated up above him. His irrational heart, perceptive of the pride of judges, sickened and said it should not be thus; and said it the more passionately since there was that in Ducane which wanted to be a judge.

Ducane knew, and knew it in a half-guilty, half-annoyed way as if he had been eavesdropping, that there were moments when he had said to himself, "I alone of all these people am good enough, am humble enough, to be a judge". Ducane was capable of picturing himself as not only aspiring to be, but as actually being, the just man and the just judge. He did not rightly know what to do with these visions. Sometimes he took them, now that he had removed himself from the possibility of actually becoming a real judge, for a sort of harmless idealism. Sometimes they seemed to him the most corrupting influences in his life.

What Ducane was experiencing, in this form peculiar to him of imagining himself as a judge, was, though this was not entirely clear in his mind, one of the great paradoxes of morality, namely that in order to become good it may be necessary to imagine oneself good, and yet such imagining may also be the very thing which renders improvement impossible, either because of surreptitious complacency or because of some deeper blasphemous infection which is set up when goodness is thought about in the wrong way. To become good it may be necessary to think about virtue; although unreflective simple people may achieve a thought-less excellence. Ducane was in any case highly reflective and had from childhood quite explicitly set before himself the aim of becoming a good man; and although he had little of the demoniac in his nature there was a devil of pride, a stiff Calvinistic Scottish devil, who was quite capable of bringing Ducane to utter damnation, and Ducane knew this perfectly well.

This metaphysical dilemma was present to him at times not in any clear conceptual form but rather as an atmosphere, a feeling of bewildered guilt which was almost sexual in quality and not altogether unpleasant. If Ducane had believed in God, which he had not done since he abandoned, at the age of fifteen, the strict low church Glaswegian Protestantism in which he had been brought up, he would have prayed, instantly and hard, whenever he perceived this feeling coming on. As it was he endured it grimly, as it were with his eyes tight shut, trying not to let it proliferate into something interesting. This feeling, which came to him naturally whenever he experienced power, especially rather formal power, over another person, had now been generated by his questioning of McGrath. And his faintly excited sense of having power over McGrath put him in mind of another person over whom he had power, and that was Jessica.

Ducane was ruefully aware that his remorse about his behaviour to Jessica was at least partly compounded of distress at cutting, as Jessica's rather muddled lover, a figure which was indubitably not that of the good man. In fact Ducane had long ago made up his mind that he was a man who simply must not have love affairs, and the adventure with Jessica was really, as he now forced himself sternly to see, a clear case of seeing and approving the better and doing the worse. However, as he also believed, the only point of severity with the past is improvement of the future. Given all this muddle, what was the right thing to do now? Could he, involved as he was in this mess of his own creating, be or even intelligibly attempt to be, the just judge where poor Jess was concerned? How could he sufficiently separate himself from it, how could he judge the mistake when he was the mistake? Ducane's thoughts were further confused here by the familiar accusing voice which informed him that he was only so anxious now to simplify his life in order to have a clear conscience, or more grossly a clear field, for his highly significant commitment to Kate. Yet was it not plain that he ought, whatever his motives for it might be, to break absolutely with Jessica and to see her no more? Poor Jessica, he thought, oh God, poor Jessica.

"I say, may I come in for a moment?"

Ducane's thoughts were interrupted by the voice of Richard Biranne, who had just put his head round the door.

"Come in, come in," said Ducane pleasantly, checking with a quick physical twitch the instant hostility which had gripped his whole body at the appearance of Biranne.

Biranne came in and sat down opposite to Ducane. Ducane looked at his visitor's clever face. Biranne had a long handsome slightly tortured-looking intellectual head. His stiff wiry hair, colourlessly fair, stood up in a wavy crest, elongated his face. His shapeless-looking mouth was twisted and rather mobile. He had a high-pitched donnish voice which was physically disturbing, as if it made objects in his vicinity vibrate and do their best to break. Ducane could well imagine that he was attractive to women.

"Droysen told me about McGrath," said Biranne. "I was wondering if you had seen that sinner and got anything out of him, if that's not an indiscreet question."

Ducane did not see why he should not discuss the matter with Biranne, who had after all seen the opening of the drama. He said, "Yes, I saw him. He told me a few things. I've got the beginnings of a picture."

"Oh. What did you get out of him?"

"He says he did the shopping for Radeechy's magical goings-on. He says the magic involved naked girls. That, with a few trimmings, is supposed to be what he spilled to the press."

"Have you got on to the girls?"

"Not yet. McGrath said he didn't know anything about them. Which I don't believe."

"Hmmm. What about the blackmail story?"

"I don't know," said Ducane. "It seems to me possible that McGrath himself was blackmailing Radeechy in a quiet way. But that's not important. There's something else. There's *someone* else."

"Someone else?" said Biranne. "I don't see why. Is that just a guess? It seems to me you've got all the ingredients for an explanation already."

"It doesn't add up. Why did Radeechy kill himself? And why did he leave no note? And why did he do it in the office? I can't help feeling that's significant."

"Had to do it somewhere, poor devil! It's interesting that you think McGrath might have been blackmailing him. Couldn't that be the reason?"

"I don't think so. But I'll soon know."

"You sound very confident. Have you got another lead?"

Ducane suddenly began to feel cautious. It disturbed him to see Biranne sitting in the chair from which the multi-coloured image of McGrath had not yet entirely faded. There came to him again that faintly thrilling feeling of mingled unworthiness and aspiration which had been occasioned by the putting of McGrath to the question. Yet Ducane had no power over Biranne. Biranne was not a prisoner in the dock.

He felt an impulse to mystify his visitor. He replied, "Yes, I've one or two leads. We'll see, we'll see."

Now he could feel, almost physically, his familiar be-devilment merging with his old dislike of Biranne. He must, at last, forget the quality of that mocking laughter. He himself had often mocked at harmless men, and indeed meant by it but little harm. The puffed up and affronted self must cease its importunities at last. He recalled Biranne's distinguished war record. Here was another motive for envy, another source of this thoroughly unworthy dislike. As Ducane gazed at Biranne, who was now preparing to depart, the dusty sunshine in the room brought a vision dazzling into his eyes of Paula and the twins, as he had last seen them together on the beach in Dorset. It had never occurred to Ducane, who liked and admired Paula, to doubt that in their divorce Biranne had been the guilty party. He had heard Biranne talking about women. But what he felt now, as he watched his visitor's departure, was something more like pity: to have had a wife like Paula, to have had children like the twins, and to have wilfully and utterly lost them.

Nine

"DO anything you like," said Jessica, "only don't say the word 'never'. I should die of that word."

John Ducane was miserably silent. His timid hangdog look had made him into another person, a stranger.

"I just don't understand," said Jessica. "There *must* be some way round this, there *must* be. *Think*, John, *think*, for Christ's sake."

"No way," he mumbled, "no way."

He was standing beside the window in the thick afternoon sunlight, shrunken up with wretchedness, rendered by misery physically appalling and strange, as if he were barnacled over with scabs and scales. He moved his head very slowly to and fro, not significantly but as an animal might, twitching its shoulders under a painful yoke. He cast a quick shrewd hostile glance at Jessica and said, "Oh my God."

Jessica said, "You want me to make it easy for you to leave me, don't you. But I can't. I might just as well try to kill myself by stopping breathing."

"My poor child," he said in a low voice, "don't fight, don't fight, don't fight."

"I'm not fighting. I'm just wanting to stay alive."

"It's become such a bloody mess, Jessica—"

"Something in you may have become a mess. I haven't changed. John, why can't you *explain*? Why are you doing this to us?"

"We can't go on in this sort of emotional muddle. We've got no background, no stability, no ordinariness. We're just living on our emotions and eating each other. And it's so rotten for you."

"You aren't thinking of me, John," she said, "I know it. You're thinking of yourself. As for ordinariness, why should we be ordinary? We aren't ordinary people."

"I mean we can't co-exist and take each other for granted. We aren't married and we aren't just friends either. It doesn't work, Jessica, it's a bad situation."

"It's been bad lately, but everything would calm down if you'd only stop making a fuss."

"We've got to simplify things. One has got to simplify one's life."

"I don't see why. Suppose life just isn't simple?"

"Well, it ought to be. All lives ought to be simple and open. With this thing going on our lives can't be either. We're like people living on drugs."

"There isn't any *thing* that's going on except that I love you. This *thing*'s in your mind."

"All right, it's in my mind then. I ought never to have let this relationship start, Jessica. The responsibility is entirely mine. I acted very wrongly indeed."

"Starting this relationship seems to me one of the better things you've ever done, however it ends."

"We can't separate it from how it ends."

"Why can't you live in the present? You live everywhere but in the present. Why can't you just be merciful to me now?"

"We are human beings, Jessica. We can't just live in the present."

Jessica closed her eyes. Her love for John was so intense at that moment it was like being burnt alive. She thought, if I could only perish now and fall at his feet like a cinder.

His sudden decision not to see her any more was utterly incomprehensible to the girl, it was a death sentence from a hidden authority for an unknown crime. Nothing had changed, and then there was suddenly this.

John Ducane had been the first great certainty in Jessica's life. She had never known her father, who died when she was an infant. The working class home of her mother and step-father had been a place which she endured and from which she ultimately escaped into an art school. But her life as a student now seemed to Jessica to have been substanceless, seeming in retrospect like a rather casual drunken party. She had been to bed with a number of different boys. She had tried out a number of new and fashionable ways of painting. No one had tried to teach her anything.

Like most of her fellow students Jessica was, to an extent which even John Ducane did not fully appreciate, entirely outside Christianity. Not only had she never believed or worshipped, she had never been informed about the Bible stories or the doctrines of the Church in her home or school. Christ was a figure in a mythology, and she knew about as much about him as she knew about Apollo. She was in fact an untainted pagan, although the word suggested a positivity which was not to be found in her life. And if one had been disposed to ask for what and by what Jessica had lived during her student days, the answer would probably have been 'her youth'. She and her companions were supported and united by one strong credo, that they were *young*.

Jessica thought, or had thought, that she was talented as an artist, but she could never decide what to do. From her education in art she had acquired no positive central bent or ability, nor even any knowledge of the history of painting, but rather a sort of craving for immediate and ephemeral 'artistic activity'. This had by now become, in perhaps the only form in which she could know it, a spiritual hunger. She and her comrades had indeed observed certain rules of conduct which had something of the status of tribal taboos. But Jessica had never developed the faculty of colouring and structuring her surroundings into a moral habitation, the faculty which is sometimes called moral sense. She kept her world denuded out of a fear of convention. Her morality lacked coherent motives. Her contacts with her contemporaries, and she met no one except her contemporaries, and her very strict contemporaries at that, were so public and so free as to become finally without taste. She even became used to making love in the presence of third and fourth parties, not out of any perversity, but as a manifestation of her freedom. After all, accommodation was limited, and nobody marked, nobody minded.

Jessica had thought herself in love on a number of occasions but in fact her attention had been very much more concentrated upon not having a baby. Perpetual change and no hard feelings was the general rule, and one which had kept Jessica, who religiously obeyed it, both inexperienced and in a sense uncorrupted and innocent. There was a kind of honesty in her mode of life. Her integrity took the form of a contempt for the fixed, the permanent, the solid, in general 'the old', a contempt which, as she grew older herself, became a sort of deep fear. So it was that some poor untutored craving in her for the Absolute, for that which after all is most fixed, most permanent, most solid and most old, had to express itself incognito. So Jessica sought to create and to love that which was perfect but momentary.

This was the zeal, this the fanaticism, which she attempted to communicate to the children whom she taught at school. She taught them to work with paper, which could be crumpled up at the end of the lesson, with plasticine, which could be squeezed back into shapeless lumps, with bricks and stones and coloured balls which could be jumbled together again; and if paint was ever spread upon a white surface it was to move like a river, like a mist, like the changing formations of the world of clouds. No one was ever allowed to *copy* anything; and a little boy who once wanted to take one of his paper constructions home to show his mother was severely reprimanded. "So it's all *play*, Miss?" a child had said to Jessica at last in a puzzled tone. At that moment Jessica felt the glowing pride of the successful teacher.

Jessica's refusal to compromise with 'the fixed', which was for her the analogue of, which perhaps indeed was, pureness of heart, and which had once made her feel so spiritually superior, had become, by the time she encountered John Ducane, something about which, although she was just as dogmatic, she was a good deal less confident. Her earliest conversations with Ducane had been arguments in which he had expressed surprise at her ignorance of great painters and she had expressed disapproval of what she regarded as the flaccid promiscuity of his taste. It appeared that he liked almost everything! He liked Giotto *and* Piero *and* Tintoretto *and* Titian *and* Rubens *and* Rembrandt *and* Velasquez *and* Tiepolo *and* Ingres *and* Renoir *and* Matisse *and* Bonnard *and* Picasso! Jessica was not far from thinking that a taste so catholic must be guilty of insincerity. When pressed by John she would cautiously admit to liking one or two individual pictures which she knew well. But really she only liked what she could immediately appropriate and use up in her own activity, and this, as the years went by, seemed to be becoming less and less.

Ducane had been the most serious event of her life. He

had made her entirely uncertain of herself while at the same time providing what seemed the only possible complete healing for that uncertainty. Jessica's disguised longing for a place of absolute rest, the longing which had been running out through her feverishly active finger tips, found a magisterial and innocent satisfaction in John. The girl loved him without reservation. His particular stability, his alien solidness and slowness, his belongingness to the establishment, his *age*, above all his puritanism now seemed to her what she had been seeking for all her life. His puritanical shyness and reserve shook her with passion. She worshipped his seriousness about the act of love.

In fact John and Jessica never really managed to understand each other at all, and this was chiefly the fault of John. If he had been a wiser man, or a man with a kind of nerve which he was too fastidious to possess, he would have taken young Jessica firmly in hand and treated her as if she were his pupil or his disciple. Really Jessica longed for John to instruct her. Of course she did not know what kind of instruction she craved; but it was in the nature of her love to think of him as wise and full and of herself as foolish and empty. And John apprehended this hunger in her too, but he instinctively feared it and did not want to find himself playing the role of a teacher. Scrupulously, he shrank from 'influencing' his young and now so docile mistress. As soon as he sensed his great power he shut his eyes to it, and herein was guilty of an insincerity more grave than that of the aesthetic promiscuity attributed to him by Jessica. This denial of his power was a mistake. John ought to have been bold enough to instruct Jessica. This would have created a more intelligible converse between them and would also have forced Ducane to reveal himself to the girl. As it was John withdrew in order not to cramp Jessica, in order to make a space into which she should expand; but she was unable to expand and worshipped across the space without understanding him. While she was almost completely concealed from him by the word 'artist', which he associated with a conventional idea to which he expected Jessica to conform, not realising that she was a new and completely different species of animal altogether.

Jessica was thinking, I can't bear this pain, he must take

this pain away from me. It must be all a nightmare, just a bad dream, it can't be true. When we stopped being lovers I thought it meant that I was to be in his life forever, I accepted it, I went through it because I loved him so much, because I wanted to be what he wished. And he let me go on loving him and he *must* have been glad that I loved him. He can't go away from me now, it's impossible, it's a fantastic mistake.

The summer afternoon London sunshine made the room hot and hazily bright and desolate and hid John's figure behind a sheet of dusty light, making it insubstantial as if it was a puppet out there that spoke his words while the real John had merged into her tormented body.

Ducane had been silent for some time, looking out of the window.

"Promise you'll come again," said Jessica. "*Promise* it or I shall die."

Ducane turned, bowing his head under the light. "It's no good," he said in a low toneless voice. "It's better for me to go away now. I'll write to you."

"You mean you won't come again?"

"It makes no sense, Jessica."

"Are you saying that you're leaving me?"

"I'll write to you—"

"Are you saying that you are going to go now and not come back?"

"Oh God. Yes, I'm saying that."

Jessica began to scream.

She was lying on her back on the bed and John Ducane was lying beside her, his face buried in her shoulder and his dry cool hair touching her cheek. Jessica's two hands, questing across the dark stuff of his jacket, met each other and clasped, holding him in a tight compact embrace. As her hands interlocked across his back she sighed deeply, gazing up at the ceiling which the slanting golden sunlight of the evening had made shadowy and dappled and deep, and the gold filled her eyes which seemed to grow larger and larger like great lakes brim full of peace. For the terrible pain had gone, utterly gone, and her body and her soul were limp with the bliss of its departing.

Ten

THERE was a loud crash upstairs, followed by a prolonged wailing sound.

Mary rather guiltily tossed Henrietta's copy of *The Flying Saucer Review*, which she had been perusing, back on to the hall table, and ran up the stairs two at a time.

The scene, in Uncle Theo's room, was much as she had expected. Theo was sitting up in bed looking rather sheepish, holding Mingo in his arms. Casie was crying, and trying to extract a handkerchief from her knickers. Theo's tea tray lay upon the floor with a mess, partly on it and partly round about it, of broken crockery, scattered bread and butter, and shattered cake. The carpet had not suffered, since the floor of Theo's room was always thickly covered with old newspapers and Theo's underwear, and into this fungoid litter the spilt tea had already been absorbed.

"Oh Casie, do stop it," said Mary. "Go downstairs and put the kettle on again. I'll clear this up. Off you go."

Casie went away still wailing.

"What happened?" said Mary.

"She said she was a useless broken-down old bitch, and I agreed with her, and then she threw the tea tray on to the floor."

"Theo, you just mustn't bait Casie like that, you're always doing it, it's so unkind."

Mingo had jumped down and was investigating the wreckage on the floor. The woolly fur which stuck out on either side of his mouth, and which he was now fluttering over the broken china, resembled moustaches. His wet pink nose quivered as he shot out a delicate pink lip and very daintily picked up a thin slice of bread and butter.

"Don't let Mingo get at the cake, please," said Theo. "It looks rather a good cake and I'm certainly proposing to eat it. Would you mind putting it on to this?" He held out a sheet of newspaper.

Mary picked up the larger fragments of the cake and put them on to the newspaper. Then, with her nose wrinkling rather like Mingo's, she began to collect the debris on to the tray. Uncle Theo's room, which he rarely permitted anyone to clean, smelled superficially of medicines and disinfectants, and more fundamentally of old human sweat. This rancid odour was alleged by the twins to be the basis of the affinity between Uncle Theo and Mingo, and Mary had come vaguely to believe this, although she regarded the aroma more as a spiritual emanation from the dog-man pair than as a mere physical cause.

The dog was on the bed again now, clasped about the waist by Theo, his four legs sticking out helplessly, his woolly face beaming, his tail, on which he was sitting, vibrating with frustrated wags. Theo was beaming too, his face plumped out with a kind of glow which was too pervasive and ubiquitous to be called a smile. Looking at them sternly, it occurred to Mary that Mingo had come to resemble Theo, or perhaps it was the other way about.

Uncle Theo puzzled Mary. She was also rather puzzled by the complete lack of curiosity about him evinced by other members of the household. When informed, as if this were part of his name or title, that Theo had left India under a cloud, Mary had, as it seemed to her naturally, asked what cloud. No one seemed to know. At first Mary imagined that her question had been thought improper. Later she decided that really no one was much interested. And the odd thing was that this lack of interest seemed to be caused in some positive way by Theo himself, as if he sent out rays which paralysed other people's concern about him. It was like a faculty of becoming invisible; and indeed Uncle Theo did often seem to have become almost imperceptible in a literal sense, as when someone said, "There was nobody there. Oh well, yes, Theo was there."

Why did Uncle Theo paralyse other people's concern about him in that way? On this problem Mary held two contradictory theories between which she vacillated. There was a shallow reassuring theory to the effect that Uncle Theo had so much animal placidity and so few thoughts that he was just not very noteworthy, in the same way in which a spider in the corner might not be noteworthy. It was true that he behaved like an ill person, at any rate he spent an inordinate amount of time in bed, always taking breakfast and tea there, sometimes lunch and dinner as well. He talked a lot about familiars whom he called his 'viruses'. But no one had ever believed that Theo had any definite, indeed any real, illness. And although he was sometimes sharp-tongued and often morose his glooms had a positive slightly buffoonish quality which forbade their being taken too seriously. Theo also had a considerable gift for being physically relaxed. He seemed a totally non-electric, non-magnetic person. Perhaps it was this air of blank bovine ease which made his neighbours rightly so incurious. There was nothing to know.

Yet there were times when Mary favoured another and more unnerving theory according to which Uncle Theo's invisibility was something more like an achievement, or perhaps a curse. At these times Mary apprehended his laziness and his relaxation not exactly as despair but as something on the other side of despair of which she did not know the name. It was as if, she thought, someone had had all his bones broken and yet were still moving about like a sort of limp doll. It was not that she caught, through the mask of Uncle Theo's behaviour, any momentary flash or flicker from some other region of torment. There was no mask. It was simply that the ensemble of Uncle Theo's particular pointlessness could take for her the jump into a new *gestalt* which showed him to her as a man who had been through the inferno and had by the experience been deprived of his will.

Mary looked at Uncle Theo now as he was, by a familiar technique, exciting Mingo by sniffing over his fur with the audible eagerness of a terrier after a rat. Unlike his younger brother, to whom his resemblance was minimal, Theo was a gaunt man and rather tall. He was partly bald, with longish strings of greasy grey hair curling down his neck. He had a large brow but the features of his face were cramped and concentrated well to the front, as if the hasty hand of his creator had absently drawn them all toward the point of his rather long nose. So although he had a large head his face looked small and poky and canine. Mary could never determine, even on fairly close inspection, the colour of his eyes. Tidying his room once she had found an old passport, and opening it to see what colour Theo himself considered his eyes to be, had found the description: 'Mud'.

Mary had been distressed to find her curiosity and concern about Theo lessening as time went on. Perhaps those invisibility rays were gradually killing her interest in him too and she would soon be just as indifferent as the others. Mary, who was accustomed to receiving confidences, had once or twice tried to question Theo about India, but he had only beamed in his dog-like way and changed the subject. She felt compassion for him and willed to help him, but her relationship to him remained abstract. The sad truth was that Mary simply did not love him enough to see him clearly. He repelled her physically, and she was one of those women who could only care deeply for what she wanted to touch.

"Will you make me some more tea, please?" said Theo.

"Yes. I'll send Casie up with it. You must make peace with her. You really do make her unhappy."

"Don't worry. Casie and I are good friends." This was true. Mary had noticed a sort of positive bond between these two.

"I wish you'd go up and see Willy," she said. "You haven't seen him for three weeks. Have you quarrelled or something?"

Theo closed his eyes, still beaming. "You can't expect two neurotic egomaniacs like me and Willy to get on together."

"Willy isn't a neurotic egomaniac."

"Thanks, dear! The fact is I gave up Willy for Lent and then found I could do without him."

"I'm just going to see him now and he's sure to ask after you. Suppose he—needs you?"

"Nobody needs me, Mary. Go and make my tea, there's a dear girl."

Mary went away down the stairs in a state of irritation with herself. I'm no good, she thought. These encounters with Theo, her inability to reach him or see him, often brought on a sort of self-pity which rendered his image even more indistinct. Mary depended, more than she might have been willing to admit, on a conception of her existence as justified by her talent for serving people. Her failure with Theo hurt her vanity.

Downstairs she found Casie, no longer tearful but furious, already banging together another tea tray for Theo. As Mary passed on toward the back door she could now hear Barbara upstairs beginning to play something on her flute.

The piercing husky hard-achieved beauty of the sound wrought on Mary's nerves. Her own utter inability to remember any tune gave music a special exasperating poignancy for her. Barbara's flute, although the child now played it well, was almost an instrument of torture to Mary. She wondered where Pierce was and whether the boy, lying in his room or hidden somewhere in the garden, was also listening to those heart-rending sounds.

The summer afternoon was very hushed in the garden and the air, thick with sun and pollen, dusted Mary's face like a warm powder-puff. The agonising sound of the flute grew fainter. Mary mounted the pebble path and let herself out of the gate in the wall and began to go up the hill between the high banks of the lane. The banks were covered in white flowering nettles, a plant which Mary liked, and she picked a few as she went along and tucked them into the pocket of her blue and white check dress. When she got to the shade of the beech wood she sat down automatically, out of a compulsive afternoon languor, upon a fallen tree, sitting astride the tree and gently rustling its skirt of curled beech leaves with her sandalled feet. The tree was smooth and grey above, but beneath the level of the leaves it curved inward with the colour and consistency of flaky milk chocolate, and as Mary sat upon it and stirred its flanks it gave off a light fungoid odour which made Mary sneeze. She began to think about Willy Kost.

Mary had for some time now been conscious of a sort of mounting distress which she connected with her relationship with Willy. She felt with him something of the same exasperated sense of failure as she felt with Theo, only with Willy it was different because she loved Willy very much and found him pre-eminently touchable. He had arrived at Trescombe Cottage when Mary was already well established as whatever she was established as at Trescombe House, and she had immediately assumed a special responsibility for him. "How's Willy?" other members of the household would tend to ask her. She had at first taken it for granted that Willy would soon confide in her and tell her all about his past, but this had not happened. No one even seemed to know for certain where Willy had been born. Ducane said Prague and Octavian said he thought Vienna. Mary had no theory, coming at last to accept Willy's sad European mysteriousness as a sort of physical quality and one which racked her tenderness more than any positive knowledge could have done.

Mary constantly told herself how lucky she was to live with so many people whom she loved and that surely so much love was enough to fill a woman's life. She knew perfectly well, with her heart's blood as well as with her mind, that loving people was the most important of all things. Yet she knew too that she was deeply discontented and she sometimes suffered fierce feral moods of confused yearning during which it seemed to her that her whole life was a masquerade and that she was piously acting the part of a kindly affectionate serviceable woman who was just not herself. Yet it was not that a rapture or a glory which had once shone around her had passed away from the world. The rapture and the glory whose hauntings she suffered had never manifested themselves in her life at all. Her love for men had always been somehow neurotic and unfulfilled, and this had been true even of her love for her husband. She had loved Alistair very much, but in a nervous, plucking, plucked at way, and though both her body and her mind had been involved in this love they had never been in accord about it. She had never been filled with her love like a calm brimming vessel. She had rather suffered it, as a tree might suffer a cold wind, and the image of a coldness was somehow mingled with her memories of marital love. Mary did not believe in analysing herself, and she had left vague the notion that sometimes came to her that this anxious unfulfilled sort of loving was the only kind of which she was capable.

Her relationship with Willy Kost was unsatisfying and even maddening to her but by now it had become very important and Mary could quite rationally hope that it would in time become better, easier, fuller. She did not any longer expect any great 'break through'. She did not expect, as she had done at first, that Willy would suddenly seize her hands and tell her all about what it was like in Dachau. In a way she no longer even wanted this to happen. But she did hope that some shrewd little genius which watched over her strange friendship with this man would see its way to bringing them, in gentleness and tenderness, much closer together.

"Willy, may I come in?"

"Oh, Mary. Come in, come in. Yes, I was expecting you. Have you had tea?"

"Yes, thanks." In fact she had not had tea, but she did not want Willy to be moving about. She wanted him still, seated in a chair, while she moved about.

Willy subsided back into his low chair by the hearth. "Some milk? I'm just drinking some."

"No thanks, Willy."

She began to roam up and down the room, as she usually did, while Willy, his legs stretched straight out and his heels dug into the wood ash, sipped his milk and watched her. They were often silent thus for a long time after Mary's arrival. Mary herself found that she needed some kind of physical recollection after she had entered Willy's presence. His presence was always a slight shock to her. In order to withstand him she had to weave her own web about his room, proliferate, as it were, her own presence to contain his.

Willy's cottage, a rectangular brick structure erected on the cheap by Octavian's predecessor, consisted simply of a large sitting-room with kitchen, bathroom and tiny bedroom beyond it at the west end. Most of the walls were covered with the bookshelves which Octavian had had the village carpenter make for the cottage after he had taken one look at Willy's crates of books. But on the south side looking toward the sea was a long narrow window with a wide white window ledge upon which various things were placed, usually by Willy's visitors, who seemed to have an urge to propitiate or protect him by the donation of often quite pointless gifts, offered or simply left, rather in the spirit of those who place saucers of milk outside the lair of a sacred snake.

Touching the window ledge automatically as she passed to see if it was dusty, Mary noticed two light-grey stones, lightly printed with curly fossil forms, probably donated by the twins, a small cardboard box full of birds' eggs, also doubtless from the twins, a mound of moss and feathers which looked like a disintegrating bird's nest, a paper bag containing tomatoes, a jam jar with two white Madame Hardy roses from a bush which grew outside Willy's door, a wooden plate with edelweiss painted on it which Barbara had brought Willy from Switzerland, a pair of binoculars, also the gift of Barbara, and a dirty tea cup which Mary picked up. As she did so she remembered the white flowering nettles which were still in the pocket of her dress. She went into the little kitchen and washed up the tea cup and one or two plates and knives which were on the side. Then she took a large wine glass out of Willy's cupboard and put the drooping nettles into it and brought them back to the window sill. Who had brought the roses in, she wondered. It would hardly have occurred to Willy to do so.

"You've brought me flowering nettles and put them in a wine glass."

"Yes."

"If I were a poet I would write a poem about that. Cruel nettles put into a wine glass by a girl—"

"They aren't cruel," said Mary. "These ones have no sting. And I'm not a girl." Willy's steady refusal to learn the flowers of the countryside, indeed to recognize the details of the countryside at all, had first exasperated and then charmed her.

"A girl, a girl—" he repeated softly.

Did Willy wish he was a poet, Mary wondered. She was beginning to want to touch him but knew that she must not do so yet. She said, "Willy, I do wish you'd go down and see Theo."

"I don't go down and see people. People come up and see me."

"Yes, I know. But I think he somehow needs you—"

"No, no. As far as Theo is concerned I am an unnecessary hypothesis."

"I don't agree. I think you're *special* for him."

"Only one person is special for Theo, and it certainly isn't me. Tell me, how are the others, how is your handsome son?"

"Oh that reminds me, Willy. Would you mind coaching Pierce in Latin again these holidays? He's awfully worried about his Latin."

"Yes, certainly. I can take him any day round about this time."

Willy banned visitors after six o'clock. He said that he was always working then, but Mary wondered. In her search for the key to Willy's interior castle she speculated often about the quality of his solitude. What was it like in the evenings and in the night for Willy? Once a violent curiosity had driven her to call on him unexpectedly about nine. The lights were switched off and he was sitting in the glow of the wood fire and she had the impression that he had been crying. Willy had been so upset and annoyed by her late visit that she had not ventured to repeat it.

"He seems to think his Greek's all right. Though I must say it doesn't seem to be a patch on the twins' Greek."

"Yes," said Willy, "the twins' Greek is indeed *erstaunlich*."

It irritated Mary when Willy used a German word or phrase. The first summer he had been there she had persuaded him to teach her German, and had spent an hour with him on several mornings a week. Willy gently terminated this arrangement after it became clear that Mary never had enough time to do the necessary learning and exercises, and tended to be very upset by her failures. Mary hated to think about this. The following summer he gave the same time to Paula, and they read the whole of the *Iliad* and the *Odyssey* aloud together. During this period Mary suffered acute physical pains of jealousy.

"What ees eet?"

"Nothing," she said shortly, but she knew that Willy knew exactly what she was thinking.

"What is the matter with Paula?" said Willy. His thoughts and Mary's often became curiously intertwined during these times when she prowled the room and he watched her.

"Is anything the matter?"

"Yes. She seemed to me to be worried or frightened or something."

"I expect it's just the end of term," said Mary. "She's overtired. Did she come up to see you?" It might have been Paula who brought in the two white roses.

"No, I met her on the beach when I was having my early walk." In the summer Willy often took very early walks by the sea before anyone was up.

Mary paused again at the window where her questing finger had drawn in the light dust a twining pattern which showed up clearly in the bright sunlight. Trescombe House could not be seen from the cottage as the wood intervened but there was a view, over the sloping tree tops, of a part of the beach, with the rust-coloured headland known as the Red Tower to the right, and to the left, over a curvy green field, a glimpse of the abandoned graveyard, the little green dome of the geometer god, and greyer and hazier in the far distance the pencil line of the Murbury sands with the black and white lighthouse at the end. Straight ahead of her Mary could see something bobbing on the sea, quite near in to the shore, and she picked up the binoculars to have a look at it.

"Ouf!" she said.

"What?"

"These binoculars are uncanny."

As she turned them into focus she could see the leaves on the trees of the wood as if they were inches in front of her face. She had never handled such powerful glasses. She moved the clear lighted circle down the hill and across the stones of the beach to pick up the object which she had seen upon the sea. She saw the faint ripples of the sea's verge and the glossy satiny skin of the calm surface and then a trailing hand. Then she had full in view the little green plastic boat which the twins called 'the coracle' after the boat in *Treasure Island*. In the boat, both dressed in bathing costumes, were Kate and John Ducane. She could see from the dark clinging look of their costumes that they had just been swimming. They were laughing in a relaxed abandoned way and Ducane had just put his hand on to Kate's knee. Mary lowered the glasses.

She turned back into the room and came to stand in front of Willy and stare at him. She thought sadly, gaiety and laughter are not in my destiny. Alistair had been gay, but somehow Mary had been the pleased spectator of his gaiety rather than a participant in it. Kate was gay and could make others laugh, even Willy. Paula had something else with Willy, a calm camaraderie of shared interests. But I just make him sad, thought Mary, and he just makes me sad.

"What ees eet, my child?"

"You," she said. "You, you, you. Oh, I do love you."

She often said this, but the words always vanished away, as if they were instantly absorbed into the infinite negativity which confronted her. She wished to pierce Willy with these words, to disturb him, even to hurt him, but he remained remote and even his tenderness to her was a mode of remoteness. It did not occur to her to think that Willy could be indifferent to her affection nor even to doubt that he found her attractive. Though not formally beautiful, Mary had as a physical endowment a strong confidence in her own power to attract. No, it was something else which kept them separate so. If Theo seemed to her like a man with broken bones walking about, Willy seemed like an inhabitant of some other dimension who could only tenuously communicate with the ordinary world. This would have troubled her less if she had not imagined his other dimension as a place of horror. Trying to make it more concrete she wondered, what could it be like to have suffered such injustice? Can he ever bring himself to *forgive them?* Mary thought that this would have been the problem for herself. But she had no evidence that it was the problem for Willy. Perhaps his demons were quite other.

She sat down now, bringing a chair up close against the side of his and sitting so that she faced him. As she did so, looking down, she saw within the front of her dress her breasts pressing together like twin birds, and she thought, I am a treasure waiting to be found.

"See, Mary, your white nettles have lifted up their heads."

"You are . . . You are . . ." she said, "a troll . . . that's what you are. Oh, you do exasperate me so!"

She began to caress him, drawing her fingers very lightly through the longish silky white hair, exciting it until it crackled and lifted a little to her touch. Then she started to caress his face with her finger tips, first lightly outlining his profile, his big faintly scored brow, his thin Jewish nose, the tender runnel above his lips, the roughened prickly chin, then moving her fingers to his eyes, which flickered shut and flickered open again, his cheeks, moulding the bones, and drawing her finger tips back along the length of his mouth: the soft feeling of the human face above the bone, touching, vulnerable and mortal. At last, with a movement which did not break the rhythm of hers, Willy captured her hand and held it with the palm flattened against the side of his head. His eyes closed now, and for a long time they sat quietly thus. Such was their love-making.

Eleven

"DO you think it's ever safe to say one's happy?" said Kate.

"I think it would be ungrateful in someone who, like you, is always happy, not to admit it sometimes!" said John Ducane.

"Ungrateful? To *them*? They have no morals and don't deserve gratitude. Yes, it's true that I'm always happy. But there are degrees of it. I feel such an intense happiness at this moment, I feel I might faint!"

They were floating in the little green coracle upon the perfectly calm sea in which they had lately been swimming. The coracle, which had no oars, was propelled by the hands of its crew. It was a suitable craft only for very still weather, as it was easily swamped and overturned.

Nearby upon the beach the twins, who had swum earlier in the day, were engaged in their perennial task of examining the stones. Uncle Theo, who disliked the stones and found them menacing, had once said that the twins behaved like people condemned by a god to some endless incomprehensible search. Uncle Theo himself, newly risen after his tea, was sitting on the beach beside Pierce's clothes. Mary forbade anyone to enter the house in a wet bathing costume and the children always undressed on the beach. Pierce, who had been swimming for some time, was lying limply on the shelving pebbles, half in and half out of the water, like a stranded sea beast. Mingo, who had been swimming with Pierce, was shaking himself and spraying rainbow water drops over Pierce's trousers and the left arm of Uncle Theo's jacket. Montrose, sitting on the jagged tooth-like remains of the wooden breakwater, had fluffed himself up into his spherical bird form, and was regarding Mingo's antics with yellow-eyed malignancy. Paula and Octavian, fully dressed now, were walking slowly along the beach discussing politics. Some natives were distantly encamped. It was Saturday.

"Yes, one must think how lucky one is," said Kate. "Think if one had been born an Indian peasant—" But in fact she could not think about Indian peasants nor think how lucky she was, she could only feel it in the slightly caressing tightening feeling of the sun drying the salt water upon her plump legs and shoulders.

"You know, I think they're all the tiniest bit afraid of you," said Kate, reverting to something she had been saying earlier. "Willy is, Mary is, Octavian certainly is. Which is what makes it so wonderful, as I'm not!"

"I can't believe anyone's afraid of me," said Ducane, but he was obviously pleased all the same.

"Your company makes me so happy. And it's partly this sense of being absolutely free with you when nobody else is! I *am* possessive, you know!"

"Just as well for both of us that I'm not!" said Ducane.

"Darling! Forgive me! But of course you forgive me. You're terribly happy too, I can feel it. Oh God, how heavenly the sun is. The twins keep saying that they want it to rain, but I want everything to go on for ever exactly as it is." Kate was in that state of elation when speech becomes a mere natural burbling, like bird song or the chatter of a stream.

The boat, which Ducane had been propelling with lazy pressures of his trailing hand upon the pleasantly resistant water, was almost motionless now. Kate and Ducane were very close together in the little boat, but not quite touching each other. He lay in the blunt stern, a little sprawled, knees crooked up and both arms over the side. She was in the almost equally blunt bows, sitting sideways with her legs half tucked under her. Between Ducane's bare foot and her knee there was about half an inch of space of which they were both pleasantly conscious, as if through this narrow strait something were deliciously and impetuously rushing.

Kate was inspecting Ducane with tender curiosity. Of course she had seen him thus stripped before, last summer in fact, only he had not then been for her the highly significant object which he had now become. How lovely it is, thought Kate, to be able to fall in love with one's old friends. It's one of the pleasures of being middle-aged. Not that I'm really exactly in love, but it's just like being in love with all the pain taken away. It's an apotheosis of friendship, it's something one thought possible when one was young and then forgot about. There's all the excitement of love in a condition of absolute safety. How touchingly thin he is, and so white, and the hair on his chest is turning grey. What is it that's attractive about men's bodies? It's much more mysterious, more spiritual, than the attractiveness of women. Why is it *heavenly*, the way the bones stick out so at his wrists? Oh dear, I don't want him to think I'm looking at him critically. He must see he's being adored. Why now he's looking at me in just the same way. She snuggled her legs a little closer under her, feeling the pleasant tight pressure of her damp bathing dress holding her breasts in close against her body. At that moment her curious exploring gaze met Ducane's and they began to laugh with mutual understanding. Ducane withdrew one hand from the sea and leaned forward and very deliberately touched Kate's knee. She felt the lingering firmness of his hand in the midst of the cool water which was now trickling over her warm leg which had become quite dry in the sun.

The boat gave a sudden heave forward. Ducane removed his hand abruptly from Kate's leg. There was a soft splashing ahead. Pierce, who had swum up unnoticed, had taken hold of the length of rope which hung from the bows and was beginning to tow the boat along.

Ducane was irritated and upset by the intrusion. He hoped the boy had noticed nothing. His thoughtless enjoyment of the present moment, the sun, the drifting, and Kate's sweet Irish voice was spoilt now. His mood was broken and the bright day gave place to a wall of blackness whose name was Jessica.

His relationship with Jessica was turning into a massacre and he could not see what could be done about it. There was as much emotion generated between them now as if they had been lovers. He had been defeated by a girl's screams. And he knew that he had given her that shot of morphia as much to spare himself as to spare her. When he thought about the matter in general he was as certain as ever that he must leave her, must finish the job. But when he thought in detail about the process he not only shuddered, he became less sure. Could it be right to inflict so much pain? If only it were over, done, without the awful doing of it.

He thought, I can't do it simply by letter. Anyway, she would just come round at once, she would come to the office.

Had he the right to be happy with Kate for a second, to take what Kate was so generously offering to him, at a time when he was causing this dreadful suffering to another person? What would Kate, with her fantasy of being nearer to him than anybody, think if she knew of this mess? What, if it came to that would Jessica think if she knew of what would seem to her his frivolous adventuring with Kate? Where, in all this, was Ducane, the upright man? Of course it was easy to see now that he ought never to have entangled himself with Jessica at all. Until even quite lately, however, he had at least been able to think of what he knew to be his sin in a fairly clear way. The pain involved in it for him, and he dared to think for her too, was at least fairly clean pain. They just had to separate and that, agonising as it was, was all there was to it. Now he was not so sure. As he lay limply on Jessica's bed with his head upon her shoulder after he had stopped her screaming by promising to see her again Ducane had felt a new kind of despair. In the clairvoyance of this despair he had seen how much his folly had already damaged both of them.

When Ducane had first begun to think of his relationship with Kate as important, and when he had decided to break with Jessica without yet considering what this would be like, he had seen it as one important aspect of his new world that he would now be able to attend properly to the needs of other people. After all he was not in love with Kate. He adored Kate and could be made happy by her, but he was not really in love with her. It was a civilized achievement of middle age. Kate could never be a burden and was not an obsession. While he had been Jessica's lover, and during the later time when he had been trying to detach himself from Jessica, he had become insensitive and unavailable and unaware. People who came to him for assistance were but absentmindedly served. He had ceased to be interested in anyone but himself. He had envisaged his world with Kate, not as a *tête-à-tête*, but as once more a populated country, only a happy one. The wonderful thing about Kate was that she was unattainable; and this was what was to set him free for ever. She would give ease to his too long wandering heart, and then he could live more fully in the world of other people, more able, because more happy, to give them his full attention.

But this was the distant landscape, the landscape beyond Jessica. Will I ever reach it, he wondered. Ought I not to withdraw from Kate, at any rate for a while? Is it even conceivably my duty to stay with Jessica? As things are at the moment I am no good to anyone. I can't think about anybody but myself. I was no good to Willy this morning. Willy had alarmed Ducane that morning by the degree of his withdrawal, his refusal even to talk. Ducane thought, if I could have given Willy my full attention this morning I would have been able to force him to communicate with me. Perhaps Willy ought to have been left in London. He's far too much alone here. Perhaps I have made a terrible mistake. If Willy kills himself it will be my fault.

By some further twist or shift of the blackness these grim reflections put Ducane in mind of Radeechy. He had still not obtained the newspaper story and it seemed likely that he would have to act without it. He had decided to visit McGrath at his house unexpectedly on this next Monday evening, and really find out everything that the fellow knew. But how much would that amount to? With a kind of bitter weariness Ducane found his mind turning to the 'whips and daggers and things' which McGrath had seen at Radeechy's house. What had Radeechy *done* with those girls? As he now felt a curious alleviation of his pain, an ability once more to see Kate's brown shoulders and her plump back, turned to him as she looked forward over the bows of the boat, he thought, how natural it is to try to cure the pains of wickedness by positive devilry, vice itself is a rescue from the misery of guilt, and there are deeper pits into which it is a relief to fall. Then he thought, poor Radeechy.

Pierce was towing the boat quite fast now, the tow rope between his teeth. Mingo, who had swum out after him, was also accompanying the boat, his ridiculous primly lifted dry head contrasting with the sleek wet head of the boy, who was dipping and slipping through the water like a seal.

"Where's Barb?" Kate called to Pierce.

"Riding her pony," he said, dropping the rope and retrieving it again spaniel-like.

"She's so mad on riding now," said Kate, turning back to Ducane, "and she's almost *too* fearless. I do hope we were wise to send her to that school in Switzerland."

"She'll get her Oxford entrance all right," said Ducane. "She's a clever girl and her French should be perfect."

"I do wish Willy would change his mind about reading German with her." Willy had unaccountably refused to help Barbara with her German.

The boat slackened speed. Pierce had dropped the rope and was swimming on toward the cliff, the easternward end of the Red Tower, which here came down sheer into the water. Ducane felt relief, as at the removal of a small demoniac presence.

"Don't go in, will you, Pierce!" Kate was shouting after him.

"No, I won't."

"That's Gunnar's Cave," said Kate, pointing to a dark line at the base of the cliff. "It must be low tide."

"Yes, you told me," said Ducane. "The entrance is only uncovered at low tide."

"It gives me the creeps," said Kate. "I have a fantasy that it's full of drowned men who went in after treasure and got caught by the sea."

"Let's get back," said Ducane. He shivered. He began to move the little coracle slowly upon the gluey gleaming surface with rhythmical sweeps of his hands. Kate shifted herself slightly so that her leg was in contact with his. They looked at each other searchingly, anxiously.

Twelve

"WHY did Shakespeare never write a play about Merlin?" said Henrietta.

"Because Shakespeare was Merlin," said Uncle Theo.

"I've often wondered that too," said Paula. "Why did he never make use of the Arthur legends?"

"I think I know," said Mary.

Everyone was silent. Mary hesitated. She was sure that she knew, only it was suddenly very difficult to put it into words.

"Why?" said John Ducane, smiling at her encouragingly.

"Shakespeare knew . . . that world of magic . . . the subject was dangerous . . . and those sort of relationships . . . not quite in the real world . . . it just wasn't his sort of thing . . . and it had such a definite atmosphere of its own . . . he just couldn't use it . . ."

Mary stopped. It wasn't quite that, but she *did* know. Shakespeare's world was something different, larger.

"I think I understand you," said Ducane, "perfectly." He smiled again.

After that the conversation scattered once more, each person chatting to his neighbour. Sunday lunch was taking place, was nearly over, at the round table in the hall. Casie was circling round the table, removing plates, talking aloud to herself as she usually did when waiting at table, and moving in and out of the kitchen, through whose open door Montrose, in his elongated not spherical manifestation, could be seen lounging in the animal basket beside which Mingo was standing in a state of evident agitation. Every now and then Mingo would put one paw into the basket and then nervously withdraw it again. Montrose lounged with the immobility of careless power.

"They treat women properly in Russia," Casie was saying as she removed the pudding plates. "In Russia I could have been an engine driver."

"But you don't want to be an engine driver, do you?" said Mary.

"Women are real people in Russia. Here they're just dirt. It's no good being a woman."

"I can imagine it's no good being *you*, but—"

"Oh do shut up, Theo."

"I think it's marvellous being a woman," said Kate. "I wouldn't change my sex for anything."

"How you relieve my mind!" said Ducane.

"I'd rather be an engine driver," said Mary crazily.

Casie retired to the kitchen.

There was no special arrangement of places at Sunday luncheon. People just scrambled randomly to their seats as they happened to arrive. On that particular day the order was as follows. Mary was sitting next to Uncle Theo who was sitting next to Edward who was sitting next to Pierce who was sitting next to Kate who was sitting next to Henrietta who was sitting next to Octavian who was sitting next to Paula who was sitting next to Barbara who was sitting next to Ducane who was sitting next to Mary.

Edward was now explaining to Uncle Theo about some birds called "honey guides" who lived in the Amazonian jungle and these birds had such a clever arrangement with the bears and things, they would lead them to where the wild bees had their nests and then the bears and things would break open the nests to eat the honey and so the birds could eat the honey too. Henrietta was explaining to Kate how there were loops and voids in the space–time continuum so that although it might take you only fifty years to reach the centre of the galaxy in your space craft, thousands of years would have passed here when you got back. ("I don't think I *quite* understand," said Kate.) Octavian, who had been discussing with Paula the prospects of reform in the trade union movement, was now anxiously asking her if she felt well, since she had eaten practically no lunch. Ducane and Barbara were flirting together in French, a language which Ducane spoke well and enjoyed any chance of showing off.

Mary, who got up to help Casie at various points during the meal, was left, as often happened, in a conversational vacuum. She liked this, feeling at such moments a sort of maternal sense of ownership toward the group of chattering persons all round her. Casie was now putting fruit and cheese on to the table. Octavian was reaching for the decanter of claret. Everyone was drinking wine except the twins who were drinking Tizer and Paula who was drinking water. Mary began to observe the face of her son who was sitting opposite to her.

Pierce too, seated between Edward and Kate, had no one to talk to. He was watching with fierce concentration the conversation between Barbara and John Ducane. Mary thought, I hope no one else is noticing him. He is looking so intense and strange. Then she thought, Oh dear, something is going to happen.

"*Quand est ce que tu vas me donner ce petit concert de Mozart?*"

"*Jamais, puisque tu ne le mérites pas!*"

"*Et pourquoi ça, petite égoiste?*"

"*Tu n'y comprends rien à la musique, toi.*"

"*Tu vas m'enseigner, alors.*"

"*Tu seras docile?*"

"*Mais oui, mon oiseau!*"

"*Et qu'est ce que tu vas me donner en retour?*"

"*Dix baisers.*"

"*C'est pas assez.*"

"*Mille baisers alors!*"

Pierce got up abruptly, scraping his chair noisily back over the paved floor of the hall. The chair fell over backwards with a crash. Pierce walked to the front door and went out through it, slamming the door behind him. There was a startled silence.

"Public school manners," said Casie.

Mary began to rise. Both Uncle Theo on one side and John Ducane on the other put out restraining hands. Mary sat down again. Uncle Theo said to Edward, "Do go on telling me about dolphins." Kate started to say, "Don't worry, Mary dear—"

Mary decided she could not stay. She got up and went out quietly through the kitchen and out into the garden. The garden was hot, brooding, and quiet, even the cuckoo was silent in the afternoon heat. Mary began to walk up the pebble path, brushing the plump veronica bushes with her hand. The bushes exuded heat and silence. She passed through the gate in the wall. It was not in her mind to look for Pierce. She knew he would have started to run once he was outside the front door. He would be half way to the graveyard by now, and there, buried in the ivy, he could lie hidden even if she were to follow him. In any case she had nothing to say to her son and she had already stopped thinking about him. His tormented nerves had wrought upon her nerves, and it was the sudden burden of her own nebulous and uncertain anguish which had made her rise from the table.

I am making a complete ass of myself, thought Mary, and it's getting worse too. I'm not eighteen. I just must not give way to these vague emotional storms of self-pity. It isn't as if there was anything definite the matter. There's nothing the matter at all.

She walked up the enclosed funnel of the lane through the smell of hot moss and reached the little wood and sat down on the tree trunk, kicking a hole for her feet in the dead leaves. Perhaps I need a holiday, she thought, perhaps it's as simple as that. Sometimes I just feel so shut in, with all those people and they've all got *something* while I've got nothing. I really ought to try to get some sort of proper job. But I suppose they do need me here, the children need me. When the twins are grown up I shall take a teacher's training course and have quite a different sort of life.

Then she thought, is this really all I have to look forward to, is this what I have to comfort myself with? Years more of managing someone else's house and then a job as a school teacher? But my wants are huge, my desires are rapacious, I want love, I want the splendour and violence of love, and I want it now, I want someone of my own. Oh Willy, Willy, Willy.

A shadow moved in the dappled light. Mary looked up. It was John Ducane. In a flurry she rose to her feet.

Mary was very fond of Ducane and admired him, but as Kate had quite accurately said she was a little afraid of him.

"Oh, John—"

"Mary, do sit down. Please forgive me for having followed you."

She sat down again, and he sat beside her, perched sideways on the log, regarding her. "Mary, I'm so sorry. I feel what happened was my fault. I behaved in a silly insensitive way. I do hope you aren't upset."

Upset—I'm frantic, thought Mary. I'm frenzied, I'm desperate. She said, "No, no, don't worry. I'm afraid Pierce behaved abominably. I do hope Barbara wasn't too hurt."

"No, she was very sensible about it," said Ducane. "I'm afraid I hadn't realised, well, quite how serious things were. I'll be more tactful in future. Please don't you be distressed. These young people have got to suffer, we can't save them from it—"

Damn their sufferings, thought Mary. She said, "Yes. Of course they have great powers of recovery."

Mary thought suddenly, this is an abomination, sitting here and having this conventional conversation when I feel so desperate and deprived and torn inside. She thought, is there nothing I can do about it? Then there seemed to be only one thing she could do about it and she did it forthwith. She burst into a storm of tears.

"Good heavens!" said John Ducane. He took out a large clean handkerchief, unfolded it, and handed it to Mary who buried her face in it.

After a minute or two, as the tears abated a little and she began to blow her nose on the handkerchief he touched her shoulder very gently, not exactly patting it but as if to remind her of his presence. "Is it about Pierce?"

"No, no," said Mary. "I'm not really worried about Pierce. It's about me."

"What? Tell me."

"It's about Willy."

"What about Willy? You're not frightened that he—?"

"No. I've never thought that Willy was likely to kill himself. It's just that—well, I suppose I've fallen in love with Willy." The uttered words surprised her. Her diffused tender agitation had not the relentless finality of her older loves. Yet it was beginning to fill the whole of her consciousness and it was, it must be, the deep cause of these sudden storms of misery.

Ducane took the information gravely and thoughtfully, as if Mary were a client explaining her case. He said after a moment, "My feeling is that I'm glad of this because it can't fail to do Willy good. What does he feel about it? Does he know?"

"Oh, he knows. As for what he feels— you know Willy as well as I do. How can one discover what he feels?"

"I thought he might perhaps behave—quite differently with you?"

106

"No, no. We seem to know each other well but I think that's just because I parade my feelings. He's affectionate, detached, passive, absolutely passive."

"He's never told you about that place?"

"He's never talked about himself at all."

"Are you going to see him now?"

"No. He said not to come today. You know how he is."

"I know how he is," said Ducane, "and I can see he's not a convenient man to be in love with. But let's think, let's think."

There was silence in the wood as they sat side by side, Mary slowly rubbing her face over with the handkerchief, Ducane, frowning with concentrated attention, leaning forward and pulverising a dry beech leaf in his hand. A pair of brimstone butterflies, playing together, passed flittering in front of them. Mary stretched out her hand toward the butterflies.

She said, "I'm sorry I've inflicted this on you. One should bear one's own burdens. I'm perfectly all right really. After all, I'm not in my first youth! It'll blow over, it'll settle down." Settle down! she thought. Yes, settle down into dreariness and quietness and forgetfulness and boredom. Yet she knew that it was not really the sharp tragic knife of passion that disturbed her now, it was some vaguer nervous storm out of her unsatisfied woman's nature. The dreariness was already with her, it had its part in her present jumpiness, her present tears. This thought was so heavy with despair that she almost began to cry again.

Then she saw that Ducane had got up. He stood in front of her, staring at her with his round surprised-looking blue eyes. He said in an excited voice, "Mary, do you know what I think? I think you should marry Willy."

"Marry Willy?" she said dully. "But I've told you what he's like with me."

"Well, change him. I'm sure it's a matter of will. You let him infect you with his passivity, you accept his mood."

It was true that she accepted his mood. "Do you think I really could—?"

"You must try, try with all the forces you can summon. You've been too humble with him. It's often an act of charity to treat someone as an equal and not as a superior! A woman in love is a great spiritual force if only she wills properly. You have no idea how much power you have over us! I've known it for a long time, that, for Willy, only you can do it. But I hadn't thought enough to see that you'd have to fight him, surprise him, wake him, hurt him even. Mary, you must try. I think you should marry Willy and take him right away from here."

Have I this power, she wondered. Ever since she had first met Willy she had been totally subservient to him. The 'parade of feelings' had not altered that. For all these gestures she had really extinguished herself in his presence, wanting simply to let him *be*. It now seemed to her that this had been all wrong, that this was the very policy which produced, for both of them, the frustrating melancholy which she had taken to be his defence against her.

"Tell yourself," said Ducane, "that anything is possible."

Mary thought, yes, I will marry Willy and I will *take him away*. With this idea so much happiness entered into her that she stood up lightly and involuntarily as if two angels had lifted her up, their fingertips underneath her elbows.

"I'll try," she said, "I'll try."

"I hear you behaved intolerably at lunch-time today."

"Who told you?"

"The twins."

"Well?"

"Well nothing. Let's have a look at your Latin prose."

"Oh Willy—I'm so wretched—sorry."

"Barbara?"

"Yes."

"And she?"

"I just annoy her."

"I have no comfort for you, Pierce. You will suffer. Only try to trap the suffering inside yourself. Crush it down in your heart like Odysseus did."

"Is it true that the first time of falling in love is the worst?"

"No."

"Oh God. Willy, I think I'll have to go away from here. If only she wouldn't play that damned flute. It nearly kills me."

"Yes, I can imagine the flute is—terrible."

"Do you mind if I walk about the room. You can't imagine what it's like when every moment you're conscious you're in the most frightful pain."

"I can a little."

"Who were you first in love with, Willy?"

"A girl, a girl, a girl—"

"What was she like?"

"It was a long time ago."

"It must be good to be past the age of falling in love."

"Like Cephalus in the first book of the *Republic*."

"Yes. I never understood that bit before. I envy you. Do you think she'll change?"

"Hope nothing."

"Is there a cure?"

"Only art. Or more love."

"I should die of more love."

"Dying into life, Pierce."

"No, just dying. Oh hell, I've broken one of those eggs the twins brought you. I'll just go and wash it off."

Why did this little shattered egg which he was washing off his fingertip, with its fragments of speckled blue shell and its fierce yellow inside make him think so intensely of Barbara? 'My name is death in life and life in death.' A love without reservation ought to be a life force compelling the world into order and beauty. But that love can be so strong and yet so entirely powerless is what breaks the heart. Love did not move toward life, it moved toward death, toward the roaring sea-caves of annihilation. Or it led to the futility of a little broken bird's egg whose remains were now being washed away by water from the tap. Even so one day God might crack the universe and wash away its fruitless powerless loves with a deluge of indifferent power.

"Sorry, Willy. Let's look at my prose now."

"I've changed my mind. I'll see your prose tomorrow. Today we will read love poetry. You shall read aloud to me and we will weep together. Here."

> "*Vivamus, mea Lesbia, atque amemus,*
> *rumoresque senum severiorum*
> *omnes unius aestimemus assis.*
> *soles occidere et redire possunt:*
> *nobis cum semel occidit brevis lux,*
> *nox est perpetua una dormienda. . . .*"

Thirteen

THE lazy sinister summer evening thickened with dust and petrol fumes and the weariness of homeward-turning human beings drifted over Notting Hill like poison gas. The perpetual din of the traffic diffused itself in the dense light, distorting the façades of houses and the faces of men. The whole district vibrated, jerked and shifted slightly, as if something else and very nasty were trying, through faults and knots and little crazy corners where lines just failed to meet, to make its way into the ordinary world.

Ducane was hurrying along, consulting a little map which he had made in his notebook to show him the way to where Peter McGrath lived. He felt a certain amount of anxiety about this surprise visit to McGrath. Ducane did not like playing the bully, and deliberate and calculated bullying was what it was now necessary to produce. He was also anxious in case he should bully to no purpose. If he had to use force he should at least use it quickly and efficiently and get exactly what he wanted. But he unfortunately knew so little about his victim that he was uncertain how best to threaten him, and once the advantage of surprise had been lost McGrath might refuse to talk, might stand upon his rights or even 'turn nasty'.

There was behind it all the unnerving fact that so far his enquiry had got nowhere. The Prime Minister had asked for an interim report and Octavian, who had had nothing to tell him, was getting nervous. The newspaper was still withholding the story, George Droysen's further investigations in Fleet Street had produced nothing, it had proved impossible to trace 'Helen of Troy', Ducane had searched Radeechy's room in the office without finding anything of interest, and the promised authorisation to examine Radeechy's house and bank account was held up on a technicality. Ducane might reasonably have complained that as his enquiry had no status it was not surprising that it was unsuccessful. But he had undertaken the task on precisely these terms and he hated the idea of defeat and of letting Octavian down. McGrath was still his only 'lead' and everything seemed to depend on what more he could now be bullied into telling. This thought made Ducane even more nervous as he turned into McGrath's road.

McGrath lived in a noisy narrow road of cracked terrace houses, some of which contained small newsagents' shops and grocers. Most of the front doors were open and most of the inhabitants of the street, many of whom were coloured, seemed to be either outside on the pavement or else hanging out of the windows. Not many of the houses bore numbers, but by counting on from a house which announced its number Ducane was able to identify an open doorway where, among a large number of names beside a variety of bells, the name of McGrath was to be seen. As he hesitated before pressing the bell Ducane felt his heart violently beating. He thought grimly, it's like a love tryst! And with this the thought of Jessica winged its way across his mind, like a great black bird passing just above his brow. He was going to see Jessica again tomorrow.

"Bells don't work," an individual who had just come down the stairs informed him. "Who d'yer want?"

"McGrath."

"Third floor."

Ducane began to climb the stairs, which were dark and smelt of cats. In fact as he climbed three shadowy cats appeared to accompany him, darting noiselessly up between his ankles and the banisters, waiting for him on the landings, and then darting up again. On the third floor there was a single well-painted door with a Yale lock and a bell. Ducane pushed the bell and heard it ring.

A woman's voice within said, "Who is it?"

Enquiries at the office had not revealed that McGrath was married, and Ducane had assumed him to be a bachelor.

Ducane said, "I wanted to see Mr McGrath."

"Wait a minute." There were sounds of movement and then the door was opened about an inch. "Don't let those rats in for Christ's sake."

"Rats?" said Ducane.

"Cats, rats, outsize rats I call them, I'm going to open the door and you must *rush* in, otherwise they'll get in too, quick now."

The door opened and Ducane entered promptly, un-
accompanied by a cat.

The person who had opened the door for him was a tall
woman with a very dark complexion, so dark that he took
her at first for an Indian, dressed in a white dressing gown,
her head wrapped in a towel. Possibly the white turban
had suggested India. There was something very surprising
about the woman though Ducane could not at first make
out what it was. The room was a little obscure and hazy,
as the curtains were half pulled.

"I can't abide cats, and they take things anyway, they're
half starving and they *scratch*; my mother told me I had one
jump on my pram and it was sitting there right on my face
and ever since if there's a cat in the room I can't get my
proper breath, funny isn't it. Have you got a thing about
cats yourself?"

"No, I don't mind cats," said Ducane. "I'm sorry to
trouble you, but I'm looking for Mr McGrath."

"Are you a policeman?"

The question interested Ducane. "No. Is Mr McGrath
expecting the police?"

"I don't know what *he*'s expecting. I'm expecting the
police. I'm expecting the Bomb. You've got a sort of
hunting look."

"Well, I'm not a policeman," said Ducane. But I'm the
next best thing, he thought with a little shame.

"McGrath's not here. He'll be back soon though. You
can wait if you like."

Ducane noticed with some surprise that his agitation
had now completely disappeared, being replaced by a sort
of calm excited interest. He felt physically at ease. He could
well believe that he had a hunting look and he wore it
coolly. He began to inspect his surroundings, starting with
the woman who confronted him.

The tall white-clad woman in the turban was certainly
not Indian. Her complexion was rather dark and wisps of
almost black hair could be seen escaping from the towel,
but her eyes were of an intense opaque blue, the thick dark
blue of a Northern sea in bright clouded light. Ducane
judged her to be some sort of Celt. She stood before him,
equally staring, with a relaxed dignity, her arms hanging

by her sides, her eyes calm and slightly vague, like a priestess at the top of some immensely long stone staircase who sees the distant procession that wends its way slowly towards her mystery.

Startled by this sudden vision, Ducane lowered his eyes. He had been staring at her in a way that was scarcely polite and, it now seemed to him, for some time.

"Don't tell me who you are, let me guess."

"I'm just from—" Ducane began hastily.

"Oh never mind. In case you're wondering who the hell I am, I'm Judy McGrath, Mrs McGrath that is, not *old* Mrs McGrath of course, she's dead these ten years the old bitch. I'm McGrath's wife, God help me; well, you'd hardly think I was his mother, would you, though I'm not what I was when I won the beauty competition at Rhyl. I *did* win it, you know, what are you looking like that for? I'll show you a picture. You married?"

"No."

"I thought you were a bachelor, they have a sort of fresh unused look. Queer?"

"No."

"Not that you'd tell me. It's their mothers that do it to them, the old bitches. Why don't you sit down, there's no charge. Drink some pink wine, it tastes like hell but at least it's alcohol."

Ducane sat down on a sofa covered with a thin flower-printed bedspread, which had been tucked down into the back of the seat. The room was cluttered and stuffy and smelt of cosmetics. A second door, half open, showed a darkened space beyond. The furniture, apart from the sofa, consisted of low dwarfish chairs with plastic upholstery and modern highly varnished coffee tables, grouped round a television set in the corner. The tables were covered with slightly dusty trinkets, little vases, fancy ash-trays, china animals. A rather expensive-looking camera lay upon one of the chairs. A white frilly petticoat was extended upon the linoleum reaching into the darkened doorway. The place had somehow the air of a shop or a waiting room, an un-confident provisional faintly desperate air, an atmosphere of boredom, an atmosphere perhaps of Mrs McGrath's boredom.

"Oh God I was so bored when you arrived!" said Mrs McGrath. "It's so boring just waiting."

What does she wait for, Ducane wondered. Somehow it was plain that it was not her husband. "No, thank you," he said to the glass of wine she was holding out to him. He noticed that she was holding something in her other hand which turned out to be a hand mirror.

"Toffee nose, eh? I'm legally married to McGrath, you know, would you like to see my passport? Or do you think I'm going to put a spell on you? I'm not a nigger, I'm as good as you are. Or are you anti-Welsh? You'd be surprised how many people are. Taffy was a Welshman, Taffy was a thief, and all that, and they really believe it. I'm Welsh Australian actually, at least my parents were Welsh Australian only they came home and I was born in Rhyl where I won the beauty competition. I could have been a model. You English?"

"Scottish."

"Christ, like McGrath, except he isn't, he's a South London hyena, he was born in Croydon. My name's Judy, by the way. Oh, beg pardon, I told you. Excuse me while I change."

Mrs McGrath disappeared into the next room, scooping up the extended petticoat as she went by. She returned a moment later dressed in a very short green cotton dress and brushing out her blackish hair. Her hair, abundant and wiry, swept down on to her neck in a thick homogeneous bundle, rounded at the end, giving her a somewhat Egyptian look.

Ducane rose to his feet. He had become aware that what was remarkable about Mrs McGrath was simply that she was a very beautiful woman. He said, "May I change my mind and have some wine."

"That's matey of you. Christ, what ghastly plonk. Here's yours. Sit down, sit down. I'm going to sit beside you. There. Mind if I go on brushing my hair? No, hard luck, I'm wearing tights, there's nothing to see."

Mrs McGrath, now seated beside Ducane, had ostentatiously crossed her legs. He sipped the pink wine. If she was indeed putting a spell on him he felt now that he did not mind it. The room had begun to smell of alcohol, or perhaps it was Mrs McGrath who smelt of alcohol. Ducane realised that she was a little tipsy. He turned to look at her.

The low-cut green dress revealed the dusky line between two round docile tucked-in white breasts. Mrs McGrath's face, which seemed without make-up, now looked paler, transparently creamy under an even brown tan. The wiry black hair crackled and lifted under the even strokes of the brush. Dark Lady, thought Ducane. He thought, Circe.

The cold dark blue eyes regarded him with the calm vague look. Mrs McGrath, still brushing, reached her left hand for her own glass. "Pip pip!" She clinked her glass gently against Ducane's and with a sinewy movement of her wrist caressed the side of his hand slowly with the back of hers. The movement of the brush stopped.

Mrs McGrath's hand was still in contact with Ducane's. Ducane had an intense localised sensation of being burnt while at the same time a long warm spear pierced into the centre of his body. He did not remove his hand.

The brush fell to the floor. Mrs McGrath's right hand collected her glass and Ducane's, holding them rim to rim and set them down on one of the tables. Her left hand now began to curl snake-like round his, the fingers slowly crossing his palm and tightening.

Ducane stared into Mrs McGrath's now very drowsy blue eyes. She leaned gradually forward and laid her lips very gently upon his lips. For a second or two they stayed thus quietly lip to lip. Then Mrs McGrath slid her arms round his shoulders and crushed herself violently against him, forcing his lips apart. Ducane felt her tongue and her teeth. A moment later he had detached himself and stood up.

Mrs McGrath remained motionless, both hands raised in the attitude into which he had flung her on rising. Her North Sea eyes were narrow now, amused, predatory and shrewd. She said softly, "Mr Honeyman, Mr Honeyman, I like you, I like you."

Ducane reflected a good deal afterwards about his conduct on this occasion and could not later acquit himself of having quite disgracefully 'let things happen'. But at the moment what he mainly felt was an intense irresponsible physical delight, a delight connected with the exact detail of this recent set of occurrences, as if all their movements from the moment at which their hands touched had composed themselves into a vibrating pattern suspended within his nervous system. He felt the outraged joy of someone round whose neck an absurdly bulky garland of flowers has quite unexpectedly been thrown. With this he felt too the immediate need to be absolutely explicit with Mrs McGrath and let her know the worst.

He said very quickly, "Mrs McGrath, it is true that I am not a police officer, but I am a representative of the government department in which your husband works. I'm afraid your husband is in trouble and I have come here to ask him some rather unpleasant questions."

"What's your name?" said Judy McGrath, relaxing her pose.

"John Ducane."

"You're sweet."

Ducane sat down cautiously on one of the coffee tables, carefully pushing a clover-spotted china pig family out of the way. "I'm afraid this may prove a serious matter—"

"You're very sweet. Do you know that? Drink some more pink wine. What do you want McGrath to tell you? Maybe I can tell you?"

Ducane thought quickly. Shall I? he wondered. And some professional toughness in him, perhaps reinforced by his natural guilt, now ebbing back through his delighted nerves, said yes. He said, giving her every warning by the gravity of his look, "Mrs McGrath, your husband was blackmailing Mr Radeechy."

Judy McGrath no longer had the eyes of a priestess. She looked at Ducane shrewdly yet trustfully. She looked at him as she might have looked at an old friend who was conveying bad news. After a moment she said, "He'll lose his job, I suppose?"

"How much did Radeechy give him to keep quiet?" asked Ducane. He held her in a cool almost cynical gaze, and yet it seemed to him afterwards that there was as much passion concealed in this questioning and answering as there had been in the flurry that preceded it.

"I don't know. Not much. Peter isn't a man with big ideas. He ate off newspapers all his childhood."

Ducane gave a long sigh. He stood up again.

While he was framing his next question there was a sound of footsteps on the stairs. They turned instantly to each other. She said in a low voice, "That's him now. We'll meet again Mr Honeyman, we'll meet again."

The door opened and McGrath came in.

Ducane's plan of surprising McGrath had certainly succeeded. McGrath stood still in the doorway with his pink mouth open staring at Ducane. Then his features crinkled into an alarmed furtive frown and he turned towards his wife with a lumbering violent movement.

"Good evening, McGrath," said Ducane smoothly. He felt alert and cold.

"Well, I'm off to the pub," said Judy McGrath. She picked up her handbag from the sofa and went to the door. As McGrath, now again looking at Ducane, did not move, she pushed him out of her way. He banged the door to after her with his foot.

"I'm sorry to intrude," said Ducane. "I find I have to ask some more questions."

"Well?"

There was a dangerous sense of equality in the air. McGrath still contained the violence of the arrested gesture towards his wife. Ducane thought, I must rush him. He said, "McGrath, you were blackmailing Radeechy."

"Did my wife tell you that?"

"No. Radeechy's papers told us. As you know, the penalties for blackmail are very severe indeed."

"It wasn't blackmail," said McGrath. He leaned back against the door.

"Well, let us say that Radeechy rewarded you for keeping your mouth shut. Frankly, McGrath, I'm not interested in you, and if you will now tell me the *whole* truth I'll do my best to get you off. If not, the law will take its course with you."

"I don't understand," said McGrath. "I haven't done anything wrong."

"Come, come. We *know* you extorted money from Radeechy. I suppose it hasn't occurred to you to wonder whether you were partly responsible for his death?"

"Me?" McGrath came forward and gripped the back of the sofa. He had started to think now and had plumped his face out with a look of upset and peevish self-righteousness. "He never minded *me*. He never worried about *me*. I liked him. We were friends."

"I'm afraid I don't believe you," said Ducane. "But what I want to know now—"

"It *wasn't* blackmail," said McGrath, "and you couldn't prove it was. Mr Radeechy gave me money for what I did. I didn't worry him at all, it couldn't have been because of me, you just ask Mr Biranne, he'll tell you what it was like up there at Mr Radeechy's place. I never threatened Mr Radeechy with anything, you couldn't prove it was black- mail, I mean it wasn't blackmail, the old gentleman just liked me, he *liked* me and he paid me generous like, that's all it was."

Ducane stepped back. His mind twisted and darted to catch the thing which had been thrown at it so unexpectedly. He controlled his face. He said coolly, "Mr Biranne. Yes, of course. He was there quite a lot, wasn't he."

"I'll say he was," said McGrath, "and he'll tell you what it was like between me and the old fellow. Me a black- mailer! Why I wouldn't hurt a fly! I was—"

McGrath went on protesting.

Ducane thought, so Biranne was lying about his relations with Radeechy. Why? Why? Why?

Fourteen

THE three women were walking slowly along the edge of the sea. The smooth sea was a light luminous uniform colour of blue, scattered over with twinkling, shifting gems of brightness, and divided by a thin dark blue line from the more pallid empty blue sky, into which on such a day it seemed that one could look infinitely far. There had been a few natives on the beach that morning, but now they had gone away in the dead time of the early afternoon. On the curve of the open green hillside just inland, like a figure in the background of a painting by Uccello, Barbara could be seen riding her new pony.

Outlined against the pale blue light, the figures of the women seemed monumental in the empty scene. They walked slowly and lazily in single file, Paula first, dressed in a plain shift of yellow cotton, Mary next in a white dress covered with small blue daisies, and Kate last, in a purplish reddish dress of South Sea island flowers. Kate, wearing her canvas shoes, was walking along with her feet in the sea. At low tide there was a little sand at the sea's edge and she was walking upon the sand. The other two walked higher up, upon the crest of mauve and white pebbles.

Paula was twisting her wedding ring round and round upon her thin finger. She had often felt inclined to throw the ring into the sea, and been prevented by some almost superstitious scruple. She was thinking now, what on earth shall I do? She had just received a postcard from Eric posted in Singapore. Something about the slow progress across the globe of her ex-lover appalled and paralysed her. Her first reaction had been one of sheer terror. Yet it was possible that she had a genuine duty here; and in the light of that word 'duty' she had found herself able once more to reflect. Perhaps Eric's mind, wounded and crippled by her fault, could only be healed by her ministration? She need not after all now marry Eric, or become again his mistress, as it had seemed to her in the first shock, and for no very clear reason, that she must. All that was necessary

119

was that she should resolutely confront him, talk to him with reason and kindness, talk if necessary on and on and on. He had gone away too quickly and she had been so cravenly glad of this. She had never *understood* that situation, she had never really contemplated it, she had shuffled it off. Perhaps if she tried now to understand it and to help Eric to understand it she would do them both some good of which at present she had not even the conception. It was simply that the idea of confronting Eric was an idea of such pure and awful pain that she could not in any way manipulate it in her thought.

I never understood what happened, Paula thought. Everything was so dreadful that I stopped thinking. I never tried to see what it was like for Richard either. If I had I might have tried to stop him from going away. But I hated myself and the muddle of it all so much, I let Richard go just because I wanted to be left alone. I ought to have fought Richard then with my intelligence. Yet it all seemed inevitable and perhaps it was. Is it fruitless to think about the past and build up coherent pictures of how one's life went wrong? I have never believed in remorse and repentance. But one must do something about the past. It doesn't just cease to be. It goes on existing and affecting the present, and in new and different ways, as if in some other dimension it too were growing.

She looked away over the sinister silent blue surface of the Eric-bearing sea. If I could think clearly now, she wondered, about what I did then could I do us all some good? Then she reflected that this 'us all' seemed to include Richard; yet there was nothing further in the rest of time that she could do for Richard except leave him utterly alone. It was Eric, not Richard, whom she might have now the power to help, and she must save her wits from crazy fear by thinking on the *problem* of how to do it. I must think it all out beforehand, she thought, and I must be in control. Eric could make me do things, that was what was so dreadful. Of course Paula had revealed her trouble to no one. She preserved it in her private heart like the awful bloody arcana of a mystical religion.

Mary was thinking, suppose I were to marry Willy and take him right away? The idea was vague, wonderful, with its sudden suggestion of purpose, of space, of change. It was a surprise idea. And yet why not? Ducane had been right when he said that she had settled down to feeling inferior to Willy. She had allowed Willy to cast a bad sleepy spell upon both of them. What she needed now was will, some freshness out of her own soul to break that spell. I've never had gaiety of my own, thought Mary. Alistair was gay, the gaiety of our marriage was all his. I am naturally an anxious person, she thought, stupidly, *wickedly* anxious. Even now, as I walk along beside this blue sea covered with sugary light I see it all through a veil of anxiety. My world is a brown world, a dim spotty soupy world like an old photograph. Can I change all this for Willy's sake? There is a grace of the gods which sends goodness. Perhaps there is a grace of the gods which sends joy. Perhaps indeed they are the same thing and another name for this thing is hope. If I could only believe a little more in happiness I could control Willy, I could *save* Willy.

In fact John Ducane's "You have power" had already made a difference to her relations with Willy. She could not yet imagine herself proposing marriage to him, though she had tried to picture this scene. Yet, between them, things were changing. I think I was too obsessed with the idea that he should talk to me about the past, she thought, about what it was like *there*. I felt that this was a barrier between us. But I know now that I can leap over the barrier, I can come close to Willy and hustle him just by a sort of animal cheerfulness, just by a sort of very *simple* love. It isn't my business to knit up Willy's past, to integrate it into a present I can share with him. It may be impossible to do this anyway. I must be loving to him in a free unanxious sort of way, even ready to make use of him to procure my own happiness! I already feel much more independent with him. Mary had felt this greater independence as a sense of almost bouncy physical well-being as she moved, differently now, about Willy's room. And she had seen Willy being positively puzzled by it. When she saw that look of puzzlement upon his dear face she laughed the best laugh she had laughed for a long time.

Kate was thinking how wonderfully cool the water goes on feeling upon my ankles, a marvellous feeling of something cool caressing something warm, like those puddings where there's a hot cake hidden inside a mound of ice cream. And what an intense heavenly blue the sea is, not a dark blue at all, but like a cauldron of light. How wonderful colour is, how I should like to swim in the *colour* of that sea, and go down and down a revolving blue shaft into a vortex of pure brightness where there isn't even colour any more but just bliss. How wonderful everything is and Octavian isn't the least bit hurt about John, I know he isn't, not the least little bit, it doesn't worry him at all. Octavian is happy and I'm going to make John happy. He's still worried about Octavian but he'll soon see that all is well, that all is perfectly well, and then he'll settle down to be happy too. How wonderful love is, the most wonderful thing in the whole world. And how lucky I am to be able to love without muddle, without fear, in absolute freedom. Of course Octavian is great. He has such a divine temperament. And then, if it comes to that, so have I. We were both breast-fed babies with happy childhoods. It does make a difference. I think being good is just a matter of temperament in the end. Yes, we shall all be so happy and good too. Oh, how utterly marvellous it is to be me!

Fifteen

"OH it's you, is it," said Willy Kost. "Long time no see."
Theo came into the cottage slowly, not looking at his host, and closed the door, by leaning his shoulder against it. He moved along the room, setting the bottle of whisky down on the window ledge. He went into Willy's kitchen and fetched two glasses and a jug of water. He poured some whisky and some water into each glass and offered one glass to Willy, who was sitting at the table.

"What's the music?" said Theo.

"Slow movement of the twelfth quartet, opus 127."

"I can't bear it."

Willy switched the gramophone off.

"A consciousness in agony represented in slow motion."

"Yes," said Willy.

Theo leaned against the long window, looking out. "Wonderful binoculars these. Did Barbara give them to you?"

"Yes."

"I can see our Three Graces walking along by the edge of the sea. Each one more beautiful than the last."

"Oh."

"You know why I haven't been for so long?"

"Why?"

"I think I'm bad for you."

Willy was drinking the whisky. "You know that's not so, Theo."

"It is. You need brisk ordinary people. You and I always talk metaphysics. But all metaphysics is devilish, *devilish*."

"There is no good metaphysics?"

"No. Nothing about that can be *said*."

"Sad for the human race, since we are such natural prattlers."

"Yes. We are natural prattlers. And that deepens, prolongs, spreads and intensifies our evil."

"Come, come," said Willy. "Very few people know of these devilish theories you speak of."

123

"They have their influence. They pervade, they pervade. They produce illusions of knowledge. Even what we are most certain of we know only in an illusory form."

"Such as what?"

"Such as that all is vanity. *All* is vanity, Willy, and man walks in a vain shadow. You and I are the only people here who know this, which is why we are bad for each other. We have to chatter about it. You and I are the only people here who know, but we also know that we do not know. Our hearts are too corrupt to know such a thing as truth, we know it only as illusion."

"Is there no way out?"

"There are a million ways out on *this side*, back into the fantasy of ordinary life. Muffins for tea is a way out. Propertius is a way out. But these are just boltholes. One ought to be able to get . . . through . . . to the other side."

"You may be right about Propertius," said Willy, "but I would like to say a good word for muffins for tea."

"Mary."

"No, no, not Mary. Mary is something else. Just muffins for tea."

"There are muffins and muffins," Theo conceded. "But let us take Propertius now. What is the point of all this activity of yours, what are you *really* after? Senseless agitation, senseless agitation, the filling of a void which for your eternal salvation had much better be left unfilled. Is your edition of Propertius going to be a great work of scholarship?"

"No."

"Is it necessary to the human race?"

"No."

"It's not great, it's not even necessary. It's mediocre, it's a time-filler. Why do you do it?"

Willy reflected for a moment. He said, "It expresses my love for Propertius and my love for Latin. Love needs to be expressed, it needs to do work. This may be something which cannot be stated in your devilish metaphysics without being somehow falsified, but it is . . . an indubitable good. And if there is an indubitable good within one's reach one stretches out one's hand."

"Permit me to correct your description, my dear Willy.

The object of love here is yourself, this is the value which you attempt with Latin and with Propertius to exalt and to defend."

"That is possible," said Willy. "But I don't see why one should necessarily know. You are a great one for not knowing things. Let's not know that, shall we?"

Theo had left the window and was standing by the table leaning down upon his knuckles and regarding his host. The front of his jacket was hanging open revealing a crumpled shirt, stained brown braces and a dirty woollen vest. From this inwardness of Theo a mingled smell of sweat and dog was beamed across the pile of open books and dictionaries. Willy shifted, rubbing a thin ankle with a small delicate hand.

"And after Propertius, what?"

"Another time-filler, I suppose."

"Did they tell you about that chap who committed suicide?"

"No," said Willy, surprised. "Who?"

"Oh, no one we know, as Kate would say. Just some meaningless fellow in my dear brother's office. They're all agog. It's the jolliest thing that's happened since Octavian's CBE. They're keeping it from *you*, you know why! You're becoming a sort of sacred object to the people down there."

"They shouldn't worry about me," Willy mumbled. "I shall stay out my time."

"Yes, I think you will," said Theo, "though I don't know why. I don't know why I do. I feel ill all the time now. And I can't stand it down there, that's why I came up here to torment you. It's getting worse down there. They're all watching each other ever so sweetly. *Homo homini lupus*, Willy, *homo homini lupus*. They're all of them sex maniacs and they don't even know it. There's my dear brother, that perfect O, getting erotic satisfaction out of seeing his wife flirting with another man—"

"Why not pardon them a little," said Willy. "They don't do much harm. You rail on us all for not being saints."

"Yes, yes, yes. And when I stop that railing I shall be dead. It is the only thing I know and I shall cry it out again and again, like a tedious little bird with only one song."

"If you know that much you must know more. There is then a *light* in which you judge us."

"Yes," said Theo. "The light shows me evil, but it gives me no hope of good, not a shred of hope, not a shred."

"You must be wrong," said Willy. "You *must* be wrong."

"You express a touching and very fundamental form of religious faith. Nevertheless there are the damned."

"Theo," said Willy. "Tell me sometime, tell me perhaps now, what really happened to you in India, what *happened?*"

Theo, his narrowed pointed face thrust well forward over the table, shook his head. "No, no, my heart, no." He said after a moment. "You, Willy, tell me sometime, tell me perhaps now, what it was like for you . . . in that place."

Willy was silent, regarding one hand and seeming to count the fingers with the thumb. He said slowly, "It might be possible . . . some time . . . to tell you."

"Bosh," said Theo. "You mustn't tell me, you must never tell me, such things can't be told, I wouldn't listen." He lurched back from the table and came round behind Willy. He put his large thick hands down on to Willy's shoulders, feeling the small cat-like bones. He kneaded the flesh with his fingers. He said, "I am a very foolish man, Willy."

"I know you are. A certain *kouros*—"

"Damn *kouroi*. You must forgive me, absolve me."

"You're always wanting to be forgiven. What do you want to be forgiven for? Presumably not for being rude and negligent and disloyal and selfish and. . . ."

"No!" They both laughed.

"I can forgive you, Theo. I can't absolve you. You must absolve yourself. Pardon the past and let it go . . . absolutely . . . away."

Theo leaned down until his brow was touching the silky white hair. He closed his eyes and let his arms slide forward over Willy's shoulders to receive the comfort he had come to receive, the close caressing pressure of Willy's hands upon his.

Sixteen

"OCTAVIAN, I've discovered something rather odd."
"Sit down, John. I must say I'm glad you've discovered *something*, odd or otherwise. What is it?"

"Listen," said Ducane. "I went to see McGrath yesterday evening at his house—"

"*Was* McGrath blackmailing Radeechy?"

"Yes, he was, but that's not important. McGrath mentioned Biranne. He said Biranne was often at Radeechy's place."

"Biranne? I thought he didn't know Radeechy at all."

"So he led us to suppose. Well, I didn't express any surprise, I just made McGrath go on talking, and I got him back on to what exactly happened when he came to Radeechy's room after the shot was fired, and something else emerged. Biranne had *locked the door*."

"Locked the door of Radeechy's room? On the inside?"

"Yes. McGrath said, 'And then Mr Biranne let me in'."

"Was McGrath telling the truth?"

"I'm assuming so."

"I suppose one might—do it instinctively?"

"An odd instinct. Of course the door could only have been locked for a moment. McGrath reached the door, he reckons, less than a minute after the shot. But why was it locked at all? However, wait, there's more. I began to think then about that scene, what might have happened in those few moments, and I noticed something which I ought to have noticed straight away as soon as I saw the police photographs."

"What?"

"Radeechy was left-handed."

"I never spotted that. So—?"

"No, you mightn't have. But one left-handed man notices another. One of the few serious conversations I ever had with Radeechy was about the causes of left-handedness. He told me he was completely helpless with his right hand."

"Well—?"

"The gun was lying on the desk beside Radeechy's right hand."

"Good heavens," said Octavian. Then he said, "I suppose he *might* have used his right hand—?"

"No. You just imagine shooting yourself with your left hand."

"Might it have fallen there somehow out of his other hand?"

"Impossible, I think. I looked at the photographs carefully."

"So what follows?"

"Wait a minute. Now Biranne did say that he'd moved the gun—"

"Yes, but he said he only moved it an inch to see Radeechy's face and then pushed it back where it was."

"Precisely—"

"Oh *God*," said Octavian, "you don't think that Biranne killed him, do you?"

"No, I don't—"

"Biranne hasn't the temperament, and besides why—"

"I don't know about Biranne's temperament. Anyway, find the motive and the temperament will look after itself."

"Of course that *could* be the perfect crime, couldn't it. Go into a man's room, shoot him, and then 'discover' the body."

"Possibly. Though consider the difficulties in this case. The shot was fired from very close quarters into the mouth. However, let me go on with the tale. I went over to Scotland Yard. You remember I asked you to get the PM to say a word to those boys over there. Evidently he did, because they were all dying to help me for a change. I wanted to check the finger-prints on the revolver, to see whether they were left-hand prints and whether they were in the right place."

"And—?"

"They were left-hand prints all right, and they were, as far as I could see, in the proper place. Not that that proves anything conclusive, but at any rate he'd had his hand on the gun in such a way that he could have fired it himself. Now Biranne said he'd touched the gun. How did he say this? Did he seem particularly nervous and upset?"

"Yes!" said Octavian. "But we were all jolly nervous and upset! We're not used to death after lunch!"

"Naturally. Well, there were Biranne's finger-prints all right upon the barrel of the gun only. You remember he gave his finger-prints to the police."

"Yes. Rather officiously, I thought at the time. None of this proves he didn't shoot Radeechy, wipe the gun clean and press the thing into Radeechy's hand. Hence perhaps the locked door."

"No. But if he'd had the knowledge to press it into Radeechy's left hand he'd have had the knowledge to leave the gun on the left side of the desk."

"That's true. I suppose that lets Biranne out. Unless it's all fiendish cunning. . . ."

"No, no, I don't believe anything of that sort. Well, to continue. I then followed up an idea I'd had. You remember those old fashioned stiff starched collars Radeechy used to wear?"

"Yes."

"Biranne's finger-prints were also on Radeechy's collar.'

"On his *collar*? You don't think there was a fight or something?"

"I rather doubt that. There was no other evidence of a fight. I think it means that Biranne moved the body."

"An odd thing to do. And he didn't say he did. Why ever—?"

"You remember," said Ducane, "that you were puzzled because there was no suicide note, it seemed so out of character?"

"You think—You think Biranne searched the body and took away the note?"

"Well, it's a possibility. If Biranne and Radeechy were *in* something together, Biranne might have been afraid of what Radeechy might have in his pockets. I feel sure he searched the body, whether to get hold of the suicide note or of something else. The mistake with the gun also suggests that Biranne was taken by surprise. He panicked, knew he'd only got a moment for his search, locked the door—a rather dangerous thing to do—and then, one can picture it, pushed the gun out of the way, pulled Radeechy back in the chair in order to get at all his pockets. Then when he'd let Radeechy fall back on the desk he instinctively put the gun beside his right hand."

"Could be, could be," said Octavian. "I thought at the time—at least I didn't *think*, it was just vaguely in my mind —how *neatly* the gun was lying beside the right hand. Whereas it might have fallen anywhere but there."

"Yes," said Ducane ruefully. "I thought of that afterwards. I'm afraid I haven't been very bright, Octavian. And I ought to have noticed at once that the gun was on the wrong side, and if I'd been *there* I might have, only in the photographs it was harder to see."

"But isn't it an odd coincidence that Biranne was there, the nearest person, when it happened? Can we be certain Biranne didn't—kill him—it's an awful idea and I can't believe it, but it is all so strange."

"We can't be *certain*, but I don't believe Biranne killed him. If he had he would have pressed the gun into Radeechy's right hand *or* laid it on the left side of the desk. He wouldn't have got one thing right and the other thing wrong. I don't believe it *anyway*. As for the coincidence— well, it might *be* a coincidence. Or Radeechy might have done it suddenly as a result of something Biranne said to him. We don't know that Biranne wasn't in the room before the shot. Or Radeechy might have summoned Biranne to see him do it."

"It's weird," said Octavian. "And pretty disconcerting. Radeechy didn't know anything which had any security interest, but Biranne knows practically the whole bag of tricks. What could they have been up to?"

"Not *that*, I feel pretty sure," said Ducane. "No. I think it's something much odder, something to do with Radeechy's magic."

"McGrath didn't say anything about what Biranne *did* at Radeechy's place?"

"No. McGrath just saw him arriving there. I think McGrath was telling the truth. I frightened him a bit."

"We've sacked the blighter now, by the way."

"That's all right. I'm afraid I've got everything I can out of him."

"What did the Scotland Yard boys think of all this? Won't they want to take it over?"

"They don't know! I took the finger-prints myself. I told them some yarn."

"Mmm. Let's not be in trouble later!"

"Let me decide this, Octavian. We *shall* have to tell the police. But I don't want Biranne startled just yet."

"You're not going to ask him to explain?"

"Not yet. I want to do this thing properly. I want another lead. I want Helen of Troy. She's the missing link now."

Ducane's Bentley moved slowly along with the rush hour traffic over the curved terracotta-coloured surface of the Mall. Clouds of thick heat eddied across the crawling noise of the cars and cast a distorting haze upon the immobile trees of St James's Park, their midsummer fullness already drooping. It was the sort of moment when, on a hot evening, London gives an indolent sigh of despair. There is a pointlessness of summer London more awful than anything which fogs or early afternoon twilights are able to evoke, a summer mood of yawning and glazing eyes and little nightmare-ridden sleeps in bored and desperate rooms. With this ennui, evil comes creeping through the city, the evil of indifference and sleepiness and lack of care. At such a time the long-fought temptation is wearily yielded to, and the long-dreamt-of crime is with shoulder-shrugging casualness committed at last.

Ducane, who was sitting in the front of the car with Fivey, felt this miasma creeping about him along the crowded pavements which were passing him by with such dream-like slowness. Everything in his life seemed to have become inflated and distorted and grotesque. He had told a lie to Jessica. He had told her that evening conferences in the office prevented him from coming to see her this week. He had promised to see her next week. He felt himself increasingly cornered by Jessica, as if the girl was an entangling power which was *growing*. At moments, almost with cynicism, he thought, grow then, and make me brutal, make me a demon with a demon's strength. Then the sense of these thoughts as utterly evil would reduce him again to an elementary confusion.

His longing to see Kate had meanwhile become alarmingly intense, so intense that he had been tempted that morning, instead of going to Scotland Yard, to tell Fivey to drive him to Dorset. But he knew perfectly clearly that any gesture of this sort would introduce an ugly and perhaps irreparable disorder into the harmonious pattern which Kate herself had so confidently invented, decreed and imposed. There was a kind of sweet and innocent unconsciousness in his relations with Kate from which the sharply problematic, even the unexpected, must be kept far away. There could be great affection, there could be deep love, but there must be no moments of frenzy. Need there could be, but steady orderly need, not clutching need. How precarious it all now seemed to him, this big golden good round which he was now arranging his existence and for the sake of which he was killing Jessica's love. I wonder if I should tell Kate everything about Jessica, he wondered, and with an *élan* of relief imagined himself kneeling on the floor with his head on Kate's knee. But no, he thought, it would hurt her terribly, and, he ruefully thought, it would expose me as being half a liar. I must tell her, but later, later, later, when it's all long finished and no longer an agony. To tell her now would be entirely against the rules, *her* rules. I mustn't involve Kate in any of my muddles. Her idea is that our relationship is to be simple and sunny, and simple and sunny I must faithfully make it to be.

The discovery about Biranne had upset Ducane more than he had been prepared to reveal to Octavian. He did not at all like having as a quarry a man whom he disliked, and whom he disliked for irrational and unworthy reasons. Ducane had for the moment lost, and this was perhaps the work of that wicked summer indolence, his usual sense of being compact and self-contained and presenting a hard working surface to the world. He felt sorry for himself, he felt menaced and vulnerable. In this state, people could 'get inside him,' knives could be inserted and turned. This was one reason why he had funked facing Jessica. There was a kind of extreme pain which Jessica could cause him and which, out of blind love, she had so far refrained from causing. He felt that if he came to her in this stripped enfeebled mood she would instinctively torment him to the utmost. Nor did Ducane now fancy having Biranne as an adversary. He shrank from the prospect of perhaps having power over the man. Whatever it was that had bound Biranne and Radeechy together it was something unpleasant, with what was to Ducane's prophetic nostrils a rather eerie sort of unpleasantness. Whatever happened, it seemed likely that Ducane would shortly be involved in some sort of personal struggle with Biranne, for which, in his present state, he felt insufficiently compassionate, clear-headed, and indeed strong.

There was also the curious matter of Mrs McGrath. Immediately after Ducane's departure from McGrath's house he had looked back on that incident with a little shame and some amusement and a certain surprised exhilaration. It was some time since the unexpected had entered Ducane's life in quite that guise and it had seemed to him rather delightful. Later on it amused him less. His investigation was nebulous and tricky and indeed unsuccessful enough already without his complicating it by acting irresponsibly and indiscreetly. He could not afford to make mistakes. McGrath was an unscrupulous man, a blackmailer and a babbler to the press, and altogether not the sort of person whose wife higher civil servants in charge of confidential enquiries should be alleged to have been kissing. Ducane did not really think that, whatever Mrs McGrath might have said to her husband, there was any serious trouble McGrath could make for him. But it was the sort of thing which simply ought not to happen. More deeply he felt in retrospect *depressed* by the scene, as if some sleepy drug which he had swallowed with the pink wine were weighing on his senses still. Perhaps it was out of the somnolent ennui of the Circean chamber where Mrs McGrath *waited* that there had followed him away that sense of pointlessness which now so much took away his strength.

The car was moving, more quickly now, along the Old Brompton Road in the direction of Ducane's house in Earls Court. While these gloomy and debilitating thoughts had been occupying his mind, Ducane had been exchanging almost unconscious chat with Fivey about the weather and the predicted continuation of the 'heat wave'. Ducane could not feel that he had made, with his servant, any notable progress, although he had in a quite physical way become more used to having him about the house and could now easily restrain his annoyance at the droning Jacobite songs and at hearing Fivey using the hall telephone to make bets on horses. Fivey had confided one more piece of information about his mother, that she had 'taught him to steal from shops'. But when Ducane had tried to lead him on into revelations about his subsequent career in crime, his fellow Scotsman had just murmured mysteriously, "It's a very hard world, Sir". And questioned by Ducane about a photograph of a woman of indeterminate age which Fivey kept in his bedroom, had merely answered mournfully, "Far away and long ago, Sir, far away and long ago". However in spite of these intimations of the bitterness of life, Fivey, also patently feeling himself more at home, was at times almost jaunty, his eyes lightening with a look of intelligence, almost amounting to a wink, as he met his master's look, as if to say, I'm a rogue, but you're one too, you know, in your own way. I doubt if there's a ha'porth of difference between us. You're just luckier than I am, that's all. This quiet insolence rather pleased Ducane.

As the car now turned into Bina Gardens Ducane was watching the slow, significant, majestic movements of Fivey's very large and copiously freckled hands upon the steering wheel. As Ducane watched, he found that his own hand, which had been extended along the back of the seat, had somehow or other found its way down on to Fivey's farther shoulder. Ducane considered the matter for a moment. He decided to leave it where it was. He even shifted it a little so that his fingers curved gently, without gripping, over the bone of the shoulder. The contact brought to Ducane the intense and immediate comfort which it now seemed to him he had been seeking for all day. Fivey gazed impassively straight ahead.

Seventeen

THE three women were in town. Paula had come up to buy books, Kate was on her usual mid-week visit, and Mary had been persuaded to come up because she 'needed a change'. Mary had also come in order to encourage Pierce to leave Dorset, having skilfully prompted a luncheon invitation for him from the Pember-Smiths, who were about to set out for the Norfolk Broads where their new yacht was waiting. Mary hoped that Pierce's school-fellow, Geoffrey Pember-Smith, might boast about the yacht to some effect over lunch, since Pierce had already been invited to accompany them to Norfolk. But she feared, or rather she knew, that her offspring would be simply counting the hours until he could rush back to the misery of his now almost complete non-communication with Barbara. Mary pitied his pain and was increasingly irritated by Barbara's ostentatious insouciance, but there was nothing she could do. At moments she came near to thinking that just this useless dragging suffering of her son made the whole idea of living with Kate into a mistake. But if it had not been Barbara it would have been some other girl, the pains of a first love cannot be avoided, and it would be ridiculous to be too sorry for Pierce. All the same the situation depressed Mary, and she was vaguely afraid of Pierce being driven by Barbara into the commission of some sort of outrageous excess.

Pierce had not of course confided in his mother, but she was glad to learn that he had confided in Willy. Willy was very fond of Pierce and discussing him with Willy she had had a deep reassuring feeling, as if Willy had already fallen into the role of Pierce's father. Since Ducane had spoken the 'liberating words' in the beech wood Mary had felt much more at ease in Willy's presence and had made him more at ease too. They talked more readily; and although their talk was still less intimate than she would have wished, Mary no longer had that doomed feeling of anguished needful separation which had used to paralyse her so much in his presence. She could touch him now more spontan-

eously, more playfully, and without desperation. She
thought to herself, in a language that was new to her, I'll
make something of Willy yet, I'll *make* something of him.

The four of them had travelled up together by train and
separated at Waterloo, Paula to go to Charing Cross Road,
Kate to Harrods, Pierce to the Pember-Smiths, and Mary
to have a quick lunch by herself in a coffee bar, for she had
a plan of her own for the day about which she had spoken
to nobody.

Mary gave up her ticket at Gunnersbury station and
walked up the ramp toward the road. The summer melancholy of suburban London, gritty, contingent, trivial, hung
over the scene like an old familiar smell and the unforesee-
able physical operations of memory made her at each step
tremble with recognition. It was many years since she had
been here.

She walked along, and although she could not before
have pictured the road in her mind, she remembered each
house. It was as if out of some depth, adorned with the
significance of the past, each thing came up into a frame
which was placed ready for it just the moment before: a
carved gate-post, an oval of stained glass in a front door, a
sweep of clematis against a trellised wall, clammy dark
green moss upon a red tiled path, a lamp post with a lonely
look upon a circle of pavement. These houses, 'the older
larger houses' as she had thought of them then, were
singularly unchanged. In the torpor of the afternoon the
remembered road had the slightly menacing and elusive
familiarity of a place in a dream when one thinks: I have
been here, yet where is it and what is going to happen?
The colours too seemed like dream colours, vivid and yet
somehow enclosed and dulled, not reflecting light, as if they
were intense colours seen in darkness. And the streets were
empty as in a dream.

Mary turned a corner and for a moment did not recognise the scene at all. Houses had disappeared. Tall blocks
of flats and huge garages had taken their place. Now there
were a few cars, but still nobody walking on the pavements.
Mary frowned away from her eyes the ghostly crowding
images of things no longer there, and thought with a sudden

surprised pain, perhaps *our* house too will have simply
disappeared. But by now she had reached the end of the little
road and could see, half way down upon the left, the small
semi-detached house where she had lived with Alistair
during the four years of their marriage.

They had been the first inhabitants of that house, which
had been built after the war. The frail municipal saplings of
the road, which she now recognised as prunus and whose
name then she had never troubled to learn, had grown into
big mature trees. Alistair, a trifle younger than his wife,
had been too young to serve in the war, and had been still
doing his chartered accountancy exams when he had
brought his young bride to the little house in Gunnersbury.
Mary steadied herself, putting her hand on to the low wall
at the corner of the road, aware, almost as if it were a
separate personality, of her hand's sudden memory of the
surface of the wall, the slightly sharp crumbly stones, and the
urban moss, which, like the moss upon the red tiled path, con-
trived to remain damp and clammy even in the hottest sun.

With the touch of her hand upon the wall there came the
unexpected image of a piano, their old upright piano long
since sold, yet now indelibly associated with the mossy wall
in virtue of some lost thought which Mary must have
thought once as she paused with her shopping bag at the
corner of the road. Alistair had a beautiful baritone voice
and they had often sung together, he playing the piano,
she standing with her hands on his shoulders, head tossed
back in an abandonment of song. This was a purely happy
memory and she could recall even now that feeling of her
face as it were dissolving into an immediate joy. Alistair
could play and sing. He was also a fairly good painter, and
a talented poet, and a writer, and he was good at chess, and
a fencer, and a formidable tennis player. As she suddenly
rehearsed these things in her mind she thought, he had so
many *accomplishments*. And it occurred to her as she caressed
the wall that she must have rehearsed these things, just as
she had done now, when she was deciding to marry him.
Only it occurred to her that the word 'accomplishments'
belonged not to then but to now, and that it was a sad and
narrowing word.

That Mary had had the nerve to come back and see the

little house in Gunnersbury was due in some obscure way to Willy. She had not spoken to him about it and indeed had never talked to him about Alistair at all. But with the hardening of her resolution to *make something* of Willy had come a sense of having somehow shirked the past, of having too cravenly put it away. She must be able to talk to Willy about Alistair and about exactly how things were and about what happened. And in order to do this she felt that she had to go back, to revive and refresh those dull old memories and those dull old pains. She had, in a quite new way which was now possible, to confront her husband.

How absolute and absorbing that confrontation would be she had not foreseen. She had not foreseen the clematis and the tiled path and the wall. Willy seemed a poor shadow now compared with the bursting reality of these things. The torpid summer atmosphere of the road whose smell, a dusty faintly tarry smell, she recognised so well, was the atmosphere of her marriage, a gradual sense not so much of being trapped as of a contraction, of things becoming smaller and less bright. Was it just that, in some quite vulgar worldly way, she had been disappointed in finding her husband less distinguished than she had imagined? Perhaps I ought not to have married him, Mary thought, perhaps I didn't love him quite enough. Yet did it make any sense to make that judgment now? What could the wall and the moss really tell her about the mind and heart of a girl of twenty-three? She recalled now, though more as a physical object than as an intellectual one, Alistair's enormous novel, which she had so devotedly typed out, and which she had retyped with less enthusiasm after the first two copies had become tattered almost to pieces after being sent to twenty publishers. The novel still existed. She had discovered it only a year ago in a trunk and had felt physically sick at turning its pages.

Mary now began to walk slowly down the far side of the road. She could see already that the yellow privet hedge which she and Alistair had planted had been taken away and the creosoted fence had been taken away and a low brick wall with a crenellated top had been put there instead. The small front garden, which she and Alistair had planted with roses, was entirely paved now except for two beds out of which large sprawling rosemary bushes leaned to sweep the paving stones with their bluish branches. Now Mary, almost opposite the house, could see with a shock the light of a farther window within the darkness of the front room. They must have knocked down the wall between the two downstairs rooms. She and Alistair had often discussed doing so. She stopped and looked across. The house seemed deserted, the street deserted. She touched the smooth close-grained surface of the now thick and robust trunk of one of the prunus trees. The next tree was still missing, the one which the swerving car had knocked over.

Mary felt sick and faint, holding on to the sturdy tree. The shape of the downstairs windows brought back to her that last evening, a summer evening with a lazy pointless atmosphere like the atmosphere which she was breathing now. She and Alistair had been quarrelling. What about? There was an atmosphere of quarrel, not serious, usual, a tired summer evening quarrel. She could see the letter in his hand which he was going to take to the post. She could not see his face. Perhaps she had not looked at his face. She had come to the window to watch him go down the path and step off the pavement and she had seen everything, heard everything: the sudden swerving car in the quietness of the road, the screech of brakes, Alistair's hesitation, his leap for safety which took him in fact right under the wheels, his hand thrown upward, his terrible, terrible cry.

Why ever did I come here, thought Mary. I didn't know it would be like this. And, as if in substance the very same, the old thoughts came crowding to her. If only I had called him back, or tapped on the window, or said just one more sentence to him, or gone with him, as I might have done if we hadn't been quarrelling. Anything, anything might have broken that long long chain of causes that brought him and that motor car together in that moment of time. Tears began to stream down Mary's face. She detached herself from the tree and began to walk on. She found herself saying half aloud what she had said then crazily over and over to the people who crowded round her on the pavement. "You see, so few cars come down our road. So few cars come down our road."

Paula was coming down the narrow stairs at Foyles. She had already spent several hours on her book-hunt and had eaten her sandwiches in the Pillars of Hercules. She had also made some purchases, which he had asked her to make, for Willy. She had not mentioned this to Mary, as she was aware that Mary was intensely jealous of anyone who performed services for Willy. This sort of discretion came to Paula quite naturally and unreflectively.

Paula was carrying a large basket full of books and also a parcel under her arm. She thought, well that's the lot, but what shall I do with all this weighty stuff now. There was still some time before the train on which she and Pierce and Mary were to travel back to Dorset. Paula thought, I'll go to the National Gallery and dump these in the cloakroom and look at some pictures. She emerged into the hot and crowded street and hailed a taxi. *Up and up. Heat Wave to Continue*, said the posters.

Paula knew a good deal about pictures and they brought to her an intense and completely pure and absorbing pleasure which she received from no other art, although in fact her knowledge of literature was much greater. Today, however, as she mounted the familiar steps and turned to the left into the golden company of the Italian primitives all she could think about was Eric, the image of whom, banished by the book-hunt, now returned to her with renewed force. Eric slowly, slowly moving towards her like a big black fly crawling over the surface of the round world. She had just had a postcard from him posted in Colombo.

Paula had an image of Eric's hands. He had strange square hands with very broad flattened fingers and long silky golden hair which grew not only on the back of the palm but well down to the second finger joint. A signet ring which he wore was quite buried in this tawny grass. Perhaps his hands had somehow decided for him that he must be a potter. Paula could smell his hands smelling with the cool sleek smell of wet clay. Eric had only just managed to make a living with his pottery at Chiswick. Paula had liked his lack of worldliness, she had liked his hands miraculously wooing the rising clay, she had liked the clay. It was all so different from Richard. Perhaps I fell in love with Eric's hands, she thought, perhaps I fell in love with the clay.

Eric had seemed to her, after Richard's mixture of intellectualism and sophisticated sensuality, so solid and *natural*. Yet Eric was terribly neurotic, she thought for the first time. He was posing as a natural man, as an artisan, with his curious smock and his great leonine head of unkempt golden hair. Big Eric, big man. So much the greater the appalling horror of his . . . defeat by Richard. How could Eric ever forgive her for that defeat? The thought came to her, perhaps Eric is coming back to kill me. Perhaps that is the only thing which can give him peace now. To kill me. Or to kill Richard.

Richard. Paula, who had been walking at random through the rooms, stopped dead in front of Bronzino's picture of *Venus, Cupid, Folly and Time*. Richard's special picture. "There's a real piece of pornography for you," she could hear Richard's high-pitched voice saying. "There's the only real kiss ever represented in a picture. A kiss and not a kiss. Paula, Paula, give me a Bronzino kiss." Paula went to the middle of the room and sat down. It was long ago, before their marriage even, that Richard had 'taken over' that picture of Bronzino. It was he who had first made her really *look* at it, and it had become the symbol of their courtship, a symbol which Paula had endorsed the more since she found it in a way alien to her. It was a transfiguration of Richard's sensuality, Richard's lechery, and she took it to her with a quick gasp of surprise even as she took Richard. Chaste Paula, cool Paula, bluestocking Paula, had found in her husband's deviously lecherous nature a garden of undreamt delights. Paula was incapable of unmarried bliss. Her married bliss had been bliss indeed.

Paula sat and looked at the picture. A slim elongated naked Venus turns languidly toward a slim elongated naked Cupid. Cupid stoops against her, his long-fingered left hand supporting her head, his long-fingered right hand curled about her left breast. His lips have just come to rest very lightly upon hers, or perhaps just beside hers. It is the long still moment of dreamy suspended passion before the spinning clutching descent. Against a background of smooth masks and desperate faces the curly-headed Folly advances to deluge with rose petals the drugged and amorous pair, while the old lecher Time himself reaches out a long and powerful arm above the scene to bring all sweet things to an end. "Did you go to see my picture, Paula?" Richard would always say, if Paula had been to the Gallery. The last time he had said it to her was at the end of the first and only quarrel they had had about Eric. He had said it to reconcile them. She had not replied.

Paula told the taxi to stop at the corner of Smith Street and the King's Road. She paused beside the grocer's shop on the corner and the grocer, who recognised her, bowed and smiled. She smiled a quick constricted smile and began to walk down the street. This was an idiotic way of torturing herself, as idiotic as the impulse she had suddenly had last year to ring Richard up at the office. She had listened silently for a minute to his familiar voice saying "Biranne", and then a puzzled "Hello? Hello?" and then she had replaced the receiver. What she was going to do now was to look again at the house in Chelsea where she and Richard had lived. She knew, from something she had overheard Octavian saying, that he lived there still.

She walked more slowly now on the shady side of the street, the opposite side to the house. She could already see the front door, which used to be blue, and which had been newly painted in a fashionable brownish orange. He's had the door painted, she thought, he's *cared* enough, he looked through books and chose a colour. And as she came closer still she thought, how very clean the windows are, and there's a window box with flowers in it that's new. And she thought, why am I surprised? I must have been assuming that without me there it would be all cobwebs and desolation. I must have been assuming that without me Richard would be demoralised, broken down, done for. Yes, I did think that. How could he have chosen a new colour for the door without me? She stopped in the shade opposite to the house. There was no danger of Richard being there at that time of the afternoon. Paula put her hand over her left breast, curling her fingers round it as Cupid had curled his fingers round the breast of his mother. She was just wondering whether she dared to cross the road and peer in at the front window when something absolutely terrible happened. An extremely attractive and well-dressed woman came briskly down the street, stopped outside Richard's house, and *let herself in with a latch key.*

Paula turned abruptly away and began to walk quickly back toward the King's Road. Hot raging tears filled her eyes. She knew now, knew it with a devouring crippling pain in her body's centre, that she had not only assumed that without her Richard was demoralised and desolate and unable to have the front door painted. She had, not with her mind but with her flesh and her heart, assumed that without her Richard was alone.

Jessica Bird had hardly ever visited John Ducane at his own house. This had never seemed to her particularly significant. John had always told her how cheerless his own house was and what pleasure he received from visiting her flat. So they normally, and of late always, met at Jessica's flat and not at the house in Earls Court.

Jessica had not felt deprived or excluded. Now, however, especially since he had spoken of leaving her, Ducane's house had become in her mind a place both mysterious and magnetic, as if it contained, in the form of some talismanic object, the secret of his change of heart. She had nightmares about the house in which it appeared vastly enlarged into a labyrinth of dark places through which she wandered lost and frightened looking for John. Jessica did not yet believe that he would leave her. She did not see the *sense* of his leaving her, given that she demanded so little. She could not quite bring herself to say to him: take another mistress, I can bear it. But by making him promise to tell her when he did take another mistress she felt that she had in some sense patently condoned his doing so. What then could have driven him into these frantic efforts to escape from her? As there was no proper cause for the frenzy Jessica could not quite believe that the frenzy was real. There must be some misunderstanding, she thought, there must be some mistake.

When one is much in love—and Jessica was still much in love—it is difficult to believe that the beloved's affection may really have diminished. Any other explanation will be accepted except this one. Besides, Jessica had already suffered her crisis of death and rebirth when John had ceased to be her lover. She had been crucified for him already and had risen again, and this had persuaded her of her immortality. Since then John had become entissued in the whole substance of her life in a way which seemed at last invulnerable since it was removed from the drama of an 'affair'. That he should want to take *that* from her seemed in him purely wilful.

There are mysterious agencies of the human mind which, like roving gases, travel the world, causing pain and mutilation, without their owners having any full awareness, or even any awareness at all, of the strength and the whereabouts of these exhalations. Possibly a saint might be known by the utter absence of such gaseous tentacles, but the ordinary person is naturally endowed with them, just as he is endowed with the ghostly power of appearing in other people's dreams. So it is that we can be terrors to each other, and people in lonely rooms suffer humiliation and even damage because of others in whose consciousness perhaps they scarcely figure at all. Eidola projected from the mind take on a life of their own, wandering to find their victims and maddening them with miseries and fears which the original source of these wanderers could not be justly charged with inflicting and might indeed be very puzzled to hear of.

Jessica felt herself so powerless and so harmless in her relation to John that she could not conceive that she was rapidly becoming as hateful to him as a boa-constrictor clutching him about the neck. She could not conceive that he had nightmares about her. Ducane could not forgive Jessica for having broken his resolution by screaming and made him so abjectly take her in his arms. This scene, which he could not banish from his mind, seemed to symbolise the way in which he had allowed himself, by a show of violence, to be trapped into a position of hateful falsity. Meanwhile poor Jessica, whose whole occupation was thinking about him, was driven by the sheer need of an activity connected with him to write him daily love letters, which he received with nausea, read cursorily, and did not answer.

What had driven Jessica, on this summer afternoon, to make the journey to Earls Court was chiefly the letter which she had received from Ducane saying that he had too much work to do this week to be able to see her. She was miserably disappointed not to see him. But she received yet another impression from the letter which was in a curious way invigorating, and this was the clear impression that Ducane was lying. She did not believe in these 'evening conferences'. She was sure that he had never lied to her before. A certainty of his absolute truthfulness with her had been a steady consolation. But the tone of this letter was something new; and Jessica was almost glad of it, since to detect him in a lie, even to know that he was lying, seemed to endow her with a certain power. It was after all very improbable that John should be so busy that he had no time in the whole week to see her. The letter sounded distinctly shifty.

Jessica had no very clear intention in her pilgrimage. She did not really want to spy on John, she just wanted the comfort of doing something, however vague, 'about him'. She considered waiting at Earls Court tube station and meeting him 'by accident' as he emerged, since he occasionally returned by train, and she did in fact wait for a while in the station entrance although it was still a little early for him to be coming home. Then she walked slowly up the road and down the short street which led to the backwater of small pretty houses where John lived.

John's road, a cul-de-sac, met the other street at right angles and opposite to this junction there was a public house which was just opening its doors. Into this pub Jessica now went and stationed herself with a glass of beer at the window with a good view of the corner and of the front of Ducane's house. She had not been there for long, and was wondering whether if she saw him she could stop herself from running out, when something happened which astonished and appalled her. An extremely attractive and well-dressed woman came briskly down the street, stopped outside Ducane's house, rang the bell and was instantly admitted.

Jessica put her glass down. She thought, he is *there*, he is *in there*, he has been lying, he has a mistress. A completely new sensation of jealousy shook her whole body in successive shudders of pain. At the same moment, by some connected miracle, the strength which had flowed into her when she had received Ducane's lying letter was increased a hundredfold, and in that quiet sleepy pub a new demon came into existence, the demon of a ferociously determined jealous woman.

Kate Gray came briskly down the street, stopped outside Ducane's house, rang the bell, and was instantly admitted. She knew that Ducane could not be at home since he was going directly from the office to spend the evening with Octavian. Kate had come to make her personal investigation of Ducane's manservant.

"I want to come in and leave some things for Mr Ducane and to write him a note," said Kate, advancing promptly into the hall. "Could you let me have some writing paper please? And perhaps I could leave these things in the kitchen. Thank you, I know the way. I am Mrs Gray. You are Fivey, I believe."

Fivey had followed Kate into the kitchen and was silently watching her unload from her basket a box of marrons glacés and a bottle of slivovitz, her offerings to Ducane and her excuse for calling.

"You keep things very neat in here, Fivey," she said approvingly. "Very neat and clean indeed. It's a pleasant kitchen, isn't it. Now these things are for Mr Ducane. You know he won't be home until late this evening, he's over with my husband."

Kate surveyed Fivey across the table. She found him very unexpected indeed. Ducane's attempts at describing, in answer to a question of Kate's, his man's personal appearance had been vague and had made Kate anticipate something a little coarse and brutish. Brutish perhaps Fivey was, but with the picturesque romanticised almost tender brutishness with which the Beast is usually represented in productions of *Beauty and the Beast*, a large touching cuddly animal which had always seemed to Kate in her childhood greatly to be preferred to the tediously handsome prince into which it had to be metamorphosed at the end. Kate marked the apricot skin, so strikingly blotched with big brown freckles, the huge inflated shaggy head, the abundant hair and moustache the rich colour of a newly opened conker, the long long slanted eyes of the purest spotless light brown, the long straight line of the lips. He must *comb* it, she thought. I wonder if I could persuade Octavian to grow a moustache, I never realised it could be so becoming.

Kate became aware that she had for some moments been staring at Fivey, who had been staring back. She said hastily, "Could you bring me some paper please, to write my note on."

Without a word Fivey disappeared and returned in a moment with some paper. Kate sat down at the table and wrote *Dearest John*. His *hands* are spotted too, she thought, lifting her eyes far enough to see one of them. I wonder if he is spotted all over. She put in a comma and poised her pen. She could not think of anything to say to John. She went on *Here I am*, and crossed it out. She wrote *I've just been to Fortnum's and I've got you some nice things*. She said to Fivey, "I don't think after all it's necessary to leave a note. Just tell Mr Ducane I delivered these."

Fivey nodded and Kate slowly crumpled the note up. Something had gone wrong. She made out that what was wrong was that Fivey had not spoken. Ducane didn't say he was *dumb*, she thought.

She said, "I hope you're happy here with Mr Ducane, Fivey?"

"Mr Ducane is a very kind gentleman."

"Good heavens!" cried Kate. "Mr Ducane never told me you were Irish!" There was no mistaking the voice. "Why I'm Irish too!"

"I took the liberty of recognising your accent, ma'am," said Fivey. His face was impassive and the slanted brown eyes were intently fixed on Kate.

"How splendid, I come from County Clare. Where do you come from?"

"I come from County Clare myself."

"What an extraordinary coincidence!" cried Kate. "Well, that's a real bond between us. Where in Clare are you from?"

"On the coast there—"

"Near the Burren?"

"Yes, ma'am."

"How astonishing! I come from quite near there. Are your people still there?"

"Only my old mother, ma'am, with her little house and a cow."

"And do you often go back?"

"It's the fare, ma'am. I send my mother a little bit of my wages, you see."

I must give him the fare, thought Kate, but how? He

looks rather a proud man. Of course I can see now that he's Irish.

"Have you been in England long, Fivey?"

"Not long at all, ma'am. I'm a country boy."

A real child of nature, she thought. How very simple and moving he is, a true peasant. Ducane didn't describe him properly at all. And she thought, I do rather wish he was *our* servant. I wouldn't at all mind *having* Fivey.

"London must be a bit intimidating. But I expect you'll get used to it."

Kate, who by now felt very disinclined to leave the house, got up and began to prowl about the kitchen, patting cups and stroking saucepans and peering into bowls. She was beginning to feel quite at ease in the presence of Fivey as if warm rays from his reassuring beast-like presence were both caressing and stimulating her nerves.

"Have a marron glacé," she said. She tore the box open and thrust it across the table towards him.

Fivey's large spotted hand descended and, still staring at Kate with unbroken concentration, he conveyed the marron to his mouth.

He does stare so, she thought, but I rather like it. Bother, now I've opened that box I can't give it to John. I'll have to take it away with me. Or else give it to Fivey!

She resumed her prowling. "What's that?" She pointed to a bowl-like steel sink with a round gaping orifice at the bottom of it.

"A waste disposal unit," said Fivey with his mouth full of marron.

"Oh. I've never seen one. Let's dispose of some waste."

Fivey came over to demonstrate. He took a soggy newspaper bundle out of the rubbish bin, dropped it down the hole, and turned a switch. There was a formidable grinding sound.

"It's rather alarming, isn't it," said Kate. As she leaned forward over the machine she rested her white nylon gloves for a moment on the edge of the bowl. Then, with a flash like the escape of a fish, one of the little white gloves slid down over the slippery steel surface and into the dark churning void below. After it, with almost equal quickness, went Fivey's spotted hand, but not quick enough to save the

148

little glove from its fate. Half a second later Kate had gripped Fivey by the wrist.

"Oh, be careful, be careful!"

They stood quite still for a moment staring at each other. Kate drew back a little, drew him back, still holding the thick hairy wrist in a firm grip. Then she released him, sat down, and reached out automatically for the bottle of slivovitz.

She said, "That quite shook me. You must be terribly careful with that dangerous thing. I think I need a drink. Could you get two glasses?"

Fivey put two glasses on the table and sat down, not opposite to Kate but beside her. With a hand that trembled slightly Kate poured out the slivovitz. She had forgotten its quite extraordinary *sexy* smell. She could still feel the texture of Fivey's hairy wrist engraved upon the palm of her hand. She turned towards him and they drank.

Kate put down her glass. Fivey had turned his chair to face her, his drink in his right hand, his left hand upon the table. The big extended relaxed hand looked suddenly to Kate like a couchant animal. It's all very odd, thought Kate, I'd quite forgotten the taste of slivovitz, it's wonderful, wonderful. She laid her own hand down very slowly and carefully on top of Fivey's hand, moving it about slightly to feel the hair, the skin, the bone. They continued to stare at each other.

Then with a kind of formal deliberation, as if he were about to take hold of her for a dance, Fivey put down his glass, moved Kate's glass out of the way, edged his chair nearer, and began to slide his arm round her shoulder. The chestnut-coloured moustaches grew nearer and nearer and larger and larger. Kate closed her eyes.

"Octavian, do stop laughing, I think you're *awful*!"

"You mean to say the fellow actually made a pass at you?"

"No, darling, I've already explained. *I* made a pass at *him*!"

"And then you slipped him a tenner to visit his old mother!"

"It was the least I could do."

"Kate darling, you're mad, I adore you!"

149

"I must say I was rather *surprised* myself. It must have been something to do with his being Irish. Or something to do with my glove falling into the waste disposal unit."

"Or something to do with the slivovitz!"

"Oh God, the slivovitz! We drank the whole bottle! I've got the most *ghastly* headache."

"Anyway, you've proved he's heterosexual!"

"I don't know about that. He might be both. He's *terribly* sweet, Octavian, just like a marvellous animal. And such a simple nature, straight out of the Irish countryside."

"His conduct seems to me to have been far from simple. London is full of men who would faint with joy if they could get around to kissing you after a year's acquaintance, let alone twenty-five minutes flat!"

"Oh Octavian, that heavenly moustache!"

"Well, you're in a proper fix now with Ducane, aren't you, with his valet as your fancy man!"

"Well, yes, I am—Octavian, do you think I ought to tell Ducane? It's rather awful, isn't it?"

"Fivey's not likely to tell him, anyway!"

"It depends what terms they're on. Maybe they're in bed together at this very moment, discussing it just like us and laughing their heads off!"

"Come, you don't think that."

"No, of course I don't. But it's all most embarrassing. Whatever would the others think if they knew what I'd been up to while they were soberly shopping!"

"Think of the scenes at the dinner table. The surreptitious glances. The hands touching when the soup arrives. I shall enjoy every moment of it!"

"Oh dear! Do you think John would be hurt?"

"Yes, I do think he would be hurt. And he'd never believe you started it. He doesn't know you like I do! And he might sack Fivey."

"You mean he wouldn't *understand*?"

"No."

"Well, in that case I can't tell him, can I? I'd hate to ge poor Fivey into trouble."

"Did you leave a note for Ducane?"

"No. And I took away the bottle and the rest of the marrons!"

150

"And you didn't tell Fivey whether or not to say you'd called? You're a very inefficient intriguer. You'd better ring him up tomorrow morning!"

"I *can't*. Oh Octavian, I *am* dreadful. No, I'll just have to leave it, and if John mentions my having called I'll say something vague."

"Well, you've certainly entertained me. Never a dull moment with you around. Ready?"

"Ready, darling. Oh Octavian, it's such *fun* being married to you."

Eighteen

PIERCE and Uncle Theo and Mingo were down on the beach together. Uncle Theo was sitting up, with Mingo's head and front paws on his lap. Pierce, who had been swimming, was extended upon his face, his arms limply stretched out above his head. For some time now Theo had been contemplating the lean stretched out body beside him, first wet, now dry, and baked to a light and almost uniform shade of biscuity brown. As there were no natives in sight Pierce had been swimming naked. Uncle Theo sighed deeply, consuming the sigh inside himself so that it should not be audible.

Uncle Theo's right hand was automatically twisting and caressing Mingo's woolly fur. Mingo was generally agreed to be more like a sheep than a dog, and the twins were convinced that he must have sheep ancestry. Mingo's eyes were closed, but a faint vibrating of his hot body, a sort of internalised tail-wag, showed that he was awake. Uncle Theo's gaze brooded upon the limp hunched shoulders, the jutting shoulder-blades, the slim sweeping waist, the thin yet firm hips and the long straight legs of what Willy Kost had called 'a certain *kouros*'. The soles of Pierce's feet, which Uncle Theo could just see by leaning forward a little, were pleasantly wrinkled and dusted over with sand. They would be nice and curious to touch, the skin hardened and yet tender. They would taste of sea salt.

Uncle Theo's left hand, in the small space between himself and the boy, fingered the mauve and white pebbles of the beach. These stones, which brought such pleasure to the twins, were a nightmare to Theo. Their multiplicity and randomness appalled him. The intention of God could reach only a little way through the opacity of matter, and where it failed to penetrate there was just jumble and desolation. So Theo saw it, and what was for the twins a treasury of lovable individuals (it grieved the twins that they could not distinguish *every* stone with their attentions and carry it into the house) was for Theo an expanse of abomination where the spirit had never come. Does nature suffer here, in her extremities, Theo wondered, or is all dead here? Jumble and desolation. Yet was it not all jumble and desolation, was it not all an expanse of senseless random matter, and he himself as meaningless as these stones, since in real truth there was no God?

The pebbles gave a general impression of being either white or mauve, but looked at closely they exhibited almost every intermediate colour and also varied considerably in size and shape. All were rounded, but some were flattish, some oblong, some spherical; some were almost transparent, others more or less copiously speckled, others close-textured and nearly black, a few of a brownish-red, some of a pale grey, others of a purple which was almost blue. Theo, rooting among them, had dug a small hole revealing layers of damp and glistening pebbles beneath the duller sun-baked surface. He lifted one up to look at it. It was a flattish grey stone with a faint fan-like fossil marking upon it. It was not worth keeping it for the twins whose vast collection already contained many such. Theo rubbed it dry on his trousers. Then with great care and gentleness he laid it upon Pierce's spinal cord, near to the waist-line, balanced upon one of those vertebrae whose delicate curving line his eye had been tracing. Pierce groaned faintly. Theo picked up another stone and laid it upon Pierce's right shoulder, and then placed another upon the opposite shoulder to balance it. Absorbed now in his task, he shifted Mingo a little and began to cover Pierce's back with a symmetrical design of flattish stones. As he laid each stone very carefully down, drying it first and warming it a little in his hands (the surface stones were too hot for comfort) the tips of his fingers encountered the warm flesh, sandy and slightly gritty to the touch. The climax of this activity, to which Uncle Theo looked hungrily forward, and which he provoked himself by deferring, was the moment when he should oh so gently and lingeringly place a stone upon the summit of each of Pierce's buttocks.

There was a sudden crunching sound and two shadows fell upon them. Pierce twisted away, scattering the stones, and sat up. *Damn*, thought Theo, damn, damn, damn.

"Please may we have Mingo?" said Edward. "We need him for our game of Feathers."

"He won't come," said Pierce. "He's in a love-state with Uncle Theo." Pierce did not cover himself for Henrietta, who was used to male nakedness.

"He'll come if we ask him *specially*," said Henrietta. "He's such a *polite* dog."

"Come on, Mingo, stop lazing," said Theo, pushing the dog off his lap.

"Seen any saucers lately?" said Pierce.

"Yes, we saw one yesterday. We *think* it's the same one."

"Funny, isn't it," said Pierce, "that no one seems to see those saucers except you two!"

The twins were dignified on the subject of their saucers.

Edward, who had been engaged in hauling the reluctant and rather floppy Mingo up on to his four paws, said "Oh how I wish it would rain!"

Henrietta was now beckoning her brother aside and whispering to him. Edward released Mingo who forthwith collapsed again. After a good deal of whispering and fumbling, Edward cleared his throat and addressed Pierce in what the children called his official voice. "Pierce. We've got something here we should like to give you."

"What?" said Pierce in an indifferent tone. He had lain down again upon the pebbles, on his back this time.

The twins came round to him and Pierce raised himself indolently upon an elbow. "Here," said Edward. "We'd like you to have *this*, for yourself."

"With our best love," said Henrietta.

Edward held out something and Pierce received it in a brown gritty hand. Theo, peering, saw that it was a fossil, a rather remarkable one, an almost perfect ammonite. The delicate finely indented spiral of the shell was clearly marked on both sides of the stone as Pierce now turned it over in his palm, and the sea had rounded the edges and blurred the pattern just sufficiently to produce a thing of great beauty. Theo knew that the gift of the ammonite must represent a considerable sacrifice on the part of the twins, who valued their stones for aesthetic as well as for scientific reasons.

"Thanks," said Pierce, holding the stone rather awkwardly.

Edward stood back, as if to bow, and then quickly turned his attention again to the animation of Mingo. Pierce got lazily up to his feet. With many "Come on"s and "Good boy"s the twins had cajoled the dog into following them, and they were just beginning to march away across the dazzling mauve and white expanse, when Pierce suddenly twitched and straightened as if he had received an electric shock. He then twisted his naked body like a curling spring, his arm flung back, rotated upon his heels, and with a mighty cast sent the ammonite spinning far out to sea.

Edward and Henrietta, who had seen what happened, stopped dead. Theo leapt to his feet. Pierce turned away with his back to the sea. The twins started walking again, and receded stiffly, followed by Mingo.

"You absolute little swine," said Theo to Pierce, "what ever possessed you to do that?"

Pierce looked at him, half over his shoulder, with a scarcely recognisable face as contorted as a Japanese mask. Theo thought, he is furiously angry, no, he is about to burst into tears.

"Steady on, Pierce."

"I'm so bloody fucking miserable."

"All right. But you oughtn't to take it out of the twins."

"Maybe. Oh what does it matter. I hate everyone. Everything's *black*."

Picturing himself taking the naked *kouros* into his arms, Theo settled down on the stones and sat firmly upon his hands. Pierce stood between him and the water, twisting and rippling his brown body like a prisoner in bonds against the luminous blue sheet of sky and sea.

"Keep the blackness inside yourself then," said Theo. "Don't pass it on."

"If I kept it all inside I think I'd die of it. Have you ever been hopelessly in love, Uncle Theo?"

"Yes." Hopelessly just about describes it, thought Theo, pressing the palms of his hands down on to the stones.

With an indolent stoop and a grimace Pierce picked up his clothes and began to walk slowly away along the beach in the opposite direction to the twins.

Theo wanted to call him back. But then he thought, oh

let him go, there's no mending a fruitless love, it just has to be endured. I endure, let him endure.

He rose to his feet, but did not follow Pierce. He walked along to where, further on, he could see that the twins had sat down, with Mingo beside them. They had not started on their game of Feathers. As he came nearer he saw that Henrietta was crying.

Mingo greeted Theo as if they had not met for a year. Theo sat down beside Henrietta. "Come, my pet, don't grieve. Pierce is very unhappy, you know that. And when people are unhappy they often make other people suffer, quite automatically."

"What did he have to do that for?" cried Edward indignantly. "If he didn't want it he could have given it back to us. It was such a lovely one."

"It was the most beautiful one of all," Henrietta wailed. "Edward didn't want to give it and I persuaded him to, just to cheer Pierce up. Oh I do wish I hadn't!"

"Never regret a good action," said Theo. "It has more power than you know. Pierce will tell you he's sorry, and you must promise to forgive him."

The twins agreed, after a little argument, that they would forgive Pierce. Henrietta was tearful for a while longer about the sad fate of the ammonite deep in the sea, until Theo and Edward joined in consoling her by picturing how happy it would be talking to the crabs and the fishes and how it would much rather be there than getting dusty up in Pierce's bedroom.

Why ever did I do that, Pierce asked himself as he stepped into his trousers. I'll tell them I'm sorry, he thought, but that won't do any good. Oh well, I don't care, I detest everybody. I believe I'm becoming bad, like Barbara said. All right, I'm bad and I'll *be* bad.

Barbara was absent at present, staying with a school friend in town. Pierce had hoped that her absence might bring some relief, even in the form of apathy, but had not reckoned with the sheer pain of the absence itself. His black mood, which during the unpredictable torment of her presence had remained incoherent, now seemed to be becoming much harder and more definite as if he were gathering himself for some final destructive assault. And his physical desire for the phantom Barbara seemed even more teasingly painful than his desire for the glimpsed girl of flesh and blood.

He had been unable to prevent himself from following her about and provoking her, until she had told him in plain terms that she was going to town for a holiday from him. They had quarrelled violently, and Pierce had returned later to his room to find lying about on his bed all the objects which he had ever given to Barbara as presents. He had retaliated by returning to her room, and breaking some of them in the process, all the things which she had ever given him, including the excellent all-purpose knife which she had brought him from Switzerland and which had been the apple of his eye.

Pierce, fully dressed now but barefoot, stood by the edge of the glossy sea. He looked down at the receding underwater stones which the sun was revealing through a panel of green, still but bubbly like imperfect glass. He thought, I shall punish her somehow, I shall have to. And then I shall go into Gunnar's Cave and jolly well stay there and *drown*.

Nineteen

MARY climbed over the low wall of the graveyard. Her blue and white cotton dress caught on a sparkling edge of warm stone and a fine shower of dusty earth spilled over into her sandal.

Willy was a little way ahead of her, moving slowly over the bouncy interlaced ropes of the ivy. He moved with a rhythmical dancer's motion, his limp imperceptible, the mysterious pliancy of the ivy floor entering into his body.

Mary leaned back against the wall. She was in no hurry to catch him up. The hot afternoon was silent with a thick powdery fragrant silence which Mary breathed ecstatically up into her head. A very very distant cuckoo call endorsed the silence like a mark or signature. Mary thought, I am lazy, I am in no hurry. She thought, today *I have him on a lead*. She smiled at the thought.

From this part of the graveyard nothing was visible except the whitish grey monuments, their tops tapering into invisibility in the over-abundant light, and the octagonal church, up whose walls Mary noticed the small-leaved ivy was beginning to climb. At some later time perhaps the church itself would simply be a mound of ivy, as so many of the gravestones had already become. Beyond the shimmering forms of the graves the afternoon sky was empty, a pale colourless radiant void.

Mary began to move, not following Willy but going parallel to him. Her sandalled feet touched the woven surface of the springy ivy, which yielded but with no sense of touching the ground below. Walking on water would be rather like this, Mary thought, one would feel the water as thick yielding stuff pressing up against the soles of one's feet. She paused and touched the iron railing which surrounded one of the obelisks, streaking her hand with brown. She was conscious of Willy near to her, moving. The substance of the summer afternoon joined their two bodies so that when he moved she felt her own flesh very gently tugged at. Today we are like Siamese twins, she thought, only we are joined together by some sort of delicious extensible warm ectoplasm.

Now Willy had thrown himself down on the ivy, falling straight back on to it in the way the children did. Mary approached and seeing that his eyes were closed sat down quietly nearby, leaning her back against one of the stones, the one from which Pierce had so carefully stripped the ivy to reveal a fine carving of a sailing ship upon it.

Willy, who had felt the ivy-tremor of Mary's coming, said "Ai".

"Ai."

Mary was quiet for a while, looking at the whiteness of Willy's hair fanned out upon the ivy. His face was so small and brown, his nose so thin, his hands so dainty and bony. She was reminded suddenly of the feel of a bird's claws as it perches on one's finger, a tender frightening feeling.

"What are you thinking, Mary?"

"Just about the graveyard." She could not tell him about the bird.

"What about it?"

"Oh, I don't know. I feel these people must have had peaceful happy lives."

"One cannot say that of any people."

"I feel their presence—and yet it's not hostile or troubled."

"Yes, I feel their presence too. But the hosts of the dead are transformed."

Mary was silent. She did not feel them as hostile or troubled, and yet the graveyard did make her afraid, with a not too unpleasant fear, especially on these afternoons which had the density of midnight. What are they transformed into, she wondered. She had no images of skulls or rotting bones. She saw them all as sleepers bound about in white with dark empty eyes, open-eyed sleepers.

"You're shivering, Mary."

"I'm all right. I think I've just got a touch of the sun."

"Let me cure you of it with my magic stone. Here, catch."

Mary clasped quickly at something green which was flying through the air. For a second she thought it was going to fall into the dark interior of the ivy matrix, but her hand nimbly deflected it on to her lap. It was a piece of semi-

159

transparent green glass, worked by the sea into an almost perfect sphere.

"Oh how lovely!" She put it to her brow. "And how cool too."

"You caught it so prettily in your skirt. You know the story about the princess who discovered the prince who was hiding among her waiting women by throwing a ball to each woman. The women all put their legs apart so as to catch the ball in their dress, but the prince put his legs together."

Mary laughed. She felt the connection between their bodies like a strong soupy swirl of almost visible substance. Willy was moving now, propping himself up against a grave, and Mary thought, oh how I wish he would lean over and lay his head in my lap.

"You mustn't let the twins see this piece of glass," she said. "They would want it so much you would have to give it to them!"

"But I've given it to you."

"Oh, thank you!" She closed her eyes, rolling the cool glass over her brow and down the side of her nose to her cheek. She said, "Oh Willy, Willy, Willy."

"What ees eet?"

"Nothing. I feel so strange. I wish you'd talk to me more. Tell me something about you, anything, any small thing, a toy you had when you were a child, your first day at school, someone who was your friend once, just anything."

"Well, I shall tell you—I shall tell you the most terrible thing that ever happened to me."

"Oh!" She thought, now it's all going to come out, all of it, everything, oh God can I stand it.

"I was six years old."

"Oh."

"We were on a summer holiday," Willy went on, "at a seaside place on the Black Sea. Every morning I went with my nurse into the public gardens and she sat down and knitted and I pretended to play. I didn't really play because I didn't know how to play like that in public and I was frightened of other children. I knew I was supposed to run about and I ran about and pretended to pretend to be a horse. But all the time I was worrying in case someone

160

should look at me and know that it was all false and that I was not a happy child playing at all, but a little frightened thing running to and fro. I would have liked just to sit quietly beside my nurse, but she would not allow that and would tell me to run about and enjoy myself. There were other children in the public gardens but they were mostly older than me and went about in groups of their own. Then one day a little fair-haired girl with a small black and white dog came to the gardens. The little girl's nurse sat near to my nurse and I began to play with the dog. I was too shy to speak to the girl or even look at her properly. She had a blue velvet coat and little blue boots. I can see those blue boots very clearly. Perhaps that was all I let myself see of her in the first days. She was just a blurred thing near to where I was playing with the dog. I liked playing with the dog, that was real playing, but I wanted much more to play with the little girl, but she would go and sit beside her nurse, though I heard her more than once being told that she might play with me if she wished.

Then she began to come near to me when I was petting the dog, and once when I was sitting on the grass with the dog lying beside me she came and sat down beside the dog too, and I asked her the dog's name. I can still feel the warm smooth feeling of the dog's back on which I had put my hand and I can see her hand near to mine stroking the dog's ears, and now I can see her face as I first saw it clearly for the first time, a round rosy rather shiny glowing face. She had short very fair hair and a funny little cross mouth and I loved her. We talked a little bit and then she asked me to play with her. I was an only child and I did not know how one played with another child. I knew no games which could be played except alone. I said I would play with her but did not then know what to do. She tried to teach me a game, but I was too foolish and too much loving to understand, and I think anyway it was a game needing more people. In the end we just played with the dog, running races with it and teasing it and trying to make it do tricks. Now I wanted every day to come to the public gardens to see the little girl and I was very very happy. I think I was happier in those days than I have ever been since in my whole life. Then one day I thought I would like to bring a present to the little girl and the dog, and I persuaded my parents to buy a little yellow bouncing ball for the dog to play with and for us to throw and for him to bring back. I was so impatient for the next morning, I could hardly wait to show my friend the yellow ball and to throw it for the little dog. Next morning then I went to the gardens, and there was the girl in her blue coat and her blue boots and the black and white dog frisking round about her. I showed her the yellow ball and I threw it for the dog and he went running after it and he caught it and it stuck in his throat and he choked and died."

"Oh God!" said Mary. She knelt up in the ivy. The climax of the story had arrived so suddenly she did not know what to say. "Oh how—Oh Willy—What happened then—?"

"I did not see all as my nurse took me away. I was in a hysteria for that day and had the next day a fever. Then it was time for us to go home. I never saw the little girl again."

"Oh Willy," she said, "I am sorry, I am so sorry—"

There was a silence. The distant cuckoo call hollowed the quiet air. The scene, like a faded brown picture postcard, hovered in Mary's mind, making the graveyard invisible. She saw the formal public garden, the gossiping nursemaids, the sedate quaintly dressed children, the frisky dog. Desperately searching for speech, she meant to ask, What was the little girl's name? She asked, "What was the dog's name?"

The silence continued. She thought, he cannot remember. She looked up.

Willy was sitting perfectly still, his arms clasped round his knees, and tears were streaming down his face. His mouth drooped, half opened, and after two attempts he said, "Rover. It was an English terrier and it was fashionable then to call them by English names."

"Oh my darling—" said Mary. She moved awkwardly, trying to lever herself upon the springy surface. She leaned against him, thrusting one arm along his back, bowing her head on to his shoulder. Willy dabbed his face with a clean folded handkerchief. Mary put her other arm round him and clasped her hands tight upon his other shoulder, her cheek crushed against his jacket. She felt his body rigid in the ring of her clasp and she thought desperately, this does not comfort him, this does not comfort him at all. She squeezed him closer and then drew away. The bright airy light surprised her as if she had been in a dark place.

She said, "Listen, Willy, listen, and don't think me mad. Will you marry me?"

"What?"

"I said will you marry me?"

Mary was kneeling opposite to him now. Willy continued to mop his face. He shifted himself, tucking one leg under him. His gaze moved slowly across the graveyard and by the time it had come to rest on Mary his face had changed completely, plumped out into the radiant, perky, puckish face which she had seen him wear once as he jigged about his room to some music of Mozart.

"Wonderful, wonderful, wonderful!" said Willy. "No one has ever proposed to me before!" Then as Mary began to say something he added in a low voice, almost under his breath, "I am impotent, you know—"

"Willy, Willy!" A shrill cry came to them across the graveyard and they turned to see Barbara climbing hurriedly over the wall. She came bounding towards them, her blue sandals scarcely touching the dark green matting.

"Oh Willy, Mary, have you seen Montrose?"

They both said no.

"I've been looking for him and he isn't anywhere, not *anywhere*. It's been so long and he's never been away like this ever and he didn't come for his milk and Pierce says he must be *drowned* and—"

"Nonsense," said Mary. "Cats don't get drowned, they've got far too much sense. He'll turn up, he's sure to."

"But where *is* he, he's not like some cats, he *never* goes away—"

"Now then," said Willy, getting up rather stiffly from his ivy couch. "We'll go back to the house together and I'll help you look for him. I expect he's quite near, lying asleep under a bush. I'll help you find him."

"But I've looked *everywhere* and it's long past his tea-time and he always comes in—"

Willy was speaking to her in a soft sing-song comforting voice as he led her away.

Mary stayed where she was. After a while she began slowly to get to her feet. With a start of alarm she remembered the piece of green glass which Willy had given her, throwing it into her lap like the prince finding the princess, only of course in the story it was the other way round. When she had sprung up to put her arms about him it must have rolled somewhere away. She began to search, thrusting her arm down above the elbow into the dark dry twiggy interior of the ivy thicket, but though she went on searching for a long time she could not find the piece of green glass again.

Twenty

THE immense literature about Roman law has been produced by excogitation from a relatively small amount of evidence, of which a substantial part is suspect because of interpolations. Ducane had often wondered whether his passion for the subject were not a kind of perversion. There are certain areas of scholarship, early Greek history is one and Roman law is another, where the scantiness of evidence sets a special challenge to the disciplined mind. It is a game with very few pieces where the skill of the player lies in complicating the rules. The isolated and uneloquent fact must be exhibited within a tissue of hypothesis subtle enough to make it speak, and it was the weaving of this tissue which fascinated Ducane. Whereas he would have found little interest in struggling with the vast mass of factual material available to a student of more recent times. There was in this preference a certain aestheticism, allied perhaps to his puritanical nature, a predilection for what was neat, enclosed, demonstrable and highly finished. What was too empirical seemed to Ducane messy. His only persistent source of dissatisfaction with his dry and finite subject matter was that the topics which interested him most frequently turned out to have been thoroughly investigated some years previously by a German.

At the moment Ducane, who had just returned from his evening with Octavian during which, contrary to their intention, they had talked shop, was sitting on his bed and turning over a paper which he had written while he was still at All Souls on the problem of 'literal contract' and wondering whether to include it in a collection of essays which he was shortly going to publish under the title of *Puzzle and Paradox in Roman Law*. He knew quite well that he ought to be otherwise engaged. He ought to be writing a letter to Jessica to suggest a time of meeting. He ought to be drafting an interim report on his enquiry into the Radeechy affair. He was putting off the former because anything he was likely to write was likely to be at least half a lie. He was putting off the latter because he had not yet decided what to do about Richard Biranne.

Attempts by Ducane's various minions, George Droysen and others, to get on to the track of 'Helen of Troy' had all so far failed. And a *sub rosa* investigation, for which Ducane had at last received a personal authority, of Radeechy's house and bank account had revealed nothing of interest. At least, there was only one thing that was odd, and that was a negative thing. Radeechy's library contained a great many books on magic, but there were no traces at all of the 'goings-on' of which McGrath had spoken. Ducane had looked forward with a certain shame-faced curiosity to examining the tools of Radeechy's curious trade; but there was nothing whatever to be seen. Ducane concluded that Radeechy must have destroyed them all before killing himself, which suggested that the suicide was premeditated and not impulsive. This piece of reasoning helped very little, however.

Ducane had put off, and was inclined still to put off, the moment of actually asking Biranne for an explanation, because he was beginning to feel that this was his last card. The report on Biranne from the security people had been, as he had expected it to be, without interest, and his own discreet enquiries and speculations had been fruitless. He could get no 'lead' at all to help him to interpret that surprising connection; and he did not want to confront Biranne without having found out a good deal more. Biranne was a very clever man and could scarcely be bluffed into thinking that 'all was discovered'. All was very far from being discovered and Biranne would certainly become aware of this. Ducane had no doubt in his own mind that Radeechy's relations with Biranne somehow contained the key to the suicide, but the evidence for this, when he came to reflect upon it, was suggestive rather than conclusive. Biranne had lied about his acquaintance with Radeechy, he had been the prompt discoverer of Radeechy's death, and he had in some way moved or fiddled with Radeechy's body. But if Biranne chose to maintain that he had lied out of nervousness and touched the body out of impulsive curiosity, what more could be said? And that his promptness upon the scene was accidental could well be the truth.

Ducane had reopened in his mind the possibility that Biranne had actually murdered Radeechy, and that the left-hand right-hand discrepancy between Radeechy's fingerprints and the position of the gun was due to either accident or cunning. But he could not satisfy himself: accident was too unlikely and cunning too devious and unclear. If Biranne had seen Radeechy 'doing things' in the course of his magical operations would he not have known that Radeechy was left-handed? In fact Ducane knew from experience that left-handedness often escapes notice; and in any case there was no proof that Biranne's visits to the house were connected with the magic at all. On the whole Ducane was not convinced by the idea of murder. He felt pretty sure that Radeechy had used the gun and that Biranne had unthinkingly moved it in the course of his search, or whatever it was he had been doing, and had instinctively replaced it beside the right hand. In the end, perhaps very soon, he would have to tax Biranne with this. But the interview, to which he did not in any way look forward, was crucial and must not be bungled. He wanted not only to surprise Biranne but to have enough information to be able in some way to trap him. At the moment, however, it simply seemed impossible to find out anything more, he ruefully concluded, short of having Peter McGrath put upon the rack.

"There's a gentleman downstairs to see you, Sir. He says his name's McGrath."

Ducane jumped. Fivey, who preferred not to enter a room if putting his head round the door would do, was leaning over, supported by the door handle, at an angle of forty-five degrees. Even his moustaches admitted the pull of gravity.

"Where is he? I'll come down."

"He's in the hall, Sir."

As Fivey stood aside Ducane apprehended a curious and unfamiliar smell, a sort of piercing sweet-sour odour, which seemed to be emanating from his servant. He hurried past and out of its range. Fivey followed him down the narrow stairs droning *Bony Chairlie's noo awa* half under his breath.

Ducane caught a quick glimpse of McGrath's orange hair and blue eyes. Then they were blotted out by the large form of Fivey who, sidestepping like a dancer, passed in front of Ducane, opened the door of Ducane's small drawing-room with a flourish, and turned the lights on. McGrath, no longer looking at Ducane, was staring at Fivey who was now leaning against the lintel of the door more in the attitude of a spectator than of one about to usher others into a room.

"Go in, please," said Ducane.

McGrath passed Fivey, staring into his eyes as he did so and pausing inside the room to stare back at him. Fivey returned the stare. Ducane followed McGrath in and inhaled once more the sinister, slightly oily smell. Fivey fell rather than stepped away from the doorway and with a murmur of *Weel ye noo come back again* faded in the direction of the kitchen.

Ducane closed the door sharply. "Rather a late hour for a visit, McGrath."

"Who's he?" said McGrath.

"My servant."

"Mmm. Posh. Looks a bit of a weirdie though. Is there something wrong with him?"

"No. Why?"

"Those spots on his face."

"Freckles."

"Looked to me as if he's had a few. A bit pie-eyed."

"Sit down, McGrath. Now tell me why you've come. I hope you've got some more information for me."

Ducane pulled the curtains. He sat down on the long stool in front of the fireplace and motioned McGrath to the chintz armchair. McGrath sat down.

"Well, now," said Ducane. "Out with it. I assure you you won't regret telling me the truth."

McGrath was leaning forward studying Ducane's face carefully. He said, "Do you mean, Sir, that you might make it—worth my while?"

That's it, is it, thought Ducane. He replied, "If you mean will I pay you for further information, I am afraid not. I rather mean that if it later appears that you have concealed anything material you may get into serious trouble."

The idea of offering McGrath a financial inducement to talk more had of course occurred earlier to Ducane, but he had rejected it. The man was totally indiscreet and was moreover more likely to talk if threatened than if cajoled. Ducane shrank from having any kind of confidential or quasi-cordial relations with the fellow, and felt persuaded that in any case his money would only buy lies.

"You're making a mistake, Sir," said McGrath. "I've told you everything I know about Mr Radeechy. It wasn't about him I came "

"Why did you speak of my 'making it worth your while' then, if you've nothing further to tell? I warn you, McGrath, you are playing a dangerous game. If you are frank with me now I may be able to help you later. But otherwise—"

"You see, Sir, it wasn't really about that at all. In fact, Sir, I was wondering if I could interest you in a sort of project—"

"I doubt if any project of yours could interest me, McGrath, except the one I've mentioned."

"Well, it does concern you, Sir, this project, and I think you *will* be interested—"

"What are you talking about?"

"It's a bit hard to explain, Sir. The fact is, Sir, I was wondering if you could see your way to continuing the little regular remittances that Mr Radeechy used to make to me, for my services that is—"

Ducane stared at McGrath. McGrath's pinkish-white face had a damp babyish look, his pale blue eyes were amiable and round, his sugar-pink mouth had snaked out into an ingratiating smile. Ducane saw him with loathing. He said, "I'm afraid I do not require services."

"I wasn't exactly suggesting anything like that, Sir, though of course I *would* be glad to oblige. But you see, Sir, I do need the money and I think it should be made up to me a bit for having lost my job. My job, Sir, and my pension."

"I am certainly not going to give you money," said Ducane, "and I am surprised that you should ask it. You must get yourself another job. I am afraid your welfare is not my concern. Now, McGrath, I'm sure you have more to tell me about Mr Radeechy. When you were at his house—"

"No, no, Sir, it's not that. I've said all I can about Mr Radeechy. I want your help, Sir, a little bit of money, just a pound or two a week—"

"You're wasting your time, McGrath," said Ducane, rising to his feet. "And now if—"

"Maybe I'd better not beat round the bush, Sir," said McGrath, "though I'm the last to want to make any unpleasantness for a nice friendly gentleman like you. Maybe you'd like to take a look at these."

McGrath was holding out two large shiny sheets which looked like photographs. Automatically Ducane reached out and took them. They were photographs. And in a moment he saw with a shudder of surprise and alarm that they were photographs of letters written in familiar handwriting.

"What on earth—"

"You see, Sir, I took the liberty of removing these two letters from your desk at the office."

Ducane looked at the two letters and a fire of fury and shame rose into his face. He took a deep breath and then said as coolly as he could, "You really have gone too far now, McGrath. This is going to be a matter for the police. What were you proposing to do with these letters?"

McGrath also rose to his feet. His pink lips flickered and he seemed a little excited but quite bold. "Well, Sir, I'd hoped to do *nothing* with the letters. I mean if you could see your way to just continuing that little allowance Mr Radeechy used to make me. Mr Radeechy and me were quite friends about it, there were no hard feelings. And what's two or three pounds a week to a rich gentleman like you?"

"I see," said Ducane. "And suppose I tell you and your little allowance to go to the devil?"

"Why then, Sir, I would be forced to send the letters to the young ladies. I mean each young lady's letter to the *other* young lady."

The letters were from Kate and Jessica.

"It's convenient, Sir, as you'll notice that the young ladies both write by hand—lovely handwriting if I may say so—and both date their letters in the way that shows the year. And of course I've got the envelopes as well with the post-marks and your name written on."

In fact the letters had been written within two days of each other.

Ducane thought quickly. Of course there was no question of his giving in to this appalling rogue. All the same he simply could not bear the prospect of Kate and Jessica—

He said, "I am afraid you have made a miscalculation, McGrath. Each of the young ladies, as you call them, is perfectly well informed of my affection for the other. You have nothing to threaten me with, since I am totally indifferent to what you propose."

"I trust you'll pardon me, Sir," said McGrath, "it's not that I want to call you a liar, but I wouldn't come to you like this all unprepared, now would I? I've made my little investigation. Like to know how I did it? As you see, each of the ladies writes on posh paper with their address and telephone number. They write their Christian names clear and legible, bless them, and it wasn't so difficult to find out their surnames. Then I ring up each of them and ask if I can speak to the other and each of them says, all surprised, they don't know anyone of that name."

"You are ingenious, McGrath," said Ducane. He began to read through the two letters.

Kate's letter ran as follows:

Oh my darling John, how I miss you, it seems an age till our lovely *weekend* arrives. I hate to think of you all lonely in London without me, but it won't be long until we are *reunited.* You are my *property*, you know, and I have a strong sense of property! I shall assert my rights! Don't be long away from me, my sweet, haste the day and the hour. Oh how heavenly it is, John, to be able to speak love to you and to know that you feel as I do! Love, love, love. Your Kate. PS. Willy Kost sends regards and hopes to see you too.

Jessica's letter ran as follows:

My dearest, my dearest, my John, this is just my usual daily missive to tell you what you know, that I love you to distraction. You were so infinitely sweet to me yesterday after I had been so awful and you know how unutterably grateful I am that you *stayed.* I lay there on the bed afterwards for an hour and cried—with gratitude. Are we not somehow compelled by love? I shall not let one day pass without giving you the assurance of mine. Surely there is a future for us together. I am yours yours yours
                                                            Jessica.

Oh my God, said Ducane to himself. How very much he did not want those girls to see each other's letters. It would be no good explaining Kate's ecstatic temperament to Jessica, or explaining to Kate that Jessica was living in a world of fantasy. Kate's letter read just like a note from a mistress. Jessica would be certain that he had lied, and he could not bear that. He could bear to part from Jessica but he could scarcely bear that she should think so ill of him. And Jessica's letter was even more suggestive. Perhaps he could try to confess it all to Kate—but the tender romantic spell would be broken and Kate would justly feel herself deceived. Would she entirely believe him, in any case? Things could never be the same again between them. Yet Ducane also saw with awful clarity that there was nothing to be done. He could not do business with McGrath, it would be an intolerable situation as well as being quite wrong. The only hope was to frighten the man.

"Understand quite clearly, McGrath," said Ducane, "that I am not going to give way to this evil proposal of yours. I am not going to pay you a single penny. And if you send those two letters to those two young women I shall go straight to the police and charge you with blackmail. You would not enjoy a long sojourn in prison, I think."

"Oh come now, come now, Sir," said McGrath, his flabby face simpering. "I don't think you can mean *that*. Why if you were to do that, Sir, I'd simply have to let the newspapers have the story. And the two young ladies would be so upset!"

"You absolute villain," said Ducane.

"Now don't take on so. After all, Sir, it's man to man now, it's your advantage against mine. Why should you weigh in the scales more than I do?"

Ducane thought, all I can do is play for time. He won't send the letters while he thinks it possible I may pay up. I'll just have to explain the whole thing to Kate and Jess, to prepare them. But oh how can I? He said to McGrath, "You are in a strong position, I don't deny it, McGrath. I congratulate you on your cleverness. I'll think over your project. We might be able to come to some arrangement, provided your requirements were very modest. And I warn you if they ever ceased to be modest I would go straight to the police. But I need time to think the matter over. Come and see me again in two or three days' time."

"Thank you, Sir, thank you," said McGrath. "I knew you'd be quiet and sensible like. May I hope, Sir, for a little bit on account, not committing you to anything like, but just to show we're friends?"

"I rather doubt if we're friends," said Ducane, "but here's two pounds."

"Oh thank you, thank you. And do remember, Sir, if I may make so bold, and that's another thing, there's always Judy, my wife you know, we understand each other, Judy and I, and Judy's always been a willing girl, philosophical you might say, and Judy took quite a fancy to you, Sir, and if you should ever feel the urge—"

"How dare you talk to me like that about your wife!" cried Ducane. "Get out of here. *Get out.*" He rushed to the door and opened it.

Fivey jumped hastily back and pretended to be tidying the hall table.

"Listening, were you!" Ducane roared at him. "Now, McGrath, clear off!"

"Yes, Sir, yes, Sir, but I'll come back like we said," McGrath murmured, scurrying into the hall. He paused for a moment in front of Fivey and they regarded each other like two dogs. Then he darted out of the hall door.

Ducane turned to Fivey. "You're drunk!" he shouted. "I can smell it on your breath. Be off to bed. And if I ever catch you eavesdropping again I'll sack you on the spot."

Fivey vacillated, caressed Ducane with a startled reproachful look of his pure brown eyes, rotated, and began carefully to mount the stairs. Ducane went back into the drawing-room and slammed the door.

He tore the two photographs into small pieces. He sat down and put his head in his hands. In fact he had been deceiving Kate and Jess up to the hilt. There was no 'explanation' of his conduct. His conduct would look bad, just as bad as it was. He was justly served. And then the scoundrel had the impudence to offer him his wife! He could not believe that Judy McGrath— At that moment Ducane suddenly thought of something which ought to have been clear to him a good deal earlier.

Twenty-one

"WHAT ees eet, Paula?"
       "Venus, Cupid, Folly and Time."
"What?"
"Nothing."
"When shall we start reading the Aeneid?"
"Later. After— Later."
"After what?"
"Later."
"What ees eet, my dear?"
"Nothing, Willy. Why, here comes Barbara to see you.
I must go. Thanks for the tutorial!"

Eric's ship is steaming northward through the Indian
Ocean, and Eric is in the prow, Eric is the ship's figurehead,
with his big varnished face and his stiff golden hair streaming backward. He leans across the brilliant sea, sending
toward the north, toward the decisive meeting, the narrow
burning beam of his will. That unappeased violence, in him
travels to the encounter. With what can it be opposed? Is
there any love still for healing, or only the need of courage
in the face of force? What profit now even to run away,
since discovery would be so certain and flight merely the
fearful waiting in a stranger's room for those inevitable feet
upon the stair? He must be awaited here with closed lips, no
single word uttered, no confession made, no assistance asked.
It is too late, and pride will not now surrender its captive.
After so much of cleverness, so much of subtlety, so much of
the insolence of reason, comes that at last which must be
dumbly faced. Eric, not now to be controlled or managed,
must, with whatever outcome, be totally endured. The
necessary courage is that full endurance in secrecy, that
being dismembered in secrecy, the willingness to surrender,
in whatever strange way it might be asked for, an eye for an
eye, a tooth for a tooth. And this had to be, not only because of
the relentless journeying ship, but because of the unredeem-
ed past buried alive in its demoniac silence. Now let a demon
courage rise to face that resurrected bloodstained shade.

But oh, the human weakness, the desire for the comforter, the frail crying wish that it had all never happened at all and things were as they once were. The bitter memory of the newly painted door and the beautiful woman entering. The bitterness of that bitterness. Oh Richard, Richard, Richard.

"Why, Henrietta, here all alone? Where's Edward?"

"He's hunting for Montrose."

"Henrietta, you're crying. What is it, my little pussy? Sit down here and tell me."

"Everything's *awful*."

"Why, what's awful? Tell me all the things that are awful."

"We can't find Montrose *anywhere*."

"Montrose will come back. Cats always do. Don't you fret then."

"And we found a dead fish in our special pool."

"They have to die sometime, Henrietta, just like us."

"And we saw a bad magpie carrying off a poor frog."

"The magpie has to eat, you know! And I don't suppose the frog really knew what was happening at all."

"I do wish the animals wouldn't hurt each other."

"We human beings hurt each other too!"

"And we found a poor seagull with a broken wing and Uncle Theo drowned it."

"That was the only thing to do, Henrietta."

"And I dreamed last night that we were back with Daddy and it was all all right again, and when I woke up I was so miserable. Why, Mummy, what is it? Why, Mummy, now you're crying too. . . ."

"I've learnt the flute quartet in D major."

"I know."

"Oh, you've been listening! It was supposed to be a surprise."

"I heard you the other day when I was walking by the house."

"May I come up and play it to you?"

"No."

"Why not? You used to let me come here and play to you."

"Not any more."

"Why not, Willy?"

"The music is too painful, dearest Barbara."

"You think I wouldn't play it properly! I *have* improved."

"No, no, I could hear you were playing it beautifully."

"Willy, why won't you teach me German? You teach Pierce Latin so why not me German?"

"Just not."

"I don't understand you. I think you've become horrid. Everyone's horrid. Pierce is horrid."

"Pierce is in love."

"Pooh! What's being in love like, Willy?"

"I've forgotten."

"Well, I suppose you are rather old. If I'm ever in love with someone I won't be horrid to them."

"That's a very good rule, Barbara. Remember that rule when the time comes."

"You remember how you used to say that I was Titania and you were the ass?"

"Did I? Well, I'm still the ass. I'm going to London tomorrow, Barbie."

"I know. You're going to stay two days with John. John told me."

"I'm going to the libraries."

"I'll come and see you as soon as you're back. I'll be lonely, with mama and papa away."

"I'll be working then. Come at the weekend."

"Why not directly you're back?"

"*Nam excludit sors mea 'saepe veni'.*"

"You keep saying things in Latin and you know I can't understand. I might understand if you wrote it down. But I can't *talk* Latin, and you pronounce it in such a funny way."

"Never mind."

"I wish you wouldn't be so horrid, Willy, just when I'm so miserable about Montrose."

"Don't worry about Montrose, Barbie, he'll turn up. He's just wandered off on an expedition."

"But he's never done it before. He's not a real tom cat. He wouldn't *want* to go away."

"I'm sure he'll come back, my dove. There now, don't cry. You upset me so much when you cry."

"I don't think you care at all. I think you're beastly."

Barbara, sitting on the floor beside Willy's chair, had twined her arms about his knees. Willy now rose abruptly, stepping out of the wreath of her arms and marching over to the window.

"*Stop crying*, Barbara."

Out of sheer surprise she stopped, and sat there snuffling and mopping her eyes, her bare feet, just visible underneath her green and white spotted dress, nestling together like two little brown birds.

Willy took hold of the window sill, pushed aside the latest stones which the twins had brought and the glass which held the now limp and drooping nettles, and began to look intently through his Swiss binoculars at nothing in particular. I shall have to leave this place, thought Willy. The agony was each time greater of not being able to seize Barbara violently in his arms.

"What are you looking at, Willy?"

"Nothing, child."

"You can't be looking at nothing. You're so dull today. I shall jolly well go away."

"Don't go, Barbie. Yes, you'd better go. I've got to work."

"All right, I shall go and ride my pony. And I'll *never* play you that Mozart."

"Do something for me, will you, Barb?"

"Possibly. What is it?"

"Go and find Pierce and be specially nice to him."

"Well, maybe. I'll see how I feel. Have a nice time in London."

After she had gone Willy Kost locked the door and went into his bedroom and lay face downwards on his bed. The sheer physical strain of the last half hour had left him limp and shuddering. He could not decide if it was worse when she touched him or when she did not. There was a raw agony of yearning which was soothed by her touch. And yet at such moments the checking of the inclination of his whole body towards hers racked every nerve and muscle. To sit there inertly while she caressed his hair or stroked his knee required an exertion of physical strength which made him ache. And all the while vivid imagery of embracing her, kissing her passionately, taking her on to his lap, surrounded Barbara with a golden aura of pain.

I thought it might have got better, Willy said to himself, but it seems to have got worse. I shall have to do something, I shall have to go away, if things go on like this I shall go mad. He began deliberately to think about Mary and at last a sweet soothing faintness began to creep over him like a light mist. He was not in love with Mary, but he loved her very dearly, and he had been more profoundly moved and delighted by her proposal than he had yet been able to express to her in the two affectionate, confused, inconclusive meetings he had had with her since the scene in the graveyard. Perhaps he would marry Mary and take her right away. Perhaps that was the solution. Why should he not even now make a dash for happiness? Was it too late? Had the past really broken him?

Willy lay motionless face downward on his bed as the sun went down toward the sea and the evening made the landward colours seethe with vividness and then faded them into a luminous blue midsummer dark. He lay there wide-eyed and listened quietly to Theo who tapped for a while upon the door and then went slowly away.

Twenty-two

"Oh shut up, Fivey!" Ducane shouted through the drawing-room door.

The kitchen door banged. The drawing-room door banged.

"Sorry, Willy," said Ducane. "My nerves are on edge."

"What ees eet?"

"Oh nothing. All this sunny weather is getting me down. It's so unnatural."

"I wonder if those curious spots will go away in the winter."

"What are you talking about, Willy?"

"Those freckles on your butler or whatever he is."

"Good heavens! I'd never thought of that. I hope not. I rather like them!" Ducane laughed. "You make me feel better, Willy. Have a drink."

"A *leetle* whisky, maybe, just for a nightcap. Thanks."

"You're very brown. Been basking in the sun?"

"Just lazy."

"You seem cheerful, Willy."

"Just crazy."

"Octavian and Kate got off all right?"

"Yes, with the usual hullaballoo."

"I hope they'll like Tangier. I thought it was just like the Tottenham Court Road myself."

"*They* will like *anywhere.*"

"Yes. They're happy people."

Both Willy and Ducane sighed.

"Happiness," said Willy, "is a matter of one's most ordinary everyday mode of consciousness being busy and lively and unconcerned with self. To be damned is for one's ordinary everyday mode of consciousness to be unremitting agonising preoccupation with self."

"Yes," said Ducane. "Kate and Octavian are hedonists,

179

yet they aren't deeply preoccupied with themselves and so they can make other people happy."

Ducane thought, this is a moment at which I might be able to make Willy talk about himself if I tried very hard. I think he wants to talk about himself. But I can't do it. I'm too burdened with my own troubles. He said, "Things all right generally down there?"

"Yes and no. I don't see them much. Paula's worried about something, she's got some sort of secret nightmare."

She's not the only one, thought Ducane gloomily. He said, "Sorry to hear that. I must try to see a bit more of Paula." How instinctively I assume that what everyone needs is help from me, Ducane thought bitterly.

"Yes, do that, John. And poor Barbara's still very upset about the cat."

"The cat hasn't turned up?"

"No."

"I expect it will. Barbie's a very sweet kid, but hopelessly spoilt of course."

"Mmm."

Ducane was feeling almost demoralised and as this was very unusual he was correspondingly alarmed. He was a man who needed to think well of himself. Much of the energy of his life issued from a clear conscience and a lively self-aware altruism. As he had had occasion to note just now, he was accustomed to picture himself as a strong self-sufficient clean-living rather austere person to whom helping others was a natural activity. If Paula was in trouble then obviously what Paula needed was the support, the advice, the compassion of John Ducane. To think this was a reflex action. Ducane knew abstractly that one's ideal picture of oneself is likely to be misleading, but the discrediting of the picture in his own case had not brought any clear revelation of the shabby truth, but just muddle and loss of power. I cannot help anyone, he thought, it's not just that I'm not worthy to, I haven't the strength any more, I haven't the strength now to stretch out a hand to Willy, I'm enervated by all this mess and guilt.

He had spent part of the previous evening with Jessica and had agreed blankly to 'go on seeing her'. They had argued in a bitter hostile way about how often Ducane should see her. Ducane had insisted that it should be only once a fortnight. Jessica had not screamed, she had not wept. She had argued shrewdly, coldly. She had interrogated Ducane, asking him once more if he had a mistress, which he had again denied. They had stared at each other with suspicion and anger and had parted brusquely. Ducane went away thinking though he was now too wary to say it: when two people have become so hard and unforgiving to each other they ought to have the wit and the strength to part. But then he felt, on reflecting on the evening, so extremely ashamed of his unkind behaviour that he took refuge in feelings of uncertainty and weakness.

He had also seen McGrath again and had given him some more money. He regretted having become so angry with the man on the first occasion, as it was at least worth discovering whether McGrath could be persuaded to sell any more information about Radeechy. Ducane noted wryly that his earlier scruples about corrupting McGrath and demeaning himself seemed to have vanished since he was now in any case on commercial terms with the fellow. McGrath, however, who was still uncertain, as Ducane intended him to be, whether or not Ducane was really settling down to pay him a regular wage for not posting the letters to 'the two young ladies', was evasive, hinted at things he might reveal if suitably rewarded, and made another appointment. In fact Ducane doubted whether McGrath had more to tell. As for the matter of the letters, Ducane told himself that he was just playing for time, and that was indeed all he could do. He must, at some suitable opportunity, inform Kate and Jessica of each other's existence and prepare them for an unpleasantness. They were rational women and it would probably pass off all right. The only serious damage would be to his own dignity and that could be salutary damage.

At least this was what Ducane thought some of the time. At other moments the whole thing was a nightmare. He writhed at the idea of their seeing him as a liar and a traitor. His behaviour to Jessica, already so inconsistent and unkind, would seem, on this revelation, that of a shabby trickster. Jessica was certain to believe that Kate was his mistress. Ducane could face being thought a brute, but could not face being thought a cold-blooded deceiver. Yet, he reflected, I *am* a cold-blooded deceiver. What I can't bear is not being one but seeming one! As for Kate, he did not really know how she would take it, and at certain terrible times he pictured himself banished from Trescombe for ever. At these times the thought flashed on him for a second: perhaps after all it would be better just to go on paying McGrath. But Ducane knew that this was the way to hell, and that he should even envisage it showed that he was corrupted indeed.

And he thought about Biranne. He thought more and more intensely about Biranne, producing not clarity but darkness. Ducane's particular sort of religious temperament, which needed the energy of virtue for everyday living, pictured the good as a single distant point of light. A similar and perhaps less accurate instinct led him to feel the evil in his life as also single, a continuous systematically related matrix, almost a conspiracy. This was perhaps the remnant in his mind of his ancestors' vigorous and literal belief in the devil. So now he felt that the muddle with the two women, McGrath's blackmail, Radeechy's death for which in a curious way he was beginning to feel himself responsible, and the mysterious and in some way obviously wicked activities of Biranne were all intimately connected together. Moreover the key to it all was Biranne himself.

Ducane had begun to have dreams about Biranne and the dreams were odd. In the dreams Ducane was invariably the pursuer. He sought for Biranne with anxiety and yearning through huge empty gardens and bombed London streets. Familiar scenes were transfigured into ghastliness by a need, an absence, the need for Biranne, the absence of Biranne. Ducane, who was not accustomed to taking dreams seriously, attempted no interpretation of these. In his waking consciousness he was sufficiently obsessed with the man, and he could note how the sheer strength of the obsession had moved him beyond his former irritations and resentments. The enquiry was important and Ducane hated failure. But what Ducane now felt as Biranne's involvement in Ducane's own life was more important still. There is the love of the hunter for the quarry. Yet was Biranne entirely a quarry? Was he not also a centre of power, a demon?

These bizarre ideas haunted Ducane's disturbed mind not as clear thoughts but rather as pressures and atmospheres. His discovery that Biranne had lied about Radeechy had started a process of development which seemed to have its own private chemistry. While Biranne was just an acquaintance who had been mockingly rude about Ducane many years ago, Ducane had simply felt a small wincing dislike of the man which he had condemned but been unable to lessen. As soon as Ducane found himself with the possibility of power over Biranne and in possession of discreditable facts about him, his interest gained not only in strength but in warmth. The mocking laughter of so many years ago had lost its power to hurt. Biranne as a sinner and as a man in a trap was no longer a menace to consciousness, and Ducane gave himself no credit for an interest which he recognized as having more to do with power than with compassion. However, the fact remained that he was becoming increasingly worried about Biranne and by Biranne. Had Biranne murdered Radeechy? This remained a possibility, and in returning to it Ducane felt a mounting anxiety. He had been putting off a direct confrontation in the hope of acquiring more information, but the sources of information now seemed to be dry. Ducane had no intention of being hustled by his own psychology. But after careful thought he had by now come to the point of deciding: I must see him. I shall have to bluff him, it's risky, but I must see him. And this conclusion filled him with alarm and with a curious deep wicked pleasure. I shall see him tomorrow, Ducane was thinking as he listened to Willy going on talking about the people at Trescombe.

"Has Theo stopped sulking, Willy?"

"Yes. He comes up to see me again."

"I wonder what happened to Theo in India. Well, I suppose one can imagine!"

"I don't know. I thought you might know, John. You are father confessor to all of us."

"Don't, Willy!"

"You are our picture of the just man."

"That's right, mock me."

"Seriously—"

"Chuck it, Willy. How are the twins?"

"*Herrlich.* They have great souls, those little ones. And they have been vouchsafed no end of flying saucers. They are the only people who are not in a turmoil."

"Dear me, are the rest of you in a turmoil? Are you in a turmoil? I'm sure Mary isn't in a turmoil. She never is."

Willy hesitated, pulled his lame leg back towards him with both hands, sat up and leaned forward. He looked at the carpet and said, "You said I seemed cheerful. So I ought to be. I have had a proposal of marriage."

"Good heavens, who from?"

"Mary."

Ducane was about to say, Splendid, I told her to do that, but stopped himself in time. If he was to have the impertinence to play at being God he must also have the discretion to conceal the fact. How pleased I am, he thought.

"How marvellous!"

"You disapprove—"

"Of course not! So you said yes?"

"I mean you disapprove of her having been so foolish as to want to marry me."

"Of course not, Willy. On the contrary, I—But you said yes, I may wish you joy?"

"I didn't say yes, I didn't say no. I was speechless with gratitude. I still am."

"Willy—light out for happiness. Yes?"

"Happiness. I don't know if that can be a goal for me, John."

"Then make it a matter of faith. Mary is—well, Mary is an ace, you know that. What's more, she needs you."

"Mary is an ace, as you beautifully put it. I know that. And I presume to love her. But I have a soul like an old cracked chamberpot. I could give no joy to a woman."

"Rubbish. Let her remake you. Have the humility to let her."

"Perhaps. I will pray about it. The gods have promised me an answer."

"Oh Willy, you lucky fool—"

I envy him, thought Ducane. He loves innocently and he is loved innocently. It is simple for him, for him and for his gods. Whereas I have tied myself up in this cat's cradle of treachery and falsehood. But I am so glad I prompted

Mary here, I am sure she would not have dared to speak if I had not encouraged her. May I have made the happiness of two good people. But Ducane's heart was strangely heavy. He thought to himself with a sort of desperation, tomorrow, tomorrow, tomorrow I shall see Biranne.

Twenty-three

JESSICA BIRD rang the bell of John Ducane's house.
A small man with a delicate brown face and a crop of
white hair opened the door. Jessica, who knew that Ducane
was at the office, took this to be the manservant.

In a firm official voice she said, "I am from Payne and
Stevens, the interior decorators. I have come to take the
measurements for the curtains in Mr Ducane's bedroom."

The small man murmured something and opened the
door a little farther. Jessica marched in. She had decided
that she could no longer live with her uncertainty about
whether or not Ducane had taken a new mistress. Or rather,
she had no uncertainty, she was sure that there was another
woman. She wanted, to make her anguish complete, the
absolute proof of it.

"Will you show me Mr Ducane's bedroom, please? I
am afraid I don't know the house." She drew a steel tape
measure from her pocket and exhibited it.

"Yes, certainly, yes—"

The small man led her up the stairs and into the room in
the front of the house above the drawing-room. Jessica, who
had never penetrated into her lover's bedroom in the old
days, had conjectured that this must be the room, but it was
better to be sure.

"Will you want anything, steps or anything?"

"No, no, I'll be all right, you can leave me to it now,
thank you. I'll just be about ten minutes or so. I've got
to make some measurements in the bathroom too. Don't
let me keep you."

The small man murmured again and went away, closing
the bedroom door.

Jessica, who had composed her plan of action carefully
beforehand, now felt so giddy with emotion that she had to
sit down on a chair. She had not realised how powerfully
Ducane's bedroom would affect her. The silence, his
trousers neatly folded upon the counterpane, his brushes
and collar studs upon the dressing table, the bare masculine

plainness of a single man's room, the bitter-sweet sense of familiarity and absence made her suddenly sick with longing. The bedroom, unlike the drawing-room below, might have been any man's room, yet it was full of the ghost of Ducane which, distilled now into a purer male essence than any she had ever encountered, assaulted her fainting senses.

Jessica's rolling eye lighted upon the bed and jealousy pulled her together like a mouthful of brandy. It was not a narrow bed. It was not exactly a double bed, but it was one of those rather broad single beds with plenty of room for two. She leapt up and began her search.

Jessica was of the opinion that it is virtually impossible for a woman to inhabit a room, even for a short while, without leaving traces. If a woman had been in Ducane's bed some sign would certainly have been left behind, some token from the transcendent region of Ducane's love life, some glittering fragment of that Jessica-excluding super-world upon which her imagination had by now so finely worked. What she would do with this talisman, whether torment herself or torment him, she had not yet thought. What she wanted was simply to have the tiny thing in her possession.

Very carefully Jessica folded back the coverlet of the bed and drew down the bed clothes. She put her face close to the pillow sniffing attentively. She had taken care to wear no perfume herself that day. Her pale streaky hair fell forward on to the pillow. How unfortunate that she suffered from hay fever. She interrogated her sense of smell. There was a faint cosmetic odour but it might have been shaving cream or even disinfectant. Inconclusive.

Leaving the bed she moved to the wastepaper basket. It contained a screw of Kleenex, a toothpaste carton, an empty cigarette packet, half a comb and a good deal of human hair. Jessica picked out the ball of hair and began straightening it out and sniffing it. It was all dark brown and looked like Ducane's hair. After a moment's hesitation she stuffed the hair into her pocket. She opened the wardrobe. The neat line of Ducane's sombre suitings confronted her in the darkness like so many shrunken male presences. The wardrobe smelt of wood and man. It was like a little enchanted house or the ark of some unfamiliar faith. Jessica stood in awe before it. Then, frowning with determination and courage, she began quickly to go through the pockets of the suits. Ducane's pockets were full of entities, papers of all sorts, parking tickets, cloakroom tickets, more hair, coins, several combs and numerous sea-rounded pebbles. There were two letters, but one was from the telephone company and the other from a plumber.

Jessica left the wardrobe and transferred her attention to the chest of drawers. Here, although there was much to make her gasp and sigh—neckties remembered from happier days, cuff links which she herself had given him—there was nothing at all in the way of 'evidence'. There were no contraceptives. There was nothing feminine. Jessica, now in a flurried rush, slid into the bathroom. There was an indeterminate smell of bath essence. A black silk dressing gown covered with red asterisks hanging behind the door had masculine handkerchiefs in its pockets and smelt of tobacco. The bathroom cupboard revealed no perfumes, no face creams. The bathroom wastepaper basket contained a detective novel.

Jessica ran back into the bedroom. There must be something to find, she thought, and I *must* find it. Certainty was so much better than doubt, and with certainty would come power, the power to hurt and astonish, the power to create again, however perversely, a bond of living emotion. Jessica began to look into corners, to search the floor. Some tiny thing, a bead, a button, a hairpin, must be hiding somewhere in the carpet. She lifted the skirts of the bed-cover and crawled underneath the bed. There as she lay full length, feverishly combing the carpet with her fingers, she became aware that the room had darkened. Then she saw two male feet and two lengths of trousered leg which had come close up beside the bed. Jessica crawled out.

"You know, what you told me just now can't be *quite* true." The speaker who uttered these words rather apologetically was the small white-haired man who had let her in.

Jessica was so relieved that it was not Ducane that she sat down on the bed for a moment and just stared. Then she said, "I was just checking the power points."

"To begin with," the man went on, "I have been looking them up in the telephone book and there is no such firm as Payne and Stevens, and secondly Mr Ducane has just lately had new curtains fitted in this room. And thirdly why have you taken the bed to pieces. That will do to begin with." The small man took a chair, placed it in front of the closed door, and sat down on it expectantly.

Jessica looked at Ducane's bed, with the bedclothes pulled down and the pillows disarranged. She looked at the chest of drawers, with every drawer open and ties and shirts hanging over the edge. Whatever was she to say? Jessica was not afraid of being sent to prison, she was afraid of being trapped by Ducane, of being kept there by force until he returned. She thought, any moment now I shall burst into tears.

"You see," the small man went on in a gentle slightly foreign voice, "I can't just let it go, can I? I mean, you might be a burglar, mightn't you? And I have to defend my friend's belongings, with which I must say you seem to have been making rather free."

Jessica found her voice. "You're not the—butler, chauffeur?"

"No. It's the butler chauffeur's afternoon off. I'm someone else. But that doesn't matter. I'm still waiting for you to explain yourself, my dear."

"I'm not a burglar," said Jessica in a small voice.

"Well, no, I didn't really think you were. I reflected on you a little bit downstairs, after I'd looked up Payne and Stevens, and I said to myself that young lady is no burglar, However you must ,be *something*, you know, and I'm still waiting to hear what it is."

Jessica sat hunched on the bed. She felt frightened, guilty and wretched. Suppose indeed the little man were to keep her here until Ducane came back, suppose he were to lock her in? Why did loving so much lead to nothing now but misery and terror? Tears filled her eyes. She thrust her hand into her pocket and brought out the ball of Ducane's hair which fell on the floor.

"Oh come come come come come." He came and sat beside her on the bed and handed her a big clean handkerchief in which she hid her face. "I'm not a monster, you know. I don't want to frighten you. I won't hurt you. But just imagine yourself being me! I must ask you some questions. And naturally I'm curious too. I simply can't think *what* you can be up to. It is all a bit *odd*, isn't it? There,

there don't cry. Just talk to me a little bit, will you?"

Jessica stopped crying and rubbed her face over. She stared into the male darkness of the wardrobe. She felt full of misery and violence. The unexpected, that at least was something. She would impale herself upon it. She said in a hard voice, "You ask me what I am. I am a jealous woman."

Her companion whistled softly, a long melodious whistle. Then he said, "Wow!"

"Mr Ducane and I used to be together," said Jessica, "but then he dropped me. And he says he hasn't got anyone else. But I'm sure that isn't true. I saw a woman coming into the house one day. I just felt I had to know for sure. So I got in, as you saw, and I've been searching the room to see if any woman has been here."

"Found anything?" he asked in an interested tone.

"No. But I'm *sure*—"

"I don't think John would tell a lie, even about that."

Jessica turned to face the small brown man. He was regarding her now with a kind of humorous glee. "Please will you tell me," said Jessica, "do you know, has he got a mistress? Well, why should you tell me. This is all fantastic."

"But I *adore* what's fantastic. No, I'm sure he hasn't got a mistress. Is that enough for you? Will you go away happy?"

"No," she said. "Nothing's enough. *Nothing*."

"The demon jealousy. Yes. I know about it too. Tell me your name, my child, your first name only. We seem to be almost acquainted."

"Jessica."

"Good. My name's Willy. Now listen, Jessica, will you forgive me if I ask you some more questions and will you give me truthful answers?"

"Yes."

"How long were you John's mistress?"

"About a year."

"And how long since he dropped you?"

"About two years."

"Have you seen much of him in the two years?"

"Yes. We've been sort of friends."

"You're still in love, and he's not?"

"Yes. And he says now he wants us not to meet any more. Because he wants me to be free. But I don't want to be free."

"I can understand that. But jealousy is a dreadful thing, Jessica. It is the most natural to us of the really wicked passions and it goes deep and envenoms the soul. It must be resisted with every honest cunning and with the deliberate thinking of generous thoughts, however abstract and empty these may seem in comparison with that wicked strength. Think about the virtue that you need and call it generosity, magnanimity, charity. You are young, Jessica, and you are very delightful—may I just take your hand, so?—and the world is not spoilt for you yet. There is no merit, Jessica, in a faithfulness which is poison to you and captivity to him. You have nothing to gain here except by losing. You wish to act out your love, to give it body, but there is only one act left to you that is truly loving and that is to let him go, and to let him go gently and without resentment. Put all your energy into that and you will win from the world of the spirit a grace which you cannot now even dream of. For there is grace, Jessica, there are principalities and powers, there is unknown good which flies magnetically toward the good we know. And suppose that you had found what you were looking for, my dear child? Would you not have been led on from jealousy through deceit into cruelty? Human frailty forms a system, Jessica, and faults in the past have their endlessly spreading network of results. We are not good people, Jessica, and we shall always be involved in that great network, you and I. All we can do is constantly to notice when we begin to act badly, to check ourselves, to go back, to coax our weakness and inspire our strength, to call upon the names of virtues of which we know perhaps only the names. We are not good people, and the best we can hope for is to be gentle, to forgive each other and to forgive the past, to be forgiven ourselves and to accept this forgiveness, and to return again to the beautiful unexpected strangeness of the world. Isn't it, Jessica, my child?"

After a long pause Jessica said, "*Who are you?*"

"My dear," he murmured. "You learn fast. Forgive me."

"Good heavens," said Jessica.

Willy had kissed her.

They were half facing each other now, with their knees braced together. Willy was holding her firmly by the wrist, while his other hand had strayed round her neck and was playing with her hair. Jessica had gripped the lapel of his jacket. They stared hard at each other.

"You are very beautiful, Jessica, and you remind me— you remind me of what I have seen in dreams, embraced in dreams. Forgive me for touching you. Really wanting to touch and to hold somebody, this is so important, isn't it? This is how we poor clay objects communicate, by looking thus, by touching thus. There should be few that you touch, and those the dearest ones."

"Please tell me who you are," she said. "You are so strange. What is your second name?"

"No, no. Let us just be Willy and Jessica. We shall not meet again."

"You can't say that when you've just kissed me. You can't kiss me and vanish. I shall ask John—"

"If you ask John about me I shall tell him that you searched his room."

"Oh! And you were saying that we should be gentle!'

"I am being gentle, my child. I am a murmuring voice a little bird on a tree, the voice of your conscience perhaps. And if there is anything else it is just a little nameless imp, or an imp called Willy maybe, who is quite momentary and has no real self at all. If I do you any little hurt may it simply make you toss your head and return again to the beautiful strange wide unpredictable world."

"But I must see more of you—you must help me—you *could* help me."

"Anybody could help you, Jessica, if you wanted to be helped. For now it is just you and me upon an island, a dream island of the unexpected, to be remembered like a dream, all atmosphere and feeling and nothing in detail. Oh, but you are beautiful. May I kiss you again?"

Jessica slid her arms strongly round him and closed her eyes. She was roused by a sound which was Willy kicking off his shoes. She kicked off hers. With lips still joined they keeled over slowly into the unmade bed.

Some time later as they lay heart to heart Jessica said softly, not anxiously, but curiously, "What are we doing, Willy, what is this?"

"This is sacrilege, my Jessica. A very important human activity."

192

Twenty-four

LIKE all true Earls Courters, Ducane despised Chelsea. The bounder would live in a place like this, he said to himself, as he turned into Smith Street and began to pass along the line of smartly painted hall doors.

He was feeling far from jocular however. He had thought of Biranne as a man in a trap. But could the trap be sprung? Biranne was a strong man and not a fool. However much Ducane attempted to surprise him or even to bluff him he was unlikely to break down and confess or by any inadvertence to give himself away. There was nothing which Ducane knew for which some innocent explanation could not be garbled up. And if, with a cold eye, Biranne produced and stuck to these explanations what could Ducane do but apologise and retire, and if he apologised and retired what on earth could he do next? When Ducane reflected upon how little, in fact, he did know he was amazed at the strength of his certainty that Biranne was guilty, at least of something. Could this not be utterly mistaken? Tonight was a gamble, he told himself. But perhaps it was time for a gamble, since more prudent methods had produced mere intuitions, ranging from suspicion of murder to conjecture of total innocence.

It was now nearly nine o'clock in the evening, and the dense dusty air, heavy with its heat, hung over London like a half-deflated balloon, stuffy and sagging. The yellow sunlight was tired and the shadows were without refreshment. Only at the far end of the street could be seen the blurred dark green of trees which hinted at the river. Ducane, too agitated to wait at his own house, had come from Earls Court on foot. He had taken an early supper with Willy, who appeared to be in a curious state of euphoria. After supper Willy had switched on the wireless and Ducane had left him dancing round the drawing-room to the sound of Mozart's piano concerto in C minor. Ducane, who was relying on surprising Biranne, had dialled his telephone number from Earls Court, silently replacing the receiver as soon as the familiar high-pitched voice answered the 'phone.

As Ducane came near to the house he was almost choking with anxiety and excitement, and had to stop several times to get his breath from the thick air, which now seemed devoid of oxygen. He stopped finally a few paces away, shook himself or perhaps shuddered, straightened his back and walked briskly to the door. It was open.

Ducane stood frozen upon the step, his hand half raised toward the bell. He lowered his hand. To his wrought-up nerves any unusual thing, even of the simplest, had an air of sinister significance. Was he after all expected? Had Biranne understood the meaning of the telephone call? Had Biranne seen him coming? Ducane stood and pondered. He decided that the open door was a matter of chance. Then he decided that he would not ring the bell. He would just walk in.

As he stepped cautiously on to the thick yellow hall carpet, however, he felt more of the sentiment of the hunted than of the hunter. He looked about quickly, guiltily, half turned to retreat, paused, listened. The silence of the unfamiliar house composed menacingly about him. He became aware, buried in it, of a ticking clock, then of his own heart beating. He stood still, his eyes moving, seeing in the goldenish evening penumbra a marquetry table, an oval mirror, a recession of glittering stair-rods of lacquered brass. An open doorway, some distance straight ahead revealed, brighter, what appeared to be a billiard room. Attempting to breathe normally and not to tiptoe Ducane opened the door upon his right. The front room, evidently the dining-room. Empty. A great many bottles on a Sheraton side-board. He moved back, breath held in, and reached for the next door. He pushed it open. The room was darkened by venetian blinds upon which the sun fell slanting, dazzling a little along the long hairlike slits of the almost closed blinds. Ducane blinked into the semi-darkness of the room. Then, on the far side, he saw a standing figure. A remarkable figure, the figure of Judy McGrath.

"Hello, Mr Honeyman. Didn't I tell you that we'd meet again?"

What was remarkable about Judy McGrath this time was that she had no clothes on.

Ducane came slowly on into the room and closed the door behind him. Collecting himself he looked about with deliberation. There was no one else present.

"Good evening, Mrs McGrath."

"You must excuse my déshabille. It's so hot this evening, isn't it."

"Exceptionally hot and stuffy," said Ducane. He sat down in an armchair and stared at Judy. He said softly, "Helen of Troy".

"I knew you'd find me out, Mr Honeyman, you're so clever. Have a cigarette? Or one of Richard's cigars?"

"No thanks." Ducane felt, this is a moment outside my ordinary life, a moment given by a god, not perhaps by a great god, and not by a good one, but by a god certainly. It had never fallen to his lot to contemplate a naked woman in quite this way before.

Judy stood in front of him with a slight awkwardness. The human body, even that of a beautiful woman, cannot easily stand in complete repose. She stood half turned away from him, one knee bent, one shoulder hunched, her chin jutting as if to see him she had to peer over something. Her body lacked the authority of its beauty and wore a little shame, the shame of what is usually hidden from the air and which greets it a little self-consciously. However used Mrs McGrath was in her spirit to taking her clothes off, her body was yet a trifle less forward. Half consciously Ducane noted this and it touched him. The sunlight dazzled in streaks along the shutters and filled the room with a thick powdery half-light, a warm golden-brown air, in the midst of which Judy McGrath's body rose up, moved slightly, a pillar of honey with a fleeting lemony radiance. The warm light caressed her, revealed her, blended with her. Her black hair, dusted over with a sheen of brown, seemed a slightly greenish bronze, and the shadow between her large round slightly dependent breasts was a blur of dark russet. Judy's eyes, brooding slits now, were almost closed. She swung her body slightly, revealing the curve of the buttock, outlined in a thin arc of fuzzy phosphorescent fire.

Ducane breathed deeply and swallowed his breath before it could become a sigh. He said, "I came here to see Mr Biranne, but you will do just as well."

"If you have a use for me, Mr Honeyman, I'm yours."

"Why did Radeechy kill himself?"

"I don't know, Mr Honeyman. Mr Radeechy was a strange man with strange habits, who got strange ideas into his head."

"Was it your notion or your husband's to blackmail him?"

"I have no idea, Mr Honeyman. I'm a woman. Look."

Ducane was looking, but his head was perfectly clear now. He noticed that the huge brown circles in the centre of her breasts were reminding him of Fivey.

"Tell me about Radeechy," said Ducane.

"I could love you, Mr Honeyman. You could love me."

"I doubt that, Judy. Tell me about Radeechy."

"You mean what we did in the vaults at night?"

"In the *vaults*—" said Ducane carefully.

"In the vaults of the office."

"I see," said Ducane slowly, thinking as fast as he could. "Of course. You used to go with Radeechy into the vaults, into the old air-raid shelters underneath the office—"

"That's right, Mr Honeyman. I thought you knew. I thought you knew everything."

"I know practically everything." said Ducane. "I just want you to tell me the rest. Why did you go to the vaults?"

"It was getting to be a bit awkward at his house, you see, with Mrs around, and the neighbours. We used to make quite a lot of noise."

"Hmmm," said Ducane. "Did Mrs Radeechy know about all this?"

"Oh yes, it was all ever so honest."

"Did she mind?"

"I don't know," said Judy. She had begun to oscillate her body in a circular movement, pivoted upon her rather large feet which were gripping the carpet with long claw-like toes. "She seemed not to. But I guess she did really."

"Was Radeechy anxious because he was distressing his wife?"

"He was never anxious when he was with me, Mr Honeyman. No man is ever anxious when he is with me."

"What did Radeechy want you to do for him," asked Ducane. "I mean apart from the things that were obvious."

"None of Mr Radeechy's things were obvious things, Mr Honeyman."

"Well, presumably he made love to you."

"Oh *no*, nothing like that. It was all very spiritualistic, if you see what I mean. Besides, Mr McGrath was there half of the time."

"Oh. You took part in rituals, magic?"

"I never understood it really, I just did what he told me, half of the time I couldn't see what was happening. Some gentlemen have very strange ideas. He was not the first."

"What do you mean by spiritualistic?"

"It was all ideas, all in his head like. There are some like that. He never touched me, not with his hands that is."

The phrase "not with his hands" produced an effect on Ducane which he took a moment to recognize as extreme physical excitement. He pushed his chair back abruptly and stood up. Judy McGrath immediately, with an electrical jerk, altered her stance, stepping forward towards him and throwing her head back. At the same time she picked up something from the table. Ducane's lowered gaze now sought out, what he had before avoided seeing, the place of the darkest shadow.

"Don't go," she said softly. "Or else take me with you. What are your things, Mr Honey? Whatever they are I could do them. And there are things I could teach you too."

"Put your clothes on," said Ducane.

Something moved in the sulphurous light between them and came to rest upon his wrist, brushing caressingly along the hairs of his arm. It was the pencil-thin tip of a riding whip, the other end of which rested in Judy's hand.

Ducane jerked his arm away and moved quickly out of the room. He blundered through the hall and swung the front door wide open and blinked in the sudden brightness of the street. As he began to walk rapidly along the pavement he nearly collided with Biranne, who was carrying a bottle. They looked at each other appalled, and before Ducane pushed past and hurried on he saw Biranne's face transfigured with fear.

Twenty-five

"WHY do animals not have to blow their noses?" asked Edward.

No one seemed to know the answer to this question or be prepared to enter into a discussion of it. Mary was cooking rhubarb, Paula was looking through a page of the Aeneid into some private worry of her own, and Ducane was engaged in composing and censoring some very private pictures of Judy McGrath.

"Uncle Theo wants Mingo please," said Henrietta who had just come into the kitchen. "Here's a postcard come for you, John."

The twins shovelled the sleepy Mingo up from his comfortable place in Montrose's basket and departed carrying him between them.

Ducane surveyed a picture of some veiled women. On the other side Kate had written, *Darling, veiled women are so thrilling, though mean to be thrilled as would hate to be veiled self. This place is super. This morning saw some dogs doing something quite extraordinary. Can't possibly tell you on postcard. Didn't know dogs had vices. Much love.*

Ducane turned the card again and looked gloomily at the veiled women. He too recalled being excited by veiled women in Tangier, and the memory mingled rather horribly with the strong aura of Judy which still hung about him. It was odd that his confrontation with the unveiled Judy should now seem to remind him of the hidden women of Africa. There was something mechanical in himself which responded to the two visions in much the same way. I am becoming cut off, he thought, I am becoming like Radeechy, it is all indirect, it is all in my mind. Then he wondered, what are my things anyway? The question was not without interest.

He turned the card over again and tried to concentrate his attention upon Kate: sweet Kate, with her halo of wiry golden hair and her affectionate and loving nature. But Kate seemed to elude his regard, and the place in the centre where she should have been seemed either empty or concealed. There was the same sense of the mechanical. I need her presence, he thought. I am not good at absence, at least I am not good at her absence.

Ducane had been disturbed not only by Judy but by what she had told him. At first sight the discovery that Radeechy's 'goings-on' had taken place in the old air-raid shelters underneath the office strongly suggested that those who feared a 'security risk' were not being idly suspicious. The magic might be simply a front, a characteristically extravagant and far-fetched façade, to conceal quite other nocturnal activities. However, on second thoughts Ducane decided this was unlikely. If Radeechy wished to remain all night in the office there was really nothing to stop him, and the additional indulgence of fantasies involving girls seemed too wantonly risky if his purposes were quite other. No, Ducane concluded, once again the thing was what it seemed. But what did it seem? That dreary sense of the mechanical came to him again. Was there perhaps no centre to the mystery at all, nothing there but the melancholy sexual experiments of an unbalanced man?

Ducane had decided that his next move was to see McGrath again and to get McGrath to show him the place in the vaults where Radeechy did what he did. Ducane did not want any further view of Mrs McGrath, so he had written to McGrath summoning him to the office on Monday. After this, obeying an almost panic instinct of flight, Ducane had told Fivey to drive him to Dorset. He was upset by the whole business and wished heartily that Octavian and Kate were not away. A message had come from the Prime Minister's office to confirm, what Octavian had earlier told him, that the Radeechy affair had 'gone off the boil', and to ask him for an early report, however inconclusive. When he received this message Ducane realised how very far, by now, his interest in the enquiry was from being a purely official one. He was deeply involved and for his own sake would have to try to understand. He felt too as if he were being drawn onward almost deliberately by a never entirely broken thread. Whenever the trail had seemed to end something had unexpectedly happened to show him the next piece of the way.

That Judy McGrath was 'Helen of Troy' and that McGrath had, not perhaps for the first time, used his wife as a decoy for a blackmail victim had occurred to Ducane a little earlier as possible. He had not expected the link between Judy and Biranne; but once the link had been so sensationally given it seemed something so suggestive as to be obvious. Ducane had been at first rather sorry that he had now given so definite a warning to Biranne and lost the possible effect of a surprise; though indeed Biranne had probably been kept informed of the direction of the enquiry by the kind offices of Judy and her husband. In all likelihood McGrath was also, in the friendliest possible way, blackmailing Biranne as well. In any case Biranne must know himself to be under suspicion and on further reflection Ducane decided that this was no bad thing. He had been greatly struck by the sudden expression of terror on Biranne's face when he had encountered Ducane in Smith Street. Ducane thought, *Biranne will come to me*. It was not an unpleasant thought.

"Where's Barbara?" Ducane asked Mary. "Is she out riding?"

"No, the pony's strained a fetlock. I think she's up in her room."

"Is she still upset about Montrose?"

"Yes, dreadfully. She was crying again yesterday. I can't imagine what's happened to the wretched creature. Cats don't just vanish or get killed."

"I heard Pierce telling her Montrose was drowned," said Ducane. "He shouldn't say things like that to Barbara."

"I know he shouldn't," said Mary shortly, stirring the rhubarb.

"Well, I think I'll go up and see her. She shouldn't be moping in her room on a day like this. We might go for a walk to Willy's. Like to come, Paula?"

"No thanks."

Paula gave him an anxious preoccupied stare. Her face seemed enclosed and grey, the face of a fencer looking through the thick mesh of a mask. Ducane thought, with a familiar pain of conscience, I ought to see Paula properly, make her talk to me and tell me what's the matter. He thought quickly, shall I see Barbara now or Paula? But by now the pain of conscience had brought the accusing image of Jessica sliding before his mind. I ought to see Jessica soon, he thought, and the idea so depressed and confused him that the energy of his sympathy for Paula was at once decreased. Inclination triumphed. Barbara could console him. He would go to Barbara. He rose to his feet.

"Try to bring Willy down to tea, John," said Mary.

"I'll try, but I'll not succeed."

Ducane left the kitchen. The sun shone through the glass panels of the front door, revealing the polished slightly rosy depressions in the worn stones of the paved hall. Ducane picked up Edward's copy of *The Natural History of Selborne* from the floor and replaced it on the table. On the lawn in front of the house he could see Casie and the twins sitting on a red tartan rug shelling peas. He felt, as his hand touched the table and he paused in the sunny familiar hallway, another and a different pang, touching, pleasant, painful, the apprehension of an innocent world, a world which he loved and needed, and surely could never altogether mislay? He thought: innocence matters. It is not a thing one just loses. It remains somehow magnetically in one's life, remains as something quick and alive and utterly safe from the mechanical and the dreary. He thought *poor Biranne*. And he thought again the disturbing strange thought, *Biranne will come to me*. He began to mount the stairs.

As Ducane reached the landing he saw at the far end of it Pierce, who had just come up the back stairs from the scullery quarters. Pierce, who had not seen Ducane, was walking rather cautiously carrying a white dish in his hand. Balancing the dish, he opened the door of his bedroom and went in. Ducane half consciously took in what he had seen and half consciously reflected on it. Then, with a sudden flash which brought him back to the present moment, he understood its meaning. He paused, considered, and then walked quickly on past Barbara's door. He gained the door of Pierce's room and flung it open. Montrose was curled up on Pierce's bed.

"Pierce, you rotten little bastard," said Ducane.

Pierce, who had just put the saucer of milk down on the floor, slowly straightened up and took off his glasses. He thrust out his plump lower lip and drew his hand slowly down over his straight forehead and long nose as if to secure the expression of his face. He waited.

Ducane picked up Montrose and strode out. He knocked on the door of Barbara's room and entered at once. The room was empty. Pierce, who had followed Ducane directly, came after him into the room. They faced each other.

"God, what a rotten thing to do!" said Ducane. He was suddenly trembling with anger. All the trouble, the anxiety, the guilt in him seemed focused into this simple anger.

"I didn't hurt Montrose," said Pierce slowly.

"No, but you hurt Barbara. How could you be so bloody?" Ducane set Montrose down on the table. As he did so he saw close to his hand Barbara's small silver-handled riding whip. The image of the whip came to him incapsulated, separate, framed, and was blotted out.

"You see," said Pierce in the same slow explanatory tone, "if she had only come to see me, come to my room like she used to do, if she hadn't treated me like a leper, she would have found where Montrose was. It was a sort of test." He put one hand on the table, leaning earnestly forward.

"You deliberately made her unhappy and wretched, and you kept it up too," said Ducane. "I think—" His hand closed on the handle of the whip and with a quick yet very deliberate movement he raised the whip and brought it down sharply across the back of Pierce's hand. The boy flinched but went on staring at Ducane and did not remove his hand.

"What on earth is going on here?" said Mary Clothier, who was standing in the doorway.

Pierce turned slowly and without looking at his mother walked past her out of the door, away down the corridor and into his own bedroom.

Mary hesitated. Then she moved into Barbara's room. She found she was having to use a lot of strength to deal with the considerable shock of seeing Ducane strike her son. She did not know what she felt. A confusion of feelings silenced her.

"I'm sorry," said Ducane, obviously confused too. "I'm sorry."

"Why there's Montrose—"

"Shut the door, Mary."

"What happened?"

"You see—shut the door. You see, Pierce has been keeping Montrose prisoner all the time we all thought he was lost."

"Oh—how very dreadful—I—"

"Yes. I'm afraid I lost my temper with him. I shouldn't have done."

"I don't blame you. It was very wrong of him. I'll go and look for Barbara."

"Wait a minute, Mary. Just let Montrose out, will you. That's right. Sit down. Sorry. Just wait a minute."

Mary sat down on the bed and looked at Ducane who was standing by the window frowning and still holding the whip. He shrugged his shoulders suddenly and tossed it on to the table and then crossed his two hands over his forehead covering his eyes.

"You're upset," said Mary. "Oh don't be! Do you imagine I'm going to be cross with you?"

"No, no. I'm upset about something, I'm not even sure what. I suppose Pierce will hate me for this."

"He's just as likely to love you for it. Young people have a strange psychology."

"*All* people have a strange psychology," said Ducane. He sat down at the table and regarded Mary. His rather round blue eyes, so markedly blue now in his bony sunburnt face, stared at Mary with a sort of puzzlement and he thrust back the limp locks of dark brown hair with a quick rhythmical movement. Mary studied him. What was the matter?

"I'm sorry," said Ducane after a moment. "I'm just having a crisis of dissatisfaction with myself and I want sympathy. One always asks for sympathy when one least deserves it."

He's missing Kate, Mary thought. She said, "I'm sure *you* have little reason to be dissatisfied with yourself, John. But let me sympathise. Tell me what's the matter."

Ducane's blue eyes became yet rounder with what looked like alarm. He started to speak, stopped, and then said, "How old is Pierce?"

"Fifteen."

"I ought to have got to know him better."

"I hope you will. But you can't look after everyone, John."

"You see me as always looking after people?"

"Well, yes—"

"God!"

"Sorry, I didn't mean—"

"It's all right. He's a very reserved child."

"He's been a long time without a father, too many years just with me."

"How old was he when his father died?"

"Two."

"So he scarcely remembers him."

"Scarcely."

"What was your husband's name, Mary?"

Oh God, thought Mary, I can't talk to him about Alistair. She recognized that particular coaxing intentness in Ducane's manner, his way of questioning people with close attention so as to make them tell him everything about themselves, which they usually turned out to be all too ready to do. She had seen him doing this to other people, even at dinner parties. He had never done it to her. She thought, I won't tell him anything, I've never talked to anyone about this, I won't talk to him. She said, "Alistair". The name came out into the room, an alien gobbet floating away into the air, drifting back again, hovering just above the level of her eyes.

"What did he do? I don't think I ever knew his profession."

"He was a chartered accountant."

"Does Pierce resemble him?"

"To look at, yes, though Alistair was taller. Not in temper."

"What sort of person was he?"

I can't go on with this, thought Mary. How could she say, he was a funny man, always making puns. He was gay. He sang so beautifully. He was a universal artist. He was a failure. She said, "He wrote a novel."

"Was it published?"

"No. It was no good." Mary had spent part of yesterday reading Alistair's novel. She had taken out the huge typescript with the intention of destroying it but had found herself unable to. It was so bad, so childish, so like Alistair.

"He died young," said Ducane softly. "He might have done better, he might have done much better."

Mary supposed this was true. It was not a thing that she felt. Perhaps it was unfair to dub him a failure. Yet somehow the judgment was absolute.

"What did he die of?" said Ducane in the soft coaxing voice.

Mary was silent. A black wall rose up in front of her. She was coming nearer and nearer and looking into the blackness. She stared into it, she entered it. She said in an almost dreamy voice, "He was run over by a car one evening just outside our house. I saw it happen."

"Oh—I'm sorry—was he—killed at once?"

"No." She recalled his cries, the long wait for the ambulance, the crowd, the long wait in the hospital.

"I'm sorry, Mary," said Ducane. "I'm being—"

"It was the accidentalness of it," she said. "Sometimes I've nearly gone mad just thinking of it. That it should be so *accidental*. If I'd just said another sentence to him before he went out of the room, if he'd just stopped to tie his shoe lace, anything, and oh God, we'd just been *quarrelling*, and I let him go away without a word, if I'd only called him back, but he went straight out all upset and the car went over him. If he'd died of an illness or even been killed in the war somewhere far away where I couldn't know I could have felt it was inevitable, but to have him killed there accidentally in front of my eyes, I couldn't bear it, I've never told anyone how he died, I told Kate and Paula he died of pneumonia and I told Pierce that too. Pierce slept through it all in an upstairs room. I loved him, of course I loved him, but never quite enough or in the right way, and I haven't been able to think of him properly since, and it's somehow because of that awful accident, because things were cut off in that particular way, it made all our life together seem meaningless, and I haven't been able to feel properly about him, it's as if he were changed into some awful ghost with which I can't make any peace. I remember an awful feeling I had when I was going through his clothes afterwards as if he were watching me, all sad and deprived and unappeased, and I've had that feeling since, it comes at odd times in the evening, and I feel as if he still wants my love and I can't give it to him. I see his faults and his weaknesses now and what made me love him has faded utterly. It's terrible that one doesn't love people forever. I should have gone on loving him, it's the only thing I can do for him any more, and I have tried, but one can't love in a void, one can't love a sort of nothing for which one can't do anything *else*, and there's nothing left any more except the novel and that's so terribly silly and yet it's him in a way. If only it hadn't happened like *that*, so suddenly and all by chance, he walked straight out and under the car. You see, so few cars came down our road—"

"Don't cry so, Mary," said Ducane. He moved beside her on to the bed and put an arm round her shoulder. "Chance is really harder to bear than mortality, and it's *all* chance my dear, even what seems most inevitable. It's not easy to do, but one must accept it as one accepts one's losses and one's past. Don't try to see him. Just love him. Perhaps you never altogether knew him. Now his mystery is free of you. Respect it, and don't try to see any more. Love can't always do work. Sometimes it just has to look into the darkness. Keep looking and don't be afraid. There are no demons there."

"Words, John," said Mary. "Words, words, words." But she let herself be comforted by them, and felt that the tears were really for Alistair which she was weeping now.

Twenty-six

"MIND the steps, Sir. This bit's rather slimy. Better take my hand."

The slowly moving circle of light from the torch revealed a short flight of steps sheeted over with a fungoid veneer of damp dust. There was a pattern of footprints in the centre, and tangles of dangling black threads at the side. Beyond them a concrete ramp went on down into the darkness.

Ducane steadied himself by pressing his knuckles against the cold brick wall. He did not want to touch McGrath who was just in front of him. They descended slowly as far as the concrete.

"You say Mr Radeechy told you to cut the electric cable at the top of the passage, where we left the air-raid shelters?"

"That's right, Sir. Mr Radeechy liked it all to be by candle light. I think he thought it was safer too, you know, in case anyone came."

"Was the door we've just come through usually locked?"

"Yes, Sir. Mr R. had a key and he gave me a key."

"Did you ever come down here without him?"

"I hardly ever came down here with him, Sir. I just left the stuff ready for him and cleared off. He didn't want me around when he was at it."

"Go on, man, lead on, don't just block the way."

"Are you all right, Sir?"

"Of course I'm all right. Go on."

The wavering light of the torch undulated forward suggesting a vista of a narrow extended sloping rectangular slot of red brick with a dark ending. Several black pipes, bunched into the corner of the roof and joined together by a heavy sacking of cobwebs, led down into the darkness. The effect was of the entrance to an ancient sepulchre and it was hard to believe that the corridors of a government department were only at a few minutes' distance.

"Did you lock the door at the top behind us?" Ducane asked. He found that he was speaking in a low voice. The concrete ramp was slightly sticky as well, and footsteps made a faint soft kissing sound. A very low almost inaudible hum seemed to be coming out of the black pipes.

"Yes, Sir. I hope that was right, Sir? I thought we wouldn't want to be interrupted down here, Sir, any more than Mr R!"

"Well, don't lose the key."

"We'd be in a rare fix then, wouldn't we, Sir! No one comes near that door. We could be down here for ever and no one the wiser."

"Get on, get on. Are we nearly there?"

"Nearly. Not that way, Sir. Straight on."

A narrow black doorway had appeared on the right of the passage.

"Where does that lead to?"

"Lord, Sir, I don't know. I didn't go exploring down here. It's not a very nice place, especially when you're by yourself. I went down to the room and up again as quickly as I could. You aren't nervous, are you, Sir?"

"Of course not. Don't wave the torch about so, keep it down."

The shape of the passage and the sharp angle of descent was reminding Ducane of kings' tombs he had visited in Greece and Egypt. He thought, I ought to have brought a torch of my own. Then he thought, I ought to have told someone I was coming down here. There was no need for secrecy. I didn't realise what it would be like. Suppose we do lose the key? Suppose we get separated, suppose we get lost? These passages can't lead to more air raid shelters, we've left the air-raid shelters behind, we're at much too low a level now. It's more likely that this is some disused part of the Underground or something to do with the sewers.

"It's steep again here, Sir, and more steps, watch out. Not straight on, this way now, follow me. Now this passage on the left. Keep close."

"Ever see any rats down here?" Ducane had a horror of rats. He was as close as he could be now on McGrath's heels without touching him.

"I saw one once, Sir, a big fat fellow. Mr R. saw several. He asked me to get some biscuit tins and that to keep the stuff in. He was afraid the rats might eat it, you see. Left again, Sir."

"Are you sure you know the way?"

"Quite sure, Sir. A bit eerie, isn't it? Just like the cata-
combs I should think. Here we are arrived. Could you
hold the torch now while I use the other key?"

They had reached a closed door. Ducane took a firm
hold on the torch. Was the battery not perceptibly fainter?
He moved the torch, revealing a black close-fitting well-
painted door and McGrath's red-golden head stooped over
the keyhole. McGrath's hairs glistened like burnished wire
in the close light. The door gave silently.

"That's right. Give me the torch, Sir."

"I'll keep the torch," said Ducane.

McGrath moved through the opening and Ducane followed, stepping carefully. There was a very unpleasant
smell.

"Well, here we are, Sir, in the holy of holies." The door
clicked to behind them.

Ducane began to shine the torch about the room but the
first thing revealed by it was McGrath. Again Ducane was
struck by the intense colour of the man's hair. The light blue
eyes stared back. There was a moment of stillness. Then
Ducane moved to examine the room. The curious idea had
occurred to him: this man could murder me down here and
no one would ever know. He did not turn his back on
McGrath.

The room was a plain fifteen-foot cube with a concrete
floor. One wall appeared to be covered with a whitish
paper, the other walls and the ceiling were red brick. A
trio of black pipes curled round the corner of the ceiling
and disappeared into the wall. Ducane had an impression
of trestle tables and chairs and some old physical memory
came to him from the war time, some recalling of dug-outs
and guard rooms. He felt at once certain that the strange
room had been something to do with the war, something
secret and unrecorded and lost.

"Shall I light some candles, Sir? You could see a bit more
then. And it would save the torch. I'm afraid it's going to
give out before long."

McGrath moved to a corner and clanked open a metal
box. A match was struck. The candle flame illumined
McGrath's hair and paper-white cheek and also the ela-

209

borate silver candlestick which held the candle. Ducane exclaimed.

"Very pretty, isn't it, Sir? Mr Radeechy had some nice stuff down here, I'll show you. You can put the torch out now, Sir."

Four candles in identical silver holders were now burning upon the trestle in the corner. Ducane moved to examine the candlesticks. Each one stood upon four silver balls held by four dragon claws, and the thick shaft was engraved all over with swirling dragons.

"Nice, aren't they," said McGrath. "Chinese, Mr Radeechy said they were. And take a look at this."

He had brought out and was holding aloft a silver-gilt chalice studded with what appeared to be very large jewels. Ducane took the cup from him and examined it. The light was too dim and he knew too little about precious stones to be sure if these ones were real. But the effect was rich and somehow barbaric.

"Have a drink, Sir," said McGrath.

As Ducane held the cup McGrath suddenly tilted some wine into it from a bottle which he had just produced. Ducane hastily put the chalice down on the table.

"It's quite all right, Sir. It won't have gone off. Quite a little feast we could have down here. We needn't starve. See, there's this funny bread, and walnuts, Mr R. was very partial to walnuts."

McGrath was taking the contents out of the tins and spreading them upon the table. Ducane saw slices of moist black bread and the nuts, their veined shells slightly green with mould. Black bread for the black mass; and Ducane recalled that walnuts were held to be magical since their double interior resembled the lobes of the human brain.

McGrath was cracking walnuts with a pair of silver nut crackers. "Here, Sir, have half. They're quite good inside."

Ducane felt the dry wrinkled morsel pressed into his hand. He moved back. Whatever he did he must not share a walnut with McGrath. That meant something too, only he could not remember what.

"Show me what there is to see and then let's get back."

"Not much to see really, Sir," said McGrath munching walnut. "This was where the candles went. I'll lay the rest of the stuff out."

McGrath placed the candles in a row along the back of another trestle table which stood up against the white wall. A narrow black mattress lay upon the table. "That was where the girl went, Sir," said McGrath in a low reverential voice.

McGrath returned to the other darkened table and then began to lay out a number of articles upon the mattress. First there were a number of well-corked clearly labelled glass jars such as one might find in a kitchen. Ducane looked at the labels: poppy, hyssop, hellebore, hemp, sunflower, nightshade, henbane, belladonna. The black bread and a pile of walnuts were laid next to them. There followed a large packet of table salt, a small silver-gilt bell, a Bible, a battered Roman missal, some sticks of incense, an elongated piece of silver on a stand with a cross bar close to the foot of it, and a slim black whip. The bell tinkled slightly. McGrath's pale red-haired hand closed over it.

McGrath placed the tall piece of silver in the centre of the table behind the mattress. Ducane thought: of course, a tau cross, a cross reversed.

"For the five senses, you see. Mr Radeechy explained it to me once. Salt for taste, flame for sight, bell for sound, incense for smell, and *this* for touch."

McGrath laid the whip in front of the cross.

Ducane shuddered.

"And then there's this," McGrath was going on.

The candles curtsied in a movement of air and Ducane withdrew his attention from the whip.

McGrath, swollen to twice his size, seemed to be struggling with something or dancing, his hands raised above his head, casting a huge capering shadow upon the brick wall. Then with a heavy plop the garment fell into place and McGrath displayed it, grinning. He was wearing a vast cope of yellow silk embroidered with black fir-cones. With a coquettish movement he turned in a circle. The sleeves and trouser legs of his dark suit protruded from the exquisite cope with an effect of grossness. The garment was much too large for him. Radeechy had been a big man.

"This completes the get-up, you see." McGrath had now produced a tall stiff embroidered head-dress rather like a mitre, and was about to put it on.

Ducane took it quickly out of his hand. "Take that thing off."

"It's posh, isn't it?"

"Take it off."

Rather reluctantly McGrath struggled out of the cope. As it came over his head he said, "Do you think I could have some of these things, Sir?"

"Have some—?"

"Well, as mementos like. Do you think I could have that cup thing?"

"No, of course not!" said Ducane. "These things are the property of Mr Radeechy's heir. The police will take charge of them. Stand out of the way, would you. I want to look around." He picked up one of the candles. "What a terrible smell."

"I expect it's the birds."

"The birds?"

"Yes," said McGrath. "The poor pigeons. See."

He pointed into the darkness underneath a trestle table on the other side of the room.

Ducane moved the candle and saw beneath the table what looked like a large cage. It was in fact a cage roughly made out of a packing case and some strands of wire. Within the cage, as he leaned towards it, Ducane saw a spread-out grey wing. Then he saw a heap of sleek rounded grey and blue shapes piled together in a corner. The feathers were still glossy.

"All dead now of course," said McGrath with a certain satisfaction. "Mr Radeechy wanted them alive." McGrath's hand reached out to touch the cage with an almost affectionate gesture. His wrist, woven over with golden wires, protruded a long way from his jacket.

"You mean—?"

"He used to kill them in the ceremony, whatever he did. Blood all around the place something shocking. It always took me quite a time to clean it up after he'd been having a go. He was very particular you see about the cleaning up."

"Where did you get them?"

"Caught them in Trafalgar Square. Nothing's easier if you get there early in the morning. Bit difficult in winter.

But I could usually catch one or two on a foggy day and carry them off under my coat."

"And you kept them here?"

"Some at home, some here, till they were needed. I fed them of course, but they seemed to be asleep most of the time. Not having any light I suppose. I'd just put that lot in when it happened, about Mr Radeechy I mean."

Ducane turned away from the little soft heap in the cage. "It didn't occur to you to come down and let them out?"

McGrath seemed surprised. "Lord, no. I didn't think of it. I didn't want to come down here more than I need. And with poor Mr Radeechy dead I wasn't going to trouble my head about a few pigeons."

Ducane shook himself. The candlestick was beginning to feel very heavy in his hand. It tilted over and hot candle grease fell on to his wrist and on to the sleeve of his coat. He felt suddenly slightly faint and it came to him that ever since he had entered the room he had been becoming passive and drowsy. He had a distinct urge to remove the objects from the mattress and lie down on it himself. He wondered for the first time how the room was ventilated. There seemed to be very little air to breathe. He took a deep gasping breath and the smell sickened him and he gave a retching cough.

"Foul smell, isn't it?" said McGrath, who was still on one knee beside the cage, watching him. "But it's not just the birds, you know. It's *him*."

"Him?"

"Mr R. He smelt something awful. Did you never notice it?"

Ducane had in fact noticed that Radeechy smelt unpleasant. He had once overheard clerks in the office jesting about it.

"Well, if we've seen what there is to see we'd better go," said Ducane.

He turned back to the altar. The golden cope with the black pine-cones had been tossed over one end of the mattress. Ducane saw in the close light of the candle that the cope was tattered and soiled, one wing of it darkened near the hem by an irregular brown stain.

"Is there anything else?"

"You've seen the lot, Sir. Look, there's nothing else in the room. Just these tins, nothing more inside except some matches and some of Mr R's cigarettes, bless him. Nothing under the tables except the old pigeons. But just you look for yourself, Sir, just you look for yourself."

Ducane walked along the edges of the room with his candle and then turned to face McGrath who was now standing with his back to the tau cross, watching Ducane intently. Ducane saw that McGrath had picked up the whip and was teasing the slender tapering point of it with a finger of his left hand. McGrath's eyes were empty featureless expanses of pale blue.

It's the dreariness of it, thought Ducane, that stupefies. This evil is dreary, it's something shut in and small, dust falling upon cobwebs, a bloodstain upon a garment, a heap of dead birds in a packing case. Whatever it was that Radeechy had so assiduously courted and attracted to himself, and which had breathed upon him, squirted over him, that odour of decay, had no intensity or grandeur. These were but small powers, graceless and bedraggled. Yet could not evil damn a man, was there not blackness enough to kill a human soul? It is in me, thought Ducane, as he continued to look through the empty blue staring eyes of McGrath. The evil is in me. There are demons and powers outside us, Radeechy played with them, but they are pygmy things. The great evil, the real evil, is inside myself. It is I who am Lucifer. With this there came a rush of darkness within him which was like fresh air. Had Radeechy felt this onrush of black beatitude as he stood before the cross reversed and rested the chalice upon the belly of the naked girl?

"What's the matter, Sir?"

"Nothing," said Ducane. He put the candle down on the nearest table. "I feel a little odd. It's the lack of air."

"Sit down a minute, Sir. Here's a chair."

"No, no. What are those odd marks on the wall behind you?"

"Oh just the usual things, Sir. Soldiers I'd say."

Ducane leaned across the mattress and examined the white wall. It was a wall of whitewashed brick and the appearance of a wallpaper had been given to it by a dense covering of graffiti, reaching from the ceiling to the floor.

The customary messages and remarks were followed here and there by dates—all wartime dates. There were representations of the male organ in a variety of contexts. The decorated wall behind the cross provided a backcloth which was suddenly friendly and human, almost good.

Then certain marks caught Ducane's eye which seemed of more recent date, as if they had been put on with a blue felt pen. They overlaid the pencil scrawlings of the soldiers. There were several carefully drawn pentograms and hexograms. Then in Radeechy's small pedantic hand was written *Asmodeus, Astaroth*, and below that *Do what thou wilt shall be the whole of law*. Directly above the cross was a large blue square which Ducane, moving the candle nearer, saw to be composed of capital letters. The letters read as follows:

```
O  Y  P  A  T  E  A
H  R  O  T  A  S  R
C  O  P  E  R  A  D
E  T  E  N  E  T  O
E  A  R  E  P  O  M
D  S  A  T  O  R  I
O  A  R  S  U  N  A
```

"What does that mean?"

"Lord, Sir, I don't know. It's in some funny foreign language. Mr Radeechy wrote it up one day. He told me to be careful not to smudge it when I was dusting."

Ducane took out his diary and copied the square of letters down into the back of it. "Let's go," he said to McGrath.

"Just a minute, Sir," said McGrath.

They were both leaning against the trestle table with the cross upon it. Lit by the candles behind it, the multiple shadow of the reversed cross flickered upon their two hands, McGrath's left and Ducane's right, which were gripping the edge of the trestle. McGrath was still holding the whip in his right hand, drooping it now against his trouser leg. Stooping a little, and with a delicate almost fastidious gesture, Ducane took the whip out of McGrath's hand and swinging it round behind him tossed it on to the mattress. As his fingers touched McGrath's he saw McGrath's head and shoulders very clearly as if inscribed in an oval of light, the red-golden hair, the narrow pale face, the unflecked blue eyes. The vision carried with it a sense of something novel. Ducane thought, I am seeing him for the first time as being young, no, no, I am seeing him for the first time as being beautiful. He tensed his hand upon the table, dragging his nails across the surface of the wood.

"Let's not quarrel, Sir, shall we?"

"I wasn't aware that we were—quarrelling," said Ducane after a moment. He took a slow step backward.

"Well, there was that little business of ours, you know. You were kind enough to help me out with a little money, if you remember, Sir. And I was able to oblige you about the young ladies' letters. I'd be most grateful, Sir, if we could now put this little matter on a proper business footing and then we can both forget all about it, see? I like you, Sir, I won't make any secret of it, I like you, and I want us to be friends. Mr Radeechy and I were friends, like, and you and I could be friends, Mr Ducane, Sir, and that's what I'd like best. There's a lot I could do for you, Sir, if I was so minded, I'm a very useful man, Sir, and a jack of all trades if I may say so, and Mr Radeechy found me very useful indeed. I'd like to serve you, Sir, and that comes from the heart. But I think it would be nicer for us both if we just settled up the other little thing first of all. A matter of four pounds a week, say, not much, Sir, to *you*, I mean I wouldn't want to charge *you* much. Just that, regular like—so perhaps, Sir, if you wouldn't mind just filling in this banker's order, I've always found that the easiest way—"

"A banker's order?" said Ducane, staring at the apparition of McGrath flourishing a piece of paper in front of him. Then he began to tremble with laughter. One of the candles went out. "A banker's order? No, no, McGrath. You've got it all wrong, I'm afraid. You're a damnable villain but I'm not a total fool. I paid you a little because I needed you for this investigation. Now that you've done all you can for me I'm not paying you another penny."

"In that case, Sir, I'm afraid I shall be forced to communicate with those young ladies. You realise that?"

"You can do what you like about the young ladies," said Ducane. "I'm through with you, McGrath. The police will communicate with you about collecting up the stuff from here and you'll be required to make a statement. You'll be off my hands, thank God. And I never want to see or hear of you again. Now we're going back."

"But, Sir, Sir—"

"That's enough, McGrath. Just hand me the torch, will you? Now lead the way. Quick march."

The remaining candles were blown out. The black door opened and let in the dark fresher air of the tomb-like passage. McGrath faded through the doorway. Ducane followed, holding the torch so as to illuminate McGrath's heels. As he began to mount the ramp he felt a curious taste upon his tongue. He realised that at some point he must have put the half walnut absently into his mouth and eaten it.

Twenty-seven

DEAREST JOHN, forgive me for writing, I've just got to write. I've got to do something which connects me with you, really, and not just in thought, and this is all I can do. Thank you very much for your dear postcard. I am so glad to think that I shall see you the week after next. But it seems rather a long time to wait. And I thought perhaps you would be glad to know that I was thinking about you all the time. Is that wrong of me? I am so happy when I think that you have somehow accepted me. You have accepted me, haven't you? I mean, you are *letting* me love you, aren't you? And that is all that I want. At least it's not all that I want but it's all that I can ask and, John, it's *enough*. I can be happy just thinking about you and seeing you now and then when you aren't too busy. Love is such a good occupation, John, and I'm beginning to think that I'm clever at it! Be well, my dearest, and don't work too hard, and if it is ever a refreshment to you to know that your Jessica is thinking loving thoughts about you, then know it indeed, because it will be true. Yours, yours, yours

Jessica

P.S. I wonder if you understand me when I say that I have a *guilty conscience*? And that I was so relieved to get your postcard and know that all was well? You are a forgiving man and I worship you for that too. (If all this is Greek to you never mind! I'll explain one day!)

John my dear,
  I am feeling wretched and I must write to you, and although I know you don't want to be told that I love you, and that this just annoys you, I've still got to write and tell you because it's a fact and one that I live with in hell. I know one averts one's attention from unpleasant things and I have no doubt you think as little as possible about the problem of What To Do About Jessica; but the problem remains, and I have to press it on your notice now and

then because *you are the only person who can help me*. I might
say too that you are the person who *ought* to help me, since
you do bear some responsibility for having awakened in
me such an immense, such a truly monstrous degree of
love. Of course I shall never recover from this illness. *But
you must just do a little more to help me to live with it.*

I suppose you know, if you use your imagination at all
about me (but perhaps you don't?), that I expect a letter
from you by every post. Idiotic, but I do; I can't help it,
it's physical. I rush down as soon as I hear the postman.
And when, as usual, there's nothing, it's like a kind of
amputation. Do try to *think* about this, John, even for two
seconds. You leave me without any news for nearly a week.
Then you send me a *postcard* suggesting a meeting in ten days'
time. This just isn't good enough, my dear. Are you *really* so
busy that you can't see me for half an hour sometime next
week? I behave very well these days, as you know—you've
trained me and I have to! Couldn't you manage a short drink
some evening? In fact, I could manage really any time of
day, anywhere. Why not telephone me? I'm in nearly all the
time now.

It would give me a *particular relief* to see you just now
because—well, I wonder if you know why? I can't help
wondering if you are not angry with me especially after
getting your postcard. If you think I have done wrong you
have got to forgive me. Because otherwise I shall die. John,
please see me next week.

Jessica

John, as you may know by now, I went to bed with somebody last week. I expect you probably know all about it and
either you are furious or you despise me utterly. I just
couldn't interpret your postcard. It had such a curious tone.
What are you thinking about me? I don't say 'forgive me'
as I don't feel penitent. You've made it so clear that you
don't want me, or rather you want me completely on your
own terms. I'm supposed to love you but give no trouble.
Well, I'm not as trouble-free as all that. And things happen
to me too. However I suppose I should be grateful that at
least you've always been totally truthful with me—and now
I'm being totally truthful with you. It is unfortunately for

us both also the truth that I love you and only you utterly and permanently and to distraction. You've just got to bear it. *Please see me tomorrow*. I'll telephone you at the office.

J.

Jessica Bird had been wandering up and down her room for some time now. The three letters, which she had spent most of the previous night writing, were laid out on the table. Which letter should she send? Which was the sincere one? She felt all of the things in all of the letters. Which was the efficacious one? She knew in her heart that not one of them would be efficacious. Any one of them would annoy John and make him harden his heart against her. He would not see her tomorrow. He might see her for half an hour next week and then postpone the appointment he had made on the postcard. It was not likely that he was angry with her; she had just become a nuisance and anything that she did, any claim that she made on his attention, was an irritant. This is perhaps the saddest experience in the demise of love and the most difficult for the imagination to encompass: to come to know that someone who loved you once now regards you as boring and annoying and unimportant. Sheer hatred might even be preferred to this. Of course she was being very unjust to John. John was a conscientious man who did no doubt worry about her welfare and it was on principle and as a matter of duty that he had suggested to her such a far off date on a *postcard*. He was trying to cure her. But this was not the way to do it. And indeed there was no cure.

It had been a sort of relief to Jessica to feel a clear and definite jealousy. The beautiful woman entering John's front door had been an indubitable percept, something novel, an occasion of quite new thoughts and hence a freshener of love; and as there is a joy of loving which lives even in extreme pain, there had been something invigorating and even cheering in this period of jealous love. However, the period of jealous love, though not exactly over, had suffered change. Jessica, amid all her other preoccupations, had been impressed in a quite factual way by her failure to find anything at all of a suggestive nature in John's bedroom: not a pin, not a smell, no cosmetics, no contraceptives.

nothing. As John could scarcely have imagined her bold and inventive enough actually to get herself inside his house, he would be unlikely to have kept his room in quite such an innocuous condition if something were really going on there. Jessica was particularly impressed by the absence of the least hint of perfume. A woman who looked like the woman she had seen would be certain to wear perfume. It was wonderful that there had been nothing to smell. Yet there *had* been, as large as life, this woman, and Jessica would have continued to devote her time to speculation about her were it not that she had been plunged into the most terrible anxiety by the extraordinary way in which her visit to Ducane's house had terminated.

The little man, Willy, had told her that he would not tell John; but could she believe him? Did men tell each other such things? Of course they did. It would be only human if Willy told her he would not tell, and even meant it, and then told. How would John take it, how *had* he taken it? What did the postcard mean? What should she do? Should she confess and risk his not knowing, or not confess and risk his knowing? Would he be angry, would he be, oh beautiful thought, jealous, would he decide to write her off altogether? This lapse might provide him with just that little extra ounce of resentment needed to make him decide to stop seeing her. Was that the meaning of the postcard? He would nurse his anger, humiliate her by the delay, and then announce to her that it was their last meeting? Or did he know and just feel utterly indifferent? Or did he not know, and was really becoming grateful for her love, ready to accept it, comforted to know that she was eternally there?

Jessica paused facing the window pane but she did not look out. The window pane might have been entirely opaque, she herself might have been wearing a black veil, for all she could see of the cars and the people and the dogs and the cats passing by in the street. Her thoughts and images enclosed her head in a field of forces which literally rendered the world invisible. The only relief from endless speculation was fantasy, and of this she only allowed herself a very little. John did not really know his own heart. He was a hopeless puritan who could not have a love affair without feeling guilty. He had broken things off because he felt too guilty to be happy. But he was gradually discovering that without Jessica his life was empty. He had made conscientious efforts to reduce their love into a friendship, but he could not stop thinking about her. One day he would realise that he could not cease to love her; and then the idea would come to him that the way to stop feeling guilty with somebody is to marry them. He would write her a long letter about it in his pedantic official style, full of careful explanations of his state of mind, asking if after all the pain he had caused her she still loved him enough to be willing to become his wife.

Jessica had also devoted quite a lot of thought to Willy. Any event is welcome to those who are unhappily in love, and Willy had certainly been an event. For a short while, before her own reflections, together with John's curious postcard, had begun to frighten her, she had even felt a sort of exhilaration about Willy. There was an odd sacrilegious pleasure in the unfaithfulness itself. But she had also *noticed* Willy, and although she was scarcely aware of this, simply being forced to see something in the world other than John Ducane had done her good. Willy had intrigued and moved her, and before the old tyranny of love had again incarcerated her poor incurious heart she had felt a very definite desire to see him again. He had never revealed his surname or told her who he was. However, her curiosity about him, which did she but know it was a little spark of virtue in her, had by now been completely quenched by her guilt and indecision about John.

Jessica looked at herself in the long mirror which hung at one end of the room. She could no longer decide whether she was beautiful. Her face had no significance now except seen-by-John, her body no meaning except touched-by-John. But what did he see, what did he touch? That he could see her as clearly as she now saw herself was a thought which terrified her. Perhaps he looked upon her now with secret disgust, noticing those hairs upon her upper lip and the enlargement of the pores about her nose. She had shortened her skirt for the new fashion, and her long legs were visible now from well above the knee, clad in lacy cream-coloured stockings. But did her long legs please him any more or was he merely annoyed that she should dress in this juvenile way and led to notice, what he had never noticed before, the bulkiness of her knees? Jessica drew back her long straggle of fair hair with one hand and put her face close to the mirror. There was no doubt about it. She was beginning to look old.

She returned again to her pacing of the room and to contemplation of the three letters on the table. The room was empty and echoing and white. She had destroyed all her objects and had not had the heart to construct any new ones. As the term was over at her school, Jessica could now devote the whole of every day to walking up and down her room and thinking about John Ducane. She did not dare to leave the house in case he telephoned.

There was a slight sound downstairs and Jessica darted to the door. The post. She sprang down the stairs three at a time and swept up the envelopes which were lying on the mat. She longed for a thick letter from John, but she also dreaded it. It might contain his long and careful explanation of why he had decided to see her no more.

There was no letter from John. The particular pain of this, the pain she had described as being like an amputation, flared through her body. No, it was not like an amputation. It was a jerking pain, more like being on the rack. She felt dislocated from head to foot. She put the envelopes on the table. In fact there was one letter for her, in a brown envelope, addressed in an unknown rather uneducated-looking hand. She walked heavily up the stairs and two tears went very slowly, as if they too were weary and discouraged, over the curve of her cheek. She wished the post did not come three times a day.

She put the brown envelope down on the table. Should she send one of those letters to John? She just *had* to see him soon. The agony of not knowing whether he knew and what he thought was becoming just physically too much. Some inner organ would give way, her heart would literally break, if she did not see him soon. Dare she ring him at the office? He had asked her never to do that. But the last time she had telephoned his house the servant had said he was not in, and she could not endure again the special unique pain of imagining that he had told the servant that he was not in to a young lady who might ring him up.

Absently Jessica picked up the brown envelope from the table and began to tear it open. There seemed to be quite a lot inside it. She pulled out a piece of lined paper with a short letter upon it, and an envelope came out too and fell face upwards on top of one of her own letters. Jessica stared at it with a shock of amazement and premonitory fright. It was an envelope addressed to John Ducane Esquire, in another and different handwriting. Why had this been sent to her? Was she supposed to pass it on to John? But she saw that the envelope had already been opened and the postmark was of earlier this month. With fascinated horror Jessica unfolded the accompanying letter. It was brief and read as follows.

Dear Madam,

in view of your emotional feelings about Mr John Ducane I feel sure that it would be of interest to you to see the enclosed.

Yours faithfully,
A Well-Wisher

Trembling violently Jessica fumbled with the other envelope and plucked the letter out of it. The letter read thus:

Trescombe House
Trescombe
Dorset

Oh my darling John, how I miss you, it seems an age till our lovely *weekend* arrives. I hate to think of you all lonely in London, but it won't be long until we are *reunited*. You are my *property*, you know, and I have a strong sense of property! I shall assert my rights! Don't be long away from me, my sweet, haste the day and the hour. Oh how heavenly it is, John, to be able to speak love to you, and to know that you feel as I do! Love, love, love,

Your Kate

P.S. Willy Kost sends regards and hopes to see you too.

Jessica sat down on the floor and concentrated her attention upon not dying. She felt no impulse to weep or scream, but it was as if her flesh were being dragged apart. Shock was more evident than pain, or perhaps pain was so extreme that it had brought her to the brink of unconsciousness. She sat quite still for about five minutes with her eyes closed and every muscle contracted to keep herself in a single piece. Then she opened her eyes and read the letter again and examined the envelope.

There was of course not the slightest doubt that this was a letter to John from his mistress. Quite apart from the tone of the letter, the reference to the significantly under-lined *weekend* put this beyond question. They seemed to be on very happy, indeed ecstatic, terms. It was not the letter of a woman who was uncertain whether she was loved. The letter moreover had been written less than three weeks ago. The date on the envelope showed clearly and the letter itself was dated with day, month and year. So at this very recent time the affair had been for some while in existence, was in full swing. This then meant that John had lied to her.

Jessica got up from the floor. She went to the drawer which contained all the letters which John had ever sent her, and took out the postcard which lay on the top.

Forgive this in haste, I am most terribly busy in the office with various rather preoccupying matters. I am sorry not to have written. Could we meet on Monday, not of next week but of the week following? I shall look forward to that. If I don't hear otherwise I'll come to your place at seven. Very good wishes.

J.

Various rather preoccupying matters, thought Jessica. *Come to your place*. How differently it read now. Of course she was not to visit him, she was never to visit him. Busy with his marvellous love affair he had coldly calculated what was the longest he could put her off for, what was the most he could make her put up with, without arousing suspicion. *Monday, not of next week but of the week following.* How care-fully it was put so as to make a shabby offer sound less shabby. No doubt he would be just back from one of those *lovely weekends*. And he would look into her eyes, as he had done on the last occasion, and tell her in that grave sincere voice that he had no mistress.

Jessica began to walk up and down again, but very much more slowly. She debated, but very slowly, an impulse to lift the telephone at once and ring John's office. She debated it slowly because she knew that it was not urgent since she would certainly not do it, and because she knew that something else, and something very important, was happening inside her. It must be given time to happen properly, to gain authority over her. So John, the conscientious puritanical John, the just and righteous John, the John-God, had coldly lied to her. She was not an object of concern to him at all, she was a person to be manipulated and deceived and put off the scent. She was perhaps, and this thought made Jessica pause for a moment in her slow perambulation, a positive danger to him, a danger to his new-found happiness, a nasty relic, a false note. *I hate to think of you all lonely in London.* Of course John would not have told the lovely lady about his obligations to poor Jessica. That would spoil things, that would never do. John had lied to the lovely lady as well.

Jessica said to herself aloud, "It is all over now with John. It is the end." She paused again to watch herself. Still no screams, no tears, no tendency to fall down in a faint. There was a line of hardness in her, a rigid steely upright as thin as a wire but very strong. She was not going to die after all for John Ducane. She was his superior now. She knew, and he did not know she knew. She sat down on the bed. She felt very tired as if she had been for a long walk. She had been for a long walk, she had been walking for days up and down her room, thinking about John, waiting for him to write, waiting for him to telephone. And all this time . . . Jessica settled two cushions behind her and sat upright and comfortable upon the bed. She fell now into a total immobility, she sat like an idol, like a sphinx. Her eyes scarcely blinked, her breathing seemed suspended, it was as if the life had been withdrawn from her leaving an effigy of wax. An hour passed.

Jessica moved and it was evening. She went to the window and looked out. A Siamese cat was walking slowly along the top of the railings. A West Indian newspaper boy was delivering the evening papers. A student was polishing his very old car. Two dogs who had just met were wagging their tails. She turned away from the window and went to the mirror and said to her image softly several times "Jessica, Jessica. . . ."

Then she turned back to the table and took up the letter again, but this time it was to scrutinise only the P.S. *Willy Kost.*

227

Twenty-eight

"I WAS wondering when you'd turn up," murmured
Ducane.

Richard Biranne was standing in Ducane's drawing-
room and had not yet taken the chair to which Ducane had
invited him. Ducane was seated beside the empty fireplace.
The lamps were lit and the curtains were drawn upon a
dark blue evening. The room smelt of summer dust and roses.

Biranne stood fingering the edge of the mantelpiece,
swaying his body restlessly and twitching his shoulders.
His long head was thrown back and averted and his
narrow blue eyes glanced quickly at Ducane, surveyed the
room, and almost coquettishly glanced again. A lamp was
behind him, shadowing his face and lighting up his fuzzy
crest of fair hair. He had arrived on Ducane's doorstep
unannounced two minutes ago.

"Well?" said Ducane. He had adopted a cold almost
lethargic composure to conceal his extreme satisfaction,
indeed exhilaration, at Biranne's arrival.

The inspection with McGrath of Radeechy's 'chapel'
had finally satisfied Ducane that Radeechy was, as far as
the 'security aspect' was concerned, innocuous. He was
certain that the necromantic activities were not a front.
There was sincerity, there was evident faith, in Radeechy's
pathetic arrangements; and if Radeechy had been up to
anything else he would scarcely have risked attracting
attention by nocturnal visits with girls. The suicide itself
remained unexplained. But the glimpse of the chapel had
been enough to persuade Ducane that such a man might
well have suicidal promptings. What had come to Ducane
in the course of that candle-lit occasion was an intimation of
the reality with which Radeechy had been meddling. Of
course Ducane did not believe in 'spirits'. But what had
gone on in that room, upon that altar, when the blood of
the pigeons dripped down on to the black mattress, was not
childish mumming. It was a positive and effective meddling
with the human mind. Ducane could not get the smell of it

out of his nostrils. and he knew that McGrath was right to say that it was not only the smell of decomposing birds. Radeechy had discovered and had made to materialise about him a certain dreariness of evil, a minor evil no doubt, but his success might very well have set him on the road to suicide.

All this made sense, and would have made reasonably complete sense if it were not for the involvement of Biranne. Biranne had tampered with the body, he had concealed his visits to Radeechy's house, he knew Judy McGrath. However Ducane was not now by any means so sure that Biranne held the key to Radeechy's suicide or knew any more about it than Ducane had already been able to conjecture. It suddenly began to look to Ducane as if his enquiry was finished, or as finished as it would ever be, and that he could with a clear conscience write a report in which Biranne was not mentioned at all. Everything that connected Biranne with Radeechy, though so odd and suggestive, could have an innocent explanation. He might have touched the body out of curiosity or solicitude and then decided it was prudent not to mention it, his relationship with the McGraths might be quite fortuitous, his visits to Radeechy's house might have had Judy as their object, and he might have concealed them precisely for this reason. In fact in so far as these things fitted together they did so in a way which tended to acquit Biranne of any sinister role.

All this was logical and rational, and Ducane should have been pleased to be convinced and to have his case thus cleanly ended. However he was not pleased, partly because he felt sure, on no very clear grounds, that there was some aspect of the matter which was still hidden and that Biranne knew about it, and partly because of what by now amounted almost to an emotional involvement with Biranne. He had become used to regarding Biranne as his quarry. He had developed a sharp curiosity about the man, a curiosity which had something of the quality of a form of affection. He very much wanted to 'have it out' with Biranne and the idea was exciting. Yet he had, in the two days which had passed since his underground journey with McGrath, hesitated to make any move. He had been delighted to find Biranne on his doorstep.

Biranne was in a state of emotion the nature of which was not easy to discern but which he could not conceal and did not attempt to conceal. He walked the length of the room and back and then stood staring down at Ducane.

"Sit down and have some whisky," said Ducane. He had already placed a decanter and two glasses upon a low table beside the hearth. He motioned to the chair opposite.

"No thanks, I'll stand," said Biranne. "No whisky."

Ducane, who had been thinking hard ever since he had seen Biranne's tense face in the blue twilight of the doorway, said in a tone which was half persuasion, half command. "You've come to tell me something. What is it?"

"I'm afraid I don't quite understand you—"

"Look here," said Ducane, "I'll be quite straight with you and I want you to be quite straight with me. You've come to tell me something about Radeechy. I know a good deal about Radeechy and a good deal about you, but there are still one or two things that puzzle me. These may be perfectly innocent things and if you can give me a satisfactory explanation I'll be the first to be pleased."

Biranne, still staring, stroked his hair back. He said, "For a man who proposes to talk straight you've used a lot of words to say nothing. I want to know why you came to my house."

"I wanted to question you."

"What about?" Biranne's high-pitched voice crackled with nerves.

"I wanted to know why you had told me certain lies," said Ducane carefully. He found that he was now leaning forward, and with deliberation settled himself back again into his chair.

"What lies did I tell you?"

"You pretended not to know Radeechy when in fact you knew him well."

"What else?"

"Why did you tamper with Radeechy's body?" said Ducane.

"I didn't tamper with Radeechy's body, I didn't touch him."

"Then how did your finger-prints get on to his collar?"

Biranne stared steadily down at Ducane. He chewed his knuckles thoughtfully. Then he walked along the room and back. "Do you mind if I have some whisky after all? May I sit down?"

"Please. Well?"

Biranne sat down and poured out some whisky, taking his time. He looked into the glass, sipped it cautiously. He said, "Perhaps it was silly of me to mislead you, but it was just that I didn't want to be involved. You understand. Maybe I ought to have told the police that I touched the body, only it seemed both unimportant and rather absurd. It was just an impulse. He was lying forward and I pulled him up a little, I suppose to see if he was still alive, and I pushed the gun out of the way at the same time. Then I put everything back the way it was before. Whatever made you test his collar for my finger-prints?"

"You didn't put everything back the way it was before" said Ducane. "You evidently didn't know that Radeechy was left-handed. You put the gun on the wrong side."

Biranne smiled faintly. The whisky had done him good. "You're wasting your talents. You ought to be in Scotland Yard."

"Why did you lock the door?"

"You are well informed. That was an impulse too. I intended in the first moment to ring up Octavian and keep the door locked until he appeared. Then I changed my mind."

"I'll tell you in a minute what I think of these explanations," said Ducane. "Now tell me why you pretended not to know Radeechy."

"That was just general discretion," said Biranne, pouring out some more whisky. "One has a certain right to defend oneself against impertinent curiosities. I don't know why the fellow killed himself. It might have had something to do with girls, it might have been anything. I didn't want to be questioned about him or called in as a witness. You'd have done the same in my place."

"I wouldn't, and I couldn't be in your place," said Ducane with a vehemence which shot him forward again in his chair.

Biranne stared at his questioner steadily, almost sternly, and then transferred his attention ostentatiously to the whisky which he was rolling round and round in his glass. He was silent.

A banging door and a snatch of *The Bonny Earl of Murray* announced the return home of Fivey after his evening out. Ducane frowned, sat back again, and said to himself, Oh Christ, he's going to get away with it.

"What about Helen of Troy?" said Ducane.

Biranne smiled cunningly and then with a raised eyebrow looked confiding. "Young Judy, yes. I gather *you* had an encounter with Judy. She seems to be in all our lives."

"She's not in my life!" said Ducane. He realised that he was beginning to get angry. The interview was going wrong. Biranne was already patently less anxious, and it was he himself who was being taunted and was answering defensively. He sat up and poured himself out some whisky. They stared at each other.

"Come, come, Biranne," said Ducane. It sounded almost coaxing.

"What do you mean 'come, come'? I don't deny that I know Judy McGrath and that Radeechy knew her too. She is a versatile lady with a wide acquaintance."

"Did you get to know her through Radeechy?"

Biranne looked cautious. "No. I got to know her through her husband. McGrath knows how to exploit a saleable piece of goods. Radeechy got to know her the same way."

"Is McGrath blackmailing you as well?"

"How do you mean as well? Is he blackmailing you?"

"No, he isn't! He was blackmailing Radeechy."

"Was he? Oh yes, I remember. Interesting. Perhaps that accounts for the suicide."

"You haven't answered my question."

"I don't think I allow your right to question me, my dear Ducane."

"Then why did you come here tonight?"

"Because you were, shall we say, getting on my nerves. Well, if you really want to know, I came here to ask *you* some questions."

"What about?"

"About how well you know Judy McGrath."

"Really!" said Ducane. He got up, jarring his chair back and almost overturning a lamp. He walked quickly to the other end of the room and back. He stared down at Biranne and then realised that they had exchanged positions.

Biranne lounged in his chair, and Ducane stood before him. There was no doubt that Biranne was a clever man. He will get away with it, Ducane thought. Why was he increasingly sure that there was something here to get away with?

"Well?" said Biranne. He seemed quite relaxed now, his hand on his glass, his legs extended in front of him, his long narrow head lolling on the cushions.

Ducane thought, he came here to find out how much I know, and I have virtually informed him that I know nothing! Damn, damn, damn. With this Ducane felt a final certainty that Biranne was guilty, guilty of something, perhaps guilty of something serious. He thought, I must frighten him somehow.

Ducane said, thinking hard, "As you are perfectly well aware, I scarcely know Mrs McGrath."

"You kissed her," said Biranne. "But of course dark horses like you often tend to be fast workers." He laughed shortly and poured out some more whisky.

"She kissed me," said Ducane. "I confess her professional ease took me by surprise. You know perfectly well that I have no interest of that sort in Mrs McGrath."

"Why should I believe you?"

"I don't tell lies."

"Really?" said Biranne. "Then why did you tell me one just now?"

"What do you mean?"

"You said McGrath was not blackmailing you."

Ducane looked down into Biranne's handsome insolent face. Then he turned away and laughed. He began to pace the room.

"All right. McGrath has tried to blackmail me, and for my own reasons I've led him on. How did you know?"

"He told me. The fellow has an engaging frankness. He tried to blackmail me too. He and Judy work as a team, as you probably realise. She ensnares people in high places with, shall we say, odd tastes, and McGrath follows close behind with his little camera. He really has quite a talent for photography."

"I see. He tried it on you. But you wouldn't play?"

"I told him that if he tried that game on me I'd kill him, and he believed me."

Ducane turned at the end of the room to look at the long relaxed figure in the armchair. He has an answer for everyone and everything, he thought to himself. I could never make a man believe that I would kill him!

"As I say," said Ducane, "I had my own reasons for encouraging McGrath." He was beginning to have an idea, an idea which Biranne himself had put into his head.

"Very compelling reasons, I daresay. With two charming girls involved. Yes, you *are* a dark horse."

"I see that McGrath's engaging frankness has known no bounds," said Ducane. He thought, this fellow knows more about me than I know about him. And I thought of him as my victim, my prisoner!

"Well, he did tell me something about two letters. He was rather proud of himself. I must say, he's a most ingenious man."

"He seems to be quite a friend of yours," said Ducane. "It will be interesting when he tells us *everything* he knows."

"He'll never do that," said Biranne easily. "No one has got anything on McGrath. No one ever will have."

"I have got something on McGrath," said Ducane.

Biranne sat forward. "What?"

"Precisely blackmail," said Ducane. "Why ever do you think I encouraged him? Those two letters are perfectly innocuous. The two young women express themselves warmly, as many young women do, but neither is my mistress, and there's no earthly reason against their knowing of each other's existence. In fact they now do know, since I've told them. That was the first thing I did when McGrath made his move. McGrath has no power over me as he has nothing to reveal. Really, Biranne, I'm surprised at you. From what you know of my character do you really think I'd tolerate blackmail? I haven't anything disgraceful to conceal, and I certainly wouldn't pay money to an object like McGrath in order to spare myself and two girls a small amount of embarrassment."

"You mean you—"

"Yes. McGrath has no power over me. But I have power over him and I am going to use it. Naturally I am not interested in convicting McGrath, but I am interested in persuading him to talk, and talk he will."

"But have you—evidence?" Biranne's watchfulness had returned and he was plucking again at his knuckles with bared teeth.

"The man was fool enough to write me a letter. And I have a tape recording. I too have been a little ingenious in this matter." For a truthful man I'm certainly having a strange evening, thought Ducane. He had come near to Biranne now and was watching him closely. Biranne was plainly uneasy.

"So you're going to put the screw on McGrath?"

"Yes. He's told me half the story already. I'll get the other half next week. Possibly with, possibly without, the help of the police. I have a feeling it will be interesting. And I have a feeling it will concern you."

"He won't tell you anything," said Biranne. He was looking down at the carpet now.

"So you don't deny he has something to tell?"

"Oh, he has plenty to tell. But not about Radeechy. Of course you can threaten poor McGrath and make him turn King's evidence. But it won't help you. He doesn't know any more about that."

"Why are you so sure?"

"Because I think he'd have told me, or at least hinted. Too much has been made of this Radeechy business. I can't think why you're all so excited about it. There's no more in it than meets the eye. Radeechy was a half crazy crank with an interest in the occult and some pretty odd tastes in sex. He's just the sort of man who kills himself. Why shouldn't he? Can't he kill himself quietly without all this to-do?"

Ducane sat down. He moved the table with the whisky on it a little out of the way and pulled his chair forward. He said softly, "Look here, Richard, I *know* you've been lying to me this evening, and I *know* you're more involved in all this than you've pretended to be, deeply involved, up to the neck. You know why Radeechy committed suicide and before you leave this house you're going to tell me. You took something off Radeechy's body and I know what it was that you took. I may not have found out very much about you, but I've found out quite enough to get you into trouble if I choose to do so."

Biranne, sitting upright now, his hands in golden light,

gripping either arm of the chair, the long cylinder of his head averted and shadowed, said, "Sorry, Ducane, I've nothing more to say to you except goodnight." But he did not move.

Ducane realised that he had used Biranne's Christian name. With this came at last a sense of having the man cornered. He thought, I've got him. He said urgently, leaning forward, "Don't be a fool. Why did you say I was getting on your nerves? You didn't just come here to find out what I knew, you came here to tell me things. I'm not bluffing you, Biranne. This damned enquiry is coming to a finale, and you're in the finale whether you like it or not. The point for you to consider is this. Up to now the thing hasn't been a police matter. It's been entirely secret and I have discretion to keep it secret and to hold back completely anything which I find which I think is irrelevant. Well, you know what my briefing was. If you tell me the whole truth I may be able to keep it dark, so far as it concerns you. Obviously I can't promise this, but I could consider it. If you won't talk I shall have to hand the whole thing over, suspicions and all, to the police. If you'd rather be interrogated by them than by me, it's up to you. And don't expect any loyalty from a man like McGrath."

Biranne drew in a very long breath. His head was bowed forward now and Ducane could see one long slit of blue eye. The stiff crest of hair glowed golden in the light of the lamp. Biranne said, half under his breath, "Let me think, let me think." Then, still not looking up, he said, "If anything I were to tell you was not strictly germane to answering the question: was Radeechy a spy? you would have discretion to withhold it?"

"Yes."

"If I were to tell you precisely why Radeechy died could you report the explanation in general terms without further naming of persons?"

"I don't know. Your question is too vague. I can't promise you silence. For instance if you tell me that you killed Radeechy."

"I didn't kill Radeechy. At least not in any sense that could bring me into a law court. Just wait a minute, will you, wait a minute."

Biranne got up. He turned his back on Ducane and

236

looked away into the darkened corner of the room. Ducane ran his hands up over his forehead and found that his hair was limp and damp with perspiration. He kept his eyes and his will intently fixed upon Biranne, focusing upon the nape of his neck, where the wiry fuzz diminished into curly blond fur. Ducane kept silent but filled the silence with will. But he knew now that Biranne wanted to talk and would talk. Perhaps he had intended to do so from the start and had just wanted, needed, to be coerced.

Biranne turned back, and his face was a good deal calmer. His thin mouth smiled faintly with an air of sardonic resolution. He said, "All right. I trust you as far as you say you can be trusted and I put myself into your power. This document, on which I'd like to make one or two comments after you've read it, will tell you everything you want to know." He held out a piece of folded paper towards Ducane and then once more turned his back.

Ducane unfolded the paper. He saw at once that it was written in Radeechy's familiar compressed hand. It read as follows:

This is to state to the police, the public, and before God if He exists, that in September of last year I murdered my wife Claudia by pushing her out of a window. I acted impetuously and without premeditated intent to kill her. My motive was jealousy of her liaison with Richard Biranne. Biranne witnessed my act and has since attempted to blackmail me. I die now by my own hand. Biranne has my dying curse.

Joseph Radeechy

I loved my wife.

Ducane was so extremely surprised and in an odd way so moved by this document that he simply wanted to crush it against his brow and close his eyes. But he had too an immediate and cautious instinct of himself as an actor, an instinct which took him back to his days in the law courts. To calm himself he got up, went to his desk, took out a magnifying glass, and examined the letter carefully under the lamp. The writing was strong and fluent and certainly Radeechy's.

Biranne was still standing with his back turned. Ducane said, "Sit down, please, Biranne."

They both sat down, Biranne breathing deeply and stretching himself out as if very tired.

Ducane said, "Perhaps you could answer a few questions."

"Anything you like."

"I am prepared to assume that Radeechy wrote this. Is it all true?"

Biranne sat up again. He said, "It's true that he killed Claudia and that I saw it happen. It's also true that he was jealous of me and Claudia. It's not true that I tried to blackmail him, at least not exactly true."

"What do you mean by 'not exactly'?"

"I'm afraid I don't come very well out of this."

"Never mind how you come out of it. Tell me the truth."

"You see, I wanted Judy McGrath."

"And since you had this hold over Radeechy—?"

"I never intended to use the hold, I never even hinted at it. It was a matter of what Radeechy decided to think. I wanted to get Judy away from him, right away, and I must have made this pretty clear, and he chose to imagine he was being threatened."

"And you let him imagine?"

"I suppose so—"

"And when was this happening?"

"My take-over bid? Two or three months ago. Not just after—"

"Quite. And is what is given here in your view the whole explanation of his suicide?"

"Yes. At least, what is a whole explanation? There's no other secret, no other particular key. But he was a weird man who lived in a perpetual condition of fear and anxiety. I think he did half believe he was communing with spirits and he was afraid of them."

"Did he love his wife?"

"Yes, I think so. But please believe me that I didn't realise this at the start."

"Did you go to bed with Mrs Radeechy?"

"Yes."

"Was she a very unhappy woman?"

"No, not really, not till the end anyway. I didn't understand this to begin with either. I took a conventional view of the thing. Claudia looked like a deserted wife. Radeechy. had quite a harem of necromantic girl friends, at least he had until Judy turned up and made him sack the rest. I think Radeechy fell properly for Judy—and this did hurt Claudia. She'd tolerated the others, safety in numbers and so on, but this was serious. I think this was what made her ready to flirt with me, and then I just rather took her by storm. It was unexpected. I didn't do it in cold blood. I was amazed by the degree of Radeechy's jealousy. I didn't think he'd care that much."

"How did you first meet Claudia, anyway?"

"Through one of Judy's predecessors. Claudia came to this girl's place to see if she could find out something about Judy, that is after she'd started to fret about her. And I, well, happened to be there."

"I see. So Radeechy was jealous and he told you to clear out?"

"Yes. And perhaps I ought to have done. But I somehow felt I had to stand up to him for Claudia's sake. I *liked* Claudia, she was somebody. And it was all getting pretty muddled by this time. I told him he didn't deserve her. And he didn't. Those other girls, you know, he didn't fuck them, not even Judy, he didn't beat them either. He was a weirdie all right."

"And you—saw him—kill his wife?"

"Yes. It was—" Biranne stared into the empty fireplace. He reached out to touch the mantelpiece with his finger, tracing a pattern in the marble. "I was rather drunk that night. I think we all three were. Claudia was in a funny state of mind. I think in a way she liked to be with both of us together. I think she'd have been pleased if we'd actually fought each other. You see she really did care for her husband, though she'd certainly fallen for me too. We'd had this sort of hysterical trio once before. You'd hardly believe it, but we actually talked the thing over, all three together. It was Radeechy's oddness that somehow made it possible. He acted a part all the time and I think this was what Claudia wanted to see. She wanted to use me to make Radeechy suffer, and she wanted to see him suffering. He'd walk up and down and shout and wave his arms, and then fall into a long silence and frown like a Russian actor. I couldn't take him quite seriously during these sessions, though at the same time he almost frightened me, and this just made me go on baiting him. I wonder if you understand at all?"

"I think so," said Ducane. "Go on."

"Well, there's not much more to tell. The second time we were all together like that, it was well after midnight and we'd been sort of arguing, all of us arguing and drinking and shouting for hours, it was almost as if we sort of understood each other and were enjoying it. Radeechy suddenly seized hold of Claudia by the shoulders. It was a hot night and the window was wide open. He pushed her across the room, shouting at her. Then before I could even get up he'd pushed her out of the window."

Biranne paused. He was still intently tracing the curling pattern of the marble. "I shall never forget the extraordinary silence and the suddenness of her sheer absence from the room. She didn't scream, she just vanished out of the window as if she'd simply flown out into the night. We didn't hear her—reach the ground. We stood there completely paralysed. I think Radeechy was as surprised as I was. I think he really didn't intend to do it."

"Was she killed at once?"

"Yes, thank God. I mean, given that she was to die, thank God. We ran down and she was lying on the stone terrace with a broken neck. As you know, Radeechy's house is fairly isolated and no one else heard or saw anything."

"What happened then?"

"Radeechy became hysterical. I kept begging him to come inside. It came on to rain. I kept trying to make him come in. I wanted to make him think out what he was going to say to the police, but he just kept on crying. Then he told me to go away. And I decided I'd better go, and went. The next day I read in the paper about the 'accident'."

"Did McGrath know anything about this?"

"No, he didn't know anything, but he guessed something. He was round the place a lot and he's an observant man. He went to Radeechy and said that I had told him that Radeechy murdered Claudia and what about it. Unfortunately he made the mistake of coming to me at the same time and saying that Radeechy had told him that I murdered Claudia and what about it."

"This was when you threatened to kill McGrath?"

"Yes. And I felt murderous enough for it to be plausible. McGrath then tried to make a joke of it, and told me that he'd been threatening Radeechy too. I wrote a note to Radeechy to tell him to pay no attention to McGrath, but I don't think he would have anyway. He was too far gone in —sorrow."

"McGrath was already collecting off Radeechy?"

"Yes. McGrath had some pretty splendid photos of Radeechy raising chalices over breasts of naked girls. He got a small regular payment for that and for keeping quiet generally. I don't think Radeechy minded. There was even a curious sort of friendship between him and McGrath. McGrath was really upset by his death."

"Did you see Radeechy again?"

"No. Though I wrote him one or two discreet notes, mainly about Judy. I hesitated to talk to him in the office, and I was afraid to go to his house. Radeechy was absurd, but he could be alarming too and by this time I really was afraid of him. I thought for a while that he might kill me. When I came to his room on that last day and saw him holding a revolver I thought he was going to kill me."

"You mean he summoned you—?"

"To see him die, yes. That was somehow characteristic. He sent me a curious note asking me to come and see him at a certain hour as he needed my help. I knew I had to go, though I was scared. Then when I had got inside the door and closed it he brought out the revolver and shot himself in front of my eyes."

"God. Then you locked the door and searched him at once."

"Yes. You'll think I'm a cold fish. Well, maybe I am. I somehow knew instantly that he must have left a statement accusing me. I thought it would be in his pockets and I lifted him up to search him but it wasn't there. It was locked into one of the drawers of the desk. I forced the lock with a steel ruler. I was afraid someone would notice the marks, but they evidently never did."

There was a silence. "Is that all?" said Ducane.

"That's all. Well, you know the rest. McGrath wrecked things by selling that lunatic story to the papers and starting up all that fuss in the office. Otherwise the thing would have died down completely. Did you ever get to see that story by the way?"

"No, but I got a complete account of it eventually from someone who'd read it. There was nothing fresh in it. It made no mention of you."

"That was another thing I was afraid of. Do you mind if I pull the curtains back? It seems terribly stifling in here." Biranne went to the window and pulled back the heavy curtains and opened the sash as far as it would go. There was a murmur of traffic from the Earls Court Road.

After a moment Ducane said, "Why did you keep Radeechy's confession?"

"Why? It may sound crazy, but I was afraid that if things began to come out I might be accused of having murdered him!"

"Quite, quite." Ducane shuddered. He said, "And you've got Judy."

Biranne took a number of deep breaths and then pulled the curtains back again. Still breathing with long sighs he came back to stand in the middle of the room facing Ducane. "I've got Judy in so far as anyone ever has."

Ducane was silent, staring at Biranne's long slightly twisted face. It was immobile, tired, serene, and lit with a faintly self-conscious nobility. Ducane thought, yes, you are a cold fish, you are a total bastard.

"What are you going to do with me?" said Biranne.

Ducane said slowly, beginning to fidget, move his feet about, pour more whisky into the two glasses, "You've put me in a difficult position." He did not want Biranne to start play-acting. Also he was genuinely puzzled and indeed overwhelmed by the story he had just heard and the situation they were both now in.

"Go on."

"When you came here tonight," said Ducane, "did you intend to tell me all this?"

"Yes, no. I'm not sure. To be quite frank, I thought you knew a great deal more than you did. I thought you knew pretty well everything. I imagined you might have got it

242

out of McGrath. I mean that he might have told you what he suspected or even said it to you as true. Or else Judy might have told you something. And of course I was never quite sure that Radeechy hadn't planted another confession somewhere else. I somehow got it into my head that you knew it all and were playing with me for some reason of your own. I thought this especially after you came to my house, that time you found Judy there. It all began to get terribly on my nerves. I began to have dreams about you. I know it sounds ridiculous. But after a while I began to *want* to tell you. Anyway I wanted to tell somebody. I've been having dreams about Radeechy too. I know you think I've behaved badly, but I've been in pretty fair hell for it. Do you think you can keep this thing quiet, I mean in so far as it concerns me?"

"I'm not sure that I can," said Ducane. "You witnessed a murder."

Biranne drew an upright chair forward from the wall and sat down upon it. "I shall think tomorrow that I've been a damn fool," he said. "You haven't been anything like as clever as I imagined. I came here so sure that you knew the lot and so determined to confess to you, I just didn't give myself time to make a new plan. I ought to have left after the first half hour. Only I was somehow—fascinated. If I hadn't told you this you might very well never have found it out at all. Were you really intending to pass on your vague suspicions and your tiny clues to the police? There's nothing they could have done with them. I could have talked my way out of it. And did you really intend to put the screw on McGrath and risk having your two girl friends in the papers?"

"I don't know," said Ducane. "I really don't know. I hadn't quite decided what to do. But I would certainly have talked to you before deciding. If you hadn't come to me I would have come to you." It was on the tip of his tongue to say, you were right to tell me. But did this make any sense? There was little point in saying it. Ducane was not a judge or a schoolmaster or a priest. What Biranne chiefly felt at the moment was the relief of a particular tension, the end of a speculative anxiety, together with the suspicion that he had committed an enormous blunder. The most merciful thing, and perhaps the only merciful thing, that Ducane could do for him was to remove, as far as possible, this latter regret. He said, "If you hadn't told me it would certainly have come out somehow. McGrath would have talked. And given that the thing was still largely a puzzle I could hardly have made a final report on it without mentioning you."

"Well, now that I've told you, are you going to mention me?"

Ducane realised that he was feeling very, very tired indeed. He wanted this interrogation to end. He wanted to be able to think about what he had learnt. He said, "I don't think that I can conceal a murder. It's a matter of one's duty. It's almost a technical point."

"Damn your duty," said Biranne. He got up, swinging the chair away from him in one hand. "Would I be accessory after the fact?"

"I'm afraid so."

"It would be the end of my career."

"Yes. I'm sorry, Biranne, I just don't see how I can protect you. Quite apart from the fact that you saw a murder committed and have been in possession of the murderer's confession, there's the completeness of my own case to consider. I said I'd be prepared to conceal anything which was really irrelevant to what I'd been asked to find out. But this isn't irrelevant. In particular this document, which I'll keep if you don't mind, isn't irrelevant. My brief was to find out why Radeechy killed himself. This piece of paper is the complete answer to that question."

"Isn't it enough that *you* know the answer to the question? You can tell the powers that be with a clear conscience that you know there was no security point involved. Of course you won't get so much kudos—"

"It's not a matter of kudos," said Ducane. "It's a matter of doing one's job properly. I'm sorry, Biranne, I don't want to break you, but you must see—"

"Yes, yes, I see. Duty, one's job. I suppose I ought to be cool about it. Or think I'm being suitably recompensed or something. But I don't hold any theory of punishment. I'm a good civil servant and I want to go on being one. I don't want to have to start my life again. In fact I haven't behaved all that badly, I've just been unlucky. It all seemed pretty innocuous at the start."

"Scarcely what I'd call innocuous," said Ducane. "And I think you ought to stop seeing Judy McGrath."

"Why? Do you want her?"

"Of course not. It's just that someone in your position—"

"According to you I'm not going to have a position quite soon. And then presumably I can associate with whom I please. However, it's yours to command. You're the boss now. You can give me any orders, you can make me any conditions—until you've turned me in, that is."

"Enough, enough, enough," said Ducane. He felt that he was beginning to be confused. There was no good reason to mention Judy. He said, "Look, you'd better go now. We're both too tired to think. I promise you I won't make any move for two or three days, and I won't make any move without seeing you again. And of course I won't mention this yet to another soul. I'll think about it carefully. Now please go."

Ducane opened the drawing-room door and they both emerged into the hall.

"Did you have a coat?"

"No, it's a warm night."

"Well—thank you for coming."

Biranne laughed shortly. Ducane opened the front door. They both stood still in the doorway.

Ducane felt the need to touch Biranne. He put a hand upon his shoulder for a moment in a gesture which was almost shy. Biranne moved away, and then turning held out his right hand. They shook hands hastily and Biranne disappeared into the street.

Ducane, turning from the closed door with a self-conscious gesture of exhaustion, noticed that he was standing upon a letter which lay on the mat. It must have been delivered by hand sometime since Fivey's return. It was from McGrath.

With a feeling of deep gloom Ducane carried it into the drawing room. The room was still tense and sinister. He tore open McGrath's letter destroying the envelope with angry fingers. The missive read as follows:

Dear Sir,

as you will no doubt have ascertained by this time I have sent off one of the articles in question to the person concerned. I still have the other one and will not send it off, subject to our arrangement, as I am sure you will agree, the figures being the same, or perhaps we could talk it over. I will take the liberty of telephone you tomorrow morning.

With all respects,
Yours truly,
P. McGrath

Which has he sent? thought Ducane. Kate was still away. Jessica had not replied to his postcard. It makes no difference, he thought. He will be sending the other one in the next few days. He hesitated, and then tore up McGrath's letter. There was no point trying to build up a case against the man, and they both knew it. He could not possibly risk exposing Jessica and Kate. The only person exposed must be himself.

Radeechy's confession still lay upon the side table. Ducane put it into his desk and locked it in without glancing at it again. His thought shied away from the image of Radeechy writing it, Radeechy full of murderous self-destructive hate. Ducane knew that he had not the present resources to pity Radeechy and there was no point in thinking about him. I feel sick, sick, he said to himself. He turned out the drawing-room lights and began to mount the stairs.

It was dark in his bedroom but there was a light on in the bathroom and he went straight in there without turning on any lamps. He undressed quickly, trying not to see himself in the mirror. The intense desire for sleep, for oblivion, came to him with a physical reminiscence of times of unhappiness in his childhood. What a mess, thought Ducane, what a Christ awful mess. But sleep now, sleep, sleep. He buttoned his pyjamas and emerged into his bedroom, switching the lights on. As he approached his bed he saw that there was already somebody in it.

"I thought you were never coming up!" said Judy McGrath.

Twenty-nine

"IT'S only little Judy."

Judy McGrath had thrust the blankets back and reposed, propped up on one arm. She was naked. She moved over and patted the white surface of the bed invitingly. "You were such a long time, I dozed off."

Ducane saw her body through a sort of haze. The lamps seemed to be giving very little light. Or perhaps he was just very tired. He took his black silk dressing gown off a chair and put it on. He said, "Did you come with Biranne?"

"What, Mr Honey?"

"Did you come with Biranne?"

"No, I just came with my own self. The back door was open and I walked in. I soon guessed which was your room. Don't be cross with me, Mr Honey."

It must be some sort of plot, thought Ducane. He said, "Where's your husband with his little camera?" As he used the word 'little' he was aware that he was imitating not only Biranne's words but even Biranne's voice.

"I wouldn't do anything like that to you, Mr Honey. This is for free. I love you."

"I doubt if you know much about love, Judy."

"You can't say that to anybody, Mr Honey."

She's right, thought Ducane. He swayed a little and then sat down in a chair. He realised that he had drunk a lot of whisky. He realised that he wanted to drink some more.

"You'd better go, Judy. Come on, put your clothes on."

"Why such a hurry, Mr H?"

"Because I'm dead tired and I want to go to bed and I can't go to bed while you're in it. Come on, Judy."

"You could lie beside me, Mr Honey. I wouldn't so much as touch you the whole night through."

"Don't be silly, girl."

"Have a drink, Mr Honey. A little drinkie. I brought some with me. Just for good fellowship."

Ducane saw that Judy had placed a leather flask and two glasses on the table beside the bed. He watched while she rolled over on her front and poured a little whisky into each glass. She rearranged herself, reclining on her side, and held out a glass towards him.

The movement disturbed Ducane intensely. Judy, seen in the haze of the room, which cast a sort of silver-gilt shadow over her long body, had seemed like something in a picture. Possibly she had actually reminded him of some picture by Goya or Velazquez. But that rolling movement with its awkwardness, its glimpse of buttocks, the grotesque bracing of her knees, momentarily wide apart, brought with it the pathetic ugliness of real flesh and also its attractiveness.

Ducane found that he had leaned forward and accepted the glass of whisky.

"That's right, Mr Honeyman. Now we can talk. Just a little talk and then I promise I'll go. We're getting to know each other, aren't we? Isn't that nice?"

"I wouldn't call it nice exactly," said Ducane. "Whatever it is, nice is not the word."

"Cheers, mister."

"Cheers, Judy."

"Now what shall we talk about? Let's talk about us." She stretched luxuriously, pointing her toes and lengthening out her mouth and eyes. Her shoulders twitched. Dappled shadows moved over her contracted stomach. Then she relaxed again.

"How did you get tied up with that devil McGrath?" asked Ducane. He was looking into his glass, but he could see the dark haze of her blue-black hair which seemed to move like a form upon golden waters.

"I was very young, Mr Honey. And he was somebody. I knew I could only marry a man who was somebody. He could make something of himself, Peter could. He's bright."

"Bright, yes. And he's made something of himself all right. He's made himself into a pretty promising crook, and he's made you into one too."

"Do you think I ought to leave him, Mr Honey?"

"No, of course not," said Ducane with exasperation. He forced himself to look at her. He tried to concentrate upon those very clear North Sea eyes. He apprehended that her face was not really dark but radiant, almost pale, beneath its shadowy honey-golden surface colour. Her body extended in a long gilded blur. Goya, Velazquez, aid me, he prayed. "I think you ought to persuade him to mend his ways before he lands both of you in prison. You wouldn't like it at all in prison, Judy." Oh God, I want to hurt her, he thought. Let her go away, just let her go away.

"I've got to leave him, Mr Honeyman, there isn't any other way. You know that. You know I can't make Peter change. I've got to leave him, Mr Honeyman, and you've got to help me." Her voice grew softer, coaxing.

Ducane stared into the supplicating blue eyes. Let me drown, he thought, so long as I see nothing else, feel nothing else. He said, "I'm afraid I can't help you, Judy. I've given you my advice. And now—"

"You can help me. Only you can help me. Only you can really save me, Mr Honey."

"Would you please stop calling me by that ridiculous name!" said Ducane. He turned his head stiffly, robot-like, and looked at the bathroom door.

"All right—dear—John."

Ducane stood up. "Now would you kindly get out?" He turned his back to her.

"In a minute, John, in a minute. Don't be cross with me. I know I've done wrong things and it wasn't all Peter's fault. Even before I met Peter I was—you know—with men. It just seemed natural. But I feel so different since I met you. You're the first man who—you're so different and good. You could save me, Mr John, and no one else could do it. I wouldn't ask anything except to know you and see you now and then, and you'd talk to me of things. You could make a difference to my whole life. And I'd do anything you liked, I'd learn something, anything. I'd become a, I don't know, a *nurse*—"

Ducane uttered a sound which might have been a laugh or might have been an exclamation of disgust. He was not sure himself which it was.

"Save me, John, sweetheart, help me. It's such a little thing for you, and such a big thing for me. You said yourself that if I stayed with Peter I'd end up in prison."

"I didn't actually," said Ducane. "But never mind. Put your clothes on."

"In a little minute, honey, John. John, you don't know

what it's like for a woman to be in despair. I'm afraid of Peter. I've no one to turn to. I haven't any friends and I only know men who are bad. People like you are safe. You're grand and everyone respects you and you have real friends. You can't sort of fall out of the bottom of the world. I'll have to leave Peter, I've just got to, and what will become of me then? Won't you be a friend to me, John, that's all I ask. Say you'll look after me a little, say you'll see me again, please say you'll see me again, just that little thing, please."

There was a whining edge to her voice. I mustn't pity her, thought Ducane. She thinks she's serious but she isn't. She would do me harm. I would do her harm. Do I see her as damned then? What does it matter what I see her as? I can do nothing for her. "I can do nothing for you," he said in a dull voice.

There was a silence. Judy said, "I'm so tired. I'll go soon." She gave a little groan and turned over on her face.

Ducane moved slowly round and regarded her. She lay prone, her face plunged into the pillow. With a sudden intensity of concentration he looked at her body, giving it the attention which he might have given, in some picture gallery far from home, to a masterpiece which he might never see again. Only this was not the gaze of contemplation.

Ducane allowed himself to realise his strong directed excitement. In fantasy he laid his hand down, very gently, upon the golden neck, beneath the dry crisp pile of dark hair, upon that particular hillock of the spine, and drew it very slowly downward, over the velvety hump of the shoulder, into the hollow of the back, which would move and shudder a little, along the glossy curve of the hip and then, more slowly still, over the firm strokeable rise of the buttock and on to the back of the thigh, which Ducane saw, as he moved now noiselessly closer to the bed, to be covered with a fleece of golden hair.

Suppose I were to fuck her? Ducane said to himself. This was a word which he never normally used, even in his thoughts, and its sudden occurrence now excited and shocked him. The word came again with the voice of Richard Biranne. Biranne had used the word, he felt sure, some time in their discussion. Well, suppose he were to? Ducane put his glass down very silently upon the bedside table. The girl was lying quite still, her face invisible, her breathing just perceptible in the faintest regular pressure upon the white sheet beneath her shadowed side. She might be asleep. Ducane's fantasy fingers stroked her body with a feathery creative touch, the light light touch of passion which conjures forth, to the last caressed detail, a presence of flesh. He leaned over her.

A faint smell arose from Judy's body. It was a not unpleasant smell, mingled of sweat and cosmetics. Ducane looked down between Judy's shoulder-blades. He saw a grey tumbled heap of dead pigeons. He opened his mouth and devoured the smell of Judy. He felt again the onrush of Luciferian lightness, and saw in Radeechy's handwriting, written across Judy's bare golden shoulders, the message *Do what thou wilt shall be the whole of law.*

At the same time Ducane felt perfectly cold. A cold watcher within him saw the scene and knew that he would not even with the most diffident or momentary gesture lay his hand upon the satiny golden back of Judy McGrath. He thought, she knows I will not touch her. She knows I will not, perhaps she conjectures I cannot. He put his hand down holding himself instead, restraining and comforting that which so much wanted Judy.

I am the perfect whited sepulchre, Ducane thought. I've fiddled and compromised with two women and been a failure with one and a catastrophe to the other. I am the cause that evil is in a man like McGrath. I cannot pity the wretched or bring hope or comfort to the damned. I cannot feel compassion for those over whom I imagine myself to be set as a judge. I cannot even take this girl in my arms. And that not because of duty or for her sake at all, but just because of my own conception of myself as spotless: my quaint idea of myself as good, which seems to go on being with me, however rottenly I may behave.

"Get up, Judy," said Ducane in a gentle voice, turning away from the bed. "Get up, child. Put your clothes on. Time to go home." He looked about the room. A white feathery heap lay beside one of the chairs. Judy's summer dress, patterned with green and blue flowers, hung over the back of the chair. Ducane picked up the pile of soft slithery perfumed underwear and hurled it on to the bed. Judy turned over and groaned.

"I'm going into the bathroom," said Ducane. "*Get dressed.*"

He went into the bathroom and locked the door. He used the lavatory. He sleeked back the thick locks of his dark hair and looked closely at his face in the mirror. His face was brown, shiny, oily. His eyes seemed to bulge and stare. He put out his tongue, large and spade-like. He could hear movements in the bedroom. There was a soft tap upon the door.

"I'm ready now," said Judy. She was dressed. The wisp of blue and green dress fitted her closely, sleekly. Her breasts, thought Ducane, oh her breasts. I might have touched them just for a moment. And he thought, how pretty she is with her clothes on. It was as if he had made love to her and now felt a calmer and more tender renewal of passion at seeing his mistress clothed.

He moved quickly past her and opened the bedroom door.

There was a quick flurry on the landing and Fivey retreated as far as the head of the stairs, hesitated, and then turned to face Ducane in the half light. Fivey, dressed in black trousers and a white shirt, looked like the leader of some Balkan revolution. He stood, a little self-consciously defiant, his huge head thrown back, his fingers slowly exploring one of his moustaches.

Ducane said, almost shouting now, "Fivey, how absolutely splendid, I'm so glad to see you're still up. You can get out the car and take this young lady home."

"Oh, but—" said Judy, shrinking back again into the room.

"Come on, out you go," said Ducane. Without touching her he walked round behind her and half ushered half shooed her out through the open door. He turned on the lights on the landing.

"Goodnight," said Ducane. "My man will drive you home. Go along, Fivey, go and get the car. Mrs McGrath will wait for you at the front door."

"Very good, Sir," said Fivey. With an air of nobility he descended the stairs.

"Go on down," said Ducane to Judy. "I won't come with you. Wait for Fivey at the door. He won't be a moment. Goodnight."

"You're not cross with me? You'll see me again? Please?"

"Goodnight, my child, goodnight," said Ducane, gesturing towards the stairs.

She passed him slowly and went on down. A minute later he heard the sound of the car and the closing of the front door.

Ducane went back into his bedroom and shut the door and locked it. He stood for a moment blankly. Then he lowered himself carefully on to the floor and lay there face downward with his eyes closed.

Thirty

"ISN'T it funny to think that the cuckoo is silent in Africa?" said Edward.

"Henrietta, have you taken that toad out of the bath?" said Mary.

"I wanted to tame him," said Henrietta. "People *can* tame toads."

"Have you taken him out of the bath?"

"Yes, he's back in the garden."

"Cuckoos can't perch on the ground," said Edward. "They have two claws pointing forward and two pointing backward. They just sit on the ground. I saw one yesterday, just after we saw the saucer—"

"Do bustle along, Edward. If you value *More Hunting Wasps* so highly, why do you cover it with marmalade?"

"Listen, he's changing his tune," said Edward. "Cuckoo in June changes his tune. Listen."

A distant hollow *cu-cuckoo cu-cuckoo* came through the open window of the kitchen.

"I wish it would rain," said Henrietta.

"Off you go, twins," said Mary, "and take Mingo with you. He's getting under my feet."

The twins went off in procession, Henrietta pushing her brother and Mingo following with a slow wag of his floppy tail for anyone who might be attending to him. Montrose, once more in curled luxurious possession of the basket, watched his departure and drowsed back to sleep. The cat was not an early riser.

"I expect we're getting under your feet too, darling," said Kate. "Come on, John, we'll go into the garden, shall we? What a heavenly morning. Gosh, it's good to be back!"

Kate picked up her Spanish basket and led the way across the untidy hall and out on to the lawn at the front of the house. The warm morning air enfolded them, thick and exotic after the cool of the house, full already of smells and textures which the hot sun, who had been shining for many hours although by human time it was still early morning,

254

had elicited from the leafy slopes and the quiet offered surface of the sea.

"Did you hear the old cuckoo this morning at about four o'clock?" said Kate. "I do hope he didn't wake you."

"I was awake anyway."

"We've had the longest day, haven't we? But midsummer just seems to go on and on."

"Midsummer madness."

"What?"

"Nothing. It's a crazy time of year."

"Beautifully crazy. I hope we didn't wake you coming in. I'm afraid Octavian made an awful row."

"No."

Ducane had come to Trescombe late the previous night, and later still Kate and Octavian had arrived back from Tangier. Today was Friday and Octavian had already had to set off for London to attend an urgent meeting.

"Poor Octavian, having to rush off like that," said Kate. "He hardly saw you at all."

"Mmmm."

"John, are you all right? You seem a bit down. Barbie said she thought you were ill or something. Nothing nasty happen when I was away?"

"No, nothing at all."

"Well, now I'm back I'll look after you and make you all plump and happy."

"Like Octavian."

"John, John, you are a grump this morning! You haven't even asked me about Tangier. Well, I shall tell you anyway. Oh what marvellous weather! I love this time of the morning in England when it's really hot. I tell you what I missed in Africa, the dew. I suppose there *is* dew in Africa. I must ask the twins. But everything was so *dusty*. Can you feel it now, the dew sort of jumping off the grass on to your ankles? It's so cooling. Well, of course you can't with your socks on. I can't think how you can bear to wear those heavy woolly socks in this weather. Why don't you wear sandals? Octavian wore sandals all the time in Tangier, they made him look so youthful. Here, let's sit down on this seat." She sat, spreading out the skirt of her red and white striped dress. Ducane, about to sit on the edge of the dress,

255

awkwardly thrust it aside.

The lawn in front of the house sloped to the leafy spiraea hedge, now in scattered points of raspberry-pink blossom. A gap in the hedge led to a small enclosed field of mown hay which fell steeply to a wood, over the top of which the sea was stretched out, filling the horizon with a silvery blue glitter. There was a strong murmuration of bees. In the deep dappled green of the wood birds called and fell about obscurely in the branches. Ducane sneezed.

"Bless you! I hope you don't mind the hay. It has a wonderfully *remindful* smell, somehow, hasn't it. Oh John, I *am* so glad to be back. One is, isn't one? I feel a bit tired though, in a nice way. The sun is tiring, don't you think. Look how brown I am. And Octavian's quite coffee coloured all over. Well, almost all over! When he wore that fez thing during the last week he looked just like that super eunuch in the *Entführung*. Oh, John, I've got a funny present for you, one of those charming Moroccan hats, I meant to bring it down, they make them in the villages."

"How kind of you."

"I just haven't managed to get around and *see* everyone yet. I hope everybody's all right? Nothing's happened here, has it? I thought somehow people were a bit nervy."

"Who's a bit nervy?"

"Well, you for instance."

"It's not that we're nervy, it's that you're relaxed. You've got vine-leaves in your hair. You're full of wine and olives and Mediterranean sunshine and—"

"Yes, yes. But after all you've had the sun too."

"It doesn't shine in my office in Whitehall."

"John, you're being childish. I believe you need a holiday. I must speak to Octavian about it. Oh look, isn't that a cuckoo, and there's another one chasing it."

Two hawk-like birds flitted out of the wood and doubled back to become invisible among the receding green hollows where the sun pierced the thick foliage. *Cu-cuckoo, cu-cuckoo.*

"Crazy birds," said Kate. "Do they think about nothing but sex? Chasing each other all day long and no responsibilities. Do you think they spend the nights together too?"

"Copulation is a daytime activity in birds," said Ducane, "At night they are quiet. Unlike human beings."

"I adore you when you sound so pedantic. Tell me, why are cuckolds called after cuckoos? That's one bit of ornithological information I can't ask the twins for!"

"Something to do with eggs in other people's nests, I suppose."

"Yes, but then the lover ought to be the cuckoo, not the husband."

"Maybe it's a past participle. Cuckoo-ed."

"How clever you are. You have a plausible answer for everything."

"True or otherwise."

"Yes, you are nervy, all of you. I must go round and *attend* to you, each one. See what happens when I go away! Everyone gets unhappy. I can't allow it! Even Mary was quite sharp with the twins this morning, so unlike her. And Paula looks positively hollow-eyed. She didn't seem at all pleased when I handed her that letter from Aden. And Barbie's in one of her antisocial moods and won't consort with anyone who isn't a pony, and Pierce is *impossible*. Mary told me some extraordinary story about his kidnapping Montrose."

"He behaved very badly," said Ducane, "but it's all over now." He kicked the strewn sheets of mown hay at his feet and sneezed again.

"You sound just like a schoolmaster. I'm not going to lecture Pierce. Anyway I expect you and Mary have already done so. I think Barbie is being horrid to him. And then there's Theo. I've never seen him looking so morose. When I said hello to him this morning he just looked through me. Why, there he is now going down the path. I bet you he'll pretend not to notice us."

A gap at the far end of the spiraea hedge led into the kitchen garden and from it a path led down beside the line of ragged hawthorns towards the wood. It was the most direct route from the house to the sea. Theo was walking very slowly, almost uncertainly, down the path.

"Theo!" Ducane shouted. His tone was peremptory and angry.

Theo paused and turned slowly round to look at them. He looked at them with the vague face of one who, on his way to the scaffold, hears his name distantly hallooed in the crowd.

"Theo!" Kate cried.

Theo eyed them. Then he lifted his arm a little, moving it awkwardly as if it were paralysed below the elbow. His hand made a floppy gesture which might have been a wave and might have been an invitation to go to the devil. He continued his slow shuffling toward the wood.

"Poor Theo," said Kate. "I think he's upset about Mary and Willy, don't you?"

"You mean he feels he's losing Willy? Possibly. I suspect Willy's the only person Theo really communicates with."

"Heaven knows what they find to say to each other! I'm so glad about Mary and Willy, it's so *right*. It's not exactly an impetuous match, but then they're not exactly an impetuous pair. I do think they're both deeply wise people. And Mary's so sweet."

"She's more than sweet," said Ducane. "Willy's lucky."

"He's very lucky and I shall go up and tell him so before lunch. It was a good idea of mine, wasn't it, matching those two. It keeps them both here."

"You think so?" said Ducane. "It wouldn't surprise me if they both went away."

"Oh no no no no. Whatever would we do without Mary? Besides, no one is to leave. You are all my dear—children."

"Slaves."

"You are a sour-puss today! Now if only we could find some really nice man for Paula. He'd have to be terribly intellectual of course. We'd have to build another house I suppose. Mary and Willy will be in the cottage. Well, Octavian did think of building another bungalow up by the graveyard, it wouldn't show from the house. Only I do like having us all under one roof. Do you know, I used to be so afraid that *you'd* fall for Paula. She's so much cleverer than me. I was quite anxious!"

"I adore Paula," said Ducane. "I respect and admire her. One couldn't not. But—"

"But what?"

"She isn't you."

"Darling, you *are* eloquent today. Oh look, there go the twins going down to bathe. Twins! I say! Do find Uncle Theo and cheer him up. He's just gone into the wood."

Trailing their white bathing towels along the dulled

prickly green of the hedge, the twins waved and went on, followed by prancing darting Mingo, who uttered at intervals not his sea-bark but his rabbit-bark.

"Those are the only two really satisfactory human beings in our household," said Ducane.

"You *are* severe with us! Yes, the twins are super. Fab, as Barbie would say. It's sad to think they'll have to grow up and become tiresome creatures like Barb and Pierce."

"Sexual creatures you mean. Yes, we are tiresome."

"*You* are tiresome. Well, now let me tell you all about Tangier. It was perfectly extraordinary seeing all those women wearing veils. And they wear their veils in so many different ways. Or should one say 'the veil' like one says 'the kilt'? It wasn't always becoming, I assure you. And there was this extraordinary market place—"

"I've been to Tangier," said Ducane.

"Oh all right, I *won't* tell you!"

Kate, who was always delighted to go on holiday, was always delighted to come back. She loved the people who surrounded her and felt a little thrill at the special sense, on her return, of their need for her, a tiny spark as at the resuming of an electrical connection. She was glad to be missed and prized that first second at which she, as it were, experienced being missed. This time, however, as she had already expressed to John, things seemed just a bit out of gear. Her people seemed preoccupied, almost too preoccupied to rejoice as they ought to at her reappearance and romp gleefully about her. She decided, I must go round and *visit* everyone, I must have a *tête-à-tête* with everyone, even Theo. She felt like a doctor. The thought restored her to good humour.

Not that she was exactly out of humour. But she had felt, ever since the cuckoo woke her from a short sleep soon after four, an uneasiness, a sense of jarring. She later traced this unusual sensation to its origin in the presence of Ducane, indeed in the consciousness of Ducane. If the others were out of sorts she could cure them. She was aware of what she called their nerviness as something separate from herself upon which she could operate externally. But John's depression, his tendency to be 'horrid', affected her intimately. Things between herself and John were for the moment, for the moment only, dislocated and out of tune. Kate reflected rather ruefully that she thought she knew very well what it was that caused this momentary disharmony. She only hoped that John did not know it too.

Kate had certainly had a splendid fortnight in Tangier. What she did not propose to explain was that she had spent a very large part of this fortnight in bed with Octavian. Hot climates affected Octavian like that. Indeed, she had to admit, they affected her like that. After a long and vinous lunch they had positively *hurried* back to the hotel each day. Octavian could hardly wait. It amused Kate to think that if Ducane knew this he would probably be not only jealous but shocked. We're as bad as those cuckoos, she thought to herself, only of course we're monogamous and good, while they're polygamous and bad! It was true that she was plump and brown and healthy and energetic and relaxed, just as John had said, full of wine and olives and Mediterranean sunshine and—Was it possible that John *knew*? He must have missed her terribly. And now on her return, at that electrical moment of resuming contact, he might especially resent her belonging to another and somehow sense in her that luxurious belongingness. He can sort of smell it, she thought. Then she wondered, perhaps he can literally smell it? Was this scientifically possible? She must ask—well, no, that was another piece of scientific information for which she could hardly ask the twins.

Kate laughed aloud.

"What is it?" said Ducane.

How peevish he sounded today. "Nothing, nothing. I was just thinking about those dogs. Never mind, I don't think their antics are fit for your ears. I haven't the vocabulary anyway, I'd have to draw it!"

Ducane did not seem disposed to pursue the matter of the dogs. He began pounding his nose with his handkerchief, staring straight ahead of him into the wood. The sex-mad cuckoos darted past again with their irregular side-slipping flight. *Cu-cuckoo.*

He looks his least attractive at this time of year, Kate was thinking. He murders his poor nose so, it's quite red, and his eyes are always watering. He doesn't look a bit like the Duke of Wellington now. His face is a nice colour, though, that reddish brown, and so glossy and shiny where the bones stick out, I think he's got even thinner. It suits him actually. How oily his hair looks, it darkens it like black rats' tails; I expect it's the heat, perspiration perhaps. Poor fellow, he is sweating. Why does he wear that ridiculous flannel shirt on a day like this? I must give him a nylon one.

We're out of key, she thought. I'm *clumsy* with him today. But it'll pass. Just being silent together like this helps. I knew from the start that I'd have to work at this. Men are so obtuse, they don't understand that one has to work at a relationship. If things aren't quite in harmony they get grumpy and desperate at once. I can't possibly kiss him yet. He doesn't desire me, she said to herself, *at the moment* he doesn't desire me. How does one know? Then she thought, and I don't desire him. But this cloud between us will pass. We must just get quietly used to each other again. I won't fuss him or press him. I'll just leave him to himself a little and attend to something else.

She said aloud, "John, do you mind if I just glance through my letters to see there's nothing awful? There's always such a pile when one gets back from holiday, it's quite a chore. I've got them all here in the basket and if you don't mind I'll just sort them out. You stay here if you like, or perhaps you'd rather walk down to the sea. You might meet Barbie coming back from her ride."

Kate up-ended the Spanish basket and strewed about thirty letters about on the dry pale yellow mats of the hay. She leaned forward and began turning them over and laying them out in rows.

Ducane, suddenly interested, leaned forward too, inspecting the letters. Then with a soft hiss he reached out a long arm and snatched up a brown envelope which lay at the end of one of the rows. Fingering the letter he turned to face Kate, frowning and narrowing his blue eyes against the sun. The frown made his face look even bonier and thinner, a wooden totem anointed with oil.

Kate felt a sudden slight alarm. He looked so stern; and her first thought was, he's jealous of someone. Who can it be? He's recognized someone's writing. Kate, who was on very affectionate terms with a number of men, preferred for humane reasons to keep her friends in ignorance of each other. However, the writing upon the envelope, a rather uncultured hand as far as she could see, seemed unfamiliar.

"What is it?" she said playfully. "You're stealing my mail!" She reached out for the letter but Ducane withdrew it.

"Whatever is it, John?"

"Will you do me a great favour?" said Ducane.

"Well, tell me what it is."

"Don't read this letter."

Kate looked at him with surprise. "Why?"

"Because it contains something unpleasant which I think you shouldn't see."

"What sort of thing?"

"It's—it's something concerning me and another person. Something that belongs entirely to the past. A malicious busybody has written to you about it. But there is absolutely no point in your reading the letter. I will tell you about the whole thing myself later on, now if you wish it."

Kate had turned sideways and they faced each other knee to knee. The hem of the striped dress brushed the hay. She did not know what to think. She was still a bit alarmed by Ducane's sternness, though relieved to find that the misdemeanour in question appeared to be his rather than hers. She thought, perhaps it's to say that he was once a homosexual. He might not understand that I wouldn't mind. She felt very curious about the letter.

"But if it's to do with the past and you're going to tell me anyway, why shouldn't I see the letter? What harm can it do?"

"It's better not to touch pitch. A really malicious letter should be read once only and destroyed, or best of all not read at all. These things lodge in the mind. One must have no truck with suspicion and hatred. Please let me destroy this letter, Kate, *please*."

"I don't understand," said Kate. "This letter, whatever it says, can do you no possible harm with me. How little you trust me! Nothing can harm or diminish my love for you. Surely you know that."

"It's a sense datum," said Ducane, "a sense datum. It's something which you would find it hard to forget. Such things can be poisonous, however much love there is. I am to blame, Kate. But I would rather explain the thing to you myself in my own way. Surely you can appreciate that."

"No, I can't appreciate it," said Kate. She had moved forward so that their knees were touching. "And I don't know what you mean by a 'sense datum'. It's much better that I should read the letter. Otherwise I shall be endlessly wondering what was in it. Give it to me."

"No."

Kate drew away a little and laughed. "Aren't you rather taxing my feminine curiosity?"

"I'm asking you to rise above your feminine curiosity."

"Dear me, we are moral today. John, have some common sense! I'm dying to know what it's all about! It can't possibly harm you. I love you, you ass!"

"I'll tell you what it's all about. I just don't want you to see this ugly thing."

"I'm not as frail as all that!" said Kate. She snatched the letter from him and stood up, retreating behind the wooden seat.

Ducane looked up at her gloomily, and then leaned forward to hide his face in his hands. He remained immobile in this attitude of resigned or desperate repose.

Kate was now very upset. She hesitated, fingering the letter, but her curiosity was too strong. She opened it.

There were two enclosures. The first read as follows:

Dear Madam,
in view of your emotional feelings about Mr John Ducane I feel sure it would be of interest to you to see the enclosed.
Yours faithfully,
A Well Wisher

The second enclosure was an envelope addressed to Ducane, with a letter inside it. Kate pulled out the letter.

My dearest, my dearest, my John, this is just my usual daily missive to tell you what you know, that I love you to distraction. You were so infinitely sweet to me yesterday after I had been so awful, and you know how unutterably grateful I am that you *stayed*. I lay there on the bed afterwards for an hour and cried—with gratitude. Are we not somehow compelled by love? I shall not let one day pass without giving you the assurance of mine. Surely there is a future for us together. I am yours yours yours
Jessica

Kate looked at the date on the letter. She felt sick, stricken, as if some heavy black thing had been rammed into her stomach. She clutched the back of the seat, turned as if to sit down, and then moved a little away and sat down on the grass, covering her face.

"Well?" said Ducane after a while.

Kate found a rather shaky voice. "I think I see now what you mean by a sense datum."

"I'm sorry," said Ducane. He sounded quite calm now, only rather weary. "There's not much I can say. You were sure it couldn't damage things and I can only hope you were right."

"But you said it belonged to the past—"

"So it does. I'm not having a love affair with this girl, though the letter makes it sound as if I am. I ceased being her lover two years ago, and was unwise enough to go on seeing her."

Kate said in a forced voice, "But of course you can see whom you like, do what you like. You know I don't tie you in any way. How could I? I'm just a bit surprised that you sort of—misled me—"

"Lied to you. Yes." Ducane got up. He said, "I think I'd better go now. You'll just have to digest it, Kate, if you can. I've acted wrongly and I have in a way deceived you. I mean, I implied I had no entanglements and this certainly looks like one. I'm sorry."

"You're not going back to London?"

"No, I don't think so."

"Oh John, what's happening?"

"Nothing, I daresay."

"Won't you—at least—explain?"

"I'm sick of explaining, Kate. I'm sick of myself." He went quickly away through the gap in the spiraea hedge.

On her knees Kate slowly gathered up the scattered letters and put them back in the Spanish basket. Tears dropped off her sun-warmed cheeks on to the dry hay. The bird in the wood cried out, hesitant and hollow, *cu-cuckoo*, *cu-cuckoo*.

Thirty-one

"THERE'S going to be a Happening," Pierce announced to anyone who was listening.

Saturday lunch was over. Ducane and Mary and Theo still sat at the table smoking cigarettes. Kate and Octavian had retired to the sofa and were talking in low voices. Paula and the twins had gone out on to the lawn where the twins were now playing Badgerstown. Barbara was sitting on the window seat reading *Country Life*. Pierce was standing in a poised ballet dancer's attitude near the kitchen door.

"What sort of happening, dear?" asked Mary.

"Something violent, something awful."

Barbara continued to be absorbed in her article.

"You've already done something violent, something awful," said Ducane. "I think you should be content with your career of crime."

"Violent to yourself, or to someone else?" Theo asked, interested.

"Wait and see."

"Oh you are *boring*," said Barbara. She threw the magazine down and went quickly out on to the front lawn. A moment or two later she was laughing loudly with the twins.

Pierce sat down on the window seat and started looking hard into the copy of *Country Life*. He was flushed and looked as if he might burst into tears. The three at the table began to talk promptly about something else. After a minute Mary got up and said something inaudible to Pierce who shook his head. She went on into the kitchen. Ducane stubbed out his cigarette and followed her. He was unutterably oppressed by the confederate presence of Kate and Octavian.

"Can I help you at all, Mary? You're not going to wash up, are you?"

"No. Casie will do it. She's just gone to the kitchen garden to see if there are any artichokes for tonight. They're so early this year. I'm taking some raspberries up to Willy."

"May I come?"

"Yes, of course."

She doesn't want me, he thought. Well, I'll just go as far as the cottage. Where can I put myself now?

The dark shut-in velvety smell of the raspberries hung over the kitchen table. Mary put a white cloth over the basket, and they went out of the back door and began to walk up the pebble path beside the herbaceous border. It was very hot. Big orange furry bees were clambering laboriously into the antirrhinums. A little flock of goldfinches which had been searching for seeds along the foot of the brick wall took refuge among the broad pale leaves of the catalpa tree.

"Look at those thistles! It's easy to see the gardener's on holiday. I really must do some weeding. Casie hates it."

"I'll do some weeding."

"Don't be silly, John. You're on holiday down here. Kate would faint if she saw you weeding. Aren't you awfully hot in that shirt?"

"No, well, I rather like to be in a bath of perspiration."

"I wish you'd talk to Pierce."

"You mean—?"

"Tell him to grit his teeth a little about Barb. He will go on annoying her and annoying all of us. I know it's awful, but he must just face it. I keep trying to persuade him to go and stay with the Pember-Smiths. They even have a yacht!"

"If you can't persuade him how can I?"

"I've got no authority. You have. You could speak to him sternly. Ever since you hit him he's devoted to you! I told you he would be."

"Well, I'll have a try."

"Bless you. And I do wish you'd have a serious talk with Paula too. She's awfully upset about *something*, and she won't tell me what, though I've positively asked her. She'd tell you. She's terribly fond of you and you've got authority with her too, well you have with all of us. Just corner her and ask her firmly what it's all about."

"I'm very fond of her," said Ducane. "I suppose I—"

"Good. And don't take no for an answer. You're marvellous, John. I rely on you absolutely. I don't know what we'd do without you."

"Oh Christ," said Ducane.

The effect of Jessica's letter had been to draw Kate and

Octavian together in a new way, a way new at least to Ducane. He had never felt sexual jealousy of Octavian before. He felt it now. He had no doubt that his faithlessness had been revealed and discussed. Of course Octavian said nothing. He went about the house smiling inscrutably and looking more than ever like a fat golden Buddha. Kate had avoided seeing Ducane alone. He had the impression that she was completely bewildered about her own feelings. Possibly she would have welcomed an effort, a desperate effort, on Ducane's part to explain, to excuse himself, to wrap up in a web of talk and emotion that so disastrous sense datum. But Ducane, who could not bring himself to return to London, could not bring himself to talk to Kate either. He also felt that he ought not to talk to her, though he was not too sure why. He was aware that his refusal to explain now, and his inability to explain at the time, probably made the thing look graver and weightier than it was.

Yet was it not grave and weighty enough? He had made it seem a small matter by deliberately chilling his own feelings and dimming his own thoughts while *permitting* Jessica to continue in the fantasy world of her wishes. It was easy to see now that it had been wrong. In receiving the force of Jessica's sense of possession Kate was scarcely receiving a wrong picture. Jessica's condition was a fact. And if Kate retained the impression that he and Jessica were still lovers, or practically lovers, this was not a completely false impression.

When McGrath had rung Ducane up at the office, Ducane had of course told him to go to the devil. Their conversation had lasted about forty seconds. Ducane had meanwhile been trying desperately to get in touch with Jessica. He had telephoned her ten times, and sent several notes and a telegram asking her to ring him. He had called three times at the flat and got no answer. This from Jessica who, as he knew with a special new pain now, had been used to sit at home continually in the hope that he would write or ring. The feelings with which he turned away from her door strangely resembled a renewal of being in love. He had had, after the third telephone call, no doubt that she had been the first recipient of McGrath's malice; and it had occurred to him to wonder whether she might not have killed herself. An image of Jessica in her shift, pale and elongated, stretched out upon the bed, one stiffening arm trailing to the ground, accompanied him from the locked door and reappeared in his dreams. However, he did not on reflection really think this likely. There had always been a grain of petulance in Jessica's love. A saving egoism would make her detest him now. It was a very sad thought.

His thoughts of Jessica, though violent, were all as it were in monochrome. His imagination had to fight to picture her clearly. It was as if she had become a disembodied ailment which attacked his whole substance. Very different were Ducane's thoughts about Judy McGrath. He remembered the scene in his bedroom with hallucinatory vividness, and seemed to remember it all the time, as if it floated constantly rather high up in his field of vision like the dazzling lozenge which conveys the presence of the Trinity to the senses of some bewildered saint. With a large part of himself he wished that he had made love to Judy. It would have been an honest action, something within him judged; although something else in him knew that this bizarre opinion must be wrong. When one falls into falsehood all one's judgments are dislocated. It was only given this, and given that, and given the other, all of them things which ought not to be the case, that it could seem plausible to judge that making love to Judy would have been an honest action. There is a logic of evil, and Ducane felt himself enmeshed in it. But the beautiful stretched-out body of Judy, its apricot colour, its glossy texture, its *weight*, continued to haunt him with a tormenting precision and a dreadfully localised painfulness.

And this is the moment, Ducane thought to himself, in this sort of degrading muddle, in this demented state of mind, when I am called upon to be another man's judge. He had been thinking constantly about Biranne too, or rather a ghostly Biranne travelled with him, transparent and crowding him close. The wraith did not accuse him, but hovered before him, a little to the right, a little to the left, becoming at times a sort of *alter ego*. Ducane did not see how he could let Biranne off. The idea of ruining him, of wrecking his career, of involving him in disgrace and despair, was so dreadful that Ducane kept, with an almost physical movement, putting it away from him. But there was no alternative and Ducane knew that, in a little while though not yet, he must make himself into that cold judicial machine which was the only relevant and important thing. Radeechy's confession could not be suppressed. It was the completely clear and satisfactory solution to the mystery which Ducane had been briefed to solve. In any case, and quite apart from the enquiry, a murder ought not to be concealed, and it was one's plain duty not to conceal it. Since these considerations were conclusive, Ducane could be more coolly aware of the danger to himself which would be involved in any concealment. Ducane did not care for guilty secrets, and he did not want to share one with Biranne, a man whom he neither liked nor trusted. And there was also the hovering presence of McGrath, who might know more than Biranne imagined. Ducane knew that if it emerged later that he had suppressed that very important document he would be ruined himself.

"Are you all right, John?"

They had walked up the lane in silence. The variety of willow herb which is known as 'codlins and cream' filled the narrow closed-in lane with its sickly smell. A wren with uplifted tail moved in the brown darkness of the hedge, accompanying them up the hill.

"I'm fine," said Ducane in a slightly wild voice. "It's just that I have bad dreams."

"Do you mean dreams at night, or thoughts?"

"Both."

Ducane had dreamed last night that he had killed some woman, whose identity he could not discover, and was attempting to hide the body under a heap of dead pigeons when he was detected by a terrifying intruder. The intruder was Biranne.

"Tell me about them," said Mary.

Why do I always have to be helping people, thought Ducane, and getting no help myself? I wish someone could help me. I wish Mary could. He said, "It's all someone else's secret."

"Sit down here a minute." They had reached the wood. Mary sat down on the fallen tree trunk and Ducane sat beside her. He began hacking away with his foot at some parchment-coloured fungus which was growing in wavy layers underneath the curve of the tree. The delicate brown undersides of the fungus, finely pleated as a girl's dress lay fragmented upon the dry beach leaves. Along the bank beside them a pair of bullfinches foraged ponderously in the small jungle of cow parsley and angelica.

"Have you quarrelled with Kate?" asked Mary. She did not look at him. She had put the basket on the ground and regarded it, rocking it slightly with a brown sandalled foot.

She is observant, he thought. Well, it must be fairly obvious. "Yes. But that's not really—not all."

"Kate will soon come round, you know she will, she'll mend things. She always does. She loves you very much. What's the other thing, the rest?"

"I have to make a decision about somebody."

"A girl?"

Her question slightly surprised him. "No, a man. It's a rather important decision which affects this person's whole life, and I feel particularly rotten about having to make it as I'm feeling at the moment so—jumbled and immoral."

"Jumbled and immoral." Mary repeated this curious phrase as if she knew exactly what it meant. "But you know *how* to make the decision, I mean you know the machinery of the decision?"

"Yes. I know how to make the decision."

"Then shouldn't you just think about the decision and not about yourself? Let the machinery work and keep it clear of the jumble?"

"You are perfectly right," he said. He felt extraordinarily calmed by Mary's presence. In a curious way he was pleased that she had not disputed his self-accusation but had simply given him the correct reply. She assured him somehow of the existence of a permanent moral background. He thought, she is under the same orders as myself. He found that he had picked up the hem of Mary's dress and was moving it between his fingers. She was wearing a mauve dress of crêpe-like wrinkled stuff with a full skirt. As he felt the material he thought suddenly of Kate's red striped dress and of Judy's dress with the blue and green flowers. Girls and their dresses.

He said quickly, letting go of the hem, "Mary, I hope

you won't mind my saying how very glad I am about you and Willy."

"Nothing's—fixed, you know."

"Yes, I know. But I'm so glad. Give my love to Willy. I won't delay you now and I think I won't come any further."

"All right. You will talk to Paula, won't you, and to Pierce?"

"Yes. I'll do it straightaway. Whichever of them I meet first!"

They stood up. Mary turned her lean sallow head towards him, brushing back her hair. Her eyes were vague in the hot dappled half light. They stood a moment awkwardly, and then with gestures of salutation parted in silence.

Thirty-two

"WHAT are you doing in there, Mary?"
　　　"Washing up, Willy."
"Don't—I'll do it later. Come and talk to me."
"I've put the raspberries in a bowl. I've put some sugar on them. We might eat them for tea."
"We might."
Meals with Willy were still rare, strange, like a picnic, like a eucharist.

Mary came back into the sitting-room wiping her hands on the drying-up cloth. The heat in the room made a kind of positive velvety silence in which one moved slowly as if swimming.

Willy was stretched out in his armchair beside the hearth. The front of his shirt was open to the waist revealing a curly mat of grey hair which looked like a shaggy undergarment. He had dug his fingers into the mat and was scratching abstractedly. Mary placed a chair between him and the table and sat down, putting one hand on his shoulder. It was not like a caress, but more like the firm grasping of something loved yet inanimate, like the steering wheel of a car.

"Is Paula coming for the *Aeneid*? I'm so glad you persuaded her to read."
"No, she scratched today."
"How far have you got?"
"Book six."
"What's happening?"
"Aeneas has descended to the underworld."
"And what's he doing there?"
"He has just met the shade of his helmsman Palinurus. Palinurus fell asleep and fell off the stern of the ship and was drowned. As his body is unburied Charon will not carry him across the Styx. But he is told that the people near to where he died will establish a tomb and a cult in his memory, and the region will bear his name. This news cheers the poor fellow up more than somewhat!"

Willy's singsong recital oppressed Mary's heart. She said, "Do you think everyone ought to descend at some time to the underworld?"

"You mean in search of wisdom or something?"

"Yes."

"Certainly not! It's very dark and stuffy and one is more likely to feel frightened than to learn anything. Let the schoolroom of life be a light airy well-lighted place!"

Mary remembered the squealing brakes and the awful cry. She ought to tell all this to Willy. Since she had told John she ought to tell Willy. Only he couldn't make it easy the way John could. And she knew that today she was to be clumsy with him and denuded of grace.

She said, "Do you think you learnt anything in that place?"

"In Dachau? Certainly. I learnt how to keep warm by rubbing myself against a wall, how to be almost invisible when the guards came round, how to have very *very* long sexual fantasies—"

"Sorry. I'm being stupid."

"No, you're not, my dear. But very few ordeals are redemptive and I doubt if the descent into hell teaches anything new. It can only hasten processes which are already in existence, and usually this just means that it degrades. You see, in hell one lacks the energy for any good change. This indeed is the meaning of hell."

"I suppose at any rate it shows one what one is."

"Sometimes not even that. After all, what is one? We are shadows, Mary, shadows."

"I'm sure *you* were not degraded."

"Come, come, this is gloomy talk for a lovely girl on a lovely day."

"Willy, will you teach me German again—later on?"

"If you wish it, my child. But why bother about learning German? It's not very important. Almost anything is more important than learning German."

"But I can't share anything with you," she said, "your memories, your language, your music, your work, nothing. I'm just—I'm just—a woman."

"A woman. But isn't that everything?"

"No, it isn't."

She got up and went over to the window. The window ledge was dusty and a dead fly, suspended on a spider's thread, hung motionless against the glass of the open casement. Mary thought, I must clean the place. The Swiss binoculars, their grey leather shafts veneered with dust, lay upon the ledge and Mary lifted them absently. In the magic circle she saw the edge of the sea, the little whitish ripple curling against the dry stones. Then there were two big dark hunched-up figures. They were Ducane and Paula, sitting just beside the water, deep in talk. Mary put the glasses down irritably.

"Mary."

"Yes, Willy."

"Come back here."

She came back, vague, uneasy, and standing over him thrust her fingers into his white silky hair at the centre of the brow.

"Mary, I can never marry you, I can never marry anybody."

Mary's fingers stiffened. Then she drew them back through the fine hair and moved them over his brow, spreading the light perspiration with her fingertips. "That's all right, Willy."

"Forgive me, my dear."

"It's all right. I'm sorry I bothered you."

"You haven't bothered me. You've done me ever so much good. You've made me twice as much alive."

"I'm glad—"

"I'm eating so much now. I shall get as fat as Octavian."

"I'm glad. I wish Kate hadn't talked so much about us though."

"It'll blow over. We shall be as before."

"Theo will be glad. He thought he'd lost you."

"Theo is an ass."

"We shall be as before." She caressed his brow, staring over his head at the bookshelves. She did not want to be as before. She wanted great changes in her life. She grappled clumsily with a great obscure pain which had risen up in front of her like a bear.

"Mary, I love you. Don't be hurt by me."

"I can't help being hurt—" she said.

"Cheer up. I can't give you anything but love, baby, that's the only thing I've plenty of, baby."

"Don't, Willy. I'm sorry I disturbed things as they were. I've been a fool."

"You've been a divine fool and you've disturbed nothing."

"It's this interminable summer. I wish it would end. Sorry, I'm talking nonsense."

"You need a holiday."

"Yes, I need a holiday."

"I think I shall get away myself, go to London maybe."

"That's right."

What has happened, thought Mary. She moved away, coming apart from him with a kind of horror, as if a human limb were to break off, softly, easily, in a dream. She knew that a certain joy which she had taken in him might never come to her again, the joy of veiled anticipation and purpose. Some precious ambiguous possibility, which would have remained intact for ever, had been taken from them.

"What ees eet?"

"I'm sorry, Willy, I'm terribly sorry."

Tears came to her now, wrapping her whole head in a quick storm. To hide them she moved to the window and picked up the binoculars again, blinking the tears away. She stared unseeingly into a bright circle of light. Then after a moment her grip on the glasses tightened. "Willy, something perfectly extraordinary is going on down there."

Thirty-three

"PAULA."

"Oh, hello, John."

"May I walk along with you?"

"Yes, surely."

"Where are the twins?"

"Out swimming with Barbie. That's them out there."

Three heads bobbed far out in the calm sea over which the afternoon sun had laid a shallow golden haze. Two natives accompanied by a spaniel clumped noisily over the pebbles. Montrose, an immobile fluffy ball upon the breakwater, watched the spaniel pass with slit-eyed malevolence. In the further distance Pierce and Mingo were standing by the water's edge.

"Shall we sit down?"

They sat on the hot stones, Paula pulling her yellow dress well down to her knees. Ducane's hand dug instinctively into the pebbles, seeking the damp cooler stones below. "Do you mind?" He took off his jacket.

"Odd how those stones are never *quite* spherical." Paula spoke in her most precise tones, sounding like one of her children. She examined a mottled mauvish pebble and then tossed it into the water.

He's in the Red Sea, now, she thought, he's steaming north. An enormous elongated Eric, all face and head, moved slowly under steam through a calm resistless sea. I must be completely relaxed, she thought. I must have no will, no purpose, I must simply *undergo* him.

I'll meet him in London, she thought. But would he want to share her bed? How would it be? Perhaps it would be better to see him down here? But she could not bear that he should come near the twins. I must be rational, she thought, I must be rational.

"Paula—"

"Sorry. Were you saying something?"

"What's the matter, Paula? And don't say nothing's the matter. I can see you're frantic about something."

"Nothing's the matter."

"Come, come, Paula. Everyone has been noticing it. Tell me what's the matter. I might be able to help."

So everyone had been noticing it. "You can't, John. I'm as lonely as a lunatic."

"Paula. You're going to tell me."

Am I? she wondered almost vaguely. She picked up and examined another imperfectly spherical stone and tossed it after the first one.

"Paula, please, my dear—"

"If I could only tell it all in a completely cold objective way," she said aloud to herself.

"Yes, yes, do that. You can. What's it about? Just tell me roughly what it's about, to make a start."

"It's about a chap called Eric Sears."

"Who is he?"

"My former lover."

"Oh."

"You probably imagine, as everybody seems to, that I divorced Richard. Well, I didn't. Richard divorced me because I had had a love affair with Eric."

"Did you love Eric?"

"I must have done."

"Do you love Eric?"

"No, I don't think so."

"Are you seeing him?"

"I'm going to. He's on his way back from Australia to see me, to *claim* me."

"You don't have to be claimed if you don't want to."

"It's—more complicated than that."

"You're bound to him in some way?"

"Yes."

"A child?"

"No, no. It's awful. I couldn't tell you."

"But you're going to tell me."

"It was how things happened with Richard."

"I imagine Richard had had plenty of love affairs before Eric came on the scene?"

"Yes. That's what they say, is it? Yes, Richard was unfaithful. But that doesn't excuse my unfaithfulness. It doesn't even explain it. I was temporarily insane."

"What's Eric like? What does he do?"

"He's a potter. He's a big blonde man with a beard. At least he had a beard. He's a demon."

"How was it that things happened with Richard."

Paula took a deep breath. She felt her face contract as if a great wind were straining the flesh backward. She said, "They had a fight."

Paula was conscious of the immense quietness of the scene. The sun shone down into clear still water revealing the pale paving of the sea. Very distant feet crunched upon pebbles. Far away an aeroplane hummed, descended. Out on the horizon the swimming children splashed, their voices all but lost in the hot air which moved very slightly above the water like a heavy canopy. "What happened?" said Ducane's voice, very very softly.

"It was quite sudden," she said. "It was at our house, in the billiard room. You know, well perhaps you don't know, at our house in Chelsea there's a big room for billiards built on at the back. Richard used to play a bit. It had a door leading into the garden. It was late one night and Richard had said he'd got to go to Paris on office business. I think he said this just to trap me. Of course I'd told him about Eric. I'd told him about Eric right at the start, in a cold blank sort of way, and he was cold and blank about it too. I didn't even properly realise that he was jealous. I thought it might even be a kind of relief to him. Eric came round to the house that evening. It was idiotic of me to let him come there, but he very much wanted to. He hadn't been before. I think he just wanted to walk around in Richard's place. We were talking in the hall. I think we were just going to leave and go to Eric's flat. Then we realised that Richard had come in through the garden and was standing in the billiard room in the darkness listening. As soon as I heard a sound I knew what had happened and I turned the light on. Eric and Richard had never met before. We all stood together in the billiard room and Eric started to make some sort of speech. He wasn't particularly put out and he was proposing to carry off the situation with a high hand. Then Richard just sprang at him. Eric's a big man, but Richard was in the Commandos, and he just knew how to fight and Eric didn't. He hit Eric somehow on the neck and I think Eric was half stunned. Then, God knows how he did it, and it happened so quickly, he pushed Eric back against the wall and overturned the billiard table against him."

"My God," said Ducane softly.

"You know what a billiard table weighs," said Paula. Her voice was almost pedantic. Her gaze was focused on a particular pebble on the floor of the sea. "The edge of the table came down on to one of Eric's feet, and the upper part of it crushed him against the wall. He began to scream. Richard and I tried to pull the table back. It was an extraordinary scene. We didn't say a word to each other, we just pulled at each end of the table. Eric went on screaming. Then the table shifted a little and he collapsed and Richard pulled him out into the open. He was practically unconscious with pain. I went and telephoned for an ambulance."

Paula was silent.

"What happened then?" said Ducane in the same almost whispering voice.

"I went with him to the hospital. The next time I saw Richard was outside the divorce court."

"And was Eric much hurt?"

"He hadn't any serious internal injury," said Paula in her exact voice. "But one foot was completely crushed. He had to have it amputated." She added, "We pretended it was an accident, of course."

Ducane said after a pause. "I see. What happened then?"

"Well, what happened then was that I abandoned Eric too. I couldn't go back to Richard, the idea didn't occur to me, and anyway he wrote to me about divorce the next day. I think he just couldn't stand it either, somehow. And I couldn't stay with Eric. His being maimed like that by Richard just snapped things off. I almost hated the sight of him, and I think he hated the sight of me. For a while everything became too terrible, one could scarcely bear to be conscious. I let go of Eric and he just moved away, sort of automatically. I went on seeing him, but it was like acting in some nightmarish play. Then he told me he was going to Australia. We were both relieved."

"And then—?"

"And then he wrote from there to say he'd met somebody

perfectly marvellous on the boat and was going to marry her. I was jolly relieved. Then I heard nothing till about four weeks ago when he wrote to say he hadn't got married after all and that the only thing he needed and wanted in the world was to see me and he was coming back. His boat's due next week."

"You're frightened of him," said Ducane.

"Yes. I always was a bit frightened of him. Funny, I was never frightened of Richard, though Richard's a violent man in a much more obvious way."

"You said Eric was a demon."

"Yes. It's odd, because he's a man one might easily see as absurd. I think I saw him as absurd at first, a sort of pompous play-actor. But he's got in some literal sense magnetism, an animal force, such as quite a stupid person might have. Not that Eric's stupid, but I mean this is nothing to do with the mind, at least not with the rational mind. It's a quasi-physical thing. Perhaps that's what attracted me. Richard is so cerebral, even his sensuality is cerebral. Eric was like a piece of earth, or maybe more like the sea. I always associated him with the sea."

"Do you in any way want to see him?"

"No. But I've got to see him. I've got to—undergo it again."

"I can see," said Ducane, speaking carefully, "that you feel you as it were owe him something. It's like a precise bond—"

"Exactly. A blood bond. I think he believes that there's a spell that only I can break. There's a sickening awfulness in his life which only I can remove. This is why I've got to face him and face him alone."

"Do you really believe that you could do anything for him? Given that you don't love him? Or do you think it possible you might begin to love him again?"

"No! I don't know if I could do anything. At times I think he wants somehow to punish me. There are days, hours, when I think he's coming back to kill me. Or it might be enough if he could find some way of humiliating me. I just don't know what's going to happen. All I know is that whatever it is it's got to happen. Next week."

Ducane was frowning into the sea light. "Who else knows this story?"

"No one. Except Richard and Eric."

"Why have you kept silent about it?"

She hesitated. "Pride."

"Yes. And this is what's made it into something dreadful. You've been infected by the demon in Eric."

"I know. The whole thing, the way it all happened, was shattering. And what it shattered most of all was some conception I'd had of myself, some wholeness. It's odd. That was why I never tried to stop Richard divorcing me. Something was utterly broken in me by that scene in the billiard room. Something which hadn't been broken by my going to bed with Eric. It was as if one's guilt had been made into a tangible object and rammed into one's guts."

"You've got to relive this thing, Paula, and not just for Eric but for yourself."

"Maybe. But when Eric comes—"

"You must use your common sense about it. I understand how you feel. And obviously you've got to meet Eric alone. But I think you ought to meet him in a sane context. I mean with other people all round you. He must meet your friends and see that you have support, a world of your own. Now I shall be in London next week—"

There was a quick crunching of pebbles and a shadow moved near them like a lizard. It was Uncle Theo.

Theo looked pale and dry in the bright sun, the big rounded dome of his skull surmounting his shrunken doggy face like a helmet. He looked down on them with a puckered expression of slightly quizzical disgust. He said, "Paula, Letters for you." Three letters fell on to the stones. He hesitated, as if awaiting a summons to stay, and then marched quickly off, stooping well forward from the waist and digging his feet noisily into the pebbles before Ducane could get out more than an "Oh Theo—"

Paula looked after him. "He seems so depressed these days. I wonder what on earth goes on inside his head? Poor Theo. John, I do wish you'd talk to him seriously. Make him tell you what's the matter. He'd talk to you."

Ducane gave a small snarling laugh.

"Oh!" Paula had just looked at the letters. "There's one from Eric. He's at Suez."

"Better read it quickly," said Ducane. He turned away

squinting into the sunlight, trying to discern the swimming children. He noticed that it must be low tide since a bank of purple seaweed, only visible at that time, was making a darker blur in the clear greenish water, which had already receded by several feet since he and Paula had sat down. Theo's aimlessly purposeful figure diminished steadily.

After a moment Ducane heard a strange sound beside him. He turned to see that Paula had covered her face with her hand. Her shoulders shook.

"Whatever is it, Paula?"

Paula went on shaking, and a low raucous sound came from behind the shielding hand. The other hand stretched out and tossed Eric's letter to him. Ducane read.

SS Morania
Suez

My dear Paula,

not to beat about the bush, this letter comes to tell you that I have met somebody perfectly marvellous on the boat and I am going to marry her. How very strange life is! I have always had a sense of being in the hands of the gods, but often they work in such unexpected ways! I knew I had to come back to England and I thought it was because you needed to see me. But how unimportant this seems now. Forgive me for putting it in this way, but I can be kindest to you by being plainest. What seemed the necessity of seeing you was really just the wanderlust, or rather the magnetism of my destiny pulling me away. Everything has worked out quite wonderfully. We are getting off the boat here and will fly to Cairo. (If you remember I have always wanted to see the pyramids.) After that we fly to New York and on to Chicago to meet Angelica's people. (Her father is a big man in the art world, incidentally, and she has a lot of money, though of course that's not important and I didn't even know it at first. She is a marvellous person.)

I am sorry, dear Paula, to burden you with this recital of my felicity, but there is no point in delaying the happy news. I know how much you must have been waiting and expecting. Believe me I have thought about your needs. But I think it would be unwise for us to meet now.

There is much that it would be hard for Angelica to understand. She is a very *unshadowed* person, and I have not upset her by any of the grimmer things out of my past. (I say this in case you should ever happen to meet her, though I imagine this is unlikely. We are going on a world tour after the marriage and will probably settle in San Francisco, which will be a good place for my work.) I feel confident that you will forgive this defection on my part. You are a woman of many resources and not given to envy, jealousy or moping. I trust and believe that you will soon be able to rejoice in my good fortune without feeling resentment at my failure to render to you an aid which you may have persuaded yourself that only I could give. May it in some way please you to hear me say: I am happy and feel set free from the past. It is my very earnest wish that you will one day be able to say the same.

Eric

P.S. Please be sure to destroy this letter.

Ducane turned to look at Paula. Paula's face was transformed. It expanded smoothly, blandly, seeming to have increased in area, with eyes and mouth extended, and he realised that she had been laughing. Her face, which had been pinched in behind a narrow mask, was relaxed and shining. As she shuddered again and gasped into laughter Ducane began to laugh too, and they laughed together, rocking to and fro and sending the mottled pebbles rolling down the slope towards the water.

At last Paula picked up the letter which had fallen between them and tore it to pieces. She scattered the fragments about her. "See how soon a bogeyman can be blown away."

"I see what you mean about absurd!" said Ducane.

"Things seem to happen to Eric on ships!"

"Good old Angelica, God bless her!"

"I think he'd really persuaded himself that I'd asked him to come!"

"Paula, you're out in the sun again," said Ducane. He took hold of the hem of her yellow dress.

"Yes. John, I can't thank you enough—"

"You don't regret having told me, now?"

"No, no. I know already that it's made a difference, *the* difference—"

Ducane got up rather stiffly. He pulled his jacket on, pushing up the collar of his shirt and rumpling his hair. He could see Barbara and the twins running along the beach towards them.

He said suddenly, "Paula, do you still love Richard?"

"Yes," she replied without a second's hesitation. And then began to go on, "But of course there's no—"

"Why, whatever's the matter? Look at the children. Barbie, what is it, what is it?"

"It's Pierce. He's swum into Gunnar's cave and he says he isn't coming out and he's going to stay there till the tide comes in, and he means it, I *know* he means it!"

Thirty-four

IT was extremely quiet inside the cave. Pierce swam
breast stroke with long quiet strokes, letting his body
glide fish-like through the water with as little exertion as
possible. He was dressed in trousers and a jersey and woollen
socks and rubber shoes. An electric torch, guaranteed water-
proof, was tucked into his trousers pocket and attached to
his waist by a string. He was wearing his watch, also water-
proof. He was already farther into the cave than he had ever
been before and the daylight from the low arc of the entrance
was becoming dim. He could see before him, almost phosphorescent, the regular movement of his hands breaking
the dark surface of the water. He could see nothing of his
surroundings.

Pierce's intent to spend the duration of a tide inside the
cave had become, in the long course of its maturing, so huge
and obsessive in his mind that it excluded any explanation
in terms of something further. It was certainly connected
with Barbara, but it might be truer to say that the idea of
the cave had swallowed up the idea of Barbara. A great
black dart pointed him into this magnetic darkness. Humiliation and rejection and despair had blended into a thrust
of desire which no longer had Barbara for its object. That
the ordeal might end in death was an essential part of its
authority. Yet the hypothesis of this factual death was
almost incidental. The concept of death had been growing
in Pierce's mind, an expanding, curiously dazzling, black
object which was not a physical possibility or even a consolation, but the supreme object of love.

The distant light from the cave entrance was shut out
and Pierce glided into a sphere of total blackness. He checked
his stroke and looking over his shoulder could see a suggestion of light upon the water but no low whitish arc of day.
He must have turned a corner in the cave. He fumbled
down for his electric torch and treading water turned it on.
The beam was long and powerful but the air seemed to have
a powdery physical quality which narrowed and contained

the light. Pierce made out the roof of the cavern fairly high above him and the sides, running sheer into the water and festooned with brown seaweed like a display of glistening necklaces. The cave seemed to be about twenty yards wide. Keeping his torch trained on the roof Pierce swam a few strokes back and the distant line of the daylight suddenly materialised in the darkness on his left, like a long flake of some whitish substance laid out close to his head. It was as if he could have touched it. At the same time the moving spot of the torch above him seemed to plunge and vanish.

Pierce trod in the water and got a better grip on the torch. He began to shine it all round him. The roof here was much higher and he realised that he was at a point where the cave divided. There were two caverns, seemingly of equal size, one leading away to the left, and the other, which he had just been following, to the right. This discovery slightly unnerved Pierce. His traditional mental picture of the cave showed a single roomy cavern penetrating upward into the cliff and culminating in a dry airy chamber possibly full of treasure. Not that treasure mattered or even dryness and air. The final chamber might simply be the last hole or cranny in which the rising tide finally kissed the roof and drowned its trapped rat in black oblivion. Only Pierce had not realised that he would have to make *choices*. The idea of a choice brought with it the idea of life, of future, and this brought a first wrench of fear.

Pierce shone the torch up at the roof of the left hand cavern. It was some twenty-five feet above water level and covered in seaweed. He turned the light on to the right hand cavern. The roof was a trifle higher, also covered in seaweed. Which fork would lead him upward? He decided, as he had no other guide, to follow the chance which had led him to the right. He switched off the torch and swam on. The flake of daylight disappeared.

He swam slowly now, trying to sense the position and closeness of the walls by a kind of radar. He felt that he was able to do it. But the darkness oppressed him. It had become even thicker and more physical, fitting over his head like a casing of black fungus. It seemed that if he lifted his hand he might be able to break off a piece. His breath suddenly became quick and short, and he had to tread water to make his breathing regular again. The water, which had seemed warmer inside the cave than out in the sea, still seemed unusually warm, and he felt no tiredness and no chill. He hauled up the torch again and shone it about, shining it back over the way he had come and then ahead.

Just in front of him the cavern divided again. Another choice. The thought came to Pierce, suppose that I survive the sea but simply get lost in this awful labyrinth and never manage to find my way back? Would the tide running out show him the way? He was not sure. He swam slowly forward and pointed the thin line of light at the cavern ahead. The torch-light seemed narrow and ragged, devoured by the dark. He could see less than before. His eyes seemed to be becoming less and not more accustomed to the thick fungoid murk. Here the left-hand channel seemed slightly wider and its wet weedy roof higher above the sea. Pierce swam slowly into the opening. He thought first right, and then left. I must remember. First right, and then left.

He shone the torch ahead of him examining the roof and walls. The cavern showed no diminution in size, but equally no tendency to rise, and the cave walls still descended sheer into the water. There was not even a projecting rock upon which one might rest. Pierce thought, it can't go *on* like this. Then he thought, why not? The cavern was winding about, bearing quite sharply away to the left. Why should not these worm holes, so neatly cleanly drilled in the rock, wind about indefinitely below the level of the high tide? They might afford him hours of this black featureless swimming before the rising waters finally pressed the crown of his head against the slow descent of the slimy roof.

A shiver of panic went through Pierce like an electric shock and he began at once to feel cold. He thought, supposing I were to swim very fast back the way I came would I be in time to get out of the cave before the tide covered the entrance? He lifted his arm from the water and shone the torch on to his watch. His watch, dripping, but with its familiar everyday face, looked weird and lonely under the black bell of the darkness. He had only been inside for fifteen minutes. He might be able to get out if he turned back at once. Pierce switched off the light and began to swim vigorously ahead of him, deeper into the cave.

He paused again and flashed the light about, wanting to be sure that he had passed no more divisions. It looked as if there was another one coming ahead. He paddled cautiously forward and came into a wider space from which there seemed to be no less than four issues, black rounds, like clenched fists above the very faintly moving water over which the torch-light slid in long fragments of pale chocolaty brown. Here Pierce saw to the right of him, as the cavern in which he was swimming enlarged itself, an irregularity in the wall which formed a sort of sloping shelf. Pierce made for the shelf and tried to haul himself on to it. This was not easy, as the rock was covered with a light green seaweed, like fine hair, which was extremely slippery. At last he managed to perch uncomfortably, half out of the water, and to use his torch with greater care. There were four openings ahead. Pierce saw that all four had roofs considerably lower than the roof of the chamber out of which they led. The cave seemed to be descending.

At that moment Pierce heard a noise in the water. It was not a noise made by himself. He was lying quite still, seal-like, stretched upon the sloping rock, and holding himself in place rather painfully with one hand clamped upon the abrupt end of the shelf. He stiffened, listening. There was a splashing sound as if something large and clumsy were swimming nearby. Pierce turned awkwardly, holding on and turning his head over his shoulder. The pale brown light of the torch moved on the surface of the water. Something was there, splashing in the water in the centre of the cavern. It was Mingo.

"Mingo!" said Pierce. He let go abruptly both of the torch and of his hold on the edge of the shelf. As he slid down, the string which attached the torch to his waist caught on a projection of the rock and snapped. The torch balanced on the edge of the rock and then quietly tilted over and vanished into the water.

Pierce lay still against the slippery rock, the water round his shoulder, one arm still clutching at the seaweed. The darkness was thick, total. The splashing sound approached and Pierce's outstretched hand touched Mingo's collar and the dry fur of his head. Mingo scrabbled at the rock, trying to get himself out of the water.

"Oh Mingo, Mingo," said Pierce. He pushed the dog up a little on to the slimy incline of the seaweed and laid his head against the wet warm flank, holding himself close to the rock with a stiffening grip. Hot tears began to run suddenly down his face.

Thirty-five

"WHATEVER shall we do?" said Paula. She looked at Ducane. Barbara clutched the sleeve of his coat. The twins clutched each other.

"A motor boat?" said Ducane.

"There's one in the village," said Paula, "but by the time—"

"It's hired out for the afternoon," said Edward. "We saw it going away."

"We'd better ring up the coastguards," said Ducane. "Not that that—How long is it since he went in?"

"It must be nearly fifteen minutes," said Barbara.

"More," said Henrietta.

"You see," said Barbara, her voice becoming high and tearful, "I didn't really believe him at first. I kept waiting for him to come out again. Then I suddenly felt sure he meant it. Then it was quite a long way to swim back."

"We were there too," said Edward. "I was sure he meant it, I said so at once."

"We may see the young fool swimming back any—"

"No, no, no!" wailed Barbara. "He's inside, he's going to stay inside, I know it!"

Ducane held his head. He thought as quickly as he could, his eyes fixed on Paula, who seemed to be trying desperately to help him. "How long is it before the entrance closes?"

"Half an hour," said Edward.

"Twenty-five minutes," said Henrietta.

Ducane looked at his watch. "Look," he said to Paula. "We'd better assume the worst. You give the alarm. Ring the coastguards, ring the village. If you see a motor boat stop it. Find out if anyone knows the cave. Find out if there's frogman gear available and anyone who can use it. Though I don't see what the hell—I'll swim round now and investigate. He may be hanging about just inside the entrance trying to frighten us."

"We'll come with you!" cried the children.

"No, you won't," said Ducane. "You're chilled, you've been in too long." All three children were shivering. "Anyway it's you Pierce is trying to impress, especially you, Barbara. If he thinks you're there he may not come out. You go along with Paula."

"John, you won't go into the cave, will you?" cried Paula.

"No, no. Just a little way. I'll probably meet Pierce swimming back. Go on, the rest of you, and don't panic."

Ducane took off his jacket and his tie. He kicked off his shoes and socks and stepped out of his trousers. "Go on!" he shouted at them.

Paula and the children set off over the pebbles at a run. Ducane put his shoes on again and began to run in the opposite direction along the beach to the point where the red cliff descended. He abandoned his shoes and slipped into the sea.

He swam with a quick vigorous sidestroke, keeping as close as he could to the foot of the cliff. He could feel the tug of one of those currents which made the region unpopular with bathers. It seemed to be coming against him and his progress was slow. He had never felt swimming to be so like an agonised strenuous standing still. He was panting already. The sleeves of his shirt, now clinging, now ballooned with water impeded him and, still swimming, he began to try to pull the shirt off. He got it over his head and abandoned it in the water. Then the current seemed to give as he turned the point of rock which took him into the next bay and out of sight of Trescombe.

Now nothing was visible except the still sea and the sky and the inward and outward curve of the cliff which hid the land on both sides. Ducane felt suddenly very small and alone. The red cliff, which close to showed a brownish terracotta streaked with slatey blue, descended sheer into the sea, looking so dry and crumbling it seemed it must dissolve at the touch of the water. A broad stripe along its lower half marked the level of the high tide, and seaweeds, baked already in the sun since the sea had last abandoned them, hung in dark ugly bunches like superfluous hair. Up above clumps of white daisies floated, adhering somehow to the rising wall. Ducane could smell their light odour mingled with the baked sea smell of the half-dried seaweed.

He could see the entrance to the cave now, an irregular dark brown streak above the water. As he approached it he looked at his watch, which seemed to be still going. On Henrietta's estimate there was just under fifteen minutes before the mouth was closed. A few more strokes brought Ducane suddenly in out of the sunshine, and as the shadow of the cliff fell upon him he called out, "Pierce! Pierce!" Silence.

The roof of the cave was about seven feet above the water at the entrance. Ducane swam a little farther in, noticing that the roof seemed to fall a little. Farther on it rose into invisibility in the darkness and the cave grew wider. Ducane swam into the larger space and called again.

Ducane had said that he would swim to the cave because that was the only thing he could think of to do. He had vaguely imagined that he would easily be able to find Pierce and would use his authority to make the boy come out. Now everything seemed different. The sheer solitude of the sunlit bay, followed by this plunge into the cool half-dark, had already done something to him. He felt removed from reality. He called again. He became aware that the sea was now running fairly fast in through the cave mouth and had already carried him farther away from the entrance. He swam a few strokes back to make sure he could easily get out again. Then he allowed the current to carry him a little farther on in the darkness, still shouting at intervals.

As Ducane swam in the great pool of the cavern he had a sudden mental image of the picture in *Through the Looking Glass* of Alice and the mouse swimming in the Pool of Tears. He had a clear memory of the grace with which Alice swam, her dress so elegantly spread out in the water. Something about that picture must have affected him when he was a child. Girls and their dresses. He called again. Silence.

'He could see more clearly now in the brown tea-coloured light of the cavern, and discerned to his left a blackness in the cavern wall which seemed like a hole. He swam towards it, breast stroke now, keeping his head well up and listening. Then it was as if someone had touched his head very lightly with a black cushion and he had swum in through the entrance of the hole.

Ducane was not afraid of the sea, but he was very much

afraid of confined spaces. He back-paddled, touching the wall. Then he called out. A very very faint cry answered. Ducane let the water sweep him back against the wall. He listened to the silence which was edged by the faint hiss of the moving water. He turned away from the dim light behind him and looked into the jet dark and called again. He had not imagined it. The faint cry replied, eerie, distant, lost.

Ducane began to have a new kind of picture. He saw Pierce somewhere at the end of the tunnel with cramp perhaps, hurt in some way, trapped in some way, calling out desperately for help. At the same time, as if the darkness itself had become a screen upon which the contents of his mind could be projected physically, he saw before him with absolute clarity the sallow anxious face of Mary Clothier. "I'm coming!" he shouted, and launched out into the current.

The faint light behind him diminished and went out. The current now took him so quickly along that he scarcely needed to swim. The tunnel seemed to be turning sharply. Ducane caught hold of something, wet smooth rounded rock, and tried to hold on. Then he was whirled away by the current and twisted around as if some great hand had spun him between its fingers. He swallowed some water.

Ducane felt panic. He reached out trying to find something to hold on to. He was afraid he might at any moment strike his head violently against some projection of rock. The thick shut-in darkness frightened him. He struck his knee against a knob of rock just beneath the water and managed by resting against it and bracing his hands against the side of the tunnel to stop himself from moving. He called out as loudly as he could:

"Pierce! Pierce!"

"*Pierce! Pierce!*"

It's an echo, Ducane said to himself. He said it coldly, uttering it articulately inside his head. He called again, "Hello!"

"*Hello!*"

I must get back, he thought. He let go of his rock and struck out vigorously to swim back the way he had come. But the strong current seized hold of him and hurried him with it, on, on.

Ducane was now very much afraid. He fought his way to the wall where the water seemed less swift and tried to cling to it. The absolute darkness confused his sense of direction, confused his sense of his body. He had to use mental imagery to tell himself how to swim. He thought to himself, strength will do it, every bit of strength I have, supernatural strength. He began half to edge, half to swim, along the wall of rock in what seemed to be the direction from which he had come. He moved very slowly, but at least now he seemed to be moving. He thought he was coming back to the place where the tunnel turned. For a moment he seemed entirely out of the current. Then he sensed a change of direction and the tunnel seemed airier, wider, and the force of the water less strong. He must be nearly back in the main cavern.

Ducane felt an enlargement and the tunnel wall, which he had been touching, disappeared. He could swim quite easily now. He took several strokes. He must have reached the main cavern. But it was dark now. There was a faint greenish line ahead of him of subaqueous light. But the low sun-streaked gap of the cavern mouth was not to be seen. The cave was closed.

Now there were new pictures. Ducane seemed to have been swimming for some time. Coloured images appeared upon the darkness with such brightness that it seemed as if he must be able to see the cavern walls by their light. He saw Alice standing upon the mantelpiece, at the moment when the looking glass begins to turn into a silvery gauze through which she can pass. He saw Mary Clothier's face, no longer anxious but looking tender and sad. We have both died, he thought, and then could not recall who 'we' were. Himself and Pierce of course. He called out to Pierce at intervals but received no reply. The sound echoed close about him as if unable to penetrate further, but telling him at least that the channel along which he was swimming was still reasonably large.

He was beginning to feel cold and his limbs were very tired, but the swimming had now become automatic, as if he were in a natural element. Something very dreadful moved along with him, just above his head, a noiseless black crow made of ectoplasm. It was fear, panic fear, such as would disfigure a man and make him disintegrate and scream. Ducane was very conscious of its presence. He tried to breathe slowly and evenly. He pictured the cavern rising, rising, into the dry safety of the cliff side. He tried not to picture other things. At least the cavern went on and there was nothing else to do but to go on with it, to go on and on as far as one could go. But so far there had been nothing to touch, as he constantly tested his surroundings with outstretched hands, except the sheer walls of wet stone containing the moving water. No cranny of pebbles, no strand, no rock even on which to rest. And now he was seeing Alice falling down the rabbit hole, falling slowly, slowly.

Ducane thought, in this sort of darkness I could pass within a yard of the way to safety and not know. It's all chance, utter chance. The current was not very fast now and he could easily swim to and fro across it touching the walls of the channel which were now about fifteen feet apart. The channel seemed to be narrowing very slightly. There were irregularities in the wall, but these were merely bumps, projections, worn to a slimy roundness by the water which proceeded onward into the depths of the cliff along its black interminable pipe. The air was still fresh, but it carried a faintly rotten sea smell, as if the water itself were decomposing, and indeed it did seem as if the stuff were becoming thicker and oilier. Amid the extinction or derangement of all his other senses Ducane smelt the smell with a monstrous clarity as if the smell itself were a black structure of gluey air and water within which, perhaps without moving at all, he made, more and more feebly, the yearning movement of swimming, of praying.

It seemed to him that he had not called out for some time and he called now, hoarsely, not very loudly, "Pierce!"

"Hello."

"*Pierce!*"

"Hello there."

The cry was from near. Ducane stopped swimming. Everything was changed. He inhabited his body again, he felt his extremities moving in the water. All round him he could feel things resuming their sizes. The darkness was no longer a stuff of which he was part, but a veil, an accident.

"Where are you?"

"Here, here."

Ducane was suddenly brought up against a ridge of rock, its surface soft with slime. He could feel the water dividing about him, holding him against the rock.

"Where?"

"This way."

Ducane edged round the rock and let the water take him. His knees suddenly touched bottom, then his hand. He was no longer swimming but crawling. He felt something touch his shoulder and grip him. The touch was painful, as if dazzling. He realised he must be almost anaesthetised by cold. He crawled further and lay full length. He could feel pebbles under his hand.

"I am terribly sorry," said Pierce's voice beside him.

The earnest serious boy's voice sounded strange in the blackness, with its ring of the ordinary world, apologising.

"Could you just try to massage me or something," said Ducane. "I feel absolutely numb." The brilliant pain returned and moved over his back. He began to twist and stretch his limbs. He now felt so tired he could not understand how a moment ago he could have been capable of swimming. "What's that?"

"It's Mingo. He followed me in. I am so very sorry—"

"That's enough. Is there any way on here?"

"I don't know," said Pierce's voice. "I've just arrived. At any rate we're out of the water, for the moment. I tried one of the other channels and it just ended in a wall and the roof was pretty low so I thought I'd better get out quick. It wasn't too easy to get back against the tide. Then I came in here and reached this—place—and then I heard you call."

"Are you all right?"

"Yes, I'm fine. Are you warmer now?"

"Yes." If I don't drown I shall die of exposure, Ducane thought. He sat up, chafing his arms and legs. His flesh felt alien to him, like ice-cold putty.

"We'd better move on," said Pierce. "This one may be a cul-de-sac too. Or shall I go ahead and look and then come back for you?"

"No, no. I'll come too." For God's sake don't leave me, he thought. He got to his knees and then to his feet. Something touched his head lightly. It was the roof of the tunnel. "What's that noise?"

"I think it's the tide running through holes in the rock."

There was a slightly irregular moaning sound nearby, punctuated by soft hollow reports.

"That's the water hitting the roof of the next cave," said Pierce. "It seems to be getting more excited."

The water, which had flowed so calmly on into the darkness, now seemed in these more confined inner spaces to be becoming violent. Ducane felt an impact at his feet. "Get on, Pierce. The bloody sea's beginning to arrive."

"Have you got shoes?"

"Get on."

They began to shuffle forward in the blackness. The ground seemed to be rising a little but in such complete darkness it was hard to tell, and Ducane's feet, contracted into rounded hobbling balls of pain, could not discern whether he was still walking in the water. The low keening noise and the echoing slapping noise continued.

"It goes on anyway," said Pierce. His voice sounded a little high and wavery. The noise behind them, which was increasing a little, was hard to bear. "You'll have to stoop here."

"It's so damn black. Keep on talking, I don't want to lose you."

"Oh God, it's coming right down. I think we'll have to crawl."

"What's the point of this," said Ducane, stopping. He had an image of crawling onward, onward, to end wedged in some narrow pocket of wet rock waiting for the tide. "If this one's packing up we'd better try another one while there's still time. The water's just behind us."

"It's here," said Pierce in a cracked voice. "Stay still, I'm coming back past you."

Ducane stood rigid and felt Pierce's hands fumble him while the wet jersey slid past. There was barely room in the space for them to pass each other. There was a damp warmth on his legs as Mingo scrabbled by after Pierce.

In a moment Pierce's voice came out of the darkness. "I'm afraid the water has practically filled the entrance. It seems to be coming up much faster now. We've had it in here one way or the other."

Ducane gripped himself, almost physically, as one might grip and shake an *alter ego*, and then realised that he had hold of Pierce who had blundered up against him. "Well, we must go on, then." Ducane's voice was high too, raised as if to cross a vast auditorium. It seemed to echo away into the hidden spaces and honeycombs of the dark.

The water was making a new noise now, a grinding sucking sound of advance and retreat over pebbles in a narrow place. Pierce, who had got past Ducane, moved away.

Ducane ran his knuckles along the slimy descending rock and began to stoop. Bent double he moved forward, reaching out to touch the limp tail of Pierce's jersey. Mingo passed him again, a long sliver of darkened warmth. The roof rose a little, then began to fall again. It was difficult to tell if they were going upward. Movement had become something different, a slow and painful pistoning of bones inside a mass of black matter.

"We are rising, aren't we, Pierce?"

"I think so."

"Are we walking in water?"

"No, we're out of the water. Watch out, the roof's coming down again."

Ducane was moving three-legged, one hand touching the pebbly floor of the cave. His head came into contact with Pierce's back. Pierce seemed to be on his knees.

"What is it?"

"It's come to an end."

"Feel, feel, feel all round," said Ducane. He moved his hands about him, stroking the smooth damp chunks of solid blackness which hemmed them in.

"No good," said Pierce in a new calm voice. "It's a dead end."

The calmness was the final tone of despair.

Ducane said, "Let's move back a bit. I can't stand this rock on the back of my neck." He thought, I would rather die standing up. As he moved back and straightened up he could feel the pebbles shifting underneath his feet. The sea had followed them.

"It'll rise quite fast in here," said Pierce. "I'm afraid we've had it." He uttered a low long-drawn-out moan.

Ducane began to take in, more from that dreadful sound than from the words, what was to be. He began to say something aloud to himself. But at that moment something extraordinary happened, something pierced through the sphere of darkness and black wet masses and noisy water. It seemed like light. But it was not light. It was the smell of the white daisies.

"Pierce, the air is fresher here, I can feel air coming down from above. There may be some cranny, some shaft we could climb up—"

They blundered against each other, their arms above their heads, feeling the blunt rock. Ducane felt as if his hands had become lumps of blackness, lumps without fingers. He could not now stop from shuddering and there was a hissing sound which he realised he must be making himself.

"There's something here," said Pierce beside him.

Ducane's groping encountered a hole. There was a faint movement of air. "Is it big enough to get up?"

"I think so. Stay where you are a minute."

Pierce disappeared from beside him. There were soft slippery sounds and grunts and then Pierce's voice triumphant from above, "I'm up. At least there's a ledge. I don't know if it goes farther."

"Are there footholds? How did you—?"

"Wait, I'm coming down. Keep clear."

There was a slithering noise and Pierce landed heavily beside him, seizing his shoulder.

"How did you get up?"

"It's a chimney. One can brace oneself. Shoulders on one side and feet on the other. It runs diagonally, so it's quite easy, sixty degrees I should think. You can get into the hole just by hitching yourself up and sitting on the edge of it. It's awfully slippery, that's the only thing. I'll take Mingo up now."

I can't do it, thought Ducane. Even as a boy he had not been able to do that particular trick. And now, out of condition, exhausted, paralysed with cold— He said, "You can't climb up and carry Mingo. You'll fall and break a leg. We'll have to leave Mingo behind. Mingo, he thought, and me.

"I'm not going to leave Mingo behind," said Pierce in a breaking voice. "I can push him. Just help me lift him into the hole. Here, feel it, feel it."

Between them they lifted the wet warm heavy dog up into the hole. Fortunately Mingo was used to being lifted about like a sack.

"Push him up, he'll slide. I'm getting in now. Just put your hand behind me, that's right, not too hard, stand by in case we tumble back."

The panting straining mass moved upward and for a moment Ducane could feel the boy's body braced like a bow and then his supporting hand was left in the air. A time passed. Then Pierce's voice: "We're up! Only just though, my God he's a weight. Stay still, Mingo, lie down. I wonder if we can—Christ, there doesn't seem to be much room. Can you come up now?"

Ducane sat on the edge of the dark hole whose blackness was no thicker than the surrounding air, and with the sense of a hopeless ritual slowly bent his knees until his feet were against the opposing wall. Even this required an almost impossible effort. He sat there. He had not the strength even to try. He moved his back against the slimy rock. His body was without force.

The sea was moving just below him in strong regular surges, grinding the pebbles forward and back. The hollow clapping noise below had merged into a soft chaotic roar. But Ducane scarcely heard the sounds, scarcely knew if they were inside his head or not. He wondered, suppose I were to let the water itself lift me up the chimney? But no. It would rush up that narrow sloping hole like a demon and come sucking down again. Anything in that confined space would be battered to pieces.

"What is it, John?" said Pierce's voice sharply from above.

"I can't do it," said Ducane.

"*You must. Try.* Keep your feet just a little lower than your head. Feel the wall for good foot places. Then just slide your shoulders and let your feet do the work like walking."

"I can't try, Pierce. I haven't any strength. Don't worry. The sea will carry me up when the time comes."

"Don't be crazy. Look out, I'm coming down."

Ducane could not move his cramped body in time.

Pierce arrived, tumbling him out of the hole on to his knees in the rising water.

"Sorry. Oh God. I could try and push you but I could only just manage Mingo. Oh God, what shall we do? If only I'd brought a rope—I never thought—"

Ducane had managed to stand up. He thought, I haven't got much longer before some sort of collapse. He could not think if this would be a collapse of mind or of body. Mind and body seemed utterly fused now in cold aching pain, and darkness. He said to himself deliberately, I must do everything that I can to survive. He said slowly, leaning back against the rock, "We might—make—a rope—of our clothes —Pierce."

"Yes, yes, quick. Can you undress? Nylon vests and pants, tear them into strips."

"I am undressed, dear boy. You'll have to do the tearing. Here."

Ducane climbed awkwardly out of his vest and underpants. He seemed to have lost the schema of his body and had to find out the position of his limbs by experiment. He began to shiver uncontrollably.

"No, keep yours till I've torn mine. Oh Christ, they won't tear. I'm losing my strength."

"Tear them along the side seams first," said Ducane. "Don't drop anything, for God's sake, we'd never find it again. Here, I'll hold the end, pull now, *pull*." There was a faint rending sound. "Good, good, now these, go on. Do you think that's enough? It'll stretch of course. Can you knot them? Reef knots."

"My hands won't work," said Pierce's voice. There was a tearful tremor.

"Think about the knots, don't think about your hands. Let me—good, you've done it. Now Pierce, listen and obey me. You go up again with one end of the rope and we'll try like this. I'll have to tie it round my waist, nothing else will do. Then just pull steadily and I'll try to use my hands and feet. Be careful not to overbalance, and if I suddenly start to fall *let go*. And if I can't get up then that's that. *Don't come down again*, it's pointless and you may be too exhausted to get back. I'll take my chance when the sea comes. Now up you go."

Pierce went from him with a faint groan. In the greater noise of the water Ducane could not hear him climbing. Ducane sat himself into the hole, paying out the limp wet rope and shuddering. The movement of the rope ceased.

"Have you still got it?" said Pierce from above.

"Yes. I think I can tie it round me, there's enough." But can I tie it, he thought? Idiotic not to have told Pierce to tie it. Very slowly he drew it round his waist and composed a knot. "Pull now, very gently, and I'll try to climb."

It's impossible, thought Ducane, utterly impossible. The sea water out of which he had just lifted himself was knee deep. A light spray seemed to be sifting through the black air. The noise inside his head now had a metallic overwhelming quality as in the feverish nightmares of his childhood. If I could only pray, he thought, if there was only some reservoir of force out of which I could draw something extra. He sat cramped in the hole. There was not enough force in his legs to lift him even an inch from his sitting position. His legs were stiff and cold and powerless, and his naked back worked helplessly, sliding a little up, a little down, on the slimy icy rock. His slippery unclothed body hung inertly between the walls, getting no purchase, exerting no force. He thought, if I could only somehow occupy my mind it might help my body, anything, erotic imagery, anything. Something white was floating in the air in front of him, close in front of his eyes, suspended in space. The face of a woman swam in front of him, seeming to move and yet to be still like the racing moon, indistinct and yet intent, staring into his eyes.

He found that he was no longer sitting but was suspended, braced between the two walls. Stay, stay, he said to the shimmering face as almost surreptitiously he paid attention to his edging feet, his braced back, and the hunched enduring frame between them. He could hear Pierce speaking above him with a disintegrated echoing wordless voice. The steady pull of the rope continued. Very very slowly Ducane edged upward. It was becoming easier. The pallid face was composing into a face that he knew.

Ducane lay upon the ledge. These stars of warmth behind his closed eyes must be tears, he thought almost abstractedly.

Pierce was rubbing him and trying to introduce one of his arms into the sleeve of the jersey.

"Wait, Pierce, wait, *wait.*"

A little while later Ducane sat up. He stretched out numbed hands touching black surfaces which might have been Pierce, Mingo, rock. The sweetish powdery celestially *dry* smell of the white daisies was stronger. The noise below had increased, seeming circular now, circular, he thought, as if water were being hurled violently round and round a huge circular vessel. He said to Pierce, hardly recognising his own voice, "Can we get on from here?"

"No. I've been trying. There are crannies, but no outlet."

"I see." Ducane listened to the noisy sea. There was this new note. The water must be entering the foot of the chimney.

"How much time has passed, Pierce? Is it nearly high tide?"

"I don't know. I've lost all count of time. And my watch isn't luminous."

"Neither is mine. Do you think we're above the high tide line?"

"I don't know."

"Is it wet in here?"

"I can't tell. I've lost my feeling. Do you think it is?"

Ducane began to move his hands again, trying to discern what he was touching. He felt something long and smooth, like a cold line drawn upon the dark. Then he put his fingers to his lips. The fingers tasted salt. But they would taste salt anyway. He licked his fingers, warming them to a small agony. Then he drew his cold dark line again and tasted again. Salt. Or was he perhaps mistaken? Or were his fingers too soaked in the sea to lose their salty taste? He said to Pierce, "I can't tell either." He thought, it is better not to know.

"Put the jersey on now, please."

"Listen, Pierce. Our chances of survival here, if we aren't drowned, depend on two things, your jersey and Mingo. It's just as well Mingo followed you in. He's a godsend. Where is he? Feel how warm he is. I suggest, if we can, that we both get inside your jersey and put Mingo between us. I'm afraid the rope isn't going to be much good to us

303

now, but we may as well wrap it round, that's right. Now can you pull the jersey over my head and then come up inside it yourself? Mind you don't go over the edge. How much space is there?"

"There's about four or five feet, but the roof slopes. Lift your arm, can you. Shift over this way. Now over your head."

Ducane felt the damp wool dragging on his shivering arm and then descending over his face. He nuzzled through it. He lay quiet as Pierce climbed up his body, driving his head up through the sweater. The neckline gave at the seams and Pierce's head was thrust against his own, bone to bone, and Pierce was fighting his arm into the other sleeve of the sweater.

"Pull it down as far as you can, John. I'll roll over a bit. Damn, Mingo's the wrong way round. We don't want to stifle him between us. Could you pull him up towards me, just pull him by the tail."

Unprotesting silent Mingo, warm Mingo, was at last adjusted with his bulky body between them, his head emerging at the bottom of the sweater. After a moment or two Ducane could feel the sparkling painful particles of warmth beginning to stream into him. A little later he felt something else, which was Mingo licking his thigh.

"Comfortable?"

"All right. You can't move any farther back?"

"No."

The water was boiling at the bottom of the shaft, rushing up it and then retiring with a noise like a cork being withdrawn from a bottle. Ducane thought, at any rate we shall know pretty soon, one way or the other. He was lying on his right side, with Pierce's head propped against his, the hard cheekbone pressing into his cheek. They lay like two broken puppets, lolling head to head. Ducane felt a faint shuddering and a wet warmth touched his cheek. Pierce was crying. He put a heavy limp arm over the boy and made the motion of drawing him closer.

I wonder if this is the end, thought Ducane, and if so what it will all have amounted to. How tawdry and small it has all been. He saw himself now as a little rat, a busy little scurrying rat seeking out its own little advantages and comforts. To live easily, to have cosy familiar pleasures, to be well thought of. He felt his body stiffening and he nestled closer to Mingo's invincible warmth. He patted Pierce's shoulder and burrowed his hand beneath it. He thought, poor, poor Mary. The coloured images were returning now to his closed eyes. He saw the face of Biranne near to him, as in a silent film, moving, mouthing, but unheard. He thought, if I ever get out of here I will be no man's judge. Nothing is worth doing except to kill the little rat, not to judge, not to be superior, not to exercise power, not to seek, seek, seek. To love and to reconcile and to forgive, only this matters. All power is sin and all law is frailty. Love is the only justice. Forgiveness, reconciliation, not law.

He shifted slightly and his free hand, now moving behind Pierce's back, touched something in the darkness. His chilled fingers explored it. It was a small ridged pyramid-shaped excrescence on the rock. His moving hand encountered another one. Limpets, thought Ducane. *Limpets.* He lay still again. He hoped that Pierce had not found the limpets.

Thirty-six

"**H**OW much longer?"
        "Only a few minutes now."
Voices were hushed.

The night was warm and the smell of the white daisies moved dustily across the water, laying itself down upon the still satiny skin of the sea's surface. A large round moon was turning from silver to a mottled gold against a lightish night sky.

The two boats floated near to the cliff. There had been every confusion, appeals, suggestions, plans. The villagers, thrilled by the mishap, had produced innumerable theories about the cave, but no facts. The police had been told, the coastguards had been told, the navy had been told. The lifeboat had offered to stand by. Frogmen were to come to take in aqualung equipment. Telephone calls passed along the coast. Time passed. The frogmen were needed for an accident elsewhere. Time passed on to the consummation of the high tide. After that there was a kind of lull.

"Now we can't do anything but wait," people said to each other, avoiding each other's eyes.

Mary was sitting in the stern of the boat. There had been other craft earlier, sightseers in motor boats, journalists with cameras, until the police launch told them to go away. There was silence now. Mary sat shuddering with cold in the warm air. She was wearing Theo's overcoat which at some point he had forced her to put on. The coat collar was turned up and inside the big sleeves her hidden hands had met and crawled up to clutch the opposing arms. She sat full, silent, remote, her chin tilted upward a little, her big unseeing eyes staring at the moon. She had shed no tears, but she felt her face as something which had been dissolved, destroyed, wiped into blankness by grief and terror. Now her last enemy was hope. She sat like somebody who tries hard to sleep, driving thoughts away, driving hopes away.

Near to her in the boat, and clearly visible to her although she was not looking at them, were Willy and Theo. Perhaps she could perceive them so sharply because their image had occurred so often during the terrible confusions and indecisions of the afternoon and evening. Willy and Theo, among the people from whom her grief had cut her off so utterly, the least cut off. Theo sat closest to her now in the boat, occasionally reaching out without looking at her to stroke the sleeve of the overcoat. Casie had wept. Kate had wept. Octavian had rushed to and fro organising things and telephoning. She supposed she must have talked to them all, she could not remember. It was silence now.

Mary's thoughts, since she had got into the coastguards' boat, now more than half an hour ago, had become strangely remote and still. Perhaps it was for some scarcely conscious protection from the dreadful agony of hope that she was thinking about Alistair, and about what Ducane had said about him, *Tel qu'en lui-même enfin l'éternité le change.* She formed the words in her mind: What is it like being dead, my Alistair? As she said to herself, my Alistair, she felt a stirring of something, a sort of sad impersonal love. How did she know that this something in her heart, in her mind, where nothing lived but these almost senseless words, was love at all? Yet she knew. Can one love them there in the great ranks of the dead? The dead, she thought, the dead, and formed abstractly, emptily, namelessly the idea of her son.

Death happens, love happens, and all human life is compact of accident and chance. If one loves what is so frail and mortal, if one loves and holds on, like a terrier holding on, must not one's love become changed? There is only one absolute imperative, the imperative to love: yet how can one endure to go on loving what must die, what indeed is dead? *O death, rock me asleep, bring me to quiet rest. Let pass my weary guilty ghost out of my careful breast.* One is oneself this piece of earth, this concoction of frailty, a momentary shadow upon the chaos of the accidental world. Since death and chance are the material of all there is, if love is to be love of something it must be love of death and chance. This changed love moves upon the ocean of accident, over the forms of the dead, a love so impersonal and so cold it can scarcely be recognised, a love devoid of beauty, of which one knows no more than the name, so little is it

307

like an experience. This love Mary felt now for her dead husband and for the faceless wraith of her perhaps drowned son.

The police launch had come back and suddenly shone a very bright searchlight on to the cliff. Everyone started. The warm purple air darkened about them. The illuminated semicircle of the cliff glowed a powdery flaky red streaked with grey, glistening faintly where the tide had just receded. Above the line of the dark brown seaweed the white daisies hung in feathery bunches, ornamental and unreal in the brilliant light.

"Look."

A faint dark streak had appeared at the waterline. Mary shuddered. The sharp hopes twisted violently within her. Drowned, drowned, drowned, her dulling consciousness repeated.

"The roof slopes down, you know," one of the coastguards said.

"What?"

"The roof slopes down. It's highest at the opening. It'll be another five minutes at least before they can swim out."

I wish he wouldn't say things like that, thought Mary. Twenty minutes from now, half an hour from now, how would her life be then? Could she endure it, the long vigil of death made visible? When would she begin to scream and cry? Would she still exist, conscious, untattered, compact in half an hour's time from now?

Octavian and Kate were in the other coastguards' boat. She could see Kate staring at the dark shadow in the water. Minutes passed. People in the other boat had begun to whisper. Drowned, Mary thought, drowned. The boats had closed in. The waters still sank. The opening of the cave became larger and larger. Nothing happened. Drowned.

There was a loud cry. Something was splashing in the dark hole, moving out into the light. Mary held her heart, contracted into a point of agony.

"It's Mingo."

"What?"

"It's only the dog."

Mary stared at the black hole. Tears of pain flowed upon her face.

There was another movement, a splashing, a swimming head seen clearly in the light, a louder cry, an answering cry.

"It's Pierce," someone said into her ear. Theo perhaps.

She could see her son's head plainly now. The other boat was nearer. Someone had jumped into the sea. He was being held, hoisted. "I'm all right," he was shouting "I'm all right."

Theo was holding her awkwardly as if she needed support, but she was stiff. *He's all right.* Now John, John.

"There he is!" It was Kate's voice.

Mary's boat had nosed to the front, the bow of it almost touching the cliff. Several people were in the water now, splashing about at the mouth of the cave. Mary saw the head of Ducane among them. Then he was bobbing close just at the side of the boat. He was being pushed up, pulled up, raised from the water. He rose up limp and straight out of the sea, the thin white heavy form of a naked man. He flopped into the bottom of the boat with a groan. Mary had taken off her overcoat and wrapped it around him. She gripped and held him fast.

Thirty-seven

"I UNDERSTAND you had an unpleasant experience at the weekend," said Biranne. "What happened exactly?"

"Oh nothing much. I was cut off by the tide."

"None the worse, I hope?"

"No, no, I'm fine."

"Well, you wanted to see me. Have you decided my fate?"

"Yes," said Ducane. "Have a drink."

It was early evening. Ducane, who had been in bed until half an hour ago, was wearing his black silk dressing gown with the red asterisks over his pyjamas. A fire was burning in the grate which he had laid and lit himself, since Fivey was unaccountably absent. He still felt deeply chilled, as if there were a long frozen pellet buried in the centre of his body. However, the doctor had been reassuring. Mingo had probably saved both him and Pierce from dying of exposure. By the decree of fate and chance the water had abated within feet of them.

Ducane was still simply enjoying being alive. Existing, breathing, waking up and finding oneself still there, were positive joys. Here I am, he kept saying to himself, here I am. Oh good!

"Thanks," said Biranne. "I'll have some gin. Well?"

Ducane moved over to close the drawing-room window. The noise of the rush hour in Earls Court Road became fainter. The evening sunlight made the little street glow with colour. Oh beautiful painted front doors, thought Ducane, beautiful shiny motor cars. Bless you, things.

"Well, Ducane?"

Ducane moved dreamily back toward the fire. He went to the drawer of the desk and took out Radeechy's confession which he laid on a nearby chair, and also a copy which he had made on a large piece of paper of the cryptogram which Radeechy had written on the wall of the black chapel.

"*Sit down*, Biranne."

Biranne sat down opposite to him. Still standing,

Ducane handed him the sheet of paper with the cryptogram. "Can you make anything of that?"

Biranne stared at it. "No. What is it?"

"Radeechy wrote it on the wall of the place where he performed his—experiments."

"Means nothing to me." Biranne tossed it impatiently on to the marble table beside his drink.

"Nor me. I thought you might have an inspiration."

"What's this, a sort of spiritual test? *Satori*—that's Japanese, isn't it? What does it matter anyway?"

"Radeechy matters," said Ducane. "Claudia matters. Aren't you interested?" He was staring down at Biranne.

Biranne shifted uneasily. Then he stood up and moved back, putting the chair between them. "Look here," he said, "I know what I've done. I don't need to be told by you. *I know.*"

"Good. I just wanted to be sure."

They stared intently at each other.

"Well? Go on."

"That, for a start." Ducane turned away, and with a long sigh poured himself out some gin. Then he poured a little dry vermouth into the glass, measuring it judiciously. Then he began to inspect Biranne again, looking at him with a sort of grave curiosity.

"Get it over with," said Biranne. "You're turning me in. Don't cat and mouse me as well."

"Cat and mouse," said Ducane. "Yes. Well, you may have to put up with being a little bit, as you charmingly put it, cat and moused. I want to ask you a few questions."

"So you haven't decided? Or do you want me on my knees? *Oro supplex et acclinis.* Yes, you *do* think you're God!"

"Just a few questions, my dear Biranne."

"Ask, ask."

"Where's Judy?"

"I don't know," said Biranne, surprised. "You told me to drop Judy." He gave a snarl of a laugh.

"And did you?"

"No. She dropped me. She just disappeared. I imagined she was with you. I must say I was rather relieved."

"She's not with me," said Ducane. "But never mind about Judy. Forget Judy."

"What's this all about, Ducane? I wish you'd get on with it."

"Listen, listen—"

"I am listening, confound you."

"Biranne," said Ducane, "do you still love your wife?"

Biranne put his glass down sharply on the table and turned away. He moved a little along the room. "What's the relevance of this to—anything?"

"Answer me."

"I don't know."

"Well, think about it. We've got plenty of time." Ducane sat down in one of the easy chairs, waving his glass gently about in a figure of eight. He took a sip.

"It's my affair."

Ducane was silent. He gazed into his glass, breathing slowly and deeply. It seemed to him that he still smelt of the sea. Perhaps he would smell of the sea now until the end of his days.

"All right," said Biranne. "Yes, I do still love my wife. One doesn't recover from a woman like Paula. And now that I've satisfied your rather quaint curiosity perhaps we can get back to the matter in hand."

"But this is by no means irrelevant to the matter in hand," said Ducane. "Do you ever think of returning to Paula?"

"No, of course not."

"Paula and the twins—"

"There isn't any road back to Paula and the twins."

"Why back? Why not on? They haven't been standing still in the past."

"Precisely, Paula's written me off long ago. She's got a life of her own. May I now ask the reason for these impertinent enquiries?"

"Pertinent, pertinent. Don't hustle me. I'm feeling very tired. Give yourself another drink."

Ducane pulled his chair closer to the fire and sipped the vermouth-fragrant gin. He did in fact feel very tired and curiously dreamy.

Biranne, who had been pacing the room, had stopped behind the chair opposite and was leaning on it, staring at Ducane with puzzlement.

"You were in the Commandos," said Ducane. He looked

up at Biranne's lean figure, his contracted slightly twisted clever face, under the dry fuzzy crest of hair.

"Your mind's rather straying around the place today," said Biranne.

"That business with Eric Sears. Is it specially because of that you feel you couldn't possibly return to Paula?"

"Good God! Who told you about Eric Sears?"

"Paula did."

"Oh she did, did she. Interesting. Well, it's a bit of a barrier. When one has deprived somebody's lover of his foot—"

"It becomes an obsession, a nightmare—?"

"I wouldn't say quite that. But it's certainly one of those events that *do* things, psychological things."

"I know. Paula felt this too."

"Besides, Paula detests me."

"No she doesn't. She still loves you."

"Did she tell you that too?"

"Yes."

"Christ. Why are you meddling here, Ducane?"

"Can't you see?"

"No, I can't."

"You said it was mine to command and that I could make any conditions. Well, this is my decision. I'll keep quiet about everything if you will at least try out the possibility of returning to Paula."

Biranne turned away and went to the window.

Ducane began to talk excitedly and fast, rather apologetically. "I remember your saying damn my duty, and I think now you were quite right, or rather there is another sort of duty. I don't want to wreck your life, why should I? It wouldn't help poor Claudia or poor Radeechy. And as for the processes of law, human law is only a very rough approximation to justice, and it's far too clumsy an instrument to deal with the situation that you're in. It isn't that I want to play God, I've just had this business forced upon me and I've got to do something about it. I really want to get right out without doing any damage. As for the enquiry, I'm certain about the answer to the question and I shall say so without the details. The thing about Paula just came as an inspiration, an extra, a felicitous conjecture. She certainly loves you, so why not try it? I'm not sentencing you to succeed, I'm sentencing you to try." Ducane stood up and banged his glass on to the mantelpiece.

Biranne came drifting back. He murmured, "I haven't much choice, have I?"

"Well, you have and you haven't," said Ducane. "I may as well reveal that I've decided not to open up this business anyway, I mean whatever you do. But since you're a gentleman—"

"I think you're crazy. It could be a disaster. I can't imagine how you see it as a good idea."

"I've talked to Paula about it—in general terms of course, I haven't told her this lot. And I think she very much wants to try again. She appears not to have got over you, either."

"No doubt you find this bizarre," said Biranne. He stood for a moment looking into the fire. Then he said, "All right, Ducane, all right. I'll try, just try. God knows how it'll be."

"Good. You have sometimes thought of going back?"

"Yes, I have, but only in a fantasy way. When two rather stiff-necked people part as we parted—"

"I know. That was why I felt a *deus ex machina* was not out of place."

"I trust you've enjoyed yourself. All right. But when it comes to it Paula may find she hates the sight of me. And I don't imagine I'll turn into an ideal husband overnight."

"Yes, yes. You'll go on being the bastard that you are."

Biranne smiled and picked up his drink again. "I'm surprised you don't want to preserve Paula from my clutches. Funny thing, I used to think that perhaps you and Paula— God, I'd have hated it! I couldn't bear the idea of any man coming near Paula, but you would have been the worst of all—"

"Well, if you want to keep other men off you'd better look after her yourself. By the way, I should have added another condition. You must tell Paula everything."

"About Radeechy and so on?"

"Yes. Of course Paula may decide to, as you put it, turn you in. But somehow I don't think she will. Here, you'll need this. I don't want it any more." Ducane held out Radeechy's confession.

Biranne put it on the mantelpiece. He said, "I think it

would be wiser if *you* told Paula. I mean, just the outline of facts. She may decide she doesn't want to see me. She may decide that anyway."

"I don't think so. But all right, I'll tell her. Should she come up here to see you, or would you rather go down to Dorset?"

"Let her decide that. Well, no, it might be better in town. I—I don't feel quite ready to face the twins."

Ducane laughed. "The twins are indeed formidable. But I expect you'll find that they forgive you. Now there's nothing to say but good luck."

Biranne, pulling at his lower lip, had made his face more than usually asymmetrical. "I suppose this is a kind of black-mail, isn't it."

"I suppose it is."

"I think perhaps I'll take this along after all." Biranne pocketed Radeechy's confession. They both laughed.

Biranne began to move towards the door.

"I'll drop you a note when I've seen Paula," said Ducane.

"Thanks. And in general, thanks."

They moved out toward the front door. As they reached it Biranne touched Ducane's shoulder. Ducane hastily held out his hand and they shook hands, avoiding each other's eyes. The next moment Biranne was in the street.

Ducane bent down rather wearily to pick up some letters which were lying on the mat. He trailed back into the drawing room and poked the fire. He noticed that all the furniture was dusty. Where the devil was Fivey? His pleasant sense of aliveness seemed to have faded and the pellet of cold lengthened within him. He had probably got some permanent illness which would shortly declare itself. He shivered and found that his teeth were chattering.

He had strangely looked forward to that encounter with Biranne. But it had passed off as if in a dream. It was true that he no longer thought of Biranne as a bastard. He had somehow inevitably come to like him. But also some tension was now relaxed which had bound them together. He no longer needed Biranne. And if Biranne went back to Paula, and indeed in any case, Biranne would in the long run resent Ducane's intervention and would see it only as another exercise of power. Perhaps it was only another exercise of power. Biranne would avoid him, and if Biranne were with Paula, Paula would avoid him too. Ducane sighed. He very much wanted someone sympathetic to talk to, Mary Clothier for instance, he wanted someone to console him. He wanted something new to look forward to. He sat down and began to look at the letters.

One was from Kate, one was from Jessica, and the third one was in an unfamiliar hand. Ducane opened this one first. It read as follows.

Dear John,

I expect you've been wondering what has happened to little Judy, and I feel I ought to write and tell you, since you were so very kind to me, and I mean that. You have changed my life, John, though I don't mean that you've converted me to the Ten Commandments. You've led me to Mr Right! And don't feel you've done badly, I'm afraid you take the marriage bond more seriously than I do, though I think that comes of your not being married. I was all set to leave Peter anyway when Ewan came into my life that night we drove back from your house and though we've known each other such a little time we know we're made for each other and we're going away together. Just guess where we'll be when you get this! On a boat going to Australia! What luck that my little nest-egg just covers the fare! As Ewan is a Welsh-Australian like me it seems just the thing, and he's going to take me back to his birthplace and his dad owns a motor business and will set us up so wish me joy! Well, that's all and I did like knowing you and I'm sorry we didn't you know! but I mustn't say that as Ewan is so jealous! I'll send you a postcard of the Sydney Bridge.

Yours very truly,
Judy

It took Ducane a moment to realise that 'Ewan' was the versatile Fivey. Well, he hoped that Judy would not have occasion to change her mind about Mr Right. It was just possible that here Fivey had met his match. And now he would have to look for another manservant. He would choose a good deal more providently next time. It was not until a week later that Ducane realised that some of his most expensive cuff links had disappeared with Fivey, together with a signet ring which had belonged to his father. He did not grudge Fivey the cuff links but he was sorry about the ring.

Now he opened Jessica's letter, which read as follows:

My dear John,

I am sorry not to have replied to your various letters, telegrams etc. and not to have answered the 'phone or the doorbell. It was a bit of a change, wasn't it, your being so keen to see me. As you probably know I have found out about Kate. There's not much to say. I am very shocked indeed that you should have felt it necessary to lie to me. It was a mistaken way to spare my feelings, since it was so much worse finding it all out. I hate deceits and concealments and I think you really do too, and you're probably relieved now that it's out in the open. I think there's no point in our meeting any more. You've said this yourself often enough and I was a fool not to agree. You see, I thought I loved you very much and the odd thing is I think I was just mistaken. I hope I don't hurt you by saying this. You're probably so damn relieved to get rid of me that you won't be hurt. Of course I feel very sad about it all, but not half as sad as I did two years ago. So don't worry about me. I've cried about it all so much, now I'm just snapping out of it. Better not reply to this, I'm not so cured yet that the sight of your handwriting doesn't make me feel ill. Be happy with Kate. I really wish you well, or I will soon. Please don't write or telephone. Good luck.

Jessica

Ducane dropped the letter in the fire. He saw Jessica's devotion now, intact, completed as it were, as a beautiful and touching thing. He did not feel any relief at the thought that she would soon be, perhaps already was, 'cured'. He had handled ignominiously something which now seemed to him intensely pure. The bitter quarrels, the hundred reasonings of the hundred moments, were past now and would soon be lost even to memory. What held him was the judgment of a court of higher instance that he had lied and bungled and had no dignity which could compare with her dignity of having simply loved him. He opened Kate's letter.

Dearest John,

I do hope you are really well and suffering no ill effects from your awful experience. It's not easy to know how to write to you, but I felt you would be expecting a word. So many things seem to have happened all at once.

Since I opened that letter which you asked me not to open I have of course been thinking very much about you and me, and in conclusion I am feeling thoroughly dissatisfied with myself. My nature has always been to eat cakes and have them, and one can try to do this once too often. I was so certain that with *you and me* our so strange, so nebulous, and yet so powerful *something* could be *managed* so that we had all fun and no pain. But the mechanisms of love have their own curious energies, and also (forgive me for saying this) I did rather rely on your not having misled me on a certain point. I confess I have found this revelation of another relationship hard to bear. As I said at the time, of course I have no *rights* where you are concerned. Yet maybe just this was our mistake, to think we could have this *something* without some degree of possessiveness. And if I had known earlier that you *had* a close relationship I would not have let myself go quite so far in getting fond of you. Though now it seems to me to have been idiotic to imagine that I could in any way *secure* someone as attractive as you without being either your wife or your mistress. But this is just what I did imagine. You will think me a fool. Anyway in view of it *all* I feel a little drawing back is in order, and fortunately this sort of thing happens pretty automatically. You probably feel a good deal of relief, as you must have had misgivings about an 'entanglement' with me which I now realise was mainly my doing. Be happy with Jessica. It is out of place to say 'feel free', since I never claimed to tie you, and yet there was a tie. But it is gone now. Please *of course* feel that you can come to Trescombe as before. Octavian sends love and joins me in hoping to see you soon.

Kate

Ducane dropped the sheets one by one into the flames. Kate's writing was so large that her letters came in huge bundles. He thought, how unbecoming to a woman is that particular tone of resentment, and how difficult it is even for an intelligent woman to disguise it. Then he wondered to himself, why am I being harder on Kate than on Jessica? The answer was not far to seek. Jessica had loved him more. It was self, fat self, that mattered in the end. Ducane idly picked up the piece of paper which remained on the table It was Radeechy's cryptogram. He stared at it without thought. Then he began to scrutinise it more closely. Something about the centre part of it was beginning to look curiously familiar. Then suddenly Ducane saw what it was. The central part of the square consisted of the Latin words of the ancient Christian cryptogram.

```
R O T A S
O P E R A
T E N E T
A R E P O
S A T O R
```

This elegant thing can be read forwards, backwards or vertically, and consists, with the addition of A and O (Alpha and Omega) of the letters of the first two words of the Lord's Prayer arranged in the form of a cross.

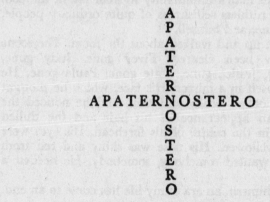

```
        A
        P
        A
        T
        E
        R
APATERNOSTERO
        O
        S
        T
        E
        R
        O
```

Who had invented, to scrawl mysteriously upon what darkened wall, that curious charm to conjure, by its ingenious form and its secret content, what powers surely more sinister and probably more real than the Christian god? And what had Radeechy done to it, to divert its power and make its talismanic value his own? Ducane studied the letters round the edge of the square. A and O again twice, only reversed. The other letters then simply read RADEECHY PATER DOMINUS.

Ducane threw the paper down. He felt disappointed, touched, upset. There was something schoolboyish and pathetic in the egoism of Radeechy's appropriation of the Latin formula. It was the sort of thing one might have carved inside one's desk at school. Perhaps all egoism when it is completely exposed has a childish quality. Ducane felt piercingly sorry for Radeechy. The solving of the crypto-gram had given him a sense of speech with him, but babbling baffled speech. After all the machinery of evil, the cross reversed, the slaughtered pigeons, the centre of it all seemed so empty and puerile. Yet Radeechy was dead, and were not the powers of evil genuine enough which had led him to two acts of violence? Ducane could not see into that world. He saw only the grotesque and the childish, and whatever was frightening here seemed to be something of limited power, something small. Perhaps there were spirits, perhaps there were evil spirits, but they were little things. The great evil, the dreadful evil, that which made war and slavery and all man's inhumanity to man lay in the cool self-justifying ruthless selfishness of quite ordinary people, such as Biranne, and himself.

Ducane got up and walked about the room. The scene had certainly been cleared. Fivey gone, Judy gone, Biranne gone, Jessica gone, Kate gone, Paula gone. He looked at himself in a mirror. His face, which he thought of as 'lean', looked peaky and thin, and he noticed the greasy unclean appearance of his hair and the dulled lock of grey in the centre of his forehead. His eyes were watery and yellowed. His nose was shiny and red from the sun. He wanted somebody, somebody. He needed a shave.

He said to himself, an era of my life has come to an end.

He reached for some writing paper and sat down and began to write.

My dear Octavian,

It is with great regret that I write to tell you that I must tender my resignation. . . .

Thirty-eight

WILL I faint when I see him? Paula wondered.
It was idiotic to meet in the National Gallery. He
had suggested on a postcard that they should meet beside
the Bronzino. Paula had been touched. But it was a silly
Richardesque idea all the same. If he had sent a *letter* and
not a *postcard* she might have suggested something else. As
it was she felt that all she could do was send another postcard saying *yes*. Fortunately there was nobody about at
this fairly early hour except an attendant who was now in
the next room.

Paula had arrived too soon. As Richard, with characteristic thoughtlessness, had suggested an early morning meeting, she had had to stay overnight at a hotel. She did not
want to stay either with John Ducane or with Octavian and
Kate. Indeed she had not told Octavian and Kate. And she
needed to be alone. She had not slept. She had been unable
to eat any breakfast. She had sat twisting her hands in the
hotel lounge and watching the clock. Then she had to run to
the cloakroom thinking she was going to be sick. At last she
rushed out of the hotel and got into a taxi. Now there was
half an hour to wait.

I might faint, thought Paula. She still felt sick and a black
canopy seemed to be suspended over her head, its lower
fringes swinging just above the level of her eyes. If that
blackness were to come rushing down her body would twist
and tilt and she would fall head first down into a dark shaft.
She felt the vertigo and the falling movement. I'd better
sit down, she thought. She moved carefully to the square
leather-cushioned seat in the centre of the room and sat
down.

The violence, the violence remained between them like
a mountain, or rather it had become more like a dreadful
attribute of Richard himself, as if he had been endowed
with a menacing metal limb. Odd to think that. It was
Eric who really had the metal limb. Had that scene in the
billiard room made Richard impossible for her for ever?

She had never really thought this, but she seemed to have assumed it. Without it she would never have left Richard. With it she had not even wondered if it was possible to stay. Was it reasonable, was it not mad, to find this thing so important, so as it were physically important?

Paula stared at Bronzino's picture. Since Richard had appropriated the picture she had deliberately refrained from making any theoretical study of it, but she remembered vaguely some of the things which she had read about it earlier on. The figures at the top of the picture are Time and Truth, who are drawing back a blue veil to reveal the ecstatic kiss which Cupid is giving to his Mother. The wailing figure behind Cupid is Jealousy. Beyond the plump figure of the rose-bearing Pleasure, the sinister enamel-faced girl with the scaly tail represents Deceit. Paula noticed for the first time the strangeness of the girl's hands, and then saw that they were reversed, the right hand on the left arm, the left hand on the right arm. Truth stares, Time moves. But the butterfly kissing goes on, the lips just brushing, the long shining bodies juxtaposed with almost awkward tenderness, not quite embracing. How like Richard it all is, she thought, so intellectual, so sensual.

A man had appeared in the doorway. He seemed to materialise rather than to arrive. Paula felt a great force pin her against the back of the seat. He came quickly forward and sat beside her.

"Hello, Paula. You're early."

"Hello—Richard—"

"So am I, I suppose. I couldn't do anything, I had to come."

"Yes."

"Well, hello—"

Paula made no attempt to talk. She was trying to control her breathing. A long breath in, now out, in, now out. It was quite easy really. She moved a little away, looking sideways at Richard, who was leaning one arm on his knee and staring unsmilingly at her. An attendant passed by. There was no one else in the room.

"Look, Paula," said Richard, in a low voice, "let's be business-like, let's make a business-like start anyway. Ducane told you about this awful thing about Radeechy?"

"Yes."

"About me and Claudia? Everything?"

"Yes."

"Well, let's separate two issues, shall we? (a) Whether you think I ought to give myself up as it were, hand the whole issue over to the police and get myself sacked and charged with being an accessory. And (b) what you and I are going to do about ourselves. If you don't mind, I'd like to get (a) settled first."

God, how like Richard this is, thought Paula, and a painful shaft of something, tenderness perhaps, memory, pierced through her. The black canopy had gone away and her breathing seemed likely to go on. But her heart was hurting her with its violence.

"Aren't the two issues connected?" said Paula. She had found herself unable to look at him and was looking at the floor.

"They're connected in the sense that you might or mightn't want to visit me in jail. Only in one of the four possible permutations of (a) and (b) and yes and no are they actually interdependent."

Oh Richard, Richard. "Is John—sort of forcing you here?"

"No, no one's forcing me. I just want (a) settled. We can't take (b) first."

"John seems to think it's all right to keep it all quiet, and he—"

"Damn John. What do you think?"

Paula had not expected this. She had been utterly appalled by the story about Claudia and Radeechy, but she had not thought that any further judgment on it would be required from her. Or rather, she had at once taken over Ducane's judgment that it was not necessary for Richard to own up. She tried to think about it now. Richard was requiring her to be objective. That in itself was extraordinary, as extraordinary as the fact that they were now sitting side by side. She looked up at the terrible figures of Truth and Time.

"I don't think it's necessary, Richard. John's quite clear that his enquiry doesn't need your evidence. You can't help—the others now. You'd be punishing yourself and I see no point in it."

Richard gave a long sigh.

She thought, he's relieved, oh God, and she felt the pain again. She looked back at the floor and let her gaze creep as far as to his feet. Metal limbs.

"Now what about (b), Paula?"

"Wait, wait," she murmured. "Let us be, as you say, business-like." She moved a little further away and began to look at him. His twisted face had screwed itself further into a contorted suspicious mask of anxiety which he touched periodically with his hand as if trying to smooth it out.

"Richard, do you *want* to come back?"

He said a short clipped "Yes". He added, "Do you want me back?"

Paula said in the same quick tone, "Yes". Their two "yeses" hovered, inconclusive and curt.

"Richard, you've been living with somebody, haven't you?"

"How did you know? Or did you just assume it?"

"I went one day—to the house—just to look—when I knew you were at the office. And I saw a rather beautiful girl let herself in with a latch key."

"God. Did you do that, Paula? God. Well, there was a girl, but it's over now. She was a tart."

"What sort of difference do you think that makes?"

"All right. None. Anyway, she's gone. She's eloped to Australia with Ducane's manservant, if you must know!"

"Did she write and tell you?"

"No, Ducane told me. Christ, you're not going to be jealous of a tart who's half way to Australia!"

"There hasn't been anyone else, just lately I mean?"

"No. What about you? Have you had anybody?"

"No."

"You're not in love with Ducane, are you?"

"No, of course not, Richard!"

"Are you sure?"

"Yes!"

"Good. Well, go on interrogating me. I can't for the life of me see why you should want me back at all."

"Richard, I must talk to you about Eric."

"Christ, that bastard hasn't turned up again?"

"No, no. He wrote and said he was going to, but he changed his mind, thank heavens."

"You don't love *him*, do you?"

"No, no, no."

"Then can't we forget him?"

"No, we can't, that's the point. At least we can't forget—what happened. I know this sounds a bit mad, but that awful scene has remained like a sort of black lump spreading poison."

"I know," he said softly, "I know."

Some Americans had arrived to inspect the Bronzino. They lingered, making learned comments, then glanced at the tense immobile pair upon the seat and hastily took themselves off.

"Paula," said Richard, "we're both rational beings. Maybe we couldn't do anything about this apart, but we might be able to do something together. Something dreadful happened for which we were both to blame. It *happened*. You know I don't believe in God or in guilt feelings or in repentance or any stuff of that sort. The past is gone, it doesn't exist any more. However, things that do exist are responsibilities occasioned by the past and also our thoughts about it, which we may not find it very easy to control. I judge that there's nothing further we can do for Eric except try to forget the bloody fool. There are things we might do for each other to make this cloud lift, if we decided that it was worth our trying to live together again. I don't think the blank lump would poison us then. I think it would just gradually go away."

As Paula looked at him, listening to his precise high-pitched voice so familiarly explaining something, expounding something, she felt a shudder pass through her which she recognised a second later as physical desire. She wanted to hurl her arms around Richard and hold him tightly. She stiffened and closed her eyes.

"What is it, Paula?"

"Nothing, nothing. You may be right. Let's go on." She opened her eyes and looked into a blue-golden blur of Bronzino. "Richard, if you were to come to me, if, if, would you go on having love affairs with other girls from time to time?"

326

After a short silence Richard said in a dry voice, "Possibly."

"I thought so—"

"Please, Paula—It's hard to say. At this moment I feel —well, hell, feelings are just feelings. I don't know what I'd do. If the old pattern continues I'd probably be unfaithful now and then. I'd have to wait and see. You know it's no use my telling you I've *decided* anything."

"I know. I expect I could stand it. Only, Richard, will you, would you, please not tell me lies?"

"You mean you'd want me to tell you every time I kiss my secretary?"

"No. But I'd want to know if you were going to bed with your secretary."

Richard was silent again for a short while, during which time a group of schoolchildren did the room with celerity. He said slowly, "It's not at all easy to make such promises beforehand, Paula. At least it's easy to make them. It's not so easy to be sure what one will do when one is being tempted by some piece of quick trouble-free pleasure."

Paula stared at the enamel-faced figure of Deceit, and at her reversed hands and scaly tail. Was it here, after all, that everything broke down and descended into a roaring shaft of shattered masks and crumpled rose petals and bloody feathers? But as she looked, clear-eyed now, she felt, infinitely stronger than any doubt, her intention to take Richard back. She turned to him.

"All right. But lies do corrupt and spoil."

"I know that. I would keep them to a minimum."

The Richardesque precision and even his intent at this moment of all moments to keep the door a little bit ajar for Venus, Cupid and Folly, touched her to an intensity of love for him which she could hardly control.

"Paula, about the twins—"

"What about the twins?"

"They're not anti-me?"

"Oh my darling, no. They've kept their love for you, nothing's touched it, I know that."

The sudden endearment, the image of the children, brought a hot rush of tears as far as her eyes. She blinked, turning away, and the thought came to her for the first time, am I still attractive to him?

"Thank God for that. When can I—? I mean, have we decided anything?"

Paula stared back, tears and all. "Richard, ask yourself, ask yourself, do you really want to?"

"Why, Paula, you're—Oh Paula, yes, yes, yes. Please give me your hand."

Paula moved towards him. Their hands touched, their knees touched. They were both trembling.

"Oh Richard, not here—someone will—"

"Yes, here."

The Americans, who had come back hoping for another look at the Bronzino, retreated rapidly.

"Paula, I'm falling in love with you again, most terribly in love."

"I've never been out of love with you, never for a second."

"Look, Paula, do you mind if we go home *at once*? I want to kiss you properly, I want to—"

They sprang up. Richard took a quick look at the attendant's back and approached the Bronzino. He drew luxurious fingers across the canvas, caressing the faintly touching mouths of Venus and Cupid. Then he seized Paula by the hand and pulled her after him. They left the Gallery at a run. The attendant turned about and began anxiously counting the pictures.

Thirty-nine

"HAVE a drink," said Ducane.
"Thanks. A little sherry."

"Do you mind the fire? It's not too hot for you?"

"No, I like it. Are you sure you're feeling all right?"

"I'm feeling much better. How's Pierce?"

"Pierce is in splendid shape. He sends much love, by the way. He said I was to remember to say *much* love."

"Mine to him. Do sit down. It's so nice of you to have come."

Mary Clothier dropped her coat on the floor and sat down rather awkwardly, holding her glass of sherry stiffly in front of her as if it were something she was unaccustomed to holding, such as a revolver. Her hand trembled slightly and some drops fell on to the stretched blue and white check of her dress and softly moistened her thigh. She looked around the room with curiosity. It was a restrained dignified pretty room full, to Mary's taste over-full, of intense quietly coloured trinkets. These lay about on polished surfaces looking more like toys than like ornaments. She looked out through the sun-drenched window at the cast-iron window boxes and brightly painted doors of the small neat houses opposite, and her heart sank. She thought, how little I know him.

"Isn't it splendid about Richard and Paula?" she said.

"Marvellous."

"I'm very glad," said Mary. "They're so happy, just like gay children." She sighed. "But weren't you surprised? I had no idea they were thinking of it. Paula is so secretive."

"Mmm. Was a bit quick. Just goes to show. Life can be sudden. All that."

Mary looked at Ducane who was trampling about on the other side of the room, in the space behind a tall armchair, like an animal in a stall, and leaning momently on the back of the chair to attend to her. He was wearing, and had profusely apologised for, a black silk dressing gown covered with spidery red asterisks, and dark red pyjamas underneath.

The garb made him look faintly exotic, faintly Spanish, like an actor, like a dancer.

"John, what was it like in the cave? Pierce won't tell me anything. And my imagination keeps on and on. I've been having awful dreams about it. Did you think you were going to die?"

Ducane said slowly, leaning over the chair, "It's hard to say, Mary. Perhaps. Pierce was very tough and brave."

"So were you, I'm sure. Can you tell me what it was like, could you describe it starting at the beginning?"

"Not now, Mary, if you don't mind." He added, "I saw your face there in the darkness, in a strange way. I'll tell you—later."

His air of authority calmed her. "All right. So long as you *will* tell me. Did you make that decision, John?"

"What decision?"

"You said you had to make a decision concerning another person."

"Oh yes. I decided that."

"And was it the right decision?"

"Yes. I tidied that business up. I've tidied up a number of things. In fact I've tidied up nearly everything!"

"Good for you."

"You don't know what you're talking about!" said Ducane. "Sorry. I'm still awfully nervy."

Mary smiled a little uncertainly. Then she said with a sudden random bitterness, "I don't know anything about you."

"You've known me for years."

"No. We've noticed each other as familiar objects on a landscape, like houses or railway stations, things one passes on a journey. We've said the minimum of obvious things to each other."

"You do us less than justice. We've communicated with each other. We are alike."

"I am not like you," she said. "No, you belong to a different race." She looked about the room at the toy-like trinkets. Outside the window the heavy sunny evening was husky with distant sound.

He looked puzzled, discouraged. "I have a feeling that you are not complimenting me now!"

330

She stared at his thin brown face, his narrow nose, the particular fall of the dry dark hair. Their conversation sounded to her hollow, like an intermittent rhythmless drum beat. She shivered.

"It doesn't matter. You are different. I must go."

"But you've only just come."

"I only came to see if you were all right."

"Perhaps I ought to have told you I'm not! You hardly flatter me by rushing away so soon. I was hoping you would have dinner with me."

"I'm afraid I have an engagement."

"Well, don't go yet, Mary. Have some more sherry."

He filled her glass. The black silk brushed her knee.

Why have I landed myself in this absurd and terrible position, thought Mary Clothier. Why have I been such a perfectly frightful ass? Why have I, after all these years, and contrary to all sense and all hope and all reason fallen quite madly in love with my old friend John Ducane?

The realisation that she was in love with Ducane came to Mary quite suddenly on the day after the rescue from the cave, but it seemed to her then that she had already been in love for some time. It was as if she had for some time been under an authority the nature of which she had not understood, though she had had an inkling of it in the moment almost of violence when she had thrown her coat about the wet cold naked man. On the following day, when Ducane had already been taken back to London by Octavian, Mary felt a blackness of depression which she took to be the aftermath of terror. She was weeding the garden in the hot afternoon. With a savage self-punishing persistence she leaned over the flowerbed, feeling the light runnels of perspiration crawling upon her cheek. She had been thinking intensely about Ducane but without thinking anything specific. It was as if she were attending to him ardently but blankly. She straightened up and went to sit down in the shade underneath the acacia tree. Her hot body went limp and she lay down flat. As she relaxed she had a vivid almost hallucinatory image of Ducane's face, together with a physical convulsion like an electric shock. She lay quite still, collecting herself.

Realising that one is in love with someone in whom one

has long been interested is a curious process. What can it be said to consist of? Each human being swims within a sea of faint suggestive imagery. It is this web of pressures, currents and suggestions, something often so much less definite than pictures, which ties our fugitive present to our past and future, composing the globe of consciousness. We think with our body, with its yearnings and its shrinkings and its ghostly walkings. Mary's whole body now, limp beneath the tall twisted acacia tree, became aware of John from head to foot in a new way. She imaged him with a turning and hovering of her being, as if a wraith were plucking itself out of her towards him. She felt his absence from her as a great tearing force moving out of her entire flesh. And she shivered with a dazzled joy.

Had she, then, not been in love with Willy? No, she had not been in love with Willy. She had loved Willy with her careful anxious mind and with her fretful fingertips. She had not thus adored him with her whole thought-body, her whole being of yearning. She had not been content to be for him simply herself and a woman. This was the old, the unmistakable state of being in love which she had imagined she would never experience again. Indeed as she lay pinned to the ground, looking up at the blotched sunlight moving upon the lined form of the acacia tree, she felt that she had never experienced it before. And she turned over groaning on to her face.

Great love is inseparable from joy, but further thought brought to her an equal portion of pain. There was absolutely nothing that she could do with this huge emotion which she had so suddenly discovered in herself. It was not only that Ducane belonged to Kate. He was a man utterly inaccessible to herself. He had been very kind to her, but that was simply because he was a good man who was kind to everybody. His attention to her had been professional, efficient and entirely momentary. She was far too plain an object to remain visible to him. On the whole he was used to her as one might be used to an efficient servant.

Of course he must never know. How long would it take her to recover? At the thought that she had known of her condition for twenty minutes and was already wondering about her recovery, tears brimmed over Mary's closed eyes and mingled with the sweat on her shining face and dripped down into the warm grass. No, she would not think of recovery. Indeed she felt that she would never recover. She would live with her condition. And he must never know. She must make no move, utter no breath, lift no finger.

Nevertheless in two days' time, after two days of pure agony, she felt that she had to see him. She would see him briefly, utter some commonplaces, and be gone. But she felt that she had to see him or she would die. She had to make a journey towards him. Sick with emotion, she travelled to London, telephoned him, and asked if she could call upon him briefly before dinner.

She sat in his presence in an ecstasy of pain and prayer. Her intense joy at being in his presence flickered through the matrix of her dullness, her stupidity, her inability to say anything which was not tedious. Oh John! she cried within herself as if for help. Oh my darling, help me to endure it!

John Ducane leaned on the back of the chair and contemplated Mary's small round head, compact as an image out of Ingres, her pale golden complexion, the very small ears behind which she had tucked her straight dark hair.

John Ducane thought to himself, why have I landed myself in this absurd and terrible position? Why have I been such a perfectly frightful ass? Why have I so infelicitously, inopportunely, improperly and undeniably fallen quite madly in love with my old friend, Mary Clothier?

It seemed now to Ducane that his thoughts had been, already for a long time, turning to Mary, running to her instinctively like animals, like children. The moment had been important when he had thought about her, we are under the same orders. But he had known, long before he had formulated it clearly, that she was like him, morally like in some way that was important. Her mode of being gave him a moral, even a metaphysical, confidence in the world, in the reality of goodness. No love is entirely without worth, even when the frivolous calls to the frivolous and the base to the base. But it is in the nature of love to discern good, and the best love is in some part at any rate a love of what is good. Ducane was very conscious, and had always been conscious, that he and Mary communicated by means of what was good in both of them.

Ducane's absolute respect for Mary, his trust in her, his apprehension in her of virtues which he understood, made the background of an affection which grew, under the complex force of his needs, into love. It is possible that at this time he idolised her, and fell in love at the moment at which he thought, she is better than me. During his gradual loss of a stiff respect he had had for himself, he had felt the need to locate in someone else the picture of an upright person. His relation with Jessica, his relation even with Kate, perhaps in a subtle way even more his relation with Kate, had left him muddled. He was a man who, unless he could think well of himself, became confused and weak of will. He had begun to need Mary when he had begun to need a better image of himself. She was the consoling counterpart of his self-abasement.

Also she was of course, he realised, a mother goddess. She was the mother of Trescombe. In this light he was able to see something almost mysterious in the plainness of her role. She had already been transfigured for him by his jealousy of Willy, a jealousy which had surprised him, appearing first as an unexplained depression, a blank want of generosity. This was a jealousy very different from the jealousy of Octavian which he had momently felt at the withdrawal of Kate. Jealousy of Octavian had wakened him to a sense of his own position as improper and idiotic. Jealousy of Willy had made him feel, I want a girl of my own. And then, I want this girl of my own.

It seemed to him now, and this added to his pain, that he had only urged her to marry Willy out of guilt and fear at his own failure with Willy. Of course she must never know how he felt and Willy must never know. Once they were married he would avoid them absolutely. I am out of the saga, he thought. He had a heavy sense of being left in total isolation; everyone had withdrawn from him and the person who could most have helped him was pre-empted by another.

He stared at Mary. His whole body ached with his sense of how much she might have done for him. To cause himself a sharp sobering pain he said, "How is Willy?"

"Oh, very well I believe. I mean, much as usual."

"When are you getting married?" said Ducane.

Mary put her glass down on the octagonal marble table. She flushed and snapped in a breath. "But I'm not getting married to Willy."

Ducane came round the armchair and sat down in it. "You said it wasn't quite fixed—"

"It's not happening at all. Willy doesn't want to marry. It was all a mistake." She looked very unhappy.

"I'm sorry—" said Ducane.

"I thought Kate would have told you," said Mary. She was still red, looking hard at her glass.

"No," said Ducane. He thought, I suppose I'd better tell her. "Kate and I—well, I don't think we'll be seeing quite so much of each other—at least not like—"

"Did you really quarrel then?" Mary asked in a slightly breathless voice.

"Not really. But—I'd better tell you, Mary, though you won't think well of me. I was formerly entangled, well in a way was entangled, with a girl in London and Kate found this out, and felt I'd been lying and I suppose I had. It was rather complicated, I'm afraid. Anyway it somehow spoilt things. It was foolish of me to imagine that I could—manage Kate."

This isn't the way to say it, he thought. It makes it sound dreadful. She'll think badly of me for ever.

"I see. A girl in—I see."

He said rather stiffly, "You must be sad about Willy. I'm sorry."

"Yes. He sort of turned me down!"

She loves him, he thought, she loves him. She'll persuade him in time. Oh God.

Mary had begun slowly to gather her coat into a bunch around her feet. "Well, I hope you'll be happy, John, happy with—Yes."

"Don't go, Mary."

"I have got an appointment."

He groaned to himself. He wanted to take her in his arms, he wanted to be utterly revealed to her, he wanted her to understand.

"Let me give you something before you go, something to

335

take away with you." He looked wildly round the room. A French glass paper-weight was lying on the desk on top of some papers. He picked it up and quickly threw it into Mary's lap. The next moment he saw that she had burst into tears.

"What is it, my heart?" Ducane knelt beside her, thrusting the table away. He touched her knee.

Holding the paper-weight tightly in her skirt and blowing her nose Mary said, "John, you'll think I'm crazy and you're not to worry. There's something I've got to tell you. I can't go away out of that door without telling you. I wasn't really in love with Willy. I loved Willy dearly, I love him dearly, but it's not being in love. One knows what being in love is like and it is a very terrible thing. I shouldn't tell you this, you've got this girl, and you've been so awfully kind to me and I oughtn't to trouble you and I meant to say nothing about it, I really did, and if you hadn't—"

"Mary, what on earth are you talking about?"

"I love you, John, I've fallen in love with you. I'm sorry, I know it's improbable, and perhaps you won't believe me, but it's true, I'm terribly sorry. I promise I'll be rational about it and not a nuisance and I wouldn't expect you to see me, well now you won't want to see me—Oh God!" She hid her face in the handkerchief.

Ducane rose to his feet. He went over to the window and looked out at the beautiful geraniums and the beautiful motor cars and the blue evening sky full of beautiful aeroplanes on their way to London Airport. He tried to control his voice.

"Mary, have you really got a dinner appointment?"

"No. I just said that. Sorry, John, I'm going now."

"I suggest you stay," said Ducane, "and talk the situation over. There's plenty to eat in the house and I've got a bottle of wine."

"There's no point in talking it over. It would only make things worse. There's nothing to say. I just love you. That's all of it."

"That's half of it," said Ducane. "Possibly over dinner I might tell you the other half."

Forty

"WAS that really it?"

"Yes."

"Are you sure you did it right?"

"My God, I'm sure!"

"Well, I don't like it."

"Girls never do the first time."

"Perhaps I'm a Lesbian."

"Don't be silly, Barbie. You did like it a little?"

"Well, just the first bit."

"Oh Barb, you were so wonderful, I worship you."

"Something's sticking into my back."

"I hope you aren't lying on my glasses."

"Damn your glasses. No, it's just an ivy root."

"You're marked all over with beautiful marks of ivy leaves!"

"You were so *heavy*, Pierce."

"I felt heavy afterwards. I felt I was just a great contented stone lying on top of you."

"Are you sure I won't have a baby?"

"Sure."

"Do you think I'll get to like it more, to like it as much as you do?"

"You'll like it more. You'll never like it as much as I do, Barbie. I've been in paradise."

"Well, I'm glad somebody's pleased."

"Oh Barb darling—"

"All right, all right. Do you think we've been wicked?"

"No. We love each other. We do love each other, don't we, Barbie?"

"Yes. But it could still be wrong."

"It could. I don't feel it is though. I feel as if everything in the world is with us."

"I feel that too."

"You don't regret it, you won't hate me?"

"No. It had to happen to me and I'm glad it's happened like this."

337

"I've loved you so long, Barb—"

"I feel I couldn't have done it with anyone else. It's because I know you so well, you're like my brother."

"Barb!"

"Well, you know what I mean. Darling Pierce, your body looks so different to me now and so wonderful."

"I can't think why girls like men at all. We're so rough and nasty and stick-like compared with you. You're not getting cold, are you?"

"No, I'm fine. What a hot night. How huge the moon is."

"It looks so close, as if we could touch it."

"Listen to the owl, isn't he lovely? Pierce—"

"Yes?"

"Do you think we'll either of us ever go to bed with anyone else?"

"No, well, Barb, you know we're quite young and—"

"You're thinking about other girls *already*!"

"Barb, Barb, please don't move away, please bring your hand back again. Darling, I love you, good God, you know I love you!"

"Maybe I do. You were horrid enough to me."

"I promise I'll never be horrid again. You were horrid too."

"I know. Let's *really* love each other, Pierce. In a good way."

"Yes, let's. It won't be difficult."

"It won't be easy. Perhaps we could get married after you've taken your A levels."

"Well, Barb, we mustn't be in *too* much of a hurry—Oh darling, *please*—"

"When are we going to do this again? Tomorrow?"

"We can't tomorrow. I've got to go to Geoffrey Pember-Smith's place."

"Can't you put it off?"

"Well, no. You see there's this chance to have the yacht—"

"What about me? I thought you loved me!"

"I do love you, darling Barb. But yachts are important too."

"Well, you could have knocked me down with a feather."

"Me too."

"What a dark horse Mary is. And after all that business with Willy."

"My dear Kate, you did rather jump to conclusions about Mary and Willy. She was never too certain about it."

"Maybe. But I'm sure she wasn't thinking of appropriating John."

"Perhaps John appropriated her."

"No, no, Octavian. It was her doing. It must have occurred to her after the thing with Willy fell through. She felt she had to have somebody. I hope they won't regret it."

"I'm sure they won't."

"You're being very charitable, Octavian."

"Well, we must forgive him, you know."

"Of course we *forgive* him. But it was a little sudden."

"It does seem to be the mating season, doesn't it."

"First Richard and Paula, and then this bombshell."

"John's certainly a remarkable peacemaker."

"You think he fixed up Paula and Richard? I doubt that. I must say, I wouldn't be married to Richard for the world."

"Paula seems pleased enough. I think they'll be happy. They know the worst, and they're terribly in love."

"Your universal benevolence is beginning to depress me, Octavian."

"Sorry, darling. Shall I turn out the light?"

"Yes, now we can see the moon properly, it's *immense*."

"Like a huge apricot."

"Listen to the owl."

"Yes, isn't he lovely."

"Where's Barbie? I didn't see her after dinner."

"Gone to bed I think."

"Thank heavens young Pierce seems to have gone off the boil a bit. He's going to stay with those Pember-Smith people tomorrow."

"Yes. Barb must be relieved. How long are the twins staying on?"

"At least another week. Paula is having the house in Chelsea redecorated."

"A rite of exorcism, I imagine."

"Fumigation. It probably needs it. By the way, what was the name of that chap, you remember, the chap who killed himself in your office?"

"Radeechy."

"Didn't you say John thought Richard was involved with him somehow?"

"It turned out there was nothing in that, at least nothing important. I believe they both knew the same girl, or something."

"Why did John resign from the office, was it because he felt he'd muffed that enquiry thing?"

"No, I don't think so. His report was a bit thin, but the whole issue was old hat anyway."

"Why then?"

"He wants to get on with his research, and maybe do some more teaching. He's been talking of resigning for years."

"I expect he wants to make a break, a new life and all that."

"I hope he'll go on coming here—I mean *they* will."

"I suppose I hope it. Octavian, I must get another housekeeper. Can we afford it?"

"Yes, darling. Only don't hurt Casie's feelings."

"Damn Casie. Well, no I won't. I wonder if anyone would understand if I advertised for a head parlourmaid? Oh Octavian, it's so sad, all our house seems broken apart, everyone is going."

"Darling, you'll soon get other ones."

"Other whats?"

"I mean, well, people."

"I think you're being horrid."

"Dear love, don't let go."

"You disgraceful old hedonist. I just can't get over John and Mary. Do you think he's the sort of homosexual who has to get married to persuade himself he's normal?"

"You think he must be homosexual because he was moderately able to resist you!"

"Octavian, you *beast*. Mary *is* rather the mother figure, isn't she?"

"I don't think John's queer. Mary just is his type, serious and so on."

"Yes. I suppose I just wasn't his type. I feel now I made an awful ass of myself about John."

"You're an affectionate girl, Kate."

"Well, don't say it in that tone!"

"John wasn't up to it. It was too complicated for him. He didn't really understand you."

"He didn't really understand me."

"John's a very nice chap, but he's not the wise good man that we once thought he was."

"We thought he was God, didn't we, and he turns out to be just like us after all."

"Just like us after all."

"Are you ready, darling?"

"Ready, sweetheart."

"Octavian, I do love you. You cheer me up so much. Isn't it wonderful that we tell each other everything?"

In fact there were a few details of Octavian's conduct, concerning long late evenings when he stayed in the office with his secretary, which Octavian did not think it necessary to divulge to Kate. However he easily forgave himself, so completely forgetting the matter as to feel blameless, and as he frequently decided that each occasion was the last he did not view himself as a deceiver of his wife. His knowledge that there was indeed nothing which she concealed from him was a profound source of happiness and satisfaction.

The apricot moon shone and the night owl hooted above the rituals of love.

"They are going," said Theo.

"Yes," said Willy.

"You are sad."

"I am always sad."

"Not always. You were almost cheerful a fortnight ago. I thought you were changed."

"Something happend that time in London."

"What happened?"

"I made love to a girl."

"Good heavens, Willy! I mean, with all due respect—"

"Yes, I was surprised too."

"What was she like?"

"A gazelle."

"And when are you seeing her again?"

"I'm not."

341

"But Willy, why not? Didn't she want to?"

"She did. But no, no, Theo. I am a dead man."

"Dead men don't make love."

"That was just a miracle. But a miracle need have no consequences. It is outside causality."

"I should have thought a miracle would have consequences by definition. And you admit to being changed."

"I don't. You said I was changed. I am just a past with no present."

"That's a cowardly lie, if ever there was one."

"What can one do with the past, Theo?"

"Forgive it. Let it enter into you in peace."

"I can't."

"You must forgive Hitler, Willy. It is time."

"Damn Hitler. No, I will never forgive him. But that's not the problem."

"What is the problem?"

"Forgiving myself."

"What do you mean?"

"It's not what he did. It's what I did."

"Where?"

"*Da unten. Là-bas* Dachau."

"Willy, Willy, Willy, hang on."

"I'm all right."

"I mean, don't tell me."

"You used to say tell me. Now you say don't."

"I've gone that much more to bits, Willy. I feel so ill all the time. All right, tell me in general terms. What happened?"

"I betrayed two people because I was afraid, and they died."

"In that inferno—. You must pity yourself too, Willy."

"They were gassed. My life wasn't even threatened."

"We are clay, Willy. There is no man whose rationality and goodness cannot be broken by torment. Do not think 'I did it'. Think it was done."

"But I did do it."

"That sense of ownership is pride."

"They were gassed, Theo."

Willy was sitting in his armchair, his lame leg extended into the soft grey powdery pile of wood ash in the fireplace. Theo was sitting with his back to the fireplace on an upright chair which he had drawn up close. He looked away past Willy's head toward the long window full of glittering blue sky. His arm lay heavily upon Willy's arm, his hand cupping and caressing the curve of the shoulder.

Willy stroked back his longish white hair and relaxed his face into a bland steely calm. "You might be right, but I can't think in your terms. It's not even like memory. It's all just there."

"All the time, Willy?"

"Every hour, every minute. And there's no machinery to shift it. No moral machinery. No psychological machinery."

"We'll see, my dear. Where there's been one miracle there could be another one. Maybe you should tell me the whole thing after all."

"Yes, I think so too."

I won't listen though, thought Theo. He's not really telling it to me.

Theo moved his hand upward a little, fingering the collar of Willy's shirt at the neck. He fixed his eyes upon the dazzling window. The sunlight seemed to have got inside the glass and the blue sky was visible through a sparkling screen of splintered light. As Willy's voice murmured on, Theo tried hard to think about something else. He thought about the seagull with the broken wing which the twins had found and brought to him. Henrietta was crying and carrying the seagull which was sitting on one of her hands, while she held and caressed it with the other. The twins came running to Theo across the stones. When an animal was hurt the twins became helpless and confused. Could anything be done, could the broken wing be mended, should they go to find a vet? Theo said no, there was nothing to be done with a broken wing. He would take the bird from them and drown it quickly. It was the kindest thing, the only thing. The bird would not know what was happening. He took the seagull carefully from Henrietta's outstretched hands and told the twins to go away. They ran off at once together, Edward now in tears as well. Theo did not pause to take off his shoes or roll up his trousers, he walked straight into the sea, his shoes crunching on the sunny underwater stones. The seagull lay perfectly still in

343

his hands, its bright eyes seeming impassive, as if calm. The bird was light, light, and the grey feathers soft, soft. Theo bent down and quickly plunged the soft grey parcel of life down underneath the water. There was a faint movement in his hands. He stood there bent for a long time, with his eyes closed, feeling the hot sun upon his neck. At last he straightened himself. He did not look down at the bedraggled thing in his hands. He dared not leave it in the sea in case the twins should see it again. He mounted the shingle and walked with wet clinging trouser legs along to the far end of the beach where he knelt and dug with his hands as deep a hole as he could in the loose falling pebbles. He put the dead bird into the hole and covered it up carefully. Then he moved a little away and lay face downward on the stones.

Willy's voice continued to speak and Theo, only half listening, pressed the thought of the seagull against his heart. There was silence in the room at last.

"Would you like some tea?" said Theo.

"Yes. Would you make it?"

Theo got up and went into Willy's little kitchen. He thought, what is the point here, what is the point. What can I say to him. That one must soon forget one's sins in the claims of others. But how to forget. The point is that nothing matters except loving what is good. Not to look at evil but to look at good. Only this contemplation breaks the tyranny of the past, breaks the adherence of evil to the personality, breaks, in the end, the personality itself. In the light of the good, evil can be seen in its place, not owned, just existing, in its place. Could he explain all this to Willy? He would have to try.

As he filled the kettle he could see, from the corner window, a girl in a blue dress with long loose fair hair coming up the path from the beech wood. He called out, "You've got a visitor, Willy."

"Is it Mary?"

"No. A girl unknown."

Willy darted up and was beside his shoulder. "Oh my God! Theo, whatever shall I do? It's Jessica."

"Who's Jessica?"

"The gazelle."

"Aren't you pleased?"

"However did she find out?"

"You can give her tea. I'll go away."

"Theo, don't abandon me! Look, Theo, I can't face it. Would you mind? I'll go and hide in the graveyard. Tell her I've left Trescombe and you don't know my address and you live here now. Will you tell her? And make her believe it. Get rid of her. Come and find me when you're certain she's gone. I'll go out the back door."

The back door banged. Theo thoughtfully made the tea. The long-legged long-haired girl came resolutely up the hill.

"Hello, Jessica," said Theo, meeting her at the door.

She looked surprised. "I wanted to see—"

"Yes, yes, you want Willy. He's not here at the moment but you can easily find him." Theo gave Jessica minute instructions about how to reach the graveyard.

He closed the door again and poured himself out a cup of tea. He felt sad, sad.

"Why look, Mingo and Montrose are sharing the basket."

"So they are. Goodbye Mingo, goodbye Montrose."

"They're too lazy to get up. I do hope Casie liked her present."

"Of course she did, Mary. She's just miserable that you're going."

"I couldn't get her to stop crying. Oh dear. Is it wicked to be so happy when someone else isn't?"

"No, I don't think so. It's one's duty to be happy. Especially when one's married."

"Then I will be your dutiful happy wife, John. Have we got everything."

"We've got a hell of a lot of things. I don't know whether we've got everything."

"I'm rather relieved Octavian and Kate aren't here. Where was it they said they were going?"

"Petra."

"Pierce and Barb got off all right. Wasn't it nice of the Pember-Smiths to invite Barb too?"

"Hmm. I suspect young Barb is going to keep young Pierce in order."

"Oh John, I'm so happy. Could you just hold my hand-bag?"

"Your bag weighs a ton. Are you still carrying that paper-weight about?"

"I won't be parted from that paper-weight."

"Come along then, you sentimental girl."

"I *think* that's everything. It's so quiet here now the cuckoos have gone."

"Come on, the car's waiting."

"Is that really your car?"

"*Our* car, sweetheart."

"*Our* car."

"You ought to recognize it by now!"

"It's so improbably big."

Ducane and Mary, laden with suitcases and baskets, walked out of the front door of Trescombe House and across the lawn to the sweep of the drive. The big black Bentley awaited them.

A red-haired man leapt out and opened the boot and the back door of the car.

"Mary," said Ducane, "I want you to meet my new chauffeur, Peter McGrath. He's a very useful man."

"Hello, Peter," said Mary. She shook hands with him.

The bundles were stowed in the boot and Mary got into the back of the car and tucked her white dress in around her knees. McGrath got into the front. Ducane, who had super-vised the loading of the boot, began to get into the front of the car too. Then recollecting himself he quickly climbed into the back beside Mary. He began to laugh.

"What are you laughing at?"

"Nothing. Home, McGrath." He said to Mary, "Watch this."

Ducane pressed a button and a glass screen rose up silently between the front and back of the car.

Ducane looked into the eyes of Mary Ducane. His married life would not be without its problems. But he could explain everything to her, everything, in time. He began to laugh again. He took his wife in his arms.

"Uncle Theo, may I have that Indian stamp?"

"Yes, Edward. Here."

346

"Edward, you pig. I *did* see it first!"

Theo quickly tore the stamp off the corner of the envelope. The writing was unknown to him. But the postmark made him tremble.

"Where are you going, twins?"

"Up to the top of the cliff. Like to come?"

"No, I'm just going to the meadow."

Theo thrust the letter into his pocket. He watched the twins depart. Then he walked across the lawn and through the gap in the spiraea hedge and sat down on the seat. Out to sea a small pewter-coloured cloud was coming up over the horizon. Theo squinted into the sunshine and pressed the letter, still in his pocket, against his side. Then with a sigh he slowly drew it out and opened it.

The old man was dead. Theo had known this from the first moment of seeing the letter. Only to tell him this would someone else have written to him now from that place. The old man was dead. He had spoken kindly of Theo just before he died. The old man was dead with whom he might have made his peace and who alone of mortals could have given him peace.

Theo had never revealed to his family that while he was in India he had taken vows in a Buddhist monastery. He had thought to end his days there. But after some years he had left, fled from it, after an incident involving a young novice. The boy was later drowned in the Ganges. Everyone who wrote to Theo about it said that it was certainly an accident.

Only the old man could release me from this wheel, Theo thought as year after year he wondered if he should go back and year after year felt it all recede from him past hope, past endeavour. He saw in dreams the saffron robes, the shaven heads, the green valley where he had thought to end his days. He could not find his way back there. He remembered the doubts the old man had had at the start. "We like to take people young," he said, "before they are soiled by the world," and he had looked doubtfully at Theo. But Theo was ardent then, like a man in love. He wanted that discipline, that silence, and the thing which lay beyond it.

I am sunk in the wreck of myself, thought Theo. I live in

347

myself like a mouse inside a ruin. I am huge, sprawling, corrupt and empty. The mouse moves, the ruin moulders. This is all. Why did I ever leave them, what was I fleeing from? What spoilt scene that I could not then endure? He had fled from a broken image of himself and from the very certainty of understanding and of being drawn back into the structure which he had damaged. He had seemed to leave his past utterly behind when with a passion which seemed a guarantee of renewed life he had entered into the community of these men. To find himself even there the same being as before shocked his pride, the relentless egoism which he now saw had not suffered an iota of diminution from his gesture of giving up the world. The place was spoiled for him. He had given it his free and upright self. He could not humbly surrender to it his broken self. Perhaps he had loved the old man too much.

Yet was it just this broken image, or was it something more terrible still which he had feared and fled from, the appalling demand made upon his nature? Theo had begun to glimpse the distance which separates the nice from the good, and the vision of this gap had terrified his soul. He had seen, far off, what is perhaps the most dreadful thing in the world, the other face of love, its blank face. Everything that he was, even the best that he was, was connected with possessive self-filling human love. That blank demand implied the death of his whole being. The old man was right to say that one should start young. Perhaps it was to calm the frenzy of this fear that he had so much and so suddenly needed to hold tightly in his arms a beautiful golden-skinned boy as lithe as a puma. What happened afterwards was hideous graceless confusion, the familiar deceitful jumble of himself breaking forth again in a scene from which he thought it had disappeared for ever. He had not really changed in those years. He had experienced joy. But that was the joy of a child at play. He had played out in the open, for those years, beside the unchanged mountain of himself.

How does one change? Theo wondered. He might have gone back some time and asked the old man that question. And yet he knew the answer really, or knew its beginning, and this was what his nature could not bear.

Theo got up and began to walk slowly back to the house.

As he came into the hall the inward smell of the house conjured up for him the image of Pierce, with his long straight strokable animal brow and nose. The kitchen was empty, except for Mingo and Montrose curled up together in the basket. The door of Casie's sitting-room was ajar and a sound came from within. Casie was watching television.

Theo entered behind her in the twilight of the contained room, and taking a chair sat down beside her as he often did. He saw that she was crying and he averted his face, stroking her shoulder with a clumsy pawing movement.

Casie said, mumbling into her handkerchief, "This play's so terribly sad. You see this man was in love with this girl and he took her out in his car and crashed the car and she was crippled for life and then. . . ."

Theo kept his hold upon her shoulder, kneading it a little with his fingers. He stared into the blue flicker of the television screen. It was too late to go back. There was a hand which could never, in grace and healing, be laid upon him now.

Yet was it not for that very reason, that it was too late, that he ought now to return? The old man would have understood this, the action without fruits. The image of return had been the image of a very human love. Now it was the image of that other one. Why should he stay here and rot? Perhaps the great mountain of himself would never grow less. But he could keep company with the enlightenment of others, and might regain at least the untempered innocence of a well-guarded child. And although he might never draw a single step closer to that great blankness he would know of its reality and feel more purely in the simplicity of his life the distant plucking of its magnetic power.

Tears suddenly began to stream down Theo's face. Yes, perhaps he would go back. Perhaps he would die after all in that green valley.

The twins lay on the cliff edge up above Gunnar's Cave. The beautiful flying saucer, spinning like a huge noiseless top, hovered in the air not far away from them, a little higher up, over the sea, in a place where they had often seen it come before. The shallow silvery metal dome glowed with a light which seemed to emanate from itself and owe nothing to the sun, and about the slim tapering outer extremity a thin line of lambent blue flame rippled and leapt. It was difficult to discern the size of the saucer, which seemed to inhabit a space of its own, as if it were inserted or pocketed in a dimension to which it did not quite belong. In some way it defeated the attempt of the human eye to estimate and measure. It hovered in its own element, in its own silence, indubitably physical, indubitably present and yet other. Then, as the children watched, it tilted slightly, and with that movement which they could never confidently interpret either as speed or as some sort of dematerialising or actual vanishing, was gone.

The twins sighed and sat up. They never spoke when the saucer was present.

"It stayed a long time today, didn't it."

"A long time."

"Isn't it odd how we know that it doesn't want to be photographed."

"Telepathy, I expect."

"I think they're good people, don't you?"

"Must be. They're so clever and they don't do any harm."

"I think they like us. I wonder if we shall ever see them."

"We'll come back tomorrow. You haven't lost that ammonite, have you, Henrietta?"

"No, it's in my skirt. Oh Edward, I'm so happy about Daddy coming back."

"So am I. I knew he'd come back, actually."

"I did too. Oh look, Edward, it's getting quite dark, it's raining out there over the sea."

"So it is. And look real *breakers* at last. How super!"

"Why it's starting to rain here now, real rain at last, lovely rain!"

"Come on, Henrietta. Let's go and swim in the rain."

Hand in hand the children began to run homeward through the soft warm drizzle.

penguin.co.uk/vintage